MW00711217

TWICE BLIND

JAMES FORESTER

BANKS & BLACKWELL PUBLISHING CO.

TWICE BLIND

This book is published by :
Banks and Blackwell Publishing Co.
P. O. Box 25
Guilford, CT 06437
(203) 458-2327

For additional books write to the address above or visit our website.
E-books available for immediate download.
Go to:

http://www.banks-blackwell.com
(Don't forget the hyphen.)

ISBN:0-9713541-1-1

Printed in the U. S. A. by arrangement with:
Morris Publishing
3212 East highway 30
Kearney, NE 68847
1-800-650-7888

PROLOGUE

Aitva could see the fiery eye of the comet huge in the telescope's field of view. Nine years before, when he and his wife Laee had first discovered the comet, they had had no notion of the monumental change it would bring to their own lives and to the world. During the twenty-two years Aitva and Laee had worked together, here in the clear air of their mountain top observatory, there had been other discoveries of importance such as the tiny tenth moon they'd found circling Kortanthe, the largest planet in the solar system. In recognition, the Council of Observations and Measurements had proclaimed their discovery of the little moon to be the most significant discovery for that five year period and in their honor the Council had designated that Aitva and Laee name the moon. Fittingly, Aitva and Laee had chosen Airell, their young daughter's name, for the beautiful little pinkish-white orb, knowing of no name they loved more or that more aptly fit the fast moving little sprite.

Ironically, finding the comet had brought them much greater notoriety, but none of the happy joy that accompanied the little moon's discovery.

The comet first appeared as a fuzzy smudge in one of the several photographs they had taken on that fateful night nine years before.

Although, they did not know it at the time, their discovery was prelude to a defining moment in human history.

Over the next few weeks, Aitva and Laee patiently measured and photographed the comet. At first, it appeared to be just another insignificant visitor from the black depths of space destined to momentarily flash down, into, and around the gravity compressed region of space near the sun before being snapped back out to the farthest limits of the sun's influence. But, as it neared the sun's fiery heat, the comet split into hundreds of parts as the substances comprising its head out-gassed in millions of small jets pushing the individual parts in different directions. Breaking apart into hundreds of individual mini comets, each giving off a distinct cloud of gas and dust, the comet became for a short period the brightest and largest object in the night sky as it left the inner solar system behind on its way back out to the deep.

The drastic change in the comet's structure drew Aitva and Laee back to

1

their telescope for a new set of observations and calculations. The results were unexpected and horrifying. The comet's head, no longer a single packed body, had change direction and become a celestial shotgun blast aimed straight at the Earth's future. Aitva and Laee repeated the trajectory calculations for the comet's next return several times before reporting their conclusions to the Council of Observations and Measurements. By then, others had also performed the same calculations and they too had arrived at the same results.

And so, the dreaded day had come and the devastating reality of Aitva and Laee's mathematical prediction of nine years before now shown menacingly through the telescope.

When the multi-headed comet had first reappeared, it had been hoped that none of its substantial pieces would strike the Earth, having spread tens of thousands of miles apart.

Unfortunately, as everyone on Earth now knew, three sizable fragments, the largest, about 4 miles across and composed of some fifty cubic miles of rock and debris, plus dozens of smaller pieces, were destined to strike the earth a hideous blow, 4 days hence. Traveling at 57 miles per second, the collisions would almost certainly result in the extinction of mankind and most of the higher forms of life on Earth.

Nevertheless, undaunted by their predicted fate, most of humanity held tenaciously to the thought of survival. Having been given nine years warning, many people around the world had worked night and day during those years to prepare to survive the approaching catastrophe. As unlikely as it seemed and as impossible as Aitva knew it to be, most people believed they would somehow survive.

Thinking of his daughter, Airell and her work with the Dandelion Project, Aitva wondered for the thousandth time if any of mankind's furious preparations would be successful.

He watched his wife as she sat at the desk against the wall quietly writing a last letter to Airell. He would soon be adding his thoughts to the letter when Laee was finished. Watching Laee for a few moments, he thought about how much he loved his wife and daughter and what the next few days would bring. He didn't mind dying. He wasn't afraid of death. His only regret was that he would not be able to look at them and laugh with them anymore. Perhaps in a little while, they would all once more be together again, but on the other side of life. Right now, only God knew what the outcome would be. In a few short days, they would know too.

Aitva and Laee, although very highly valued for their scientific knowledge and experience were too old to be included in a dandelion. Still, they had spent the last couple of years preparing astronomical archives, one for each of the 25 dandelions people had built around the world. The information, it was thought, would help future generations more quickly recover if anyone survived the catastrophe. For themselves, Aitva and Laee entertained no such fantasy. They knew their lives on this earth were effectively over and they were resigned to their fates.

For their daughter, Airell however, they still held hope. She was young and strong and healthy with her whole life still ahead of her. Fortunately, their standing in scientific and political circles had been sufficient to get Airell's husband, Cleese, an engineer and Airell, a biologist, places in the Dandelion Project. And although there was no certainty that being sheltered underground in a dandelion when the comet struck would allow people to survive, it was mankind's best hope for a future.

Cleese and Airell held hands as they walked down the entrance tunnel for the last time.

Twenty-seven years had past since the comet's impact. During that time, the planet's ecocosm had stabilized enough to allow the humans, animals and plants protected by the dandelion to once again live on the surface. So long their home, but now no longer needed, the immense shelter was going to be sealed up and abandoned today. As the chief engineer of the shelter, Cleese had one more small task to perform. Knowing this would be her last time underground, Airell had decided to accompany him while he did it.

When they reached the stone pedestal standing solidly in the middle of the tunnel, they stopped. Cleese released Airell's hand and set his tool bag on the ground. This last small chore would only take a few moments. He took the engraved gold plate Airell had carried for him and set it in the recess carved into the top of the pedestal. He then closed the metal cover to protect the engraving. Last, he removed a small torch and a bar of welding metal from his tool bag and welded the cover's straps to the metal collar lower down on the pedestal. Standing back, he inspected his work and decided it was satisfactory. Now, no matter what happened, floods, winds, or earthquakes, the engraving would have a very good chance of surviving the onslaught of time, carrying its message safely into the future.

2

Kioro Itara's scanned the boardroom and the men seated before him. He smiled inwardly knowing they were waiting patiently for him to speak.

Each man had been carefully chosen for his particular talents and abilities, his political views, and his absolute loyalty to Kioro Itara. And, though none of them had actually seen Kioro Itara face to face for several years, each man stiffened slightly as the camera shifted, knowing he was being slowly and carefully scrutinized by their unseen leader at the other end of the video link. Not one of them looked comfortable when it was his turn to be examined, and that was as it should be. And none looked up directly into the lens, both out of respect and fear. That also, was as it should be.

Before him sat the brightest and the best their country had to offer and the sight of them sitting together, ready to do his bidding gave Kioro Itara great pleasure. All was in readiness. Before him, he saw the new government of Japan, the government he had hand picked to lead the people of Japan forward into the new world he was about to create. He paused to think about that, and how long it had taken, and the enormous effort that had been expended to reach this day.

Since the humiliating end to the Second World War, Kioro Itara had been working patiently, ceaselessly, unerringly toward his goal. Now, many decades later, as head of Hinode Worldwide (pronounced hee-no-day, which means sunrise in Japanese) Japan's largest industrial combination, Itara was still as committed to his goal as the day he'd begun. Perfectly methodical in following his plan, he had carefully crafted each minute step, meticulously reviewing every detail, honing his people, his organization, and himself like the edge of a sacred kitana sword.

As he thought back, bitter memories assailed him and he remembered for the thousandth time the terrible moment when he and his family sat sharing their last meager meal, the day the gaigin had taken away all that was precious to him. He also remembered the terrible moment when he had awakened in that filthy hospital to find himself paralyzed from the waist down and his family dead. Remembering the terror, sadness, and pain momentarily overwhelmed him and he shuddered. In his aching loneliness, he had often wondered as a young man, why he had not died with his family. Having survived his despair all these years, he was now sure of the reason.

On that morning so long ago, fate had chosen Kioro Itara as Japan's son of destiny; her invincible deliverer. Even amidst his great tragedy, he had sensed that there might be a purpose to his life. Realization of this began while he lay on the cold tile floor of the hospital amidst the stinking burned bodies of his countrymen and with that realization had come his reason to live—revenge.

Since then, Kioro Itara had been a man transformed by the dark fires of revenge. For him, revenge was the sanctifying focus of his life, burning away all the unnecessary, the irrelevant, the frivolous and it had filled him with a singleness of purpose and malignant energy that was terrible to behold. To this, he had added utter ruthlessness, and the combination had always brought him success as he swept all obstacles from his path. And now, after a lifetime of work, only days away from the ultimate destruction of Japan's enemies, Kioro Itara savored his thoughts with hungry anticipation.

No longer would irresolute and weak men control Japan, holding their country in shameful subjection to arrogant and barbarous foreigners. No longer would the mighty land of the rising sun submit to anyone. For Japan's glorious sunrise was once more upon them, a time of refreshing, a time to renew the best of the old ways, a time when Japan would prevail completely and stand on the corpses of its foes.

3

During the build up to the short sharp war in Kuwait, two young reserve officers, Dexter Gordon and Syman Pons, were recalled to active duty and assigned to work at Intelligence Headquarters in Saudi Arabia. In that high pressure, sterile environment, Gordon and Pons began the dynamic relationship and resilient friendship that would serve them so well in the years ahead.

Although as different as salt and pepper, they shared the common dream of developing computers that could learn and think without assistance from their human creators. In their off hours, stranded as they were in the midst of an immense sea of sand, the two men spent a good deal of time together discussing their thoughts and ideas on the subject and as the months passed, each recognized in the other, a man of truly unique understanding and creative genius.

As the international coalition of countries opposed to Iraq's invasion of Kuwait solidified, each man had been called away from his Doctoral studies in advanced computer science. Gordon had been working at Cal Tech in Pasadena on computer and network electronics and communications. Pons, already a cryptographic software expert of international renown, had been working at MIT in Cambridge, Massachusetts where he was doing fundamental research on machine intelligence (thinking) and recognition (vision).

Together, Gordon and Pons were given the responsibility for assembling, maintaining, and managing the formidable array of computers and allied communications gear needed by IHQ, Saudi Arabia.

****

Arriving in Saudi Arabia, at age 29, Dexter was a handsome, 5' 11", blue eyed, blond. Although a little heavier, he was still the epitome of the well muscled and tan beach boy he'd been growing up in Shell Beach, California.

Dexter's father, an electronics engineer, had worked for a large Santa Barbara based aerospace company for more than 30 years and as such, had become their special projects director at Vandenberg Air Force base, about 35 miles south of Shell Beach. This meant he was the civilian head of the spy satellite projects his company built for the U.S. government that were launched on their polar orbits from Vandenberg.

As a boy, Dexter and his father had spent a lot of time together building kit electronics projects. As a result, computerized what-nots, radio controlled model cars, boats, planes, rockets and other assorted electro-mechanical gadgets, had all haunted the environs around their home and neighborhood. Thus, Dexter had come by his fascination with electronics honestly and at a very early age.

Dexter's mother was a fairly typical California housewife, who had married a middle management technocrat working his way up in a large California corporation. She was devoted to her family, and her husband's success. Running endless errands, while managing and maintaining house and home, Mrs. Gordon often had to be both mom and dad when her husbands responsibilities required that he work another hundred hour week on a project. This was a fairly common occurrence when Dexter was growing up. Bermuda shorted and halter topped much of the year, she was a busy, hard working station wagon mom, constantly on the go attending to the needs of her husband and their growing brood of three children.

As a teenager, most of Dexter's time was absorbed going to school and working. Still, he found time to beach, boat, surf, swim, date girls and cruise in his father's restored Ford Fairlane convertible with his friends. Hang gliding, volleyball, computers, and freehand rock climbing, an extremely taxing and dangerous sport at which Dexter excelled, also found prominent places in his adolescence. All in all, Dexter's childhood was California normal.

When Dexter first met Syman Pons a decade plus later and half a world away in the Saudi desert, his outer appearance had changed little, but looks can be deceiving. His boyish good looks and his easy going manner belied the considerable martial skill he had acquired as a U.S. Navy SEAL, communications/electronics expert with a unit whose specialty was black operations.

Black operations are those of a secret and often quite unsavory nature that the government will use sometimes when all other methods have failed. Behind closed doors, politicians mockingly refer to them as diplomacy by blunt instrument. Nevertheless, they depend on them as a last resort when the nation or its citizens are in real danger and the other party is being intransigent.

Upon graduation from California Polytechnic Institute, San Luis Obispo, Dexter had decided to enlist in the Navy. Two factors led him to this decision.

First, Dexter had wanted to continue his education at California Institute of Technology, but with two other college bound kids at home his parents could no longer afford to support him in school. At that time each branch of the military offered a 'You make a commitment to us and we'll pay for your education when you get out' program. Only the Navy said it would pay for his graduate education.

Second, because Dexter was a college graduate when he enlisted, and because he possessed a sophisticated knowledge of electronics, the Navy gave him a broader choice of postings. He was drawn to the SEAL special forces by an opportunity to work in communications. At the time, there was a technical revolution going on in all branches of the military, caused by the introduction of portable computers, miniaturized electronics and satellite communications equipment as they became part of the basic field equipment. Special forces units were on the cutting edge of these changes and Dexter was able to take particular advantage of these developments.

Dexter's first real action was as part of the covert advance unit put into Grenada preceding the United States' invasion in 1983. They were to observe and report on the disposition of the Grenadian security forces. The members of his SEAL team flew into the main airport dressed as tourists. It was a strange way to start an invasion, but it got them and their equipment in without any problems.

Near the end of his hitch, his unit was sent to Central America to monitor the military buildup in Nicaragua, Honduras, and El Salvador. It was generally quiet duty, but at one point his team had been ordered to sink a barge with a very large consignment of weapons provided by the USSR via Nicaragua and destined for El Salvador.

Shortly after this Dexter's tour was over and he went home to California and on to grad school at Cal Tech. The respite however was short lived with the Navy interrupting his graduate studies in 1989. He was recalled from reserve status to active duty with his old unit when the U.S. went into Panama where it again did covert advance work prior to the invasion. This time they didn't arrive as tourists and during the actual invasion Dexter was wounded while rescuing a child caught in the middle of a fire fight. Although badly hurt, he was able carried the little girl out of danger before he collapsed.

Working with his SEAL unit, Dexter had always been a good team member, loyal, dependable, and completely determined to meet the objectives. Very capable, both physically as a SEAL and with the electronics and communications gear, he fulfilled his responsibilities with a minimum of wasted time or effort.

A man of very direct methods, Gordon possessed a razor sharp intellect, which gave him a remarkable ability to quickly cut through the superfluous cloud of information that surrounds any problem and bring into clear focus the essentials to be mastered. Put another way, Dexter was very good at identifying the critical 20 percent of necessary activity that produced 80 percent of the desired result. This particular talent had been noted as outstanding in his service record. It was this, in combination with his proven ability with computers, electronics/communication gear, that had landed him at IHQ, Saudi Arabia.

An enormous amount of information flowed into and out of IHQ through a vast array of equipment. A very smart and energetic man was needed to keep it all working properly and Dexter Gordon was the right man for the job.

These same talents also helped him become the astute business person who would so shrewdly manage Thinking Machine International, the phenomenally successful computer company, he and Syman Pons would form after the war.

****

When Syman Pons arrived at IHQ Saudi Arabia, he was 32 years old, 6' 3" tall, and weighed 175 pounds. He had received his gray-green eyes and his black-auburn hair from his Jewish mother, but was possessed of the thin lithe body of his French-Canadian father. He was a fitness devote, who alternated days of running 4-6 miles with days when he did hour long Tai Chi workouts. Over the years, these two regimens had given him a sinuous feline grace that was unusual in a man so tall and thin.

Pons' responsibility at IHQ was as overall systems manager for the theater making him Gordon's immediate superior. Syman hated this management position, as he hated all management positions, but he had been tasked with a very important assignment and to the best of his ability he brought to bear the full weight of his considerable intellect and his well developed ability to cross every t and dot every i.

As a boy, when Syman first began working seriously with computers, he'd soon realized the importance of the steadfast discipline needed to write faultless computer programs. Faultless programs saved time and a lot of headaches. With tongue in cheek, an adolescent Syman had adopted the humorous little ditty, "Perfection will do nicely, thank you," as his personal motto and standard of excellence and from that early age onward he refused to accept from himself always and from others in most instances, anything less. Consequently, his resolute commitment to excellence made him very, very good at anything he did. And so it would be at IHQ for Syman Pons.

Still, given the choice, Syman would have much preferred to have served in his old Air Force squadron flying missions. Had he been younger, he might have done just that. But now, recognized as the world's leading cryptographic computer program designer, he was much too valuable to serve his country as a front end birdman.

Syman's genius with cryptography surfaced while he was working on his Masters degree at Rensselaer Polytechnic Institute in Troy, New York. As a somewhat bookish boy, he had always loved puzzles and mazes, magic and mysteries, but most of all, he'd loved secret codes. During the long frigid

9

winters of his boyhood in upstate New York, as one of his several childhood pursuits, he'd labored countless hours creating and breaking and investigating codes and his preoccupation with them remained strong into adulthood. As a direct result, Syman had chosen to go to college at Rensselaer Polytechnic Institute so he could study under Professor Charles Hortnier, a world famous theoretician and Doctor of Mathematics whose area of expertise in mathematics was randomness theory, an area of arcane knowledge that is intimately connected to modern practices used in coding information.

During World War 2, Professor Hortnier had worked in England in the mathematics group that had worked with Ultra, the code breaking operation that had so successfully decrypted Germany's coded radio messages. As Syman's mentor he was fully qualified and versed in the state of the art of information encryption and electronic information systems security.

But studying under Professor Hortnier had been a rude awakening for Syman who found his mentor a distant and cold man. Filled with a sense of his own self importance and little given to help his students in any real or meaningful way, the esteemed academic fully destroyed any vestige of respect Syman had for him with a blatant act of self service.

Before publishing his thesis, Syman was required to have Hortnier review it. In his thesis, Syman described a machine language encryption method about an order of magnitude (10 times) better than anything in existence at the time. Hortnier instantly recognized the caliber of Syman's work and its significance.

Since the second world war, Hortnier had been retained by the Office of Strategic Services (the predecessor to the CIA) the CIA, and finally, the National Security Agency as a consultant on encryption techniques. Working in this capacity, he had helped to create the most sophisticated codes used by the U.S. intelligence services and they were the best in the world at that time.

What Hortnier had realized immediately was that Syman's work made the best government coding techniques obsolete.

Syman's insights were revolutionary and the fact that this 28 year old student, working alone, could demonstrate this in his masters thesis both fascinated and worried Professor Hortnier. The Professor immediately sent copies to the cryptography experts at the NSA, where their people are able to closely monitor all developments in the art with the helpful connivance of people like Professor Hortnier.

After several top people at the NSA studied Pons' work, it was decided it should be classified with a CaTaRaCT, triple 'a' designation, the agencies highest, to immediately forestall further dissemination of Syman's method. It was obvious to Professor Hortnier and the experts at NSA that Syman Pons was to computer cryptography what Albert Einstein was to physics. Thus, Syman Pons was no longer just an ordinary citizen. His genius with computers made him a national resource.

The Agency asked Hortnier to discuss the matter with Pons and to tell him they wanted the exclusive rights of use to his work. The implied 'or else' was that the Agency got what it wanted or his work would never see the light of day, having already been classified.

At first Pons was furious that the government had been so heavy handed and he had talked to a lawyer. But, as it turned out, the NSA had the legal authority to do what it had, based on an obscure paragraph of the National Security Act relating to the peacetime use of encryption techniques for electronic data.

Although, technically legal, Pons did not believe the government had the moral justification to do to him what it had done and unknown to the NSA officials, Pons had very good personal reasons to resent such dictatorial treatment from his government.

His mother, Suszette deCoen Pons, was Jewish, a Nazi concentration camp survivor and the last living member of her family. As a displaced person after the war, no longer having any relatives to whom she might return, she had traveled to Paris, where she had met Rene, Syman's father.

Rene had come to Europe to fight with his Canadian army unit. When the war ended, Rene was stationed in Paris while he waited to be shipped home. With few duties to attend to, Rene and Suszette spent much of their time together. It didn't taken long before they'd fallen in love. They married a week before Rene returned to Canada and Suszette following him, arrived in Montreal shortly thereafter.

Then, after a few years in post war Canada, Suszette and Rene decided to immigrate to the U.S. where the employment opportunities were better.

Born in the U.S., Syman served in the Air Force after high school. He was a loyal and patriotic citizen who had considered it a duty and a privilege to have served his country. However, knowing many of the intimate details of his mother's war time experiences with a dictatorial government, Syman could not fail to see similarities of method and justification. He was never again so naive as to trust in the eternal benevolence of his government, and thereafter he felt uneasy when he remembered the summary way in which he'd been treated.

As well as no longer trusting his government, the experience with the NSA left Syman feeling demeaned and insulted. The government's motives assaulted Syman's idealism. Having developed a fundamentally new way to secure computers from unauthorized snooping, Syman believed his work would benefit everyone by protecting their right to privacy.

The government however, wasn't interested in protecting people's right to privacy. Nor did it have any regard for Syman's right to freedom of speech or his right to freely use and disseminate his intellectual property.

It was all very frustrating. Still, as frustrating as it was, Syman was determined not to let the government get the upper hand concerning his work.

11

Supremely cool headed by nature, Syman took time to thoroughly think through the options open to him. He could not lock his method back up. Hortnier, that nervy, treacherous bastard, had made that impossible by showing Syman's thesis to the NSA people without Syman's permission.

Because Syman's advances were in method rather than technology, the government cryptographers could now develop their own crude form of his program, no matter what Syman said or did. Even a crude form of his program would increase the government's computer system's security by a factor of 3 or 4. And he would still be forbidden to release his method in the United States unless he wanted a great deal of trouble from the government. This aspect of the situation was now beyond Syman's ability to change. However, being the genius that he was, Pons saw a way to make the most of this distressing situation by retaining two points of advantage to himself. One was known to the government. The other was not.

First, he negotiated a thirty-five million dollar a year royalty for the government's exclusive use of the finished program, which he would provide and update as needed. The government negotiators were opposed to paying this amount and the people at the NSA were not sure they wanted him so intimately involved. But Pons told them to hell with their veiled threats and their stonewalling. In considering his options, he'd found a loophole. They'd have to do it his way or he would simply copyright his work in Europe and Japan, effectively releasing it worldwide. At the time, there was no way they could stop him from doing just that.

What Syman had discovered with the help of one W. Raymond Fitzsimmons, a very savvy intellectual properties attorney who specialized in software copyright law, was that copyrighting one's material in a foreign country was a contingency not then covered under the National Security Act.

Because the U.S. was not at war, Syman's action's with his work, even though it had been classified in the U.S., were not specifically constrained outside the U.S.

The NSA continued to bluster and threaten, but in the end they reluctantly complied with his conditions. They also eventually had the law changed, but by then it was too late to do anything to Syman. And so, in this way Syman Pons became a well paid consultant to his Uncle Sam.

Syman's second advantage, the one unknown to the government, was a trapdoor, a hidden entry point, woven into the fabric of his encryption program that allowed him unfettered access to any computer protected with his encryption software. He accomplished this by changing his program's basic format to include a subtle, multi-layered, timed data retrieval method not mentioned in his thesis.

Syman was able to invisibly embed a small sub-program in the general program that built itself up into a larger sub-program only after Pons entered his access code. This larger sub-program then opened an entry point upstream of the security measures built into the general program.

In this way, Pons could gain entry to any computer that was using his security program with the password, PWDN,TY!, the first letters of his motto (Perfection will do nicely, thank you!).

Syman's method was similar to hiding the jigsaw puzzle pieces of a smaller picture inside a larger one. The individual parts of the smaller picture were spread separately throughout the larger one and they would only come together after Syman entered his password. As each part was added to those already gathered, a new address and command were generated which brought the next piece until the entire smaller picture was assembled. The beauty of the method was that each part of the smaller picture was a legitimate piece of the larger picture. Nothing looked added or out of place.

Once inside a system, Pons could give himself system manager privileges and do anything he wanted, including negate all record keeping functions. Thus, there was never a trace of the system's having been entered or used.

After several hundred hours of study and familiarization with the finished program, the NSA's best computer people failed to detect a trace of Syman's sub-routine.

They also failed to find any flaws in the overall program. A program normally undergoes debugging when it's first installed on a system. But there were no bugs in Syman's program and that really surprised the experts. It also made them uneasy. They had never used a new program that didn't have problems at first, but then, they had never dealt with anyone like Syman Pons.

As time went on and the excellence of Syman's encryption program was demonstrated, it was installed on almost all the government's computers. In this way, the U.S. government, unwittingly, made Pons one of the most powerful men on earth. There was virtually nothing, from launching a nuclear missile attack, to erasing all the IRS' computerized records that Pons could not do with the computers using his security programs.

By the time Syman reached Saudi Arabia, he was amused by the irony of his secret mastery of his heavily computerized government. Still, though he was amused, he was not susceptible to the allure of the power so easily and literally available to him at his finger tips. Except to test his access periodically, he never tampered with the government's computers.

With the implementation of Syman's security programs the money began to pour in. It was a stupendous benefit for the son of two blue collar workers from upstate New York. He never again had to worry about money and neither did his parents.

Ironically, Syman had never cared much about money one way or the other. His world was intellectual, not material. He had always just assumed that the money would come to him if he did excellent work. As it turned out, he was right.

Although, generally not self indulgent, this veritable river of money did allow him to embrace his second great love—flying. It was Syman's only extravagance.

Syman was a man who loved soaring, both intellectually and physically and he reveled in every form of air transport—jet fighters, ballooning, para-foils, airplanes, helicopters, gliders; it didn't matter.

Being off the earth, in the air, free-wheeling, unencumbered to glide and loop and roll and dive, while watching an unfolding panorama before him, was an enchantment that always captivated Syman Pons.

So, it came to pass that these two uniquely talented men began a friendship that would one day affect all people across the wide world. But none of this they suspected as each man stoically fulfilled his duties in the barren wastes of Saudi Arabia.

4

Dexter leaned back and pushed himself away from the middle of his desk, rolling his chair to the right to position himself in front of his desk top comparitor. As he focused on the comparitor's blank screen, his thoughts blended in a running series of memories and feelings about these mass produced super computers, he and Syman had invented, that were so greatly changing the world.

The eleven years Thinking Machine International had been making and selling, software, hardware, and finally the comparitor, had been hectic and exciting to the point of exhaustion.

During their first six years in business, Syman and Dexter led the 'A' Team at TMI, composed of the company's management, marketing and software eagles, while it firmly establish the company in the lucrative software market.

Then, using the enormous profits generated by their software sales, the 'B' Team, the company's research and development group, again, led by Syman and Dexter, worked furiously to develop revolutionary hardware products.

The culmination of their long years of hard work was the comparitor, the first true thinking machine capable of learning from its own activities.

Fundamentally different from earlier computers, a comparitor possessed peripherals that allowed it to sense and interact with its surroundings. Sight, smell, hearing, and an insatiable curiosity caused a machine to devour information in unbelievable amounts.

Mechanical manipulators, (hands), and the ability to speak, further increased the machine's ability to gather information as it interacted with its surroundings.

So vast was the comparitor's ability to learn that it took the technicians at TMI nearly two months, working round the clock, to load a new comparitor's basic knowledge program.

During the second half of the programming, a machine was allowed to experiment with its peripherals and through them learn to relate to the outside world. Interacting with the world in this way gave a comparitor perspective and wisdom gained from experience.

The technicians, who monitored the new machines during this critical part of their programming, referred to it as 'letting the baby learn'.

Although similar in form, the results were more immediate. With its memory filled with virtually every bit of human knowledge catalogued, filmed, or recorded, a fully programmed comparitor just out of the box possessed the judgment and decision making capabilities of a brilliant, but naive twenty year old human being. Fortunately, sophistication came with experience.

Although comparitors were machines, from the first they evidenced quirky human-like characteristics that surprised their creators. Each machine manifested its own unique proto-personality. The idiosyncrasies in the individual machines were due to the small differences in the machine's initial programming experience. Some machines were a little comical, some were slightly annoying, some overly literal, some bland, and some pedantic. When a machine was new, the variations were subtle. But as time went by, the variations became more distinctive as a machine developed its own unique patterns of response and behavior.

Consequently, after becoming familiar with a comparitor, more than one person reconsidered their fundamental assumptions about what it meant to be alive.

As mechanical helpmates, comparitors could do anything and everything a computer could do and a thousands things more.

However, the way they accomplished their tasks was entirely new and Syman and Dexter coined the name comparitor to emphasize the different way the new machines worked.

Early on, in the research, Dexter and Syman had decided a fundamental change in computer hardware, rather than the software, was needed to enable a machine to truly think and synthesize new information. They had trusted their 'techs' intuition' rather than the experts and they were right.

As development progressed it occurred to them that computers, which do all their work by manipulating enormously long strings of on-off electrical pulses called bits, never held an image of any real thing in their memories the way a human being does.

Seeing this as a fundamental design flaw in computers Syman and Dexter decided the central processor and memory for TMI's machine needed to handled information as complete images and concepts, instead of bits. And, as it turned out, their success at creating just such a machine was the key breakthrough in artificial intelligence research that had been sought for more than twenty years. As a result the comparitor became the new paradigm for computers.

The three dimensional magneto-optical memory core/processor was the heart of TMI's machine and its first significant breakthrough. A four inch cube of silica aerogel containing a billion individual spatial nodes and their connecting pathways, the memory core/processor embodied the most sophisticated electronic component ever manufactured. It was like a million microchips stacked one atop another allowing hundreds of millions of individual two and three dimensional images to be stored as magneto-optically biased shadows of themselves. Ready to brightly manifest when energized, combinations of images could be rotated, enlarged, stretched, joined or otherwise changed. In this way a comparitor could manipulate complete images both in perception and memory.

A second key breakthrough was realizing that a comparitor needed two of these miraculous memory/processor cores to think. This allowed one core to hold an image while the other studied it, deciding what changes were to be made. The images were handed back and forth between the two cores very rapidly while small modifications were initiated with each pass. Thus, using this technique of sequential comparison, comparitors became the first machines able to manipulate and more importantly, comprehend complete images and concepts. And because the machines dealt with images and concepts of real things, they were able to relate to the world in the same way as their human creators.

In principle the solution had seemed simple enough, but a working prototype had cost more than a billion dollars and had taken hundreds of thousands of man hours to perfect.

Expensive though they were at first, the opportunities to profit from a comparitor's unique abilities were quickly recognized and sales of the machines had taken off with big business buying the first million odd machines to handle their most onerous and complex jobs like running an entire production facility. As time went on the cost of a comparitor came down markedly as its production numbers went up. Now, a desk top comparitor like Dexter's cost only a few thousand dollars.

With TMI selling millions of comparitors world wide, the company was experiencing a growth rate similar to that of IBM, when it first began to manufacture electronic computers earlier in the century.

Thinking about TMI's phenomenal success always made Dexter a little nervous and thinking about it now was no exception. Syman and Dexter had been riding the rocket of success since their second year in business and Dexter was only too aware of how easily they could crash and burn if he or Syman made a few wrong decisions.

As President of TMI, it was Dexter's responsibility to run the company day to day. Although it was a little daunting at times, he loved the challenge of it. He worked in one of the most creative business environments in the world with some of the best and brightest people anywhere. The pace was blistering and the pressure was sometimes immense, but the satisfaction from what they had accomplished in so short a period of time was more exhilarating to him than anything else he'd ever done. And being one of the hundred richest men on earth didn't exactly hurt either.

Dexter's reverie was curtailed when his comparitor beeped and announced in a pleasant tenor voice, "Syman would like to speak with you."

"Yes, George, with visual, please," Dexter automatically replied. At once the comparitor's view screen lit up with Syman's smiling face.

"Hola, amigo. Como esta?"

"Hi, Sy. I'm fine. Que pasa?"

"One of us has to go to the bank today with the papers for that plastics company acquisition," Pons replied.

The comparitor's screen showed him standing in the office of the Servidor development group, still dressed in his jogging clothes. It was apparent from Syman's informal attire that he'd come straight to work after his early morning, (probably five am), run. Although both Dexter and Syman lived only a mile from TMI's plant in the little beach community of Lordship, it seemed lately that more often than not Syman ended his five mile morning runs in the Servidor R & D lab, rather than at home.

Servidor was the generic name, not a very original one, that had been coined for the humanoid robots that had become a possibility with the creation of the comparitor to direct them. It was the obvious next step in the comparitor's development and at present, several hundred of TMI's best research and development people were working feverishly to perfect the first production model of the world's first intelligent mechanical man. Dexter could see some of TMI's R & D people busy on the other side of the glass partition behind Syman.

R & D was Syman's favorite area in the company and he spent as much time working there as he could make available from his demanding schedule. Coming in two hours before the business day began was just one way to guarantee him some time to do what he loved.

Sometimes, when Syman was enthralled with a particularly difficult problem, he might spend several days straight working, taking time only to eat an occasional sandwich, catnap on the couch in his office, and shave and shower in the private bathroom between their offices.

At such times, Syman's office would take on what Dexter called its dormitory air, with dirty clothes dumped on the floor and with papers, half eaten food, spilled coffee, electro-mechanical parts, wires, unidentifiable gizmos and just plain stuff overflowing surfaces everywhere.

As he stared at Syman's craggy, still unshaven image on the comparitor's screen, Dexter wondered if one of Syman's work marathons was coming on. When they did, it was almost impossible to get him to pay attention to the management of the company. Sometimes it was infuriating as well as difficult, because usually Syman didn't give a happy damn about Dexter's acute business problems while operating in R&D mode.

18

It also bothered Dexter because more and more he was preoccupied with business allowing him almost no time in the R&D lab, a place he enjoyed working almost as much as Syman. Today, fortunately, Dexter thought, there was nothing overly pressing that needed Syman's attention.

"I'm working on something here and I don't want to stop right now. I wanted to know if you'd deal with the acquisition?"

"Ah, el softo toucho!" said a leering Dexter, with stage emphasis. He wagged his index finger at the comparitor's camera. "Your problem, Pons, is that you're all brains and no greed! You never will want to work in the business end of this place!"

"Umm, nope. You're right about that, pal," replied Pons, laughing at Dexter's Groucho-esque performance. "But I really am in the middle of something here."

"You're always in the middle of something there, Syman," Dexter said, in a way that revealed he thought Syman was taking advantage of him.

"And besides," continued Syman, "you sort of enjoy business management, while I, as you well know, can't stand it. And it's more efficient this way. You're President of this company. I'm the head of development."

"Yeah, well you're also the CEO and the majority stock holder in this enterprise. Technically, negotiating acquisitions is your responsibility," retorted Gordon, sourly. He really didn't want go to the bank this morning.

"Now don't go pulling low rank on me, pardner."

Gordon said nothing for a few moments, scowling at Pons the whole time, trying to make him feel guilty for weaseling out of the meeting by dumping it on him. It had no effect on Pons, who stood passively waiting for Gordon to acquiesce.

"I'll do it this time," Gordon said, finally. "But, you owe me a time swap, at my discretion. I'm sure I can find some suitably distasteful task for you in the future."

"OK," replied Pons. "Sometime when you have the flu or something. I'll make it up to you."

"George?" Syman said, quickly initiating action in the desired direction before Dexter changed his mind. "Ask Esmirelda to print a copy of the proposal for the Snelling Plastics Company acquisition for Mr. Gordon."

"Yes, Syman," replied the ever ready machine.

After a few moments of interaction with Esmirelda, (Pons' desktop comparitor), George replied, "Esmirelda wants to know what color file folder you would like?"

"Just like a woman," said Gordon, venting on the machine instead of the human. "Put it in a black folder and put everything in a manila envelope."

"The file will be printed in 1 minute and 40 seconds. Esmirelda would like to remind you that she has no remote manipulators and is therefore incapable of assembling the file in a folder or an envelope," replied the machine somewhat pedantically. "She merely wished to make a notation for the person who will assemble the completed package. She would also like to remind you that gender related insults are passé and..."

"Be quiet, George!" said Gordon, impatiently, cutting the machine off.

"Will you be in the office this afternoon, Sy? There are some other b-u-s-i-n-e-s-s matters we have to work on together."

"Should be," replied Pons, with a nod of his head.

"See you later, then. Off, George." The comparitor's screen went blank.

Gordon got up from his desk and went into his private bathroom to off load some of that morning's rented coffee. When he was finished, he walked through the connecting door between his and Pons' offices.

As he entered the room, Esmirelda said, "Good morning, Dexter."

"Good morning, Essy. Ask supply to send a black file folder and a manila envelope over here."

He went to the printer and picked up the copy of the contract for the purchase of the plastics company.

"They are already here in Syman's receiver," said the comparitor.

"Good. Thanks." said Gordon, absently as he read walking over to a sliding panel in the wall of Syman's office. Opening it, he retrieved the traveler that had delivered the stationary.

Micro-seconds after learning what was desired, Esmirelda, the comparitor in Pons' office was telling Cleophys, the comparitor in charge of TMI's automated materials and supplies warehouse to send the items to the main office building. Forty seconds later, from 1/2 of a mile away the stationary was in a traveler moving at 85 MPH under one of the enormous parking lots used by the employees of TMI. As it neared the main office building, it was slowed to 35 MPH and switched through to Syman's office receiver. Travel time, 51 seconds. Time from order placed to order delivered, 91 seconds. With the ever watchful and helpful comparitors, things sometimes happened so quickly and effortlessly that it was a little unnerving. At the moment however, having accepted the annoying banking chore, Dexter was too preoccupied with his thoughts about the up coming meeting to notice.

5

Osmid Bandar removed the large manila envelope from the stainless steel safe deposit drawer. He also removed a computer diskette which he put in the envelope. Keeping his important papers and valuables in here had been inconvenient during his stay in the U.S. It required him to come to the bank at least twice a week. His having to live in a hotel room for eight months, while he filled the Islamic Brotherhood's order, had left him no choice. He could take no chances that a nosy or dishonest hotel employee, or anyone else, might go through his things in his hotel room. If what he was working on were ever discovered his life would be worthless. If the authorities in the U.S. didn't lock him away for the rest of his life, then the Islamic Brotherhood would assassinate him for allowing others to discover their plans.

He comforted himself with the thought that he would fulfill his obligations to the Brotherhood this week. He would only have to come here once more to remove the rest of the drawer's contents. Then he could leave the now somewhat tiresome United States and return to his home in Pakistan. He sorely missed his wife and children.

Previously, he had always enjoyed his visits to the U.S. because of the pleasures he could indulge in here and because of the money to be made so quickly here. But eight months living alone amidst the hustle and bustle of this enormous land was more than enough for Osmid.

Flying thousands of miles a week to locate, purchase, and arrange to ship all the hundreds of items requested by the Brotherhood had taken its toll on both his stamina and his patience. And that is to say nothing of the countless lonely hours on the phone and working with his computer in his hotel room. The paper work was endless and he had had to travel to dozens of places to carefully inspect each item he had been instructed to acquire. This was by far the largest job he had ever undertaken and he was no longer a young man.

It was a shame it would be his last time in the United States. If he succeeded in filling their order there was every chance, that the Brotherhood would succeed with their plans and in a very short time there would be no more United States to visit again. It was a shame and a terrible waste really, but there was nothing he could do to stop them and still continue to live.

Surely they would kill him if he hesitated perceptibly or failed to accomplish the mission they had given him.

As a young man, Osmid had gotten his start smuggling opium from the Afghanistan border to Marseilles, France. He had made his first small fortune in this trade. But as time went by, the trade got messy and difficult and the competition from Southeast Asia and Latin America for the U.S. market, where the bulk of it was destined, had made it less lucrative.

When the Russians had invaded Afghanistan he had begun to trade in arms. It was easier work on the whole. The profits weren't as big but there was less risk and bother. While the arms trade was not strictly legal, it was not violently illegal like trading in opium.

And because the rebels controlled all of the border crossings he used, he didn't have to cross the border to do business. His customers came to him and took their goods away themselves. Before the Russians pulled out of Afghanistan, Osmid began selling ancient artifacts illegally pilfered from countries all over the Mid-East to an American dealer living in Paris. Having always been a pragmatic man, Osmid was open to any favorable opportunity and as the years went by, artifacts had become just one more of the lucrative commodities he handled.

Never having had any real interest in things political, his loose connection to the Islamic Brotherhood was more convenience than conviction. Osmid had begun his association with the Brotherhood while trading arms to the Afghanistan rebel forces. The clandestine activities of the Brotherhood and the shady characters who were its members, formed an endless supply of couriers, laborers, information sources, and secret connections covering much of the world. Osmid often made good use of them in his various business transactions. After more than thirty years of successful smuggling, Osmid now had a very good reputation as a fixer who could find, acquire, and move anything anywhere. Weapons, electronics, machinery, chemicals, industrial information, securities, diamonds, currency—he did not care.

Having accumulated more money than he could ever fully enjoy in a dozen lifetimes, Osmid kept at it mostly for the challenge, although this job for the Brotherhood was not an option for him. It was repayment for the help they had extended him over the years. With his responsibilities to them nearly fulfilled, Osmid was very relieved that it had all gone so well and would soon be behind him.

Osmid closed the drawer and walked out of the vault through the security gate. He stopped for a moment to tell the vault attendant he was finished. Then he walked across the lobby toward the front door of the bank. Just as he reached it, a man carrying a hand gun and wearing a ski mask burst in the door, confronting him. Osmid saw wild eyes through the holes in the mask just before the man swung the weapon around viciously, hitting him in the side of the head. His vision flashed white as the weapon connected. The force of the blow spun Osmid half way around as he fell to the floor unconscious. The manila envelope he was carrying flew from his hand and disappeared behind the potted plant next to the front door.

A second masked man carrying a shotgun followed close on the heels of the first who had barely paused as he dealt with Osmid, clearing his way. The first man stepped to the middle of the lobby and started yelling, ordering everyone to come and lie down on the floor in front of him. He waved his gun around menacingly to frighten everyone into submission. Seeing the gun and the man lying on the floor by the front door, people quickly obeyed, although one old woman began protesting her arthritic knees.

"Shut up, you old bag!" the first robber shouted as he advanced on her. "Just stand there and shut yer yap." He was pointing his big handgun at her, and the old lady stopped talking, sagging against the counter, wide eyed and momentarily silenced by fear.

Having previously cased the bank, the first robber walked over to the woman he knew was the teller manager while the other stood guard at the front door, shotgun in hand. Leaning over, he grabbed her by the arm yanking her painfully to her feet. He ordered her to take him to the cash safe in the vault.

This one was a looker, he thought, catching a glimpse down the front of her suit as she stumbled to her feet. Maybe he'd do her in the vault after he'd loaded the cash. He'd done that once before in Massachusetts and it had been great. But when Leon, his partner, heard about it on the TV later that night in their motel room, he'd threatened to kill him for risking the extra time.

Following the woman, he considered her backside. Maybe, he could bring her along as a hostage. Then they could share her all night and Leon wouldn't get all pissed off again.

As they stepped into the vault he was not quite sure which excited him more, the soft curves he could see under her skirt, or all that cash within arm's reach. Well, they were both his for the taking now!

"Load the bag!" he commanded, pushing his gun at her. She shrank back against the cold metal wall, but then reversed with a little jerk at its touch. Turning away, she fumbled with her keys. She started crying quietly but when the door opened, she quickly began shifting the wrapped bundles of money into the bag.

Leon was never comfortable standing around the front door of a bank so exposed, but there was no choice. He had to make sure no one came in or went out and that there was no monkey business. Art handled the cash and he handled the crowd. That was the way they always did it.

The old woman with the arthritis was leaning against the counter on his right mumbling quietly to herself. She had never really stopped talking, only having paused momentarily, when Art threatened her. Suddenly, she began babbling loudly, gesticulating and making the sign of the cross. Her noisy outburst drew Leon's attention from the door. Just at that moment, Dexter Gordon walked through it.

Startled at finding a well dressed business man standing next to him, Leon hesitated just a second and then began to bring the shot gun's muzzle to bear on Gordon.

Taken equally by surprise, Dexter struggled to comprehend the meaning of the specter with the mask and the gun standing in his way. Focusing on the gun, Dexter instantly drew on the training so thoroughly and deeply ingrained in him during his days as a navy SEAL. Stepping forward, he snaked his left arm between the gun's stock and the bandit's body, clamping it tightly under his upper arm, drawing the man very close to him. As the bandit struggled to pull his weapon free from Dexter's unbreakable grip, Dexter continued with one smooth unhesitating motion to reach his other arm around the back of the bandit's neck, bringing his forearm around the front and across the man's throat. Dexter now had the gun under his left arm and the bandit's head under his right. Bringing his right knee up with rib breaking force, Dexter simultaneously yanked violently down with his right arm, snapping the robber's neck in one quick motion. The second cervical vertebrae parted with a loud crack.

The entire take-down was over in less than two seconds. And it had been accomplished with the grace of a well choreographed dance step; just one of the many lethal steps in the dances of death so precisely taught to every U.S. Navy SEAL.

The body went limp. Dexter held on to the shotgun but let the body drop to the floor. All eyes had been on the confrontation and a couple of people had whimpered their fright when they heard the sharp crack, as one man so quickly killed another. The bank manager, who knew Dexter personally having done a considerable bit of business with TMI over the years, got up off the floor and cautiously approached Dexter. He kept looking nervously toward the back of the bank.

"There's another one in the vault with our head teller, Mrs. Gilmore," he whispered to Dexter, obviously awed and looking at him as if for the first time. The bank manager wasn't sure he wanted to get too close to Dexter having just seen him kill someone.

Dexter could sense the manager's self righteous distaste and it annoyed him.

"He has a hand gun," The manager added.

"OK," said Dexter, checking the shotgun's safety and its load. He quickly removed his coat, tie, shoes and socks.

"Show me where they are."

"The cash vault is through the gate, past the safe deposit area, inside the main vault. Go down the hall there and to the left," the manager whispered, pointing, but making no move toward the area himself.

Disgusted by the man's obvious cowardice, Gordon ordered, "Call the police. And get everyone out of here fast and keep them quiet!" Dexter pointed at a side door that was not in a direct line of sight from the hall leading to the vault and asked, "Can you open that door there?"

The manager nodded.

"Good! Do it!" Dexter said, as he put the contents from his pockets on a nearby counter.

In the vault, Mrs. Gilmore put the last of the wrapped bundles of bills in the duffel bag.

"Zip it!" Art commanded, loudly.

Mrs. Gilmore obeyed with shaky hands.

"Now turn around. Put your hands together behind your head and bend over with your head against the wall there." He pointed to the end wall of the vault. Mrs. Gilmore did as she was told.

Art came up behind her. "Don't move or I'll blow your pretty head off, honey," he commanded brutally as he put the barrel of the gun to back of her head. She flinched when it touched her.

"What do you want?" she asked, with a voice like a frightened child's. "What are you going to do?"

Art laughed deep in his throat. His lust had overcome his fear of Leon's retribution or of being caught. He had decided to have his way with her quickly, not wanting either to forego his pleasure with her or deal with her later as a hostage or a body. With his free hand, he hiked her skirt up over her hips onto her now horizontal back.

Mrs. Gilmore cried quietly.

After fondling her from behind for a few seconds, Art ripped her panties off.

Mrs. Gilmore started sobbing now, uncontrollably, and pleading with him. "No, no, oh please God, no!"

Art laughed his insane laugh and reached for her again. He could feel her trembling with fright. This excited him greatly. He loved to brutalize woman and force them to submit to him. He rubbed his hand back and forth between her legs, exploring her. He was totally in control of this helpless woman, and he loved it. His lust and rage felt like a drug coursing through him, making him very high. He fumbled with his zipper, completely engrossed, as he stared at her nakedness. As he moved toward her, he bent his knees slightly.

A bright red flash lit his awareness. Rolling across the woman's back, he fell to the stainless steel floor of the vault—dead.

Mrs. Gilmore shrieked in startled terror when she felt his weight.

In his maniacal frenzy of power madness and lust, Art had not noticed Dexter Gordon as he crept up from behind. His lack of attention cost him his life, giving Gordon the perfect opportunity to ram the shotgun's butt, with a surgeon's skill, into the exact juncture at the back of his neck between skull and spinal column. The violent blow instantly separated the nerves of the spine from the base of the brain, insuring that the rapist could not reflexively pull the trigger of the gun he was pointing at his victim.

Looking down at the man on the floor, Dexter felt not the slightest twinge of remorse. Having just express mailed the scumbag's soul back to God was a pleasure. Gordon was completely intolerant of society's weak kneed concern about the rights of violent criminals. He could not fathom the lack of compassion and concern for the rights and feelings of the thousands of innocent victims who are forced to endure the terror of the vicious, senseless brutality dished out by men like these two he had just dealt with.

"You're safe now, Ma'am," he said softly, as he turned away from Mrs. Gilmore in an attempt to preserve, if possible, some small shred of her dignity.

Seeing Gordon standing there, barefoot, with his back to her, holding a shotgun, she pulled her skirt down and ran, fleeing out of the vault, wracked with shuddering sobs.

Osmid Bandar's head throbbed with pain when he tried to lift it from the floor. A woman was kneeling next to him asking inane questions about how he felt. He ignored her as he looked around. He could see the masked man laying on the floor a few feet away. There was a wet stain across the crouch of the man's pants and his eyes were staring up at the wall over Osmid's head with the glassy sightless look of surprise that only the recently dead can achieve. Bank employees were milling around in small groups, huddled together, talking quietly. He didn't see any customers, but the bank's manager was talking with a man who was barefoot and holding a shotgun. Fear began to rise in Osmid's chest until he noticed no one seemed to be afraid of the man. Osmid took all this in as he rose on wobbly legs with the assistance of the woman. He could hear sirens outside coming closer. The last thing he wanted to do was to talk to the police and get tangled up in this mess. The woman was still holding tightly to his arm. Osmid shook her off and began looking around on the floor for his envelope. He saw the envelope Dexter Gordon had dropped as he entered the bank, confronting the robber. Not realizing his mistake, Osmid picked it up and without a backward glance, stepped through the front door, wanting only to get away from the bank as quickly as possible.

Lieutenant Salvano had been sent to head the crime scene investigation when it became known that someone had died there.

The bank manager had been emphatic, almost accusatory and not a little disapproving as he describe Gordon's actions. With lifted eyebrows, the manager had told him how Mr. Gordon had killed the robbers and rescued the woman in the vault. But he made it sound as if Gordon was a criminal and that surprised Salvano. However, after interviewing everyone else involved and speaking with the man himself at length, finding him to be quiet and rational, the lieutenant decided to let Gordon go.

In contrast to the bank manager, Lieutenant Salvano was impressed by what Gordon had done. Having been a Green Beret in Viet Nam, he was not surprised that Gordon, a retired SEAL, had dealt so swiftly and effectively with these two gun toting punks. He was well aware of just how effective the training was and how easy it was to disarm and kill an untrained man if you could get to within arms reach of him. Actually, he wished he had been there to watch or better still, to help.

The Lieutenant, of course, kept these thoughts to himself, his being restrained from acting in the same way in a similar situation by the police force's regulations on 'unnecessary use of force.' Still, as far as he could tell, as an unarmed citizen, Gordon's actions were appropriate. Gordon had been confronted with the muzzle of a shotgun and had defended his life in the way that seemed best to him at that instant. Having dispatched one of these animals, he realized, he could not stop there, not knowing what the other one would do with his hostage when he saw his dead partner. With this in mind, Gordon had decided to continue and try to stop the robbery turned kidnapping/rape in progress in the vault. Amazingly, he had dispatched both criminals and rescued the woman without a scratch to the hostages. Truly, it was a difficult job well done in Salvano's opinion. Of coarse, a lot of diaper clad bleeding hearts would holler about his endangering the hostages, etc., (as if they weren't already in greater danger to begin with), but no SWAT team could have done a better job.

As he mulled these thoughts over in his mind, it occurred to him he was wasting his time. Whether or not Gordon's actions were completely justifiable was not his concern. He was just a cop. That cat fight would have to be taken up at the inquest

6

Dexter walked through his office to the private connecting door between his and Syman's offices. He knocked and after a moment heard Syman's muffled, "Come in."

As Syman watched his partner cross the room, he sensed a subtle tension in Dexter's manner and wondered if he really had been upset about having to go to the bank.

"I wasn't able to do the deal," Dexter said without preamble. "I walked in on a bank robbery and everything got very exciting after that."

Syman motioned toward the chair in which Dexter normally sat when they met in his office. Dexter tossed the envelope he had brought with him toward Syman's desk as he sat down. It Frisbeed onto the desk after one complete turn in the air. A blue plastic computer disk slid most of the way out of the open top as the envelope came to rest.

"And I killed the two men who were robbing the bank. It's been quite a morning."

Syman looked hard at Dexter, narrowing his brows, thinking Dexter was pulling his leg as revenge for having had to go to the meeting. "You're joking, right?"

"No, I wish I were. I really did just kill two guys at the bank. I stepped into the lobby and one of them was standing just inside the door, not four feet away with a shotgun. He started to bring it to bear on me and I just reacted to the situation without thinking."

Dexter kept talking, spending the next several minutes telling Syman the whole story of the morning's events. When Dexter was finished, Syman sat looking at his friend wondering what to say. Nothing helpful or relevant came to mind.

"Why don't you take the rest of the day off," Syman finally suggested.

"No, I'll be all right. I'd rather be here doing something. Some familiar routine will bring me back down to earth." After a moment's pause, he continued. "I guess I'm feeling a bit edgy and needed to talk about it a little."

"That's understandable," said Syman, while thinking to himself, 'It isn't every day that one goes around killing a couple of people. I wonder how I would react in the same situation.'

Sensing in Dexter's silence his desire to drop the subject, Syman picked up the disk laying in front of him. "What's this?" he asked, holding it up for Dexter to see.

"I don't know. I didn't put a disk in the proposal."

Syman looked more closely still, focusing on the label. An illegible scrawl was penned across its top line. "Can't read the chicken scratch on this label," he informed Dexter handing it to him for inspection.

Pons then picked up the manila envelope and pulled out a sheaf of computer printout. He could feel something odd on the bottom of the pack. Turning it over he saw a large glassine envelope with a square yellow sheet showing through the paper. Although not rigid, it was not flexible like paper either. It felt surprisingly heavy as Syman separated it from the printout. Apparently Dexter had mistakenly picked up someone else's property. Still, his curiosity impelled him to look more closely at its peculiar contents, which he now knew to be a thin metal plate.

"What have we here?" Syman wondered out loud, as he removed the plate from its envelope.

Diverted from his scrutiny of the disk by Syman's remark Dexter's attention was also drawn to the metal plate.

"What the hell is that?" Asked Dexter incredulously. "This isn't our acquisition proposal."

Lightheartedly, Syman said, "Ah, mi amigo, you have a keen grasp of the obvious."

About eight inches square, the now uncovered metal plate glimmered with a rich gold hue in the warm afternoon sunlight coming through the French doors behind the desk.

Wanting a better look at the mysterious object, Dexter rose from his seat. He put the disk back on the desk as he came around its side to stand next to Syman.

The plate was engraved with a myriad of small, very finely lined drawings, each of which was proceeded by a highly polished square about the size of a postage stamp. The engraved lines showed a silvery base metal under what was apparently gold plating. The small silvery tracings were pictographs of common things; a tree, the naked form of a man and woman, a cow, a disembodied hand pouring a cup of liquid. There was one that looked like a picture of the solar system as viewed from the top. Another showed a circle with lines radiating out from it with a crescent moon shape next to it. There was a group of geometric shapes; a square, circle, triangles of different shapes, a cone and so forth.

To the left of each pictograph was one of the highly polished postage stamp size squares. Above each of the squares was the same odd little set of symbols:

etched through the gold plating revealing the plate's silvery substrate.

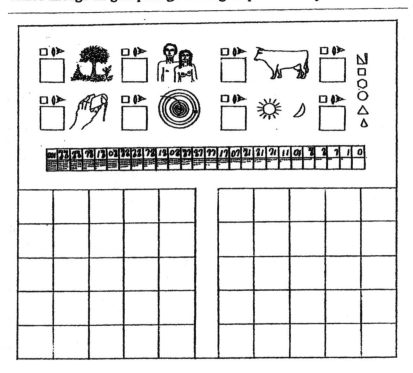

About midway down the plate there was a series of connected boxes divided into top and bottom rows. The result looked vaguely like a couple dozen tiny, half by quarter inch dominos laying side by side across the plate. In the far right domino, the upper box contained a circle. The connected box beneath, was empty. In the next domino to the left, the top box contained a diagonal slash. The lower box directly under it contained a single dot. In the next domino to the left, the top box contained a diagonal up-side-down U. And its lower box contained two dots. The upper box of the forth domino contained a misshapen backward S. The lower held three dots. The fifth domino's upper box contained a figure that vaguely resembled an up-side-down &. Below it were four dots. This progression continued across the plate with different combinations of the five symbols as the number of dots increased by one with each subsequent box. The lower box of the last domino at the extreme left held five rows of five dots.

Syman studied its orderly progression and pointed it out to Dexter. "This clearly demonstrates a base five number system."

"Yes, I see it, too," Dexter concurred after a few moments. "This thing is fascinating, like a puzzle of some kind. These little pictures," he said, pointing, "look a little like hieroglyphics."

"Puzzling, yes. The numbers appear to be user friendly, but the hieroglyphics seem to be quite enigmatic," Syman said.

"Maybe it's not a base five number system," suggested Dexter.

"Or maybe the hieroglyphics are really easy to understand and we just haven't studied them long enough," Syman countered.

Dexter and Syman had instantly become absorbed in studying the strange object and for the moment were no longer concerned with the untoward events at the bank or the more pedestrian demands of their business. Like two children, they had become totally immersed in the intriguing analysis.

If it is a number system, then the people who made this read and write their numbers from right to left." Syman observed.

"Don't the Chinese do that?" inquired Dexter.

"I believe they do," agreed Syman, "but none of this looks Chinese. It all looks, as you have already noted, more like Egyptian hieroglyphics or perhaps early Sumerian pictograms. They strike me as more mid-Eastern than far-Eastern but I'm no authority."

"Early Sumerian pictograms?" said Dexter with disbelief in his voice. "Look Pons, I know you're brilliant, but how the hell would you know the difference between early Sumerian and any other kind of pictograms. For that matter, how do you know what Sumerian pictograms look like?"

"Well, while you're out chasing loose women every night, I'm home reading a lot of weird stuff. How do you think?" Syman said, laughing.

Dexter replied with mock indignation, "Stop trying to change the subject with pejorative comments about my love life, bookworm."

Syman smiled wryly.

It was an old and familiar game. The comic relief and silly jibes kept them both from taking themselves or anything else too seriously. In the high pressure world of American corporate business, a sense of humor was an important key to mental health.

Returning to the subject at hand, Dexter said, "If it weren't so sophisticated, I'd think it was the work of some kids. Perhaps it's a fake artifact, some kind of hoax or something." Considering this line of thought, he picked up the heretofore ignored printout. Opening it, he began scanning through it, looking for some clue to the owner's identity but instantly realized, he couldn't read any of it. It was all written in a foreign language.

"Well, Mr. Pons, the plot thickens," Dexter said, theatrically.

Syman looked up from the plate and saw Dexter looking at the printout. "Did you discover the owner?"

"No I didn't. But I can say with some certitude that the owner speaks a foreign language fluently." Dexter handed the open printout to Syman. "It's obviously some kind of a list, but I can't make anything else out of it.

"I think this is Arabic," said Syman. He picked up the hand held scanner connected to his comparitor and ran it across the page. "Essy, what language is this?

"It's Arabic, Syman," the machine answered in its quiet, soothing, feminine tones.

"Good. We can put the whole thing through the document scanner and have her translate it," suggested Dexter.

Instead, Syman picked up the disk and said, "Let's see what's on this first." He pushed it into a disk slot in the front of Essy's cabinet, which stood on the right side of his desk.

"Maybe the printout's on it and then we won't have to scan it to get a translation. Save some time."

Syman raised the top of the cabinet which was the machine's display screen and said, "Scroll the disk please, Essy." The screen lit up. Orderly 5 letter groups of gibberish streamed by line after line. "It's encrypted."

Once more Syman addressed the comparitor, "Essy, can you identify the publisher of the encryption program?"

"Yes, Syman. You are the publisher and author of this particular program. This disk has been encrypted with TMI's 'Silent Ponds-No Ripples,' Series 7, Format 4ag, Text Encryption Program."

"Ah, excellent luck," said Syman. He pulled out the keyboard and rapidly typed: Esmirelda, run entry program: password PWDN,TY! He tapped the enter button with one last definitive thump!

Years before, when Syman was sure he could trust Dexter completely, he'd informed him about the trap door he'd installed in all his encryption programs. At first, Dexter couldn't believe Syman had done such a thing. But when Syman had explained everything to him, he changed his mind and decided it was a good idea after all. Eventually, Esmirelda and George were also told about the hidden entry points, but the machines were strictly forbidden to use them themselves. They were also strictly forbidden to reveal any trace of their existence to another machine or human being without express permission from Dexter or Syman. Until a few moments ago, that particular permission had never yet been given.

The gibberish on the screen disappeared and was replaced with an electronic copy of the first page of the printout they already had.

"Half way there," said Dexter, peering over Syman's shoulder.

"Yeesss," said Syman drawing the word out, paying more attention to his thoughts than his answer. "Essy, put an English translation on the screen and print hard copy for us, please."

The printer began to chuff out one page after another, showing the same listing format, but now it was in English.

Syman and Dexter watched the display screen intently. Across the top of the document were normal column headings of the type one would expect to find in any well organized spread sheet. The words 'Item Number' were at the head of the first column. Next in order came: Description/ Notes, Date Ordered, Date Purchased, Cost, Destination, with the last and most narrow column headed with a check mark. Written above the top line was the heading: Building Materials, page 1 of 17 pages.

It occurred to Pons that it was a little strange that someone would go to all the trouble to encrypt a list of building materials, but then people did a lot of nutty things.

"Essy, scroll next page, top half of page with heading. Time interval 15 seconds, through document."

"Yes, Syman," replied the machine, as the next page's heading appeared with the top half of the page.

Dexter and Syman both read 'Building Materials, page 2 of 17 pages,' before scanning down the page. Then 'Building Materials, page 3 of 17 pages,' came up on the screen.

A dense list of lumber; lengths, sizes, and type flashed on and off the screen. Fasteners, paint, adhesives, masonry supplies and every conceivable type of construction material in box car size quantities came and went. 'Building Materials, page 17 of 17 pages,' arrived. There were several dimensioned mechanical drawings for structural steel components at the very end of the list.

The next page heading read: 'Construction Tools and Equipment, page 1 of 8 pages,' After this came: 'Vehicles and Heavy Equipment, page 1 of 3 pages.'

As Syman scanned the pages something nagged at the edge of his awareness. There was something his subconscious was trying to tell him. He closed his eyes and forced all thoughts from his mind. He visualized complete nothingness and quiet, invoking his Tai Che training. With no conscious thoughts to clutter his mind, the unconscious nagging resolved itself into the realization that there were only two destinations for all this material. That was significant. Syman looked at the destination column to get the names.

"Dex, have you noticed that there are only two destinations for all these things?"

"No, I hadn't. I'm too busy trying to make some sense of all this stuff."

Syman read out loud, "Ilhas Desertas. Essy," he queried the comparitor, "where is that located?"

After a few moments a map with a blinking cursor materialized on the comparitor's screen obscuring the list text and the machine said, "The Ilhas Desertas are a collection of small islands southeast of the Island of Madeira in the Atlantic Ocean. Madeira and the Ilhas Desertas are possessions of Portugal. Do you want the latitude and longitude coordinates Syman?"

"No, Essy, just the general position, please."

"The island group is located approximately four-hundred-fifty miles west of the city of Casablanca. Casablanca is located on the northwest coast of Africa and is a main seaport for the country of Morocco."

As they watched, the map showing the Madeira Islands group shrank and the east coast of the African continent came into view at the right side of the screen revealing Morocco with the city of Casablanca highlighted.

"That's good, Essy," said Syman. "Now, where is Nalut, Libya?"

The details on the map of northwest Africa shrank more and the cursor traversed to the east as Esmirelda narrated, "The town of Nalut is located on the extreme western edge of the country of Libya, about ten miles from its border with the country of Tunisia, and about one-hundred-thirty miles southwest of the capital city of Tripoli.

In the past, when the climate was wetter, Nalut was the site of Allah's garden, an area several thousand acres in extent of great fertility, once watered by natural springs arising in the hills to the south and flowing down through the Nalut area. Cultivation around Nalut began about 4400 BC. As the climate became more arid one of the ancient world's longest and deepest qanats was constructed underground in an effort to resist the effects of the encroaching Sahara desert."

As Essy continued her narration, a window opened on the screen, showing an oblique cut-away picture of the underground structure of a typical qanat, running from some hills to a town with irrigated fields. Running through the earth was a horizontal bore with vertical well like shafts, extending to the surface every so often all along its length.

"Built about 700 B. C. E. the underground tunnel from the hills is as much as 300 feet under the surface in places. Although increasing aridity is steadily reducing the flow of the springs, the Nalut qanat still carries water the 12 miles from the springs in the southern hills providing the only water for the oasis town, which is now comprised of about 500 people."

"It's hard to believe men could have built such a thing 2700 years ago," said Dexter with obvious admiration.

"Men were just as intelligent and resourceful 2700 years ago as they are today," said Syman. "They just lacked the technically sophisticated understanding inherent in the accumulated stored knowledge we have today. That is to say, they simply lacked books."

Esmirelda had become quiet. When Syman stopped talking, she asked, "Do you want me to continue?"

"No, that's good for now," Syman replied.

Essy's VDS returned to the list.

'Workshop tools-hand, 3 pages,' appeared on the screen.

"Why would anyone want to ship all this stuff to some god forsaken place in the middle of the Sahara desert?" Dexter wondered out loud.

"That's just what I was thinking," said Syman, as he watched the list slip by on the screen.

'Workshop tools-machine, 4 pages,' (with specifications for some very sophisticated machinery Syman noted), came and went. And: 'Laboratory Equipment-Electrical/ Mechanical, 6 pages.' 'Fixtures, 4 pages.'

Dexter looked over at Syman and said, "What kind of an outfit do you suppose this is?"

"Pardon the cliché, Dexter, but your guess is as good as mine at this point."

They continued to scan through the document, the next headings being: Laboratory Supplies, 3 pages; Laboratory Chemicals, 6 pages.

"This would make some chemistry set!" Said Dexter as they read through the list.

Syman opened his mouth to say something but then closed it again, still engrossed in what he read. "We seem to have a list for everything needed to build an industrial lab of some kind. Perhaps this equipment is going to be used to develop a mineral deposit in the desert. That would explain a lot of things."

The next page appeared on the screen. It was headed: 'Bomb Parts and Supplies, page 1 of 11 pages.'

"E-i-e-i-o!" exclaimed Dexter, "Lookie here!"

Syman ignored the exclamation. "Essy, stop scrolling," he commanded. "Scroll this document starting with page 1 of 11 pages, full page, 60 second interval."

The image on the VDS lengthened as the obedient machine complied. Item 1 on the list under the heading: 'Description/Notes' read: Plutonium, Isotope 239, 6.66 kilograms, 98+% enrichment. The 'Date Ordered' was six months earlier. The 'Destination' was listed as Nalut, Libya. The 'Cost' as calculated in US dollars by the comparitor was $8,131,274.84. The line ended with a bold check mark declaring its successful acquisition.

"Shit Syman, the things in this envelope aren't the property of any industrial laboratory. Whoever put this little wish list together is trying to make an atomic bomb!" After a moment he concluded, "This can't possibly be for real."

Syman continued to read down the list considering possibilities.

"It's got to be a hoax or a fake of some kind. It's probably something innocuous like a prop for a play or movie," said Dexter, not wanting to accept the obvious implications.

"I see four facts that point toward this document having a more sinister origin," said Syman. "First, it's encrypted with one of our security programs costing over a thousand dollars. Second, the encrypted text is in an Arabic language. Third, the destination for a lot of the materials on this list are a little city out in the wastes of Libya. And last, but by no means least, the quantity of plutonium indicated can have only one possible purpose. I think you've stumbled onto the Libyan effort to make an atomic bomb, Dexter."

"That's the obvious conclusion, although not necessarily the correct one," said Dexter, in a last effort to deny the apparent truth of Syman's succinct reasoning.

"Considering the inherent danger, I think we would be wise to err on the side of caution and assume the worst. If we are wrong, then there's no harm done. But if by some sordid turn of fate you have stumbled onto Libya's atomic bomb project and we mistakenly dismiss it, the consequences do not bode well for the hapless target, which is likely to be some city in our country or Israel."

"Well," said Dexter, "suppose we do hypothetically accept this obvious conclusion as based in fact, the next question is: What do we do with the information?"

Syman pushed himself away from his desk. He leaned back in his chair and looked up into his partner's steady bright blue eyes. Dexter was now partially sitting with one cheek on the corner of Syman's desk. He sat thus, with his arms crossed over his chest, looking back at Syman as he considered an answer to the question he had just raised.

Dexter spoke again, "John Claire at the Defense Intelligence Agency comes to mind. He's an elint analyst."

"Elint, as in electronic intelligence?" Syman asked.

"Yes."

"I thought he only did satellite photo interpretation." Syman continued.

"Well, that's one type of elint. Anyway, he's been working in the intelligence community for twenty odd years so he'll know who to show this to."

"I know a couple of high level guys at the NSA," countered Syman.

"Why don't we try Claire first and see what he thinks. If he can't handle it we can talk to the people at NSA."

"Okay," agreed Syman, "It's a first step."

"Essy," said Dexter, "Get the phone number for John Claire, that's C-l-a-i-r-e, at the Defense Intelligence Agency in Washington, DC from George and then put a call through to him for me, please."

"Yes, Dexter," replied Essy, having already consulted Dexter's desk top comparitor, George, for three ten-thousandths of a second and initiated the call.

Next, Syman addressed the comparitor. "Are there other documents, beside this one on this disk?"

"No, Syman, there are no other documents on the disk," replied the machine.

Syman opened the lower right drawer of his desk and took a new disk from its flip-tray container and inserted it into Esmirelda's #2 disk drive. "Essy, make a copy of all data from the original disk on the new disk, please." The familiar whining hum of the disk drives was clearly audible in the otherwise quiet room.

Dexter and Syman resumed their reading of the Bomb Parts list, although Syman now read with focused intent, looking for a specific thing. It didn't take him long to find it.

"Here's some polonium, Dex." Syman pointed to the screen. Dexter looked at him blankly waiting for more explanation. Syman realized his discovery didn't mean anything to Dexter and for some reason that annoyed him. "It's hard to believe you and I are partners in the world's fastest growing computer manufacturing company and you're still such a technological illiterate."

"Give me a break Syman," said Dexter, defensively. "I know polonium is a rare radioactive element, but I don't know what it's used for. Why's it so important?"

"Polonium is a radioactive metal," explained Syman, "used in conjunction with the metal beryllium to make a component called an initiator. It's like the primer in a rifle cartridge. When the metals are brought together the polonium knocks large quantities of neutrons loose from the beryllium. This is accomplished in the core of a nuclear device at the moment of ignition during the first few critical nano-seconds and guarantees that there are a half dozen or ten neutrons flying around free inside the core to initiate the chain reaction. Hence, the name initiator. Without it the device might fizzle instead of explode."

"Lovely," said Dexter, feeling the sting of Syman's criticism, but still not quite sure he wanted to know this particular bit of highly arcane information. He retaliated, speaking his mind, "Didn't you have a childhood Pons? I mean, how did you ever find enough time to learn all the arcane crap you've got stored away in that brain of yours?"

"Most of what I know about nuclear devices, I learned in the Air Force. We were taught a lot about the tactical nukes they expected us to drop if the need arose," Syman said seriously, ignoring Dexter's sarcasm. "I ..."

"Mr. Claire is on the telephone, Dexter," said Esmirelda, interrupting Syman.

"Conference mode please, Essy," said Dexter.

Dexter and Syman heard the distinctive clicks and sounds of an open phone line come from the comparitor's speaker.

"Hello, John. This is Dexter Gordon."

"Hi, Dex! Long time. How are you doing?"

"I'm fine, thanks," replied Dexter. "How about you?"

"Goin' along, you know. The kids are growing like weeds. Nina and I took them to Disney World for a week. Just got back yesterday. The place was mobbed. You married yet?" Claire asked, abruptly changing the subject to Dexter.

"Not yet. Got to meet the right girl first. Listen, John, I'm calling because I've accidentally come across a document I think you and the folks at DIA might find interesting."

"How so?" Asked Claire, his tone all business now.

"I'd rather not discuss it over the phone. The document contains sensitive information that might be very important to the security of the United States."

"Can you tell me anything about what you think you've got?"

"I'd really rather not say anything over a wire. I wanna fly down to Washington this afternoon and show it to you."

"This sounds serious, Dexter."

"It is, John."

Claire looked at the picture of his family on the desk, while he considered his schedule for that afternoon. He knew Dex Gordon was no alarmist. "Can you catch the 3PM from La Guardia to Dulles? I can pick you up just after five."

"No. I'll be flying our company jet to Washington National.

We use the Signature terminals at National and Dulles." Said Dexter. "I can rent a car and drive to your office."

"Okay, Dex. I guess that'd work. It's about 12 o'clock now. I've got a meeting in a few minutes with our department supervisor that I can't postpone. Can you make it after 2PM?"

"Sure. That'd be fine," replied Dexter.

"Dexter. Is this business related?"

"No," said Dexter, "I'm sorry I'm not more forthcoming, but you'll be glad when you see what I have."

"Okay, Dexter. Do you need directions to find your way here to my office?"

"No. I have the address. I know my way around DC."

"Good enough. See you soon," said Claire and hung up.

"Essy, please call our aviation manager, Mr. Levanti, and ask him to prepare N273 for a flight to Washington, DC. Tell him to file a flight plan to Washington National, ETA 2 PM."

"Yes, Dexter," said the comparitor.

TMI maintained a hanger for their small fleet of air delivery aircraft at the Bridgeport airport across the street. Syman's love for flying not withstanding, the plant's close proximity to the airport was one of the main reasons TMI had acquired the abandoned Lycoming aircraft manufacturing complex for the site of its manufacturing operations. Now, more than ever, time was money, and TMI tried hard to be lightning fast with its delivery, service, and repair responses.

Syman had been quietly looking at his friend, while the comparitor did its work. Then he removed the disks from the comparitor, and handed them to Dexter. "What are you going to do?"

"I figured I'd spend the afternoon with Claire, and show him what we've found. And then maybe I'll take the family out for dinner. I haven't seen them in a couple of years. I'm godfather to their oldest son, Jason."

"No, I mean, what are you going to give him?" Syman asked.

"Oh. I'll give him the copy of the disk and the English translation of the printout. I think we should keep the originals. Did Essy make a decrypted copy of the disk?"

"No," replied the machine, even though it had not been directly addressed.

"Got to change that." Dexter handed the disks back to Syman, who put them back in the machine.

"Essy, I need a copy of the encrypted disk to be a perfect Arabic copy, but I want all traces of the encryption algorithms removed."

"Yes, Syman." The disk drives could be heard again.

"The hard copy is in English. I'll give that to Claire."

"While you're in DC," said Syman, "I think I'll go to New Haven. I want to show this metal plate to Royce Aldrich. I don't know why, but I don't think it's related to this list."

"I don't think it is either," said Dexter, "but maybe it's some kind of secret code or something."

Royce Aldrich was an archaeologist at Yale University in New Haven about 20 miles to the east of Stratford, up the coast of Long Island Sound. As an expert in ancient civilizations, he could probably tell them exactly what type of pictograms they were, if in fact they were pictograms.

Royce Aldrich was also a sailboat enthusiast, who had become a good friend, working a crew position on TMI's ocean racer 'Thmink'.

The official line was that TMI sponsored the boat because it was a great tax write-off as an advertising expense. The truth was, Gordon and Pons both loved sailing her in the Atlantic Cup or any other ocean races, when they could find the time. And ocean races had been the only real vacation time they taken from work over the years.

The boat's screwy name 'Thmink' was a goof on the now famous motto 'Think' adopted by Thomas Watson Sr., the founder of IBM, the twentieth century's first great computer company. It was also a play on the words, 'The Mink,' which aptly described the boat; one of the sleekest, fastest and most expensive sailing yachts afloat.

Esmirelda beeped, when the copying was finished. Syman once again removed the disks. He handed them to Dexter and said, "Nearly let the proverbial cat out of the proverbial bag."

"Wouldn't have taken Claire long to realize we can also decrypt the security programs we sell the government. Probably make him nervous," Dexter said, with a mischievous grin.

"Yes, I should think it might," said Syman, also smiling.

"So, you want to take our new puzzle and go play with Royce tonight?" Dexter said, deciding to needle Syman a little. "I'll never figure it out. You always get to go have fun while I have to go work. I really need to sit down one of these days and come up with a way to get you securely in harness. Then I can relax for a while." Opening his eyes wide, smiling maniacally, and rubbing his hands together in mock anticipation, Dexter leered at Syman.

"Well, you're the one who stumbled on the bad guys," said Syman, ignoring Dexter's pseudo-histrionics, "so you can't say it's my fault. Do you want to go talk to Royce instead of me? I'll go see Claire."

"No, you go ahead. I'll talk to Royce later, after he's had some time to look it over."

Just then, Essy said, "Dexter, the receptionist downstairs is trying to locate you."

"Conference mode with the receptionist, please, Essy," requested Dexter.

Syman and Dexter heard ringing.

"Reception. This is Carl."

"Hi Carl. This is Mr. Gordon."

"Hello, sir. There's a gentleman here who would like to speak with you. He says it's urgent. He thinks that you and he may have mistakenly swapped envelopes at the bank this morning."

Dexter was quiet for a moment, thinking about what to do, then said, "Carl, tell the gentleman I'll be glad to see him in a few minutes, when I'm finished with my present business. I'll call you when I'm ready."

"Yes, sir," said Carl, and hung up.

"Do you think we should return this stuff to him, Sy?"

"No, I don't. He doesn't know you have his envelope for sure. He can only suspect you might. It sounds like he picked up our proposal. Otherwise, how would he know to come here?"

"Maybe he talked with the people at the bank," said Dexter, "but, either way, it's not important. What is important, is that he can't be sure I have it, so I can deny it. And that will give the government boys time to figure out what's really going on."

With disks and printouts in hand, Dexter walked toward his office. At the door he turned and said, "What a day!"

Syman shrugged in empathy, as if to say 'There's no help for it,' and said instead, "Have a good time in Washington."

"See you later," Dexter said, and walked through the door into his office.

He took a charcoal gray briefcase from the closet and put it on his desk. As well as carrying his papers, it also doubled as his overnight bag on short business trips. Dexter had long ago learned the sagacity of traveling light. He opened it and put the two disks and the English copy of the printout in the compartment in the lid of the briefcase. He paused for a moment looking at the Arabic copy of the printout and decided not to take it. Why haul along the additional weight? He opened the second drawer down on the right side of his desk and dropped it in. After closing the drawer, he lifted the partition covering the bottom compartment of the briefcase. He could see at a glance that there was a fresh laundered shirt, clean socks, underwear, and his toilet case. He pulled a small flashlight from its clip-holder and checked to see if it worked. It glowed brightly. "Ready for blastoff!" He said, replacing the light and snapping the case shut. He walked back into the closet with the case and set it on the floor. Then he opened his safe and took out $400.00 in fifty dollar bills and put them in his money clip. Dexter had every major credit card, but he always liked to have plenty of cash in his pocket. It was simpler, faster and no one ever refused it.

"Just say cash and it's yours," Dexter sang musically, parroting a familiar jingle advertising one of the mega-banks.

He closed the safe and went back to his desk and sat down.

"George, I want to monitor and record the meeting I'm about to have. Use the room's remote cameras to get high definition pictures of the gentleman I'm meeting."

"Yes, Dexter," the machine replied.

Because every area of TMI's grounds was covered with cameras monitored by a security comparitor, George was able to take control of the two hidden cameras in Dexter's office. George also had (as had any comparitor), a camera mounted in the front of his cabinet, giving him a view of the operator as well, but it was facing the wrong direction.

"Call reception for me, George."

After a moment Dexter heard, "Reception. Carl speaking."

"I'm ready to see our visitor now, Carl."

"Okay, Mr. Gordon. I'll send him up."

"Thanks, Carl." The phone hung up.

Dexter raised George's video display screen. "George, I'd like to speak to Mr. Pons." A few moments later Syman materialized on the screen.

"I'm set to monitor and record the meeting," said Dexter. "I figured you would like to see our mystery man. I know Claire will want to."

"Yes, that would be good, Dex."

Dexter addressed his comparitor again, "George, please share the video and audio of my meeting with Essy and Mr. Pons. I will not receive any calls during the meeting."

"Yes, Dexter."

Syman's visage vanished as Dexter lowered the VDS.

There was a knock at the door.

"Come in."

Osmid Bandar walked into the office and found himself facing the man he had seen that morning in the bank lobby barefoot and holding a shotgun.

"Good day, Mr. Gordon," said Osmid, as he advanced toward the desk. "My name is Sabir Hassan."

"Hello," said Dexter, trying to sound relaxed and hospitable. His eyes were drawn to the angry purple bruise on the left side of Osmid's face. "What can I help you with, Mr. Hassan?"

"There is a possibility that we have mistakenly picked up one another's property this morning at the bank. I have an envelope that belongs to your company."

"Well, thank you for taking the time to come here and return it, Mr. Hassan."

Osmid held out the envelope he had brought with him. "I was told by the people at the bank that you found a similar envelope behind the plant by the door. I believe it belongs to me." There was cool evenness in his voice.

Dexter had not reached for the envelope, so Osmid put it on the desk between them.

Dexter's mind was in overdrive as he considered what to say.

"The envelope I found was some old trash that someone had dropped behind the plant," he said, not very convincingly. "I threw it away. They must have a lousy janitorial service clean their bank. I was just about to call the bank and see if they had found my proposal when you arrived."

Osmid looked directly at Dexter through snake eyes. No emotion showed on his face except for the slight lift at the corners of his mouth. Nevertheless, his freeze-dried smile of insincerity failed to belie his true feelings. In a mighty effort to maintain his composure, he said, "I seem to have barked the wrong tree," misquoting the misunderstood Americanism. Fear and anger constricted his chest. He knew Gordon was lying to him. Violence welled in him and it was all he could do not to strike out at Gordon right then, to make him return his property. Instead, he said, "Thank you for your time, Mr. Gordon," and then turning, he quickly left the office.

Dexter watched the swarthy little man leave his office and felt relief. He knew his denial had been anything but convincing. Still, without any real proof to the contrary, there was nothing Mr. Hassan, (probably not his real name, Dexter realized), could do about it.

Osmid walked through TMI's corporate headquarters building, taking the stairs down instead of the elevator. He was furious, frustrated, and frightened. He needed to walk off some of the adrenaline coursing through him. That stupid, greedy American probably wanted to keep the artifact. Osmid cursed himself for keeping it with the project list. But then, it had never entered his mind that he might loose them. Osmid was not sure what action to take, but he realized he must not, under any circumstance, allow this meddling American to find out, or interfere with, what he was doing.

He got into his car and drove back toward his hotel. As he drove, he thought about what he should do. Instead of taking the downtown exit in Bridgeport back toward his hotel, he decided he'd drive the sixty odd miles to his cousin's place in New York City. A plan was beginning to form in his mind. With his cousin's help, he could hire some outside assistance. His cousin knew the right kind of people here in the U.S. They'd break into Gordon's office tonight and search for the envelope. The office should be relatively easy to get into. If he found it there, then his problem would be solved. If not, then they could go to Gordon's house and rough him up in private and force him to hand over his property.

One way or the other, he'd get the envelope back and no one would ever know. Thinking it over, as he drove along, Osmid was almost beginning to feel good again.

7

The mechanism was insidious in its simplicity, yet devastating in its effectiveness. And without a doubt, it was the most economical weapon for mass murder ever devised. It had only two parts: a clockwork release mechanism and a pressurized tank of aerosols. The aerosols had again been refilled at 4 am as it had every Friday morning for the past six weeks.

Now, exactly 8 am, the mechanism hissed a two second puff of its vile fog into the air stream moving along the ventilation duct. It would continue to release its lethal contents every thirty seconds until its pressurized tank was empty.

Moments later, along the hundred yards of duct beyond the atomizer, the air exited through louvered openings in the ceiling of the airport terminal corridor.

Just then, Sumiko Fujita, a software engineer from Santa Clara, California, on her way home from a business conference in Tokyo, became the first of many this Friday to walk through the tainted air. During the rest of the day, hundreds of other passengers flying Hinode Worldwide Airlines to destinations around the world would also walk down that loathsome corridor.

8

Dexter sat quietly while John Claire read through the parts of the document Dexter had marked.

Finally, Claire looked up at him and said, "This is amazing, Dexter. People have died trying to get this information in Libya and you just pick it up off the floor of a bank."

"You're assuming it's related to Libya," countered Dexter.

"Well, of coarse. The radioactives are being shipped to Libya. What other conclusion should we draw from this?"

"Perhaps this is a hoax or part of a theatrical performance or something totally out in left field that we haven't considered yet."

"There's always that possibility, but this Sabir Hassan we were looking at on your security tape seems like a pretty grim fellow and not a very good actor, judging from his expression at the end of your meeting with him. I'd put my money on your having stumbled onto Libya's bomb project," concluded Claire. "We'd be damn fools if we didn't follow this up, thoroughly. The problem is you don't know where he went."

"You can call the bank and see if they have his address," Dexter suggested half seriously.

"Yeah, sure. Maybe they have his phone number, too," Claire said, with a laugh.

"Well, now you've got the general idea, what do you think should be done with it?"

"I'm going to have to go higher up with this, you understand? If there's any chance that this information is real, we've got to investigate it from every angle," said Claire, definitively.

"Does that mean you can take it from here?" Dexter asked.

"Coming to me was a smart move, Dex. Things will start popping immediately. You don't have to worry about it from here on." As an afterthought, Claire looked at his watch. It said 4:20. "Would you mind talking to my boss and telling him what you told me? I think we should put this problem in the hopper right now."

"No, I don't mind. This thing is scary as hell. The sooner we get it taken care of, the better," said Dexter with sincerity. Then, changing the subject he asked, "I hate to bring this up, John, but I haven't eaten anything since breakfast. Do you spooks have a commissary or a soda machine or something around here that has some food?"

His friend laughed, "Sure. We can stop there on the way to my bosses office, but don't eat too much. I called Nina and told her you were coming to visit and she's fixing a special dinner for us. She's also preparing the spare room for you to stay the night."

"Hey, that's really great John. I wanted to have dinner with all of you, but I can't stay the night. I rescheduled the meeting I missed this morning at the bank for tomorrow."

"What ever you say, Dex. I guess dinner will just have to do. Let's go see my boss before he leaves. I don't want to miss him, he'd have my butt."

The two men rose from their chairs. Claire picked up the purchasing manifest, the floppy disk and the security video of Sabir Hassan Dexter had brought with him.

"Can we keep these?" Claire asked, as they left his office.

"That's the plan," said Gordon

9

Syman left his office and walked across the street to the TMI hanger. Dexter had flown off to Washington in one of TMI's company jets to see John Claire. Swayed perhaps by the power of suggestion, Syman decided to fly his helicopter to New Haven to see Royce Aldrich. The flight would only be ten minutes each way, but it would be relaxing and maybe Royce would like to fly out to the Plum Club on Long Island for dinner and a drink. If so, then Syman could enjoy an hour or so of flying all together.

Syman had bought himself the Bell CF-4 commuter helicopter the year before. It was a small four place craft. He loved to fly it and any slim justification was a good enough excuse to roll it out and take off. Sometimes, when he took a rare day for himself, he would just fly off into the sky and tool around New England with no particular destination in mind. He kept a disassembled bicycle in the helicopter's luggage compartment, so he could get around easily in some of the little towns he visited. He'd found some great places earlier in the spring, but lately, he'd been too busy with the servador development to do much flying and he missed it.

After performing a preflight inspection, Syman climbed into the pilot's seat, buckled himself in and started the engine. He let the machine warm up for three minutes. When Syman advanced the throttle, the Bell leapt into the air like a flushed quail. He put the machine into a tight turning climb to the east, giving the aircraft full power.

After six minutes of uneventful flying Syman was nearing New Haven and he could clearly see the tall high rise physics building that sat on top of the hill in the midst of Yale's New Haven campus.

Some people thought the physics tower was an icon of the modern Yale University forging boldly into the Twenty-first Century. Some people thought the building was a tasteless eyesore. To Syman it didn't matter either way. For him, it was just a landmark that showed him the way to the Yale campus.

Syman gazed over the rest of the city. He could see the rusty red ridge of East Rock looming to the north and the harbor with its scrap piles and oil tank farms to the right as he turned north away from Long Island Sound heading for the physics tower.

Syman noted that the evening air over New Haven seemed remarkably clear. The usual dirty pinkish-gray twilight smog was absent over the old factory city.

A minute later, Syman set the 'copter down on the grass next to the physics tower. The school of archaeological studies was just down the hill from where he landed. It wasn't the first time Syman had gone to see Royce this way.

He always enjoyed the response from people, when he landed. Helicopters are uniquely fascinating and people always gathered around, wherever he landed the Bell. This time was no different.

As he brought the helicopter down, he could see people scattering to get out of the way. Once he was on the ground people began to edge back to get a closer look. Syman shut the machine down. The gas turbine became quiet, but the rotor blade continued to turn for a few more moments. He gathered up the valise from the co-pilot's seat and swung down from the cockpit, carefully stepping on the little step outrigged from the landing strut. He was particularly cautious about this, because the last time he'd flown, he'd slipped off the step skinning his shin as he tumbled out of the cockpit onto the ground. He'd been lucky he hadn't broken something important. As it was, his scraped shin had turned an angry purple and it had hurt like hell when anything brushed against it. He wasn't going to be so careless, today. Besides, he thought, he'd really look like a horse's ass if he fell out of the helicopter in front of all these college kids.

Syman walked down hill to the archaeology building. Unlike the starkly modern physics building, the Gothic style of the archaeology building, in keeping with the traditional style of Yale's original buildings, looked more like a wing of an English castle than an American university building. It gave the appearance of great age, although it was little more than one-hundred years old. Nevertheless, the buildings deeply worn slate steps bespoke its use by thousands of students over the years. Arriving at the third floor landing, Syman pulled open the steel fire door and stepped into the hall. He went to his left. Royce's office was down the hall four doors on the right. Syman stopped in front of the door and knocked. He had called earlier in the day and Royce would be expecting him about now. He heard a muffled "Come in," through the door. As Syman stepped into the room, Royce Aldrich looked up from his desk. Their gazes met in a warm, friendly greeting as Syman crossed the room.

"Syman, how have you been?" Royce asked, rising and extending his hand.

"I've been well, thanks," Syman replied, as they shook.

"Was that your sky car I heard a few minutes ago?"

"The very same."

"It's been a while since we last got together. I've been wondering how you and Dex have been doing."

"Lately, Royce, we haven't been doing much, except work. TMI is bringing its first servidor robot out of the lab and onto the production floor."

"I didn't know you guys were building robots," Royce said, seriously. And then with a big smile, he asked, "Do you think they could teach undergraduate archaeology?"

"Maybe," said Syman, laughing at the thought. After a moment, he continued, "It's always complicated getting a new product going. Sometimes it's not much fun, but we'll get the bugs worked out in the next few months and then hopefully, life will return to something more like normal."

Syman put his valise on Royce's desk. Opening it, he began leafing through its contents, searching for the envelope containing the plate.

Watching Syman, Royce tried to imagine what normal might be for the TMI twins, letting his thoughts retrace some of the history of his relationship with Dexter and Syman.

TMI offered several education and research grants each year to anyone attending or teaching at one of Connecticut's many universities.

Several years earlier, Royce had applied for a research grant. He'd first met both men at the company's headquarters in Stratford, Connecticut at a meeting in which Royce explained his proposal to them.

Royce had been working at the site of the original harbor for the ancient city of Carthage in North Africa. He'd made some spectacular discoveries in the two years he'd been developing the site, but his original grant was running out and he'd needed a new grant to continue. Dexter and Syman had listened to him patiently, asked some insightful questions and then asked him to wait in the outside office, while they discussed a few things. When they called him back to the conference room, they told him, they liked what he'd done so far and they made a substantial commitment ($1,600,000), handing him a check on the spot.

Royce had been floored at the unorthodox way they had proceeded. The check was for four times the amount he'd requested, and it exactly matched his total projected expenses for field work at the site for the lifetime of the dig.

They let him stand speechless for a few moments and then Syman explained that they had done a good deal of investigating about Royce's previous work, and its significance. The caliber of Royce's work had impressed them and they had already made up their minds to support his work if they were favorably impressed with Royce, when they'd met face to face. They had been.

They also told him that his work was of such historical significance that they were going to fund his grant privately, rather than through the company's grant program, and that the support would continue as long as Royce thought the work was progressing satisfactorily. Their only request had been that he write once a month and keep them abreast of his progress.

Syman and Dexter had then thanked him for contacting them. They told him, they considered it a privilege to be able to support him in his work.

A while after that unusual first meeting, Dexter invited Royce to a dinner party he was hosting at his house in Lordship. During the inevitable small talk, Dexter learned of Royce's love for sailing and invited him out for a weekend sail aboard 'Thmink' TMI's racing yacht. Dexter was also impressed with Royce's sailing abilities and before long, he was crewing with Dexter and Syman, (when he wasn't working in Tunisia at the dig).

Coming back to the present, Royce asked, "What's this mysterious artifact you want me to take a look at?"

"Well, Royce, we're not sure what it is. That's why I'm here, dinner and a drink with a good friend notwithstanding, of course."

Syman slid the plate from the envelope and handed it to him. Royce turned on his desk lamp and held the plate close to the light to get a better look. "This is very unusual, Syman. Where did you get it?"

"Dexter picked it up under some odd circumstances. It's complicated. I'll tell you about it during dinner, but, suffice to say, the previous owner didn't give us any information concerning this thing"

"Well, that's too bad. Did he tell you where he got it?"

"No. He didn't tell us that either."

Then Royce asked, "What exactly would you like me to do for you?"

"We want you to see what you can learn about it. The first thing we want to know is whether this is an artifact or an object of modern origin. You're an expert in ancient languages and inscriptions. We were hoping you might recognize something."

"Right off the bat, Sy, I don't recognize any of this. At least not in the way it's presented here." Royce was quiet for a moment, while he studied a particular area on the plate intently. "Some forms of Sumerian pictograms are similar," he said without looking up, "but similar is the operative word. They're not quite the same."

Syman smiled, when Royce told him this, as he thought about Dexter's sarcastic comments at the office earlier in the day.

"Dexter and I think this row of dominoes is a base five numbering system." Syman pointed to them on the plate. "It's demonstrated clearly from right to left."

"Yes, I see that, now that you've pointed it out," said Royce, in agreement.

Syman continued, "There are combinations of five distinct characters in the upper row. They repeat in the same regular way as our own base ten counting characters, except we use ten digits, zero through nine. Whoever inscribed this, only used these five."

"This thing is fascinating," said Royce with enthusiasm. I have some time on my hands now that the spring semester is over. I'll see what I can discover for you guys."

"Thanks Royce, that would be great. If there is any expense, just let us know and we'll take care of it. And we'll pay you of course."

"Well, we'll worry about that after I've had some time to study it. I wonder what these squares are?" said Royce pointing to several of them. "See this set of three symbols above each one. They're positioned like titles, but if they are, they all apparently say the same thing."

"Yes, I noticed them the first time I looked at the plate, too. In fact, I was thinking about them on the way over here and an idea has occurred to me. The first symbol on the right, if we read them as writing in the same way we think we're reading the base five progression, looks a little like the cross section side view of a human eye."

"Yes, I see what you mean," said Royce.

"Viewed in this way it suggests that something is either being looked at or that something should be looked at," continued Syman. "The next symbol to the left looks like the side view of a typical convex magnifying lens. It would be a pretty nearly universal symbol to anyone familiar with optics."

"And of course, the little square represents the bigger square below it," said Royce with mounting excitement.

"Right," continued Syman. "In each case the message is the same and reads 'Look at this square under magnification.'"

"You just might be right about that, Syman. Let's have a look and see. I just happen to have a microscope handy," he said, as he walked to the closet. Royce brought out the microscope and set it up on the desk. Then, he slid the plate carefully under the lowest power lens, positioning one of the squares directly beneath. After carefully adjusting the desk light and focusing the instrument, he stepped back and motioned Syman to have a look.

Syman saw a field of tiny micro-squares row upon row, rank after rank.

"We need to try a higher magnification," he said, as he stepped back to let Royce change the lens.

Royce spent a half a minute adjusting the instrument a second time.

"Wow! Look at this," he said, stepping back to let Syman look once more.

The images were faint because the magnification was high and the desk lamp was not really bright enough, but this time Syman saw dozens of pictures and pictograms, similar to what was already visible on the plate without using a microscope. Obviously the little micro-squares were some type of sophisticated micro-recording or photo-micrograph.

"We're using 500X magnification, and we're only looking at part of one of these squares, Sy. There are hundreds of these things on this plate."

"Stranger and stranger," said Syman, as he straightened up.

10

Osmid Bandar had been right. His cousin did know the necessary people and how to find them quickly. When Osmid had left Gordon's office, that afternoon, he had gone to his cousin Mhusa's apartment in the Bronx and now he was back. He was accompanied by his cousin Mhusa, two nameless men Mhusa had brought along for muscle, and a locksmith named Burt, who supplemented his income after regular work hours by occasionally helping himself to other people's property.

Osmid glanced at his watch. It was just 1 AM. He felt vaguely afraid, but he also felt exhilarated by the danger of being caught. It brought back memories of the old days, when he'd crossed remote mountain passes guiding pack animals while smuggling drugs from one country to another. It had been years since he had taken such a blatant and naked risk as he was tonight. But, if he didn't want to end up dead, he'd have to find the envelope and quickly.

Surprisingly, they were able to drive directly to the parking lot behind TMI's head quarters building without encountering anyone. It was the middle of the night and there were no security guards. It seemed strange, but then why would the company bother with security guards for an office building? Osmid had driven through a gate earlier in the day and had assumed it would be closed, when they got there, but it wasn't. They had planned to cut through the fence he'd seen next to the building, cross the intervening parking lot, and approach the building from the back, but that had proved unnecessary.

Sherlock, the security comparitor responsible for monitoring all of TMI'S property twenty-four hours a day, recorded the Ford van as it parked behind the corporate head quarters building. There was light enough from the parking lot's lights to allow Sherlock to get good pictures of the two men, who got out of the van and walked up to the entrance door. The comparitor dutifully recorded the video images and the license number of the van in a new file it had initiated when the vehicle first appeared. This was standard procedure for every new vehicle or person that came on TMI's 300 acre property. As the men walked toward the entrance door their movements were simultaneously recorded by eleven different cameras inside and outside the building.

It had taken Burt just a few seconds to open the lock with one of the keys he carried. He was very good at what he'd been hired to do, Osmid noted with satisfaction. Burt had studied the entrance door for a few moments and then selected one of the keys he had on a large ring. The first key didn't work, but the second key he tried worked perfectly.

Once inside the building, Lucricia, the comparitor responsible for climate control in all of TMI'S forty-one separate buildings, automatically turned up the lighting as Osmid led the way to Gordon's office. Having the lights go on and off as they walked through the building was unnerving, but Osmid reassured himself that people might work any hour of the day or night in a large business's corporate offices.

Standing once more in front of Gordon's office door, Osmid could feel a bitter resentment rising in him. He pointed at the door and stepped aside. Burt studied the door's lock for a moment and tried turning the handle. The door swung open. It was unlocked. Osmid was amazed at the total lack of security. Americans were so arrogant. If a building like this one were left completely unprotected in his country, there would be little left of its contents by the next morning. Stepping past Burt, Osmid walked into Dexter Gordon's private office.

"Look for a safe and see what is in it," Osmid said to Burt in a whisper.

Burt began methodically checking the large bookcase covering the wall facing Gordon's desk for a safe or secret compartment. After quickly finding only books, he moved on and carefully inspected the other walls. The walls were of solid cherry paneling hung with several exquisite paintings. On the wall between Dexter's and Syman's office was hung a fifteenth century Venetian tapestry worth a small fortune. Osmid immediately recognized the tapestry's quality and thought about stealing it.. It was a truly beautiful piece and he liked the idea of getting the best of this Gordon and taking something personal. It appealed strongly to his Oriental sense of revenge.

After his quick survey of the room, Osmid began his search with the desk. He walked around it and sat down in the chair. He pulled the center drawer open and glanced at the contents. His envelope was obviously not there. He pulled open the large top drawer on the right. It was full of files and miscellaneous paperwork. Gordon was apparently a very neat man. Both drawers had been well organized. Osmid methodically leafed through the contents, but the envelope was not there. "Damn this American," he cursed to himself. He opened the second drawer. Sitting right there on top, lay the dog-eared envelope, the object of their search.

"Ah ha!" Osmid said loudly. "I've found it."

"That's good," replied Burt. "I just found a safe here in this closet. Now I won't have to open it"

Osmid opened the envelope and immediately realized that the disk and the gold plate were missing. He didn't care about the golden artifact really. Losing that wouldn't get him killed. He just wanted the disk and the list. He dumped the list on to the desk top to make sure the disk wasn't hidden in its sheaf of pages. He fanned it and shook it. No disk.

"Open the safe anyway," he said to Burt. "A computer disk is missing from the envelope. We must keep searching until we find it."

Burt complied by taking a miniature stethoscope from his jacket pocket. Holding the instrument's pickup with his left hand, just under the safe's combination wheel, he slowly turned the combination wheel with his right. After an intense minute of work, Burt turned the handle with a satisfying click and the safe's door opened wide.

"It's open, Mr. Hassan," Burt said, quietly over his shoulder.

Osmid, who had been busy going through the remaining drawers of the desk and all the rest of the furniture in the room, sighed in resignation, having failed to locate the missing disk. He crossed to the closet, squeezing in along side Burt in the confined space. After taking everything out of the safe, it was clear that the disk was nowhere to be found in the office. And if it wasn't here, Osmid still had a big problem. Where did the meddling American have the disk?! Kneeling on the floor of the closet, staring at the open safe, feelings of impotent frustration alternated with flashes of hot rage. In his mind, he could feel his hands around Gordon's neck as he clamped down strangling the life from him. "If only," he thought.

Burt spoke to him, distracting him from his fantasy. "There's about twelve thousand dollars here. Should we take it or leave it?"

It took Osmid a moment to hear what Burt had said. He didn't care about the money.

"Take the money," he finally said, deciding maybe it would hurt this bastard American, who was causing him such dreadful problems.

"We're done here. We're going to have to pay a visit to the man himself and have him to tell us where the disk is."

Burt looked at Bandar. He wasn't sure he liked the sound of what he'd just heard. Burt was just a thief. He didn't want to get mixed up in any rough stuff. And besides, it was late. He had to get up early and go to work at his shop.

11

Karrie Gordon lay back in bed and pondered her life in its present form. She considered the turning point she had reached upon her recent graduation from Yale law school and how her life would now change. There were important and life changing decisions to be made soon and she wanted to be sure she was really in touch with her feelings and that she had an accurate perspective on her life before she made them.

She loved living in her brother's house here in Lordship, the unique little beach community located on Long Island Sound at Stratford point. The house was enormous, with something like thirty rooms and it was unlike any house she'd ever seen. It sat on a low hill directly back from the beach in the midst of three huge spreading silver maple trees surrounded by two acres of lawn. The house had five bedroom suites, each with its own sitting room, dressing room and glass roofed bathroom. There was a large library and a glass roofed ballroom which Dexter had turned into an enormous greenhouse, filling it with unusual plants from all over the globe, including several red wood seedlings he intended to plant in the yard in a few years. There were two kitchens, two dining rooms, (one formal, one normal), a great hall with a ten foot wide fire place and gas lighting, and three smaller parlors adjacent to both the library and the great hall for more intimate gatherings.

An underground boathouse had been built beneath the house and was connected to Long Island sound by a hundred foot long, water filled, steel doored tunnel.

With a penchant for tunnels, the original owner had also built a second tunnel from the main house to the carriage house, where the servants quarters were located upstairs. This allowed for secret travel between the two buildings. The house had been built during prohibition, and it was obvious that the original owner had been a big time bootlegger. The tunnels provided the perfect way to transfer large quantities of hooch from a boat under the house to the garage, where a waiting truck could be conveniently loaded out of sight.

Karrie thought it was all very romantic and not just a little mysterious and she loved everything about the place.

She'd once asked Dexter why he'd chosen to live alone in such a large house. Laughing, he told her, that one day, when he had some free time, he planned to find himself the right girl and fill the house with kids. She'd laughed too, but secretly she worried about her brother being lonely.

Although her brother Dexter had become one of the wealthiest men in the U.S. and despite the property's extensive servant's quarters, he'd chosen to live here alone for the first several years, enjoying the peace and quiet and privacy it afforded him.

That had changed a little when Karrie moved into the big house with him at the beginning of law school. Still, even with the two of them living there, the house was all but empty.

As children growing up, Dexter and Karrie had always been close, he the adored older brother, but they had inevitably grown apart when Dexter left home. Sharing this large house in Lordship, they had gotten to know each other again, but as adults.

Before, when she had been living and working in New York, they had seen each other occasionally, but Karrie had not realized what a really special person her brother had become.

Like Dexter, Karrie was blue eyed and blond. Five feet, seven inches tall, her willowy frame had been perfectly suited to the modeling career she had successfully pursued for the eight years prior to her attending law school at Yale. When Karrie turned thirty-one, she'd felt restless and dissatisfied with the world of beautiful bodies. Though successful, being a model had become boring. She longed for something more interesting and challenging.

At a deadly dull dinner party, while rubbing elbows with some of New York's rich and influential, Karrie had met Sheila Jenkins, a prominent advocacy lawyer. After spending most of the night talking together, Karrie and Sheila had become fast friends. One thing led to another and before long Sheila had gotten Karrie involved as a volunteer with some advocacy legislation she'd been shepherding through the State Legislature. The first project Karrie worked on eventually resulted in state funding for after-school centers for kids. When their legislative proposal had been passed into law, Karrie realized just how much she enjoyed both the process and the results. She had helped do something important and it whetted her appetite to become an advocacy lawyer herself.

Sheila gave her hearty encouragement, but warned her the pay would never be great. Low pay, however, was no concern. Karrie didn't need the money. She had been investing in Thinking Machines International's stock since the day the company first went public, and as a result she had become a fairly wealthy woman. Over the years, she'd invested a little over two-hundred-fifty thousand dollars. Some had come from her modeling income, but most of the money had been given to her at various times as gifts from her brother Dexter. The phenomenal growth of TMI had done the rest.

Now, finishing law school at age thirty-five, her present net worth was about 3 million dollars, so money was not a problem.

Karrie yawned and stretched. She could feel the soothing mist of sleep gently embrace her consciousness, but she resisted the urge to let go.

Karrie began thinking about Syman Pons and their relationship. Originally, she had planned to move back to New York to work with Sheila Jenkins once she'd gotten her law degree. That plan had failed to take her growing closeness to Syman into account.

They had started spending some serious time together two years ago and since then their feelings for each other had become very strong. She had never been so in love with anyone before. And now that she and Syman had become so close, the idea of being away from him for more than a day or two made her feel sick inside. She was not sure that she still wanted to go back to New York to work. Laying there in bed, Karrie knew what she really wanted was to meld her life with Syman's and live happily ever after. Dreaming about that course of action made her feel great, and she savored the dream for long minutes, knowing in her heart, what the right direction for her life would be. Immersed in the feelings of warmth, happiness, love, and security she and Syman could share together, Karrie dropped off to sleep with the light still on.

Karrie awoke with a violent shock. Two strange men were standing at the foot of her bed staring at her.

"What are you doing here?" she shrieked. "Get out or I'll call the police!" she yelled, with false threat.

A short, swarthy man spoke to Karrie in quiet tones, but with a strong accent she didn't recognize, "We are not going to harm you. We are looking for Dexter Gordon. It appears he is not home. When do you expect him to return?"

Without thinking Karrie said, "He's out of town over night. He won't be back until tomorrow."

"That is too bad," the man said, as he considered what to do next.

"What do you want with my brother?" Karrie demanded.

"Ah, so you are Mister Gordon's sister," he said, with a slight bob of his head and a reptilian look that sent a shiver through Karrie. She realized belatedly that letting these men, who ever they were, know that Dexter was her brother and that he would not be home tonight, may not have been a good idea. Well, she thought to herself, she'd been asleep, and she still wasn't clear headed even though she'd nearly had a heart attack finding two strangers in her bedroom in the middle of the night.

After a few moments pause the little man said, "You are going to have to come with us, Ms. Gordon."

Karrie freaked at the thought of going anywhere with these two creeps. Without thinking, she rolled off the side of the bed and ran through the doorway into the adjoining bedroom. She slammed the door before either man could intercept her. Fumbling for the lock, she snapped it shut, just as the first one grabbed the knob. Crossing the room, she ran out the door to the hall, straight into another man holding a gun. She froze. She'd never had anyone point a gun at her.

12

Dexter looked at his watch. It was a little after 2 A.M. His eyes felt gritty. He started the Jeep and quickly backed out of the parking space headed for home. The flight back from DC had been uneventful, but getting back to the DC airport had been difficult. A gasoline truck had tipped over on the highway just before the exit to the airport and he had been stuck in traffic for two hours. He finally got the jet off the ground at 1:30. Dexter realized he probably should have stayed the night at the Claire's, but aside from the visit with his friends, he'd had a tough day and just wanted to get a good night's sleep in his own bed. Fortunately, the drive from TMI's hanger to his house was only just over a mile.

Dexter parked the Jeep in the driveway next to the kitchen door at the back of the house. The spring night was clear and fresh with a thousand bright stars. The moon had just set and the night sky was very black. The kitchen door was unlocked. That was strange. Karrie usually locked the doors at night. Lights had been left on downstairs and that too was unlike Karrie. Dexter wondered if she wasn't feeling well. He went up the back stairs from the kitchen to the second floor to check on her and see if she was okay. As he approached her room, he could see light showing through the partially open door.

"Sis, are you okay?" he called out, quietly. There was no reply. He gently opened the door to her room and looked inside. The bed was mussed, but unoccupied. Dexter called out, "Sis, it's me, Dex. Are you okay?" Still, there was no reply. Dexter was concerned now. He crossed the room to the bathroom and opened the door without pause. No Karrie! Dexter walked quickly out of the room, going from one room to the next. She wasn't anywhere upstairs. He went downstairs again. At the bottom of the stairs was the front entrance foyer. A cherry table sat against the wall with a telephone on it, along with a pad of paper and some pens and pencils. This was were Karrie normally left notes for him. There was a note. He sighed with relief. She must have just gone out somewhere, maybe for a walk down the beach. It was a beautiful night. Dexter read the note and his blood ran cold as he realized what it said.

'Mr. Gordon,

> you have my property. I want it returned to me. I have your sister. When you return my property, I will return your sister. Do not tell anyone and no police or you will never see your sister again. I will call you at your office at precisely 12 noon with instructions.'

Dexter read the letter over again several times as alternating emotions coursed through him. He felt helpless and frightened and tired, but most of all, he was angry. Though sick at heart with worry for his sister's safety, he vowed that if anything happened to her there would be no place on earth where this thug could hide from him. Reflecting on his vow a few moments, he realized he was concentrating on the wrong thing. What he needed to do, was return the stuff as quickly as possible and get Karrie safely away from this guy.

Dexter immediately thought about calling Syman. The note said not to tell anyone else about this. He decided there was no way this Hassan or what ever his name was, would find out that he had talked to Syman. Dexter took his cell phone from his jacket pocket and punch the number '3' and then hit the speed-dial button.

A groggy Syman Pons answered the phone. "Hello."

Dexter quickly explained to him that Karrie had been kidnapped. In a few moments Syman was fully awake, with a wave of heat spreading across the skin on his chest, neck, and face. "You want me to come over to your place?"

"No. I just got in from D.C. I'll drive over there. We've got to figure this thing out and get it fixed, Syman."

"Right. See you in a few minutes."

Dexter drove the half mile across Lordship to Syman's ultra-modern house. It was also on the beach. Large, low, and round, Syman's house resembled nothing so much as a flying saucer that had crashed into an enormous sand dune on the beach.

The first to move to Lordship, Syman had picked the site and designed the house himself. A hundred feet back from the water's edge, Syman had created a large sand mound into which he had nestled the rear of the house.

He'd purchased six other properties and eventually razed their buildings to gather the acreage he wanted around the house, but when he first presented his plans to the city's zoning commission feathers flew and he was lambasted in the local newspaper as a destroyer of local history.

To Syman, who was not used to the acidic Yankee temperament of his new neighbors, it was all slightly perplexing and more than a little annoying. After pointing out to the idiots on the local zoning board that TMI and its 11,200 job's and billions of dollars of technology could be moved elsewhere, Syman quietly received the approvals he needed to build his odd house.

Once completed, its view's were spectacular and it couldn't have been more convenient to TMI, only a mile away.

As Dexter pulled up next to the house, he was thinking about none of this. The outside light came on and the kitchen door swung open where he saw Syman standing barefoot tucking the Armani dress shirt he'd worn to work that day into his bluejeans.

Syman yawned, covering his mouth with one hand as he waved to Dexter with the other. Then he turned and went back inside leaving the door open for Dexter.

It was going to be a long night.

13

Syman hovered the Bell a discreet 2000 yards away from the meeting point at an altitude of 1200 feet. The Bell was a commuter's helicopter and possessed two features that were more than a little helpful to Syman as he watched Dexter meet with Karrie's kidnapper.

Intended to fly extensively over heavily populated areas, the Bell had been designed to be very quiet and was equipped with a sophisticated electronic sound nullification system.

By generating sound waves of appropriate frequencies and amplitudes that were the exact complements to the sound waves generated by its turbine engine, lift rotor and tail rotor, the nullification system filled in the valleys in the sound waves with more sound. Thus, the variations in the sound waves, to which the human ear is sensitive, disappeared, making the machine very quiet. The technology had originally been developed to a high degree for the U. S. navy as part of its submarine stealth program and was quite effective.

Hovering at 500 feet, the Bell made about as much noise as the average family car traveling on an interstate highway at 65 miles per hour.

A second feature was the craft's auto pilot which held it steady as Syman watched Dexter drive to the meeting point on the south side of the abandoned Stop and Shop food warehouse next to I-95 in Norwalk Connecticut. The area was a rundown industrial zone full of forlorn and empty buildings. The streets were lined with abandoned cars, trash, and gutted buildings of every description. Only here and there, did an occasional business still struggle to hang on amidst the decrepit industrial wasteland.

It was a perfect place for the bad guys and it made Syman nervous. There was absolutely no one around to help Dexter and Karrie if they needed it in a hurry. And Syman could be no help hanging in the air a mile away watching the exchange through his Ziess binoculars. Syman didn't like the setup, but there was no alternative. Dexter was going to exchange the disk for Karrie and Syman was going to watch.

Through the powerful glasses Syman could clearly read the license number, 'TMI 2' on Dexter's Jeep as he drove through the narrow streets toward the meeting place. The binoculars were so deceptive. It was frustrating to be able to see Dexter so clearly, yet not actually be with him. Syman almost wished he'd forced Dexter to take him along, but Hassan had been most emphatic on the phone about killing Karrie if Dexter didn't follow his instructions exactly. They couldn't take the chance.

As he watched, Syman went over the telephone call once more in his mind. It had come at the office at exactly 12 noon, just as the note had said it would. Hassan had only demanded Dexter bring the computer disk. The gold plate apparently wasn't important to Hassan or perhaps he had forgotten to mention it. Syman prayed that that was the case because they had not been able to reach Royce Aldrich to get the plate back from him for the exchange. Royce was off doing something and nobody knew where to find him.

Syman watched as the Jeep came to a stop directly in front of the abandoned building's office door as per instructions. There were two other vehicles also parked there, nose in to the building. Syman quickly typed their license numbers into his laptop computer. One was a Ford van that had seen better days. Syman was sure it was the same one he and Dexter had seen in the security tapes that George, Dexter's office comparitor, had shown them that morning. The other was a maroon Honda 4 door sedan. There were three men sitting in the Honda as far as Syman could tell. He couldn't see into the Ford van at all.

Dexter climbed out of his jeep. A man waving a rifle stepped from the office door of the warehouse. Dexter raised his arms and another man climbed out of the front seat of the Honda. He walked over close to Dexter. Dexter turned around and put his hands on the hood of his Jeep. The second man frisked him from behind. He lifted up Dexter's jacket and pulled a gun from the holster Dexter had stuffed into the back of his pants. As Syman watched with horror, the man hammered Dexter in the back of the head with the gun, knocking him to the ground. Although anger and the fierce desire to do something filled Syman, he was frozen by uncertainty. He still didn't know where Karrie was and until he did, there wasn't anything he could do to help either of them. He couldn't take decisive action until he had a definite advantage or he might get his friends killed.

As he continued watching, the other two men got out of the Honda and another man climbed from the back of the Ford van. The man from the back of van was huge. Lumbering over to the Jeep, he picked Dexter up and carried him across the lot to the back of a trailer truck Syman thought was an abandoned hulk. He opened one of the double doors of the shipping container on the truck and dumped Dexter's unconscious form inside and closed the door.

For a fleeting moment, with the sunshine streaming inside, Syman had seen Karrie kneel down next to Dexter just before the door was again locked shut.

Well, now Syman knew where Karrie was, but the situation still presented him with no good options.

As Syman watched, two of the men, one who looked like Hassan, opened the doors of the Jeep. They were looking for the computer disk. It wouldn't be hard to find. Dexter and Syman had put them into a yellow envelope similar to the original one. The man on the passenger side pulled it from the Jeep and waved it in the air.

When they had arrived at the office that morning, George had given them a full recounting of the burglary, complete with a screening of the security surveillance tapes he and Sherlock had recorded. Dexter and Syman watched and listened to the entire thing. They saw Hassan find and remove the original envelope from Dexter's desk drawer and they watched the two men leave the office with the cash from the safe and the tapestry from the wall. Obviously, they were trying to make it look like a normal burglary. It seemed bizarre to Dexter and Syman. Syman asked George why he hadn't alerted the security guards patrolling in the manufacturing buildings at the back of the property.

"They had keys," George had told them.

Syman then asked George, why he hadn't alerted the guards when he heard them discussing the money and George explained, they had opened the safe in the normal way. It had only taken them a little longer than it took Dexter. George had assumed the men (humans), had permission to do what they were doing. No one had told him otherwise. After all, they were human.

Syman realized just how limited the comparitor's judgment was in situations like these and he made a mental note to work on the problem after this fiasco was over. It was very hard for a comparitor to second guess any human without very specific instructions and guidelines. It was one of their major shortcomings.

As Syman continued to watch the scene below, the huge guy got into the truck's cab, started the engine and drove the truck out of the lot. Weaving through the littered streets, the truck made its way to the nearest northbound entrance to Interstate 95 with the other two vehicles close behind.

Syman turned off the auto pilot and began to tail the little convoy back in the direction of Stratford. It wasn't hard to keep track of the truck. The name Carrier Service Company Ltd. was painted on the sides of the shipping box in two foot high letters, and the number 7155 was painted on its top. Smaller versions of this same number were also painted on its sides and ends.

For a moment as the vehicles began traveling northeast on I-95, back toward Stratford, Syman entertained the thought that Karrie and Dexter would be released when they reached Stratford. Recognizing this for the wishful thinking it was, Syman abandoned the thought. Next, he considered why they had kidnapped Dexter. Why hadn't they just taken the disk and let Karrie and Dexter go? The implications were very bad. Obviously Hassan had never intended to let Dexter go. Perhaps Hassan was afraid that Dexter might have stumbled onto something, exactly as he had. Or perhaps Hassan was just being careful. Syman wracked his brain, searching for the smallest shred of information, hoping to gain a clearer insight into Sabir Hassan's intentions. Those were his two best friends in the world down there, locked up in that miserable box and Syman would be damned if he would lose them to a violent little turd like Hassan. In that moment, he resolved to do whatever it took to get his friends back safely, even if he had to kill someone to do it. Stepping back from his anger, he made a concerted effort to regain some objectivity. It was so frustrating not to be able to do something definite to help his friends this moment. Syman thumped the 'copter's telephone pad, punching the number 7 and then the speed dial button. He heard the phone ring once and then Esmirelda, Syman's office comparitor answered in her soft feminine voice, "Hello."

"Hello, Essy. I need you to connect me to John Claire in Washington again, please."

"Yes, Syman," answered the ever pleasant, ever obedient comparitor.

Syman wasn't sure why he'd decided to call Claire, except he felt out of his depth. Also, 'There was wisdom in the council of many' and all that. It seemed that it might be the time to get the police or someone involved. Dexter and Karrie couldn't be in much more danger than they presently were. Maybe, John would know what to do in a situation like this.

"I also need to find out who owns two automobiles and a truck or at least who registered them and quickly." Syman glanced at his laptop, which was sitting in a special bracket at the side of the control panel. He read the numbers to Esmirelda.

He wasn't sure why he wanted the information about the vehicles. Obviously, it would be of little or no use at the moment, but Syman was primarily an intellectual animal, and it was always second nature to him to gather as much information as possible when confronting any problem. One could never tell when some little insignificant tidbit might prove to be the critical morsel needed to solve a difficult problem. It was Syman's way, and he was usually very good at discovering important things others had missed. As he flew along behind the three vehicles, he could feel several questions nagging at the back of his mind. As he often did, he cleared his mind to give his subconscious some maneuvering room. After a few moments, a picture of the shipping container emerged in his mind and he suddenly understood what was bothering him. It was unnecessary for the kidnappers to bring Karrie to the meeting if they'd never intended to release her in the first place. Why had they done it? Having her in the vicinity would only complicate abducting Dexter if that was what they had intended all along. Perhaps they'd kept her in the truck since they'd kidnapped her. That made some sense. Nobody would have heard her inside the container in that wasteland industrial zone. Syman realized that they had only needed Karrie as bait to get Dexter to come to them with the disk. There had never been any real need to bring her to the meeting. That much was now clear. So, the critical questions were; Why were they: (1) driving away with Dexter and Karrie; (2) alive and; (3) in the container?'

Syman pondered these questions as he flew along. Perhaps, they were taking Dexter somewhere more private where they could question him. Why hadn't they questioned Dexter immediately? When they'd finished, they could have simply killed them and left their bodies in the abandon building where they'd met? Syman was very relieved that they hadn't killed his friends, but he still wondered why not.

There was another thing that didn't make much sense, admittedly it was only a small concern, but they'd left Dexter's Jeep sitting there, an obvious loose end.

It appeared these men were not worried about loose ends. Also, the Jeep was worth a small fortune. Apparently, money wasn't a significant concern either or they would have taken the Jeep. But, if that were so, why had they taken cash from the safe?

Syman seemed to be tilling up more and more questions but few answers— too much input. He wished he could sit down with paper and pencil and take them one at a time, but now wasn't the time for such elegant methods.

Syman punched the phone pad and called Essy again.

"Essy, get the address for the old Stop and Shop food warehouse in Norwalk, Connecticut. The warehouse is abandoned now, so you'll probably have to search through old phonebooks to find it."

Syman kept trolling in the back of his mind for lowest common denominators while he talked to Essy about the Jeep.

"It's 314 Houton Street, Syman. It was in a four year old phonebook in our main data archive," said the comparitor before Syman could frame his next sentence.

"Good Essy. Now call our vehicle maintenance department and ask them to send a tow truck to that address to pick up Mr. Gordon's Jeep."

Although Syman felt funny worrying about Dexter's automobile right now, he was sure that leaving a thirty thousand dollar customized Jeep in the middle of a Norwalk slum would guarantee its quick disappearance. As ironic as it seemed, Syman knew Dexter would really be pissed when it was all over if Syman let that happen to it.

"John Claire is unavailable, Syman, but I left a message for him to call you as soon as possible."

"Where the hell is the government when you need it?" Syman muttered angrily under his breath.

"I don't know Syman," said the machine.

"Sorry, Essy. That was a rhetorical question not requiring an answer."

The machine made no reply.

Syman noticed that the little convoy was getting off at the harbor exit in Bridgeport. He slowed the Bell, flying sideways to the north of the interstate as the vehicles drove south. This way he could watch them without being easily seen by them. He wondered if they were going to take the ferry to Long Island. No chance of that. Too dangerous, he realized. Someone might hear Dexter and Karrie inside the container.

All of a sudden, a curious thought surfaced. Maybe these guys were concerned about something other than the police and that was why they got moving so fast. After mulling this over for a minute, Syman had second thoughts. What had triggered this idea in his mind? And then he figured it out. They'd left the warehouse parking lot within 60 seconds of Dexter's arrival. But, if they were in such a big hurry, then why flee in a trailer truck? Not exactly the quickest getaway they might have arranged, even under the worst of circumstances. If they were worried about getting away from the police, they wouldn't have used a 40,000 pound trailer truck. Even that old beater of a Ford van they were using, would have been a better get-away vehicle. It was a trivial point, but there was something odd in the way the kidnappers had gone about all of this.

"I have the information about the vehicles you requested, Syman," the comparitor said over the open phone connection.

"Go ahead."

"The Honda is a rental vehicle belonging to Hertz Incorporated. The Ford van belongs to Burt Casowitz, doing business as the Good Neighbor Locksmith Company, in Staten Island, New York. The truck is a 1987, model 41, White trailer, belonging to Hinode International, Tokyo, Japan, but it's registered to Carrier Service Company Ltd., Brooklyn, New York."

"Thanks, Essy," said Syman.

Although none of this information was of any value at the moment, Syman filed it away in his mind.

14

Karrie thought she might lose her mind. They'd kept her in this dark container for a very long time. She was hungry and tired. All of her screams and curses and threats had brought no response. At daybreak, little pin pricks of light had begun to show through various holes. It was the only light she'd seen until they'd dumped Dexter unconscious onto the floor a few minutes before.

"What in the world was going on?" she wondered for the umteenth time. As she sat on the bare cold floor of the container cradling Dexter's head in her lap she began to cry. Questions, rage, and frustrations swirled through her, mixed with more than a little fear. Overwhelmed, her feelings of helplessness made her nauseous.

Just after Dexter had been put into the container with her the container had begun to move. The rumbling of the truck on the road, had become very loud. With nothing in the container to dampen the sound, it was like being inside a large drum. Every time the truck hit a bump in the road, the container made a booming thrum as it jolted up and down.

Karrie realized with a shock that she was living through the worst experience of her life. At first, she had been preoccupied with her own misery, but now she was worried about Dexter. She didn't know how badly he was hurt. She felt the sticky wet blood on the back of his neck, but sitting in the darkness, she couldn't tell if the bleeding had stopped. The more she thought about their predicament, the more depressed she got. "Dexter, Dexter, please don't die," she sobbed softly.

A few minutes later, she felt Dexter stir in her lap.

"Oh, God, my head hurts," Dexter said in a hoarse voice just loud enough to be heard by Karrie over the rumbling. Swirls of gray mist were spinning around in his mind. He rubbed the back of his head and neck where he'd been hit.

"Dexter!" Karrie cried. "I was afraid you were dying." The relief was evident in her voice.

Dexter struggled to figure out where he was and what was going on. He was very disoriented. He'd heard a woman's voice but he hadn't understood what she'd said. He could hear a loud humming noise and everything was vibrating. He opened his eyes. At least he thought he opened his eyes, but all he saw were bright little lights. After a moment, a terrible fright of realization went through him. "I'm blind!" He said loudly. "All I see are little lights!"

Dexter sounded a little hysterical to Karrie. He struggled to sit up, but, she held him tight. "You're not blind, Dex," she said, reassuringly. "We're locked in the back of a truck."

"Karrie?" he asked, hesitantly, recognizing her voice finally. And then, after a moment, he asked, "What's going on?" He could feel he was laying with his head in someone's lap. It must be Karrie's lap. Karrie's voice had been close to his ear, but he couldn't see her.

"I don't know what's going on Dexter. I thought you would know." She answered him in a controlled voice, but a strong wave of fear went through her.

Dexter tried to think back to the last thing he could remember. He felt like he wanted to throw up. The feeling passed as he lay quietly trying to organize his thoughts. The rumbling and jarring of the container sent waves of pain through his head. Despite the pain, he began to remember what he'd last been doing and why.

Without preamble, he told Karrie, "Yesterday I found a copy of Libya's plans to build an atomic bomb."

"You did what?" Karrie asked, not sure she had heard him correctly.

"At the bank. I accidentally picked up the wrong envelope. When I got back to the office, Syman and I discovered we had a copy of a list of things that were being bought in the U.S. and shipped to Libya. The list contained about fifteen pounds of plutonium, some other radioactive chemicals and a bunch of stuff that you would only want if you're building an atomic bomb of some kind." Dexter fell silent. It hurt to talk.

Karrie could hardly take in what Dexter had just told her. She knew what plutonium was. She had protested the start up of the Diablo Canyon nuclear power plant when she was in high school. Built right on the coast only 8 miles north of their house in Shell Beach, the power plant's reactor containment building had been sited directly over an active earth quake fault that runs out into the Pacific Ocean. Pacific Gas & Electric had not known about the fault when they had built the plant. It was discovered just days before the reactor was scheduled to load its plutonium fuel rods for the first time.

Karrie had protested the startup vigorously with thousands of other Californians, but to no avail.

Dexter continued, "These people wanted their disk back and when they didn't find me at home last night, they kidnapped you to use as leverage. Syman and I were going to return it to them in exchange for you, but something's gone wrong."

"Where's Syman?" Karrie asked with new concern in her voice. "You said, you and Syman..."

Dexter cut her off. "Syman was watching the exchange from his helicopter so he knows what's happened."

Feeling a wave of hope surge through her, Karrie said excitedly, "He must be following us in the helicopter right now! He'll get us out of here."

There was no reply from Dexter. He'd passed out again.

15

Syman thought hard about his options as he watched the container truck thread its way toward Bridgeport's harbor area. Alone, he could not very well assault Hassan's group to release Dexter and Karrie. There were at least five of them. It was definitely time to get help. The question was who should he call? With faint hope he had Essy dial John Claire again. Syman considered calling the local police or the FBI, but he knew it would take a long time to explain and get them to act if they would believe him at all. He began to get angry thinking about the problems he would have and the time it would take to get any police agency to help rescue Dexter and Karrie when John Claire suddenly came on the line.

"Hello, Syman," Claire greeted him enthusiastically.

"John, we've got big problems," Syman said, ignoring the salutation. "Dexter and his sister Karrie have been kidnapped by the Libyans or whoever they are."

"Syman, slow down. I don't follow you."

Syman explained the situation to Claire while he continued watching the little caravan on the ground. As he talked, the truck drove onto a dock and parked directly under a shipside crane. A dock worker and the big guy driving the truck quickly fastened cables from the crane to the container and, it was unceremoniously loaded aboard a dilapidated container ship in less than two minutes.

"And as I watch, they are loading the container onto a ship in Bridgeport harbor." Syman said, concluding his explanation.

"This is bad, Sy. I'm sorry I wasn't available to you or I could have done something..."

"Yes, well, I'm sure you're a busy man," Syman said, cutting him off impatiently.

"Hey, take it easy, Syman. It's me your talking to, remember?" said Claire, defensively. "Dexter's a good friend of mine and I'm not going to let anything happen to him."

"Okay, John. Sorry. What are we going to do?"

"You said you're in your helo watching, right?"

"Yes."

"How long can you keep watching?"

Syman considered that for a moment after looking at the aircraft's fuel gauge. Doing a quick computation in his head, he replied, "I've got enough fuel for about three hours. That's the limiting factor right now."

"Good," said Claire. "That will give me just about enough time to get an operation together."

As Syman watched, he saw dock workers slip the enormous hawsers holding the ship to the dock

"We got another problem, John. The ship is leaving the harbor, right now."

"Damn!" said Claire, angrily. "Can you follow them at a discreet distance?"

Syman thought the newly developing situation over for a few moments before answering. "Assuming, they're headed for the Atlantic, I'll be running out of fuel just as they clear Long Island Sound, whether they go west, out through New York harbor or east, past Orient Point, Long Island. We're about in the middle of the Sound here in Bridgeport. Can you call the Coast Guard?"

"I can," said Claire. "But, I need to know if this ship has a boiler or diesel engines?"

Syman wondered why Claire wanted to know this. He could see a large stubby smokestack in the middle of the ship and it had just started giving off quantities of thick black smoke.

"I can't tell you how it's powered, but the ship's name is the Hana Maru," Syman said, by way of answering Claire's question. "Why's it important?"

"We have to go slowly, Syman. We need to do this the right way. If we try to stop them, the Libyans might kill Dex and Karrie and throw their bodies into the ship's firebox, if there is one. There'd be nothing left of their bodies in 30 minutes. They could easily stall our boarding party for that long. Dexter and Karrie would be gone and there'd be no evidence they were ever aboard the ship. On the other hand, if the ship has diesel engines, they'd have a hard time disposing of the bodies. They couldn't dump them over the side, while we were trying to board them. I've been through this before with drug smugglers. I helped track a ship for customs a while back. They burned the drugs, several tons of drugs before anyone could get aboard. I don't think a frontal assault with the Coast Guard is the smart way to go about this until we know if the ship has a boiler."

Without discussing it with Claire, Syman addressed Essy, who had been facilitating the call. "Essy, please find information concerning the Hana Maru for us. Specifically, does it have a boiler or diesel engines?"

"Yes, Syman."

"Hey what are you doing, Syman?" asked Claire. "Is there someone else listening in on our conversation?"

"That's my office comparitor, Esmirelda. She can get that information from Lloyd's Registry for us in a few moments."

"That's a computer?" Claire asked. He'd thought it was Syman's secretary who had arranged the call. Surprised, he realized he'd been talking to a machine.

"Yes," Syman said. "John, I want to know if this ship can be boarded, right now."

"Sy, it's helpful that we know about the ship now, but I have to talk to some other people, first. I can't just order the Coast Guard to board a ship and search it. I don't have that kind of authority.

"Syman," said Esmirelda, "The Hana Maru is a Dorchester class cargo vessel build in Belfast, Ireland in 1956. She was originally commissioned as the Royal Argyle by Edington, Lambert, and Smythe, shippers of bulk cargo, 114 Bryant Court Road, London, England. The ship was sold to Hinode Worldwide, a Japanese consortium, corporate address, 12 Ipa, Tokyo, Japan in 1986, when she was refitted as a container freighter and renamed the Hana Maru. The ship flys a Liberian flag and is crewed by a mixed group of 30 to 40 sailors from countries all over the world. The Hana Maru is 612 feet long, displaces 17,230 tons, is powered by 2 oil fired boilers developing 27,000 horse power and has a maximum speed of 24 knots.

"Thanks, Essy. Well, now we know she has boilers. That means we have to hit them fast, before they can do anything with Dexter and Karrie."

"What do you mean 'we' Syman? Slow down! I've got to talk to my boss about this situation, before doing anything. You realize that, right Syman?"

"Yes, of course I realize that," replied Syman.

"It's going to take some time. I'll call you back, as soon as I can."

"That's not good enough, John," said Syman, with an angry tone.

"Syman, we'll get them back! But right now, you have to keep a sharp watch on the ship and that container. If they take Dexter and Karrie out of it, we need to know. I won't lie to you, Syman. It's going to take me some real time to get something going, now that they're leaving the dock. It puts a whole new spin on everything, but I swear to you, we'll get them back, as quickly as possible."

"Why don't I find your repeated assurances comforting?" replied Syman cynically, as he watched the ship moved away from the dock.

"Look, I'll try to call you back in a few minutes. Okay? Just as soon as I know something." And with that, he hung up.

Frustrated, angry and more than a little afraid for Dexter and Karrie, Syman watched from his lonely vantage point as the Hana Maru moved out into the harbor heading for Long Island Sound.

16

Osmid Bandar disliked being aboard the Hana Maru. It was his forth time. In the age of jets it was a waste of time, but he had no choice in the matter. He had to deliver this last shipment to the island. He walked down the long corridor and up the stairs leading to the ship's bridge. As he walked, he thought about his predicament and about how quickly it had turned into a big problem. He was thinking that he might have done the wrong thing bringing the Americans aboard the ship. He was also very tired. Worried, he'd been too keyed up to sleep during the night, waiting for Gordon to bring him the disk. Originally, he had only intended that Gordon return the disk to him before he'd release the sister. But after thinking it over, it occurred to him that Gordon had probably made a copy of the disk, wondering what was on it that was important enough to justify kidnapping his sister. After a long sleepless night, Osmid finally decided that bringing the Americans gave him some control in the event Gordon had discovered something. But he was still unsure if that had occurred. He had tried to question the American. The man would not talk to him. He didn't like bringing the Americans, but he didn't know what else to do. It was simply the lesser of two evils. In consolation, Osmid comforted himself with the thought that in two weeks it wouldn't matter anyway, because the United States would no longer exist.

He arrived at the door of the bridge. He needed to have a word with the Captain. Walking toward the Captain, Osmid began speaking without invitation.

"I have put the man and the woman in cabin 4 on deck G," he said, with an air of supposed authority. "I will need some of your men to help stand guard outside the door."

The Captain looked at the pompous little man and grunted disgustedly.

"Bandar, my men have more important things to do than watch over your damn prisoners."

"I need guards!" said Bandar angrily.

"If you hadn't brought them aboard..."

"Do not question my judgment!" Bandar said, cutting him off. "You will provide men."

"If you want men," replied the Captain with contempt, "you can hire men who are off watch and pay them with your own money. But, if you harass any of my men, I'll throw you and your damn prisoners over the side myself. If no one wants the extra duty," he continued, "then you don't get any men. Now, get the hell off my bridge!"

"You will regret this when we get to the island, Captain," Bandar said, darkly, before turning to leave the bridge.

17

Syman shadowed the ship all afternoon. After leaving Bridgeport harbor the Hana Maru traveled east in its effort to gain the open sea. It had been a beautiful, sunny day and Long Island Sound had been placid as a duck pond. The excellent weather made it difficult for Syman to tail the ship without showing himself conspicuously. Rather than stay in the air, Syman landed the Bell several times at desolate places along the Connecticut shore, moving every half hour or so when the ship was almost out of sight. This strategy had the added advantage of conserving the flying machine's fuel. The disadvantage was that Syman could not keep a close continuous watch on the container that held Dexter and Karrie, but there was no help for it. If he tried to keep too close a watch, the helicopter would certainly be seen and God only knew what would happen then.

Moving up the Sound at 16 knots, the ship took not quite 4 hours to clear Orient Point, the farthest reach of land at the eastern end of Long Island. When the ship had traveled about half the way, Syman flew the Bell to Long Island. The ship steered to skirt the north shore as it passed the Point, moving further away from Connecticut.

Syman had spoken with John Claire several times during the afternoon waiting with increasing impatience to hear what was going to be done to help Dexter and Karrie. As the Hana Maru moved out into the open Atlantic, Syman felt a heavy curtain of failure settle over his spirit. With the sun setting behind him, Syman lifted the helicopter into the air for the last time in the vain hope that following the ship as long as possible might somehow make a difference. In frustration, he again called Claire.

"What are we going to do, John? The ship just reached the open ocean and I only have about 45 minutes of fuel left, before I have to turn back."

"I have some good news, finally, Syman. We've arranged for continuous surveillance of the ship, so you can go home."

"What do you mean by continuous?" Syman asked suspiciously.

"We've reoriented some satellites so we can watch the ship night and day."

Syman felt the heat rise in his face as he realized why the government had gone to the trouble to reorient satellites. It meant that their first priority was keeping an eye on the terrorists. It also meant that rescuing Dexter and Karrie was not their primary concern. "You don't have a rescue plan for Dexter and Karrie, yet, do you?" he said, to Claire accusingly.

"Hold on Sy. We do have a plan, but I can't talk to you about it over the phone."

"Why not?" asked Syman, with anger in his voice. "It's an encrypted transmission. You're stalling."

"Syman, that's not true. You seem to keep forgetting that Dexter is a good friend of mine, too. You've got to trust me a little more."

Syman was silent for a few moments. He did some quick calculations in his head and then said, "I want to meet with you, John and find out what you're planning to do. I'll fill up and then fly down there to Washington. It's 6:30 now. It will take me about two hours to get there."

Claire considered this new development for a moment and then responded, "All right, Syman. Come ahead."

18

Sumiko took her hands from the keyboard and held the edge of her desk. Nausea and dizziness swept over her. She'd been feeling like she was getting her period all morning, but that wasn't likely. She'd just finished her last period two days before, on the day she'd returned from Japan.

No sooner had the nausea past than it was followed by an intense hot flash and an even stronger bout of nausea. Fearing she would vomit sitting at her desk, Sumiko heaved herself out of her chair and stumbled toward the women's bathroom. Vomitous boiled up her throat. She fought it down, desperately gulping and swallowing. It came up again. Gritting her teeth, she rushed through the bathroom door straight into a stall, where she fell to her knees just as the contents of her stomach erupted from her mouth. In her foggy half awareness, she congratulated herself for reaching the safety and privacy of the bathroom. All the while, she violently wretched, gagging again and again in agony as her cramped digestive system contracted into an excruciating knot.

Wave after wave of hot flashes pummeled her leaving her skin moist and clammy as the loathsome smell evoked more vomiting.

After ten minutes, the last dry heave subsided leaving Sumiko weak and shaking. With her eyes tightly shut, she felt for the handle. She flushed the toilet, so she wouldn't have to confront the revolting sight she knew it contained. When she finally opened her eyes, she felt disgusted at herself seeing slimy drool hanging from her face into the toilet. She also felt frightened, when she saw what looked like red spatters of blood higher up on the dry part of the toilet's porcelain bowl. Rising to her feet, she walked on shaky legs to the sink. In the mirror, she saw watery blood on her lower lip and at the corners of her mouth.

19

Royce rubbed his eyes with the balls of his hands. They burned and they felt gritty. It was now a little after 10 P. M. and Royce had worked without interruption since early afternoon examining the curious artifact that Syman had brought to him the previous day. His stomach grumbled its protest at being empty. He had not eaten since lunch.

When he'd awakened that morning, he'd called Francois Tibedeaux, a friend whose professional specialty was micro-photography. Francois was an expert at capturing unique details in the realm of the ultra small using polarized and laser light to increase contrast and definition in the minute.

Over the years Royce had turned to Francois many times for help in recording the microscopic details of his archaeological finds. Most recently, Francois had photographed a small scarf like piece of very fine quality silk contained in a sealed funereal jar that Royce had unearthed at Carthage. While photographing the silk's fibers, Francois discovered the remains of mites in the cloth's threads. There was nothing unusual in that except that, upon further investigation, it was determined that the mites which Francois photographed, could only be found in one area of North America around the Chesapeake Bay, while the silk was from China.

Royce knew from the site's archaeological strata that the silk must have been sealed in the jar with the human remains and buried no later than the year 240 B. C. According to modern understanding of history these facts were irreconcilable.

It was a fortuitous discovery for Royce and an entertaining one for Francois, who greatly enjoyed the controversy that ensued. As circumstantial evidence it lent further support to the developing theory that the Phoenician sailors who had founded the city of Carthage were at that time sailing completely around the world to do business with many ancient peoples including the Chinese.

The world wide trade theory had many vociferous detractors, but it was the best answer to one of the great unanswered questions of the ancient world: Where did Carthage get the immense amount of gold needed to finance the hundred year long Punic war she fought with Rome? It had been established that her fighting men were paid in gold, but Carthage possessed no gold mines. Blocked from trading at most ports in the Mediterranean by their furious Roman adversaries, a growing body of evidence suggested that the trader-sailors of Carthage sailed out through the Straits of Gibraltar to gather their much needed gold from a world wide trading network that included the peoples of North, Central and South America, India, Southeast Asia, and China as well as Africa.

This prehistoric shipping trade could also account for some other curious historical and archaeological mysteries that had become evident over the years, such as the world wide spread of Negroid peoples to South America, Central Asia, and the Indonesian archipelago.

The Phoenicians were renowned for their metalwork, particularly bronze. The earliest known bronze was from East Asia. It was possible that long before the time of the Punic Wars early Phoenician traders brought the knowledge necessary to make and work bronze home with them to the Mediterranean basin.

It was also possible that after trading bronze and other goods to the native people of Africa for slaves, early Phoenician ships sailed away to any of several wealthy foreign ports around the world where their very valuable human cargo could be exchanged along with other trade goods for gold, food, and needed travel provisions.

Their prehistoric worldwide trading might also account for how tobacco, a plant originally native only to the Americas, came to be used as one of the herbs in the mummification of the dead in Egypt at the time of the Pharaohs.

All this went through Royce's mind in a moment, as he thought about his day's work. He realized that he'd slipped into his 'Carthage think' mindset without conscious effort. That was happening a lot lately. Having worked so long and hard on Carthage, it had become second nature to him, but Carthage had also become a little stale. He needed a break from it.

Conveniently, Syman Pons had arrived with his enigma at just the right time and the problems presented by it were a refreshing change.

He looked down at his desk once more, and with an effort, hauled his thoughts out of the ruts of familiar Carthage, back to this new challenge. Working with the 8 by 10 photo-micrographs of the inscribed plate that he and Francois had taken that morning, rather than straining to see it through his old microscope, made the plate's inspection an easy and pleasant task. They'd photographed and printed 38 images in 3 hours, after which, Royce had taken them out for a brass rail lunch and beers at Christopher Martin's Pub.

In the eight hours since lunch that Royce had been examining the photos, he'd developed some startling preliminary conclusions about Syman's mystery artifact. The plate appeared to be a sophisticated textual and graphic presentation, specifically designed to make its decipherment easy. It was like a pictorial dictionary that tutored its students as they went along, one simple step at a time. There were thousands of unambiguous line drawings of everyday things. Each was labeled in what appeared to be the alphabet of whomever made the plate, but it was an all together unknown alphabet as far as Royce could tell. And as an experienced archaeologist, Royce had more than a passing familiarity with most of the world's forms of writing and scripts, including pictographs and hieroglyphics.

At first, he had thought that the myriad pictures on the plate were simple pictographs, but as he became more familiar with their unusual style of presentation he quickly realized that they were really pictorial representations for the written names, labels and descriptions that were uniformly inscribed above them.

Understanding of the system used by the plate's creator came as Royce studied a line of six figures and the symbols above them.

The pictograph of a man had the symbol ╱. above it.

The pictograph of the woman had the symbol ⌒◡ above it.

The pictograph of the dog had the symbol ⌐⌒ above it.

The three pictographs showing the man, woman, and dog running had the symbol sequence ⌒◡ after what, Royce believed, were their name symbols.

Thus, ⌒◡╱. meant running ⌒◡ man or man running if one read it from right to left, as the plate's creators apparently did.

It was such a straight forward way of presentation that Royce was suspicious of the people who made the plate and their motivation for going to all the trouble to create such a thing.

In some ways it seemed almost childish in its design. It was almost too easy to decipher. But the enormous number of the images and the complexity of the plate represented thousands of man hours of work. And the plate could only have been created using very sophisticated and expensive equipment. College students might have been able to do it, but there were few universities with the facilities to etch the photo-micrograph onto anything, and no students would have the extra time needed to do the work. Someone working in a microchip manufacturing plant could do it easily on a piece of silicon substrate, but Royce doubted that the same tools could be used to etch a metal plate. A determined person, (and whoever made the plate was certainly determined), could find a way and in fact did, to engrave the photo-micrographs into the metal of the plate and then coat it with an ultra thin layer of glass to protect it.

Although this information did not immediately reveal who had made the plate, nevertheless, it was significant and might eventually help reveal the identity of the plate's creators.

Now that he understood the key to deciphering what was written on the plate, he needed to do as much of a translation of the labeled pictographs as he could. It would be a time consuming task but he could hire some summer students to help. With TMI footing the bill he would have no trouble finding students to work. He had also asked Syman to give him one of TMI's comparitors to help with the translation. Syman had said he would send one over in a day or two. Using a comparitor would greatly speed up the work. In fact, Royce hoped that with a comparitor's help, he wouldn't need to hire any students. Having student assistants was always problematic.

Once the labeled pictographs were catalogued, Royce could develop a translation program. The translation program could then be used to decipher the dense pictureless pages that filled the lower half of the plate's front and all of its back.

Royce savored his plans. The game was afoot and Royce loved the chase. He knew he was going to enjoy the detective work involved in the deciphering. And of course, he was very curious about what the plate would say when its secrets were finally revealed.

20

Syman struggled with his vertigo as he arrowed through the pitch black night straight down toward the unseen ocean, 11,000 feet below. His desire to rescue his friends and his love for flying not withstanding, he wondered if allowing himself to be pushed backward off the open cargo ramp of a C-130, while strapped into a special forces ADART, (air delivery and recovery transporter), configured in its stealth ultralight airplane mode, had been the right decision. There was the very real possibility that he might die a few short seconds from now. It felt like he'd been dropping for too long. With the altimeter still unlit, there was no way to check. With a growing certainty, his pilot's sense told him something had gone wrong with his plane. The plane was supposed to deploy its wings and begin to fly, but he was still dropping like a rock. Rising fear tightened his chest making it difficult to breathe as every muscle in his body involuntarily tensed in preparation for a 200 mile per hour crash into the icy waters of the Atlantic. He was helpless as he plummeted toward the sea. Syman had, of course, been told in minute detail about the ultralight's ejection and transition procedure and what he could expect to happen a few seconds after it dropped away from the cargo plane. That he had been told, however, had prepared him not at all for one of the most frightening experiences of his life. And as the seconds dragged by in the darkness, Syman realized he was about to die. But fate had other plans for Syman Pons, and the ultralight aircraft's computer finally opened the vehicle's carbon fiber and fabric wings and started its 167 horse power engine at the preprogrammed altitude of 5000 feet. As the five curved blades of the pusher propeller bit into the air the little plane began moving forward with ever increasing speed.

ADARTs were amazing vehicles, created to provide transportation and raw muscle to help American special forces units reach any destination and accomplish any mission. Built from modules, a standard eight man team could join the modules from their four, two-man crafts together to create several different types of vehicles or base support equipment.

If four vehicles were used together, a light capacity wheeled cargo truck suitable for traveling through mountainous terrain could be built. Assembled in a different way, the result became a heavy lifting hovercraft capable of carrying 3 tons of cargo over almost any kind of level terrain at 45 miles per hour.

In a third configuration, an eight man unit could assemble a small vertical take off and landing vehicle that could quickly deliver the men and their basic equipment to the top of a mountain.

If need be, an all weather shelter complete with heat, light, and sleeping hammocks, capable of protecting the men from temperatures of 40 degrees below zero to 120 degrees above, could be erected in two hours and could shelter them for weeks.

In addition to the ultralight configuration, used singly, each ADART could be transformed into a two man amphibious ground assault vehicle capable of going almost anywhere.

Because of the range and flexibility of the ADARTs, the speed, versatility, and fire power a unit in the field could bring to bear was truly awesome.

All of this had been explained to Syman during the planning and briefing session earlier that day, but knowing these things about the ADART did nothing to bolster Syman's confidence in the machine's ability to fly properly. However, as the miniature aircraft leveled out and began responding to its control surfaces, Syman's fear subsided and the normal self assurance he felt at the controls of almost any type of flying machine began to assert itself.

Seeing the two faint red lights at the back of Master Chief Lufkin's ADART several hundred yards ahead, Syman centered up on them and gunned his throttle to close the distance. When the two red pinpoints of light were exactly as far apart as the two green dots glowing in his helmet's sighting reticle, Syman knew he was flying at the right distance behind Sergeant Lufkin's aircraft. He could see absolutely nothing else, beside his own instruments and the twinkle of a few stars through the high patchy clouds above them. Lacking a frame of reference brought the tendrils of vertigo back in little wisps, but Syman concentrated on the two little red dots in front of him with grim determination, knowing that at 170 knots they would travel the 20 odd miles to the cargo ship quickly. After a few minutes, Syman saw the lighted ship directly out in front of them and a long way down.

As they began to drop toward the lighted ship, Syman could just barely discern Chief Lufkin's craft about 500 feet in front of him as its ghostly silhouette flew in a direct line between himself and the freighter. The ships lights blinked out and then reappeared as Lufkin's plane crossed back and forth between Syman and the ship as they closed the gap. When Syman got to within a mile of the ship, what he saw below him looked very familiar. He recognized the bridge, the forward and upper decks, stairs, loading hatches, boom cranes, rows of stacked containers, and most importantly, container 7155 at the forward end of the 170 foot long after deck, where they were going to land.

Because of the ship's forward speed of 18 knots through the calm night air, the ultralights could land in a space approximately 40' long, needing to maintain a relative air speed just slightly more than twenty knots faster than the ship. They were fortunate that there was no following or cross wind which might greatly multiply the landing distance needed or make it impossible to land at all.

Lufkin, still in the lead was coming up to the stern of the ship. From their perspective, they could now see the full length of the freighter stretching away in front of them. The table like after deck was nearest. Next forward, there was a mountain of trailer truck and rail car sized shipping containers stacked on deck, row upon row, looking like so many children's blocks, all their different dull colors jumbled together, their muddy, rust streaked and battered outsides not quite clearly discernible in the ship's deck lights.

Forward of the containers about 1/3 of the ship's length from the bow, the bridge rose into the night's darkness towering above all else shipboard. Soft lights shone through its windows at about their height as they prepared to land. Syman prayed no one was looking backward as they dropped into view illuminated by the after deck lights.

Above the lights, they had been invisible in the inky blackness of the midnight sky. And when they came to rest after landing, they would be hidden in the shadowed blind spot directly behind the containers stacked up between them and the rear bridge windows. The critical 20 or so seconds, when they were directly in the light and in obvious sight of any crew man who happened to glance their way was upon them.

Except for a raft of freeloading sea gulls loitering on the after deck a few feet in front of the railing, there was no other living thing in sight.

Centering up on the ship's stern Master Chief Lufkin goosed the motor to push his 'DART the last 50 yards over the rail and onto the deck beyond. Just as his plane neared the rail, the gulls were spooked by the sudden appearance of the enormous pterodactyl like flying creature looming up out of the darkness and as one they jumped into the air, wheeling left and right, scattering in a panicked effort to evade the frightening apparition.

Lufkin was chagrined at the birds furious movements, desperately hoping the cloud of white suddenly vacating the deck wouldn't catch the peripheral vision of the night's watch officer in the bridge.

The birds sudden movement at this time of the night was like a large white flag waving across the stern. Their behavior would be considered unusual and a good seaman would investigate anything unusual that happened aboard his ship.

"Well," he thought, "There's not a damn thing I can do about it now."

Just as the nose of Lufkin's plane came abreast of the rail, he saw one of the last gulls flash past above his head. There was a sharp 'whap!' and the 'DART began to shutter violently. Reflexively, Lufkin reduced the speed of the motor. The vibrations lessened, but so did his air speed.

"One of those miserable gulls just went through my prop," Lufkin thought, angry and a little frightened by the strong vibrations still shaking his plane.

The bird had broken off one of the five blades of the propeller and because of the loss of power the 'DART was loosing headway and dropping down toward the foaming water 40' below.

Pons watched in horror as a single gull disappeared into the spinning maelstrom of the propeller on Lufkin's plane. The bird just vanished and was instantly metamorphosed into a blur of light colored fluff and darker, heavier jetsam that flew in all directions. He clearly saw the shadowy shape of the propeller's broken blade flick away into the darkness. He watched helplessly as Lufkin's 'DART dropped into the frothing white wake just behind the ship's stern.

Pons realized with frustration, there was nothing he could do to help. He had to follow through and land his own plane. Syman didn't like the idea of abandoning Lufkin, but at just that moment there were zero options available to him. Lufkin was on his own. He had a life jacket on and an emergency location transponder as did Pons for just such a contingency. Ironically, Lufkin was also carrying the Zodiac inflatable boat and the outboard motor they were supposed to have used to get away from the freighter, once they had rescued Dexter and Karrie. A part of Syman's mind began to consider how Chief Lufkin could get the boat and motor loose of the 'DART while floating in the ocean as he lined up on the after deck.

Gliding in just above the stern rail, Syman needed to give his full attention to landing his 'DART so he stopped thinking about Lufkin's plight and focused solely on the deck and fast approaching wall of shipping containers.

All at once Chief Lufkin found himself tumbling about submerged in the furiously foaming horizontal column of water created by the freighter's enormous propeller. The noise of it thrashing in the water just a few scant feet away amplified the terror of the situation. He had no sense of position or direction. Lufkin, normally stalwart and brave as a lion, experienced real fear at the thought of being sucked into that raging piece of metal. Absurdly, a part of his mind viewed the entire situation as if looking at it from the outside as an uninvolved observer might have seen it. That part of his mind considered the similarity of the gull, moments before, and his experience now. There was every possibility of his suffering a similar fate in the next few seconds. He had never felt more helpless in his entire life.

Unexpectedly, he found himself bobbing up through the surface of the water, buoyed by his life vest. He remembered yanking the cord on his chest to inflate it and unfastening his seat harness buckle just before hitting the water. The impact must have thrown him forward and clear of his 'DART, but not into that murderous propeller.

"Oh, thank you, God," he thought to himself as he watched the ship slide further from him as each second past.

Still shaky from fright, he felt down his left side for the transponder in his thigh pocket. He used both hands as he removed it, and then holding onto it with a death grip in his right, he clipped its short lanyard to the metal utility ring on the shoulder of his flight suit intended for that purpose. Having accomplished that simple operation, he was greatly relieved.

If by some grim bit of misfortune, the transponder had slipped from his grasp and floated away out of reach before he had secured it, he would have found himself alone and adrift in the pitch black Atlantic unable to contact the rescue sub. It would have guaranteed his death.

He pushed the button on the top end of the little radio beacon . It made no sound, but a small blue light began blinking on and off as it transmitted. After watching it for a moment, he slid it into the pocket on the shoulder of his flight suit next to the ring. Then he looked around to see if his ADART was floating anywhere nearby.

Syman dropped his craft lightly to the deck about 30 feet past the rail allowing it to roll right up close to the containers. Stacked four high, the containers formed a giant wall like a sheer cliff, 40 feet high. They spanned the entire width of the ship except for the narrow alleys left along the sides next to the rails for the crew to pass along.

Container 7155, the container in which Dexter and Karrie had been locked, was sitting on the deck to Syman's right.

Syman jumped out of the 'DART and ran to the container. The doors were closed tight but there was no lock on them. Syman grabbed the handle to the twin doors. Heaving up on the handle, he yanked the container open. It was empty. Syman sagged as a great feeling of disappointment washed through him. Dexter and Karrie were gone. Guilt, mixed with feelings of anger, momentarily replaced Syman's normal optimistic self confidence. Although he knew it was not true, Syman could not help feeling that he had failed Dexter and Karrie. After a moment Syman realized he was feeling sorry for himself. "That won't help," he said, out loud, remonstrating himself. And then he said,

"Get to work." He didn't know where they were now, but he was going to find out. Taking firm control of himself, he banished all negative feelings. With that, he went back to the 'DART and began getting organized to search the ship.

A quick look at his watch told him it was a little after 2 am. He felt drained. Bending over and straightening up a few times, he shook his arms and his head to drive out the numbness that had begun to gather in his hands and behind his eyes. It had been a very long day and it was far from over yet. His wits needed to be sharp now, but he felt dull headed from all the adrenaline and the lack of sleep.

Looking around, he considered his next actions. Lufkin's landing in the drink changed things. Syman needed to contact the submarine to apprise the captain of the situation. He considered the two options available to him.

Syman's plane carried enough food and water for a couple of days, their weapons, and the communications gear they'd been issued to contact the rescue sub shadowing the Hana Miru. But that was not quite all.

Not content to be entirely dependent on the government Syman had also brought along a small water tight back pack of personal gear that he normally kept with him when he sailed aboard the Thmink. Among other things, the pack contained a Sat-Link mobile phone, which could be used over most of the world's surface between the arctic circles. He knew he did not want to use the special forces satellite phone they'd been given. With its folding parabolic dish antenna, it was a bulky, complicated, and obsolete piece of junk compared to the Sat-Link. Its only advantage was its ability to talk directly to the rescue sub. Syman reached into his water tight pack and pulled out the Sat-Link. He pushed 2 and then the dial button. The satellite phone immediately connected him to Esmirelda. Because no one else used the number, the machine knew it would be Pons calling.

"Hello, Syman," the simulated female voice purred over the line.

"Hello, Essy," he replied. "I need you to call this number. Area code 888. 424-5158. Tell whomever you get that it's an emergency call from me. Here's the message I want you to give them: 'Lufkin was forced to land in the water approximately 5 minutes ago. He needs immediate pickup'. Mark the time Essy and pass that along also. 'I'm down safe and have checked container 7155. It's empty. I'll proceed alone with the plan and maintain contact through this back channel.' Tell them you're calling for me, Essy."

"Okay Syman. Is there anything else I can do for you?"

"Yeah, you can pray I'm successful at finding Dexter and his sister and at getting them off this rust bucket of a ship."

"I do not understand the concept of praying, Syman, therefore I do not think my actions will effect the desired..."

"Forget the praying, Essy. See you later."

Syman turned the phone off and put it back in the water tight pack. Looking at the ADART ultralight airplane, he groaned inwardly, realizing he would have to disassemble the damn thing and throw its pieces overboard so the crew wouldn't discover the ship had been boarded in the night. He wasn't sure he could do it. He and Lufkin had done one trial disassembly together earlier that evening to familiarize Syman with the procedure, but it was hardly an adequate demonstration. In addition, the heavy parts of the machine probably weighed more than Syman could lift alone. Wanting time to think, he unpacked the 'DART, laying the cargo on the deck. He considered the ramifications of just leaving the ADART where it was, but there were problems with that. First, they'd been told explicitly not to let the secret machine fall into the enemy's hands and second, it would loudly announce his presence aboard.

In his minds eye, Syman could picture a 'Keystone cops' like beehive of frantic activity aboard the ship if they discovered the plane in the morning. With a wry smile, Syman concluded that letting that particular cat out of the bag would be a mistake.

Next he turned his thoughts to a novel idea. Given, that he could find and release Dexter and Karrie before morning, could he fly them off the ship? Carefully measuring the after deck with his eyes, he could see there wasn't enough room to take off. Next, he considered reconfiguring the ADART into one of its other vehicular forms, but he realized he didn't know how to do that. Finally, he thought about stowing the ADART in the empty container. If he did that, at least it would solve half his problem. He wouldn't have to lift its heavy parts more than a foot, which he was sure he could handle, but he'd end up letting the contraption fall into the wrong hands. The container seemed like the best solution available to him and it would be fast. He was anxious to find Dexter and Karrie and get the hell off this ship as quickly as possible. Let the Navy board the ship if they were so intent on keeping the ADART a secret.

Just when he'd decided to use the container, Syman saw a better solution to his problem. There, directly in front of him not fifty feet away under the nearest deck light was the ten foot wide gated opening for the ship's stern gang way. If he simply rolled the 'DART through the gate, his problem would literally be solved in the blink of an eye.

Pleased, Syman leaned over the 'DART and pushed the button that caused the wings to fold together above the machine. Then he walked over to the gate. After a quick glance to make sure no one was looking out the rear facing bridge windows, Syman reached up and unscrewed the light bulb above the gate. When the bulb had winked out, he ducked back behind the container stack. Peering carefully up at the back of the bridge again, he still saw no one. After watching for a full minute he went back to the gate and secured its two halves in their open position. Another quick look at the bridge told him his luck was holding. Walking back to the ultralight, he positioned himself next to the pilot's seat, so he could steer the craft as he pushed it toward the open gate. When he'd almost reached the opening in the rail, but was still behind the containers, he took one more good long look at the bridge window. Seeing that the coast was clear without a moment's more hesitation Syman pushed the $200,000 war machine into the abyss. Quickly closing the gate, he moved back behind the containers. Just before he lost sight of the bridge windows, a capped head came into view. Had he been seen? After a moment, he peeked slowly over the upper edge of the containers to check. He saw a man, probably the night watch officer, placidly smoking a cigarette while staring back over the stern of the ship. The officer stood thus for several minutes, obviously unperturbed.

Syman breathed a long sigh of relief, knowing he had not been seen.

He set to work stowing the gear he'd unloaded from the 'DART in the empty container. There were three green canvas duffel bags. One held food and water. One held the special forces satellite communications gear and some tools, including bolt cutters, in case they'd found Dexter and Karrie still locked in the container. The third held weapons.

Securely out of sight of the bridge inside the container, Syman used his small flashlight to find the equipment he wanted to take with him on his search through the ship. He removed four plastic half liter bottles of spring water and a box of twelve assorted fruit, grain and nut bars. Realizing he was hungry now, Syman wolfed a package of peanut butter crackers, washing them down with a bottle of orange juice. As the sugar from the food poured into his bloodstream he felt a surge of energy. He put the bottles of spring water and the food bars in his back pack and considered the rest of the provisions. He didn't know how long it would take him to find Dexter and Karrie and he didn't know if he'd be able to return to the container again. He finally added three foil pouches of corn beef to his pack and all the rest of the peanut butter crackers. It was a lot of weight to carry along, but it might take a couple of days to search the whole ship without being caught.

He didn't expect to find Dexter and Karrie well fed and they would have to be strong if they were going to get away safely.

Considering their safety caused Syman to momentarily entertain the thought that he might not find them because they'd been killed. "No negatives," he admonished himself knowing that in his situation his own mind and emotions would be his worst enemies if he did not keep them in check. He forced himself to concentrate his attention only on what was necessary to find them, leaving no room for discouraging thoughts.

From the com gear duffel, Syman took a large flashlight and extra batteries. From the weapons duffel, Syman took a box of rounds for the Air Force issue, 45 caliber, survival revolver he wore strapped to his leg. He didn't want to shoot anyone on the ship if he could help it. It would be too noisy and give his presence away. Nevertheless, it might make the difference and help get them out of a tight spot. He removed the gun and put it along with the ammo into the bulging back pack. For a moment, he considered taking some other weapons, but in the end, he decided against it. He wasn't here to engage in a fight. He was here to find his friends and get them safely off this ship ASAP. In the pack, along with the Sat-Link, Syman also had a laptop computer. Connected to the mobile phone, the laptop could link directly to his powerful comparitor at TMI in Connecticut. He had not had a specific purpose in mind when he had decided to bring it along with the phone, but he always kept them together in the pack aboard Thmink. On shore he'd reasoned the phone and computer might come in handy if something unforeseen happened as it already had. Still, Syman considered if he wanted the extra weight, now that he had filled the pack with other things. He didn't know how it might help him, but he decided to keep it anyway. He could always give it the old heave-ho, if necessary.

Finally, after digging a little, Syman removed a black cloth roll of small tools from the bottom of the pack. Although he had not used them in years he had brought them along on a hunch that they might also be helpful. These were no ordinary tools. These were the secret tools Syman had used while performing Houdini like escapes as a young stage magician during his now nearly forgotten adolescence. He'd not done any magic since he'd entered college, but Syman was pretty sure he'd not completely lost his touch. Holding the roll, memories from the past flooded his mind.

In addition to the many hours he'd spent as a child studying puzzles and mazes and codes, Syman remembered the hard work he'd done developing his talents as an amateur magician and escape artist. His interest in these provocative subjects began at age eleven when Syman read a book about the life of Harry Houdini that really captured his imagination. Syman became preoccupied with the man and his unusual talents and set about learning all he could. He haunted the town library that summer searching for books on Houdini and other magicians and escape artists in his endeavor to learn Houdini's art, making and gathering whatever equipment and knowledge he could.

By the time Syman had reached high school, he'd become a fairly adept amateur magician and escape artist himself, perfecting several different 1/4 and 1/2 hour performances, which he performed at parties and other occasions. While his class mates worked in local businesses after school, Syman earned money performing. Pulling odd things from his clothing, out of boxes, from behind peoples ears and doing startling card and rope tricks delighted children and adults alike. However, as much as people enjoyed his magic tricks, it was his escapes people enjoyed the most. Practicing in his bedroom, hour after

91

lonely hour, Syman ultimately mastered many of Houdini's simpler techniques and tricks. Hand cuffs, padlocks, cabinet, and door locks were all easy prey under an assault from the small picks and tools held in the black cloth roll.

Laying the roll on the floor of the container, Syman put his small flashlight between his teeth, freeing his hands. Then he unrolled the tool kit and removed three small tools that were generally the most useful; two picks and a flattened L-shaped wire about 4 inches long. Before leaving Connecticut, he'd also put on his magician's belt, which was the companion to the cloth roll of tools. It was a normal enough looking leather belt, except that it had cloth pockets on its underside for secretly storing little tools and keys. He now deftly secreted the three tools in the belt, putting the rest of the tools away in the backpack.

Taking a last look at the equipment, Syman swung the now hefty backpack onto his shoulder.

Stepping out of the container, he latched the door. It was time to find Dexter and Karrie

21

Karrie lay on her back in the dim light looking up at the grubby ceiling. As she lay there thinking, the ship surged gently every few seconds, like a dolphin in a bow wake. One part of her mind was ever aware of the ship as it rode up over a caught wave crest, then down into the next trough. Then up again, in endless repetition as the ship made its way over the following swells at 20 knots.

She and Dexter had slept most of the time, in fits and starts, since being taken from that miserable container and locked in this stuffy dark cabin. They were somewhere in the bowels of this ship, but they didn't have the slightest idea where, because after first handcuffing Dexter, their captors had blindfolded them. At the time, four men had stood around them pointing guns at Karrie to guarantee Dexter's quiet cooperation. And then, they had half dragged and half pushed them through the ship to their present accommodation. Though not much better than the container, they did have dingy sheetless cots to lie on. And though Karrie was miserably uncomfortable and unhappy, she was still feeling better than her brother who, whenever he sat up, became woozy from the concussion the brutal bastards had given him. Adding insult to injury, literally, they had handcuffed Dexter to a small steel ring on the wall next to his cot. He hated it, but in an odd way, it was good for him. So restrained, he was forced to sleep. He couldn't do anything else and he needed sleep if he was going to get better.

They'd been given water and a little food the two days they'd been aboard. Each morning Karrie had been locked in a bathroom for fifteen minutes. Dexter had been forced to use a bucket next to the cot. Karrie sensed the head creep was really afraid of Dexter because he apparently didn't want Dexter to be unhandcuffed unless absolutely necessary. Using the bucket had been humiliating for Dexter, but he had laughed about it with her when they were alone. He said he'd been put through worse in the SEALs to prepare him for just this sort of abuse. Karrie was surprised at Dexter's upbeat attitude in the midst of their ordeal. She suspected that too was the result of his training, because she hated what was happening and couldn't help being cranky about it. Her feelings ran the gamut from rage to frustration to fear to depression, liberally seasoned with weepy bouts of tears.

22

Syman walked quickly down the right side of the ship. Keeping close to the containers, he was hidden from the men on the bridge. He walked toward a covered porchlike hallway along the rail where the superstructure of the upper works joined with the side of the hull. He moved toward a door at the far end, hoping no one would suddenly step through it and see him. Reaching the back of the superstructure, he stopped and listened carefully, but heard nothing except the deep rumble of the engine. As Syman advanced, he could see two other doors in the wall of the companionway on his left. Reaching the first, he looked through its wire impregnated glass window. On the other side was a dimly lit landing with stairs going up and down. He passed by and went to the next door. It had no windows, but he wanted to check to see where it led. Taking a deep breath, he carefully cracked the door to have a look. It was dark and quiet. He shined his small flashlight inside. Seeing nothing, he entered cautiously to inspect the area, letting the door close behind him. Once inside, he could see it was a large storage room full of paint, foul weather gear, folded tarps, tools, coiled rope and other things needed for the daily maintenance of a ship. He allowed himself to breathe again. It smelled of must and decaying sea things, but the pungent sweet smell of linseed oil from the stored paint was the dominant scent. The smells reminded him of days sailing Thmink.

Just as he turned to leave, Syman heard faint muffled voices coming through the bulkhead from the stairway. Then he heard the creak of the stairway door through a small open window above the locker's door. He buried the lens of his light in his shirt and quietly snapped it off. The voices grew louder, coming to a halt outside the locker's door, just as the stairwell door slammed shut. Had he been seen boarding the ship, after all? Syman's heart raced as he waited for the door to open. Nothing happened. Listening intently, he could plainly hear two men talking.

"...two hundred fer a fou' hour watch," one of the men said. "I start the watch in half a' hour."

"I thought about it," said a second voice.

"Sure beats the hell out a takin' a watch in the boiler room fer extra dough," said the first.

Syman saw a flare of light on the ceiling and after a moment he smelled cigarette smoke. When he realized they weren't coming to get him, he relaxed slightly. They were just a couple of the crew taking a break for some fresh air. It struck Syman as illogical that they would go outside for air and then smoke a cigarette, but Syman had never smoked a cigarette. He couldn't relate.

The second man said, "I could sure use the cash, but I don't like the idea of shootin' no woman. I mean, what the hell is that all about? I didn't think nobody still got shanghaied."

Syman was instantly all ears. He knew who the woman was.

"Shit, you stupid o' sompin'", said the first voice. "You don't got to shoot nobody. You got a gun, but ya don't even see 'em the whole time. Higgins told me, they was handcuffed to the bulkhead. How the hell they gunna go anywhere like that?"

"I don' know," said the second voice. After a moment he continued. "I heard the cap'n was mad as hell at that feren guy 'n threw his ass offa the bridge. I don wanna piss the cap'n off or nothin' like that."

"Screw the Captain!" said the first voice. "He's an asshole and he don't pay my wage. I don't gotta put up with no bullshit from that fat bastard. I do my work good! What I do on my own time ain't none of his business. Who the hell ya think he is anyway, Captain Bly? The trouble with you Cornie, is you ain't got no balls."

"Yeah? I ain't got no balls? Well, fuck you. I autta bust you in the face, you little bastard, for talkin' to me like that," said the second voice angrily.

"Hey take it easy!" said the first man. "I didn't mean nothin' by it. I just meant you gotta take risks sometimes, if ya wanna get ahead fast. I seen you jump in after Sorensen and pull his soggy ass aboard during that storm. I don't mean you ain't got them kind of balls," said the first man, trying to calm the second man down.

"The trouble with you, Roy," said the second man, still unmollified, "is you gotta a big goddamn mouth an' you ain't got no family to take care of, so you don't give a shit about nothin' 'cept yerself."

"Whada ya mean I don't care 'bout nobody? Whada ya think I'm tryin' to do helpin' ya make a little easy money?" countered Roy.

"Yeah, sure. What's in it for you?" asked Corny, suspiciously.

"There ain't a goddamn thing in it fer me." said Roy.

Having stung each other, they were both quiet for a while. Finally, Roy warmed to the subject once again.

"Higgins tol' me he didn't have ta do squat. He just sat outside the cabin door fer four hours lookin' at magazines, until that feren guy come back and give him two hundred bucks cash, when his time was up. It's a racket and I'm gonna get me some of it. I had the feren guy put me down fer the four to eight."

The men on the other side of the door were quiet for several minutes. All the while, Syman was keenly aware of the fatigue he was now carrying like a heavy weight. He desperately wanted to sit down and rest, but he didn't dare move. Any noise would bring the sailors down on him in a flash.

Finally, Roy said, "I gotta get down to G deck. I don't wanna miss the feren guy. He might git someone else to do my watch."

"They keepin' em on G deck?" Corny asked.

"Yeah, in cabin four," answered Roy.

"Hot as hell," said Corny. "Right over da boilers. I wouldn't wanna hafta bunk down there. Those is the shittyist berths on the ship."

"Yeah well, whadda ya 'spect. They ain't gonna keep 'em in the owner's stateroom," said Roy, laughing.

"'Spose not," said Corny, without humor. "I got to get back to work. Don't get off til 7."

"I'm sure glad I'm outta that shit hole for the night. I hate workin' in the boiler room. Now fer some easy money!" said Roy, gleefully.

Syman heard the stairway door open with its wheezy squeak and then slam shut again. The men's foot falls were quickly lost in the background rumble of the ship's propulsion machinery.

He cautiously stepped out on deck. Looking around, he saw no one. He waited several minutes before opening the stairway door to follow the men. Standing on the landing listening, Syman saw a large black 'E' was stenciled on the back of the door designating the deck. Now he knew where to look for Dexter and Karrie. 'E' deck was the weather deck, the main deck of the ship. From what Syman had overheard, he now knew Dexter and Karrie were located two decks down, over the boilers. He walked quickly down the stairs to 'G' deck, stopping in front of the fire door. He peered through the window and saw a poorly lit hallway with dingy yellow walls and a dirty linoleum floor with several of its square green tiles missing. He opened the door and walked down the hall. The hall went all the way across the ship to an identical fire door and stairway. Syman saw that from this hall there were three halls running forward and two halls running aft. He saw no one, just a few doors leading to the different rooms and spaces on this deck. Because Syman knew the boilers would be forward of his present position, he gave the aft facing halls only scant inspection as he passed them. Reaching the opposite side of the ship, he turned right and walked the length of that hall carefully looking at everything as he went along, while trying to look casual in case he came upon someone.

He was dressed in black jeans, a blue T-shirt and nondescript boots. Syman and Chief Lufkin had been similarly though not identically dressed, with the idea of passing themselves off as a couple of newly hired merchant sailors in the event they met other sailors during their search.

The plan was, if they were lucky and the right situation presented itself, they'd grab Dexter and Karrie and head for the hills without a fight. But, if they encountered difficulties, then they'd use some of the heavy arms they'd brought and force their way. Without Lufkin, Syman knew force was now out of the question. He'd have to get them out of there some other way.

As Syman neared the end of the corridor, he approached a wide doorway with blue-white fluorescent light flooding through onto the hall's tile floor. Pausing momentarily to glance into the room, he saw it was a lounge with chairs, tables, a TV, and vending machines full of stale looking sandwiches, candy and soda. It was no surprise that at 4 o'clock in the morning there were no people. What was a surprise, however, was the service counter in the corner with a sink and a coffee machine with what looked like a full fresh pot of coffee on its burner. Syman looked at the coffee longingly, but passed on, not willing to slow his search for Karrie and Dexter.

Continuing on his way, he followed the corridor to its end where he had to turn right into another transverse corridor back across the ship. He was now traveling the third leg of the foursquare of hallways. He could see there were only two corridors on the left going forward toward the bow from this transverse corridor. He wondered why there were only two instead of the three. He tried to imagine the structure of the ship at this point along its length. Then he understood. The two corridors here made sense because the center area was taken by the ship's smoke stack. He could also feel the air was decidedly warmer here than further back in the ship. He knew he was nearing the boilers.

As he reached the first corridor leading forward, he glanced sideways and saw two men talking at the far end about 80 feet away. Without breaking stride, he bypassed the corridor the men were in. Neither man seemed to notice Syman or at least they hadn't looked in his direction. Syman had also noticed an unoccupied chair against the left hand wall. The men were too far away for Syman to get a good look at their faces, but he was almost certain one of them was Hassan. He had seen him in the security tapes at TMI. The other man was surely one of the foul mouthed crewman he'd heard on the other side of the paint locker door. Syman reached the second corridor running parallel to the first. He saw that it was empty, but he passed by that one as well. He'd decided to walk all the way around the four hall square, until he returned to the lounge, where he could wait for Hassan to leave without causing suspicion. Syman was sure Hassan's cabin would not be in this hot part of the ship and that Hassan would soon leave the guard there to watch, going up and forward to the more comfortable part of the ship.

With nothing else he could do, Syman decided now was the perfect time to enjoy a guilt free cup of coffee while he waited. Going to the coffee machine, he poured himself a cup. He picked up a dog-eared copy of a magazine from a rack on the wall and made himself comfortable at one of the tables. Sipping the hot black liquid was sinfully pleasurable and he reveled in it.

Staring blankly at the pages of the magazine, he considered ways to get to his friends. The most direct method was to walk up the corridor to cabin 4 and simply cold-cock the guard. It was blunt and effective, but it would remove the guard from his post, so an alert would probably be sounded sooner rather than later.

Getting safely off the ship presented them with a problem Syman had tentatively decided to solve by using one of the ship's Stimson inflatable lifeboats. With Dexter's and Karrie's help a Stimson could be tossed over the side into the sea. Then, they would follow. But there was a problem with this plan. The only Stimsons he'd seen were in a surveillance photograph taken the day before and they were on the bow of the ship. Still, he figured if they had enough time, they could work their way forward and launch one. Time was the key. He didn't want anyone to know Dexter and Karrie were gone for as long a time as possible. Unless he killed the man and Syman had no stomach for that unless absolutely necessary, there was no way to guarantee the guard wouldn't quickly alert the ship.

Syman considered various ways of talking the guard away from his post, but realized he didn't know enough about the ship to tell the man a convincing story. They needed time and he didn't know how to get it.

Looking at the coffee in his cup, a solution came to him that made him smile.

Knowing that Karrie and Dexter were nearby, Syman decided to stash the backpack here in the lounge. They could pick it up later, when they were together and on their way topside. Looking around for a likely spot, he decided the double-doored cabinet under the coffee machine would work. Downing the last of his coffee in a gulp, Syman went to the coffee machine. He opened the cabinet and put the pack inside. Then he poured two more cups of the steaming liquid. He ladled a lot of sugar into both cups and stirred them. Heading out the door, coffee in hand, Syman made a bee line straight for cabin 4. When he reached the first corridor, he peered around the corner. He saw the small man slouched splay legged in the chair with his arms crossed over his chest. Hassan was nowhere in sight. Syman stepped around the corner and walked toward the guard. The guard watched Syman approach, but regarded him with no apparent interest. Syman walked along holding the coffee out in front of him, appearing to be headed somewhere else. As he came up to the seated man, he moved to the right side of the narrow corridor as if to pass by. Looking the man directly in the eye, with a slight nod of the head Syman said, "Mornin'," in a pleasant way and then stumbled himself dumping both cups of the hot sticky liquid on the seated figure. As he fell to the deck, Syman veered off to the right side, landing on his hands and knees as the guard leap out of the chair raging in surprise and pain.

"You goddamn clumsy bastard!" he screamed at Syman. Then he demanded, "What the fuck is wrong with you?!" All the while he was dancing around pulling furiously at the hot wet fabric of his shirt with one hand while grabbing in a similar vain effort at the crotch of his pants with the other.

"Oh, man! I'm really sorry," said Syman trying to sound sincere.

"What the hell good is sorry," said the little man. "You burned the shit outa me!"

For a moment, Syman said nothing, while the other man glared down at him.

"You're right," said Syman. He was climbing back to his feet now. "Saying I'm sorry don't put things right."

"Yeah!" said the sailor with less vehemence now that the coffee had cooled to a tolerable level. "You got that right." Then after a moment, he continued, "How the hell am I s'pose to sit here on watch fer four hours soakin' wet?"

"Why you sittin' here on watch?" Syman asked, looking quickly right, then left in feigned ignorance.

"I'm guardin' them prisoners the Arab brought aboard. Pays two hundred bucks fer a four hour watch," the little man said, momentarily forgetting his problems.

"Ah, I heard some scuttlebutt 'bout that. Now I understand." Then after a moment Syman asked, "Where the prisoners at?"

"In there," said the sailor, pointing to the door of cabin four.

"Listen," said Syman, "Whyn't ya go change your clothes. I'll stay here and keep watch 'til you get back."

"Hey, what the hell ya tryin' to pull?" asked the sailor, bristling. "You tryin' ta muscle in on my action?"

"No!" said Syman, in vigorous denial. "I don't want no money and I sure don't want no extra duty," Syman added, trying to mimic the other man's ignorant speech patterns a little. "I'm just tryin' to help fix what I screwed up. It's the least I can do after dumpin' hot coffee all over ya."

"Yeah!" said Roy, thinking it over, but still suspicious.

"Look, if ya won't let me help ya then take this," said Syman, applying a persuasion, he was sure would work. He reached into his pants pocket. "My ol' man always tol' me, 'put my money where my mouth is, 'specially when making amends, so here's twenty bucks for the trouble I caused ya." Syman made like he was going to leave. He hoped his good ol' boy act was believable.

Roy's greedy little eyes lit up as Syman handed him the bill. "'saright," he mumbled, snatching the bill from Syman's outstretched hand. He wasn't smiling, but his whole demeanor changed as soon as money entered the situation. Once he had it, he said, "You really mean what ya said 'bout keepin' watch for me, whilst I get me some dry duds?"

"Yeah, sure," Syman said, with utter sincerity. "Like I said, it's the least I can do."

"Okay then. It'll take me 'bout 15 minutes to get forw'd, change, an' get back," the sailor said, now figuring Syman for a real chump.

"Take yer time. I'll wait right here 'til ya get back. Ya might wanta wash off."

"I don't know 'bout washin' off. What's yer name, anyway? I ain't seen you aboard before."

"Name's Leonard Stimson," said Syman, using the first names that came to mind. "I just come aboard in Bridgeport."

"Yer alright, Leonard," Roy said, patronizing Syman. He liked the idea of his having the upper hand over this tall, skinny, obviously not very bright clutz. "I'll be right back."

"Okay," said Syman. "I'll be waitin' here."

With that the little sailor left.

Syman waited a minute before doing anything. Hearing nothing, he tried the door knob. It was locked. Taking two of the three little tools from his belt, he set to work. Twenty seconds later, the knob turned and the door opened.

The room was dark, lit only from the hall lights behind him. He ran his hand over the bulkhead next to the door until he located the light switch. Snapping it on, Syman found himself looking at a surprised and blinking Karrie and Dexter.

"Syman!" Karrie cried, as tears began pouring down her cheeks. She rolled off her cot and flung herself into his arms, kissing him fully on the mouth. Momentarily overwhelmed, he surrendered to her tight embrace, allowing himself to enjoy the satisfaction of finding them alive and apparently in good shape.

"You old pirate," Dexter croaked out, as he tried to sit up and failed.

Seeing his friend's predicament, Syman gently freed himself from Karrie to bend over Dexter. He popped the handcuff's latch with the little flat wire he still held in his hand. The cuffs clanked down against the wall, dangling from the handhold.

"God, that feels great!" Dexter said, with obvious relief. He rubbed the black and blue bracelet of battered skin around his left wrist. "Sy, how'd you do that?"

"It's a little trick I learned as a kid," Syman answer, his friend.

"During a larcenous past you've neglected to tell us about?"

Syman smiled. "You ready to go?"

Dexter answered, "Yesterday wouldn't have been soon enough," then asked, "How'd you get aboard this ship?"

"Later compadre," Syman said. "We've got along way to go and a short time to get there." Dexter and Karrie waited expectantly. Syman continued, "Here's the plan. I persuaded the guard to leave his post by dumping hot coffee all over him. Then I told him I'd wait for him here, keeping his watch while he went and changed his clothes."

"We heard the ruckus, but didn't know what was going on," interrupted Dexter.

"We can leave the ship using one of the inflatable lifeboats, but there's a catch. The only ones I've seen are on the bow. We're in the middle of the ship here, so we have to get to the bow, dump a boat over the rail and then jump after it."

"What happens to us once were in the lifeboat?" asked Karrie.

"There's a nuclear submarine following this ship. I have a transponder and some other gear stashed in that container they brought you aboard in. The sub will pick us up."

"What are we waiting for?" said Dexter. "Let's get going!"

"There's one more thing," Syman said, not moving. "I'm going to take you back to the container, and then, I'm coming back here to wait for the cretin who was guarding the door. The door will be locked and he won't know you're gone. That will give us about one undisturbed hour to get off the ship and away and we're going to need it."

"Why don't we just go, Sy?" protested Dexter.

"We won't have enough time to get a lifeboat over the side. They'd be all over the ship in ten minutes looking for us, and we need at least that hour. We don't want to be seen going over the side. They'd just turn the ship and run us down. It's imperative that we aren't seen."

Dexter was quiet for a moment after Syman stopped talking and then said, "You're right. Lead the way."

Syman opened the cabin door and pointed down the hall. When Dexter and Karrie were past, he checked the lock and closed the door firmly. Slipping past them in the narrow corridor, he quickly led them to the original stairway he'd descended. They ran up it two stairs at a time. At the E deck door Syman motioned for them to stay put. He stepped out onto the deck and stood just the other side for a few moments reconnoitering. When he was satisfied, he signaled to his friends to come and they continued on their way back to the hated container. In three minutes, they were standing inside the aluminum box.

"I can't believe I'm glad to be back in this goddamn shipping container, again," said Dexter.

"I'm not glad," said Karrie. "Syman are you sure you have to go back?"

"Yes, Karrie, I'm sure. It will be getting light soon and going back uses up precious darkness, but we have to maintain secrecy if we want to get away from this ship successfully."

"Oh, god, I don't want to let you go back down there," she said.

"There's no choice," said Syman. "There's some food and water and other stuff in the bags. Take a look while I'm gone"

"I love you, Syman." She embraced him.

"I love you, too," he said, before turning to go.

"See you back here in a few minutes, Sy," Dexter said, as Syman nodded, then disappeared outside.

Syman returned to the chair in the hall without incident. With only an hour and a half until dawn, Syman fidgeted as he sat waiting for Roy to return. There were some magazines next to the chair on the floor. Syman could see that the bottom ones had wicked up some of the coffee he'd dumped and had become sodden messes. He considered trying to read one, but he was too anxious. He looked at his watch for the fifth time in as many minutes. It was 3:30 am. Where was that ignorant little man? His fifteen minutes were up. Looking around at the walls, Syman tried to imagine what it must be like for a merchant sailor living aboard a ship like this, traveling all over the world. 'Goddamn boring' was the first thought that came to mind. 'Tedious' and 'uncomfortable' were second and third on his mental list.

He realized this line of thinking was unprofitable and dropped it. Instead, he reminded himself about the importance of retrieving his back pack from under the coffee machine on his way back to Karrie and Dexter. He didn't want, in fact couldn't afford, to forget it. They would need the Sat-Link to get picked up. He supposed he could use the SEAL satellite com gear, but he didn't know how he could keep it steady enough to find the satellite. Now that he thought about it, he realized the plan to use it in the first place was flawed. This made him doubly glad he'd decided to bring his phone. Omni-directional, the Sat-Link didn't need a steady platform to work properly. With the vastly improved communications gear available these days, Syman wondered why the armed forces didn't appropriate some of it for themselves. He decided he'd asked John Claire about it when he got back.

Time dragged by slowly. Half an hour later Syman finally picked up one of the magazines. It was last week's Time. He was antsy and barely able to concentrate on what he was reading. Out of habit, he turned to the science section. He quickly saw there was nothing of interest in it and turned the next page to the section on medicine. There was nothing of interest in it either, except a short piece on the growing world wide influenza epidemic. It was spring and Syman was struck by the flu's appearance at this time of year. It was odd for a flu epidemic to appear in the spring and his interest was more than academic. An unusual number of people working at TMI had contracted the flu. The company doctor had just sent him a memo calling his attention to it. The article said it had been identified as a relatively nasty strain lasting two to five days. It also said that although no fatalities had been reported, it appeared to be extremely contagious and was showing up in cities around the world. He wondered if it could be the same strain.

Syman heard foot steps coming his way just before Roy swung around the corner at the bow end of the hallway. He glanced at his watch and saw that it was ten after four. The ignorant little fellow had been gone much longer than Syman had hoped, almost an hour. Sunrise was around five. It was going to be a near thing, getting off this tub unseen, Syman thought, feeling exasperated.

"I decided to take that wash you was talkin' about," Roy said, by way of a greeting.

Roy had put on a dirty shirt and a pair of greasy wrinkled blue jeans and Syman could see his hair was dry and his face still had a smudge of dirt from his previous watch in the boiler room. Syman doubted the man had washed. He'd probably been goofing off.

"Well, just as long as everything worked out okay," said Syman affably. "I'm glad you're back."

"Yeah, I'm all set," he said coming up to Syman, who had vacated the chair for him.

"See ya around," Syman said, with a wave, as he backed away.

Roy nodded curtly and said, "Yeah, later."

Syman turned on his heel and walked back in the direction of the lounge to retrieve his back pack.

Four minutes later, he was back at the shipping container, despite having grabbed the back pack on the way.

"Dex, Kar?" he hailed in the dark as he opened the door.

"God! What took you so long?" Dexter asked.

"We were beginning to think something happened to you, Syman."

"No. Nothing happened. It was just that the repulsive creature who was guarding you took his sweet time returning, but here I am and it's time to get going."

"You've got that right, pal. It's going to be dawn in a few minutes."

They gathered the equipment duffels, slinging them onto their shoulders and trooped out the door. They came to an instant stop.

Standing in an arc twenty feet away was a frowning Osmid Bandar with three brutish sailors holding guns. One, Syman could see, was Roy, the cretin, smiling broadly, gun in hand.

"Put your equipment on the deck," Bandar ordered.

They dropped the bags.

"You will accompany us," said Bandar, waving his pistol in the direction of the front of the ship.

Crestfallen, Dexter, Karrie and Syman did as they were instructed. The guards moved to the side to open the way.

"How did you know?" asked Syman, stopping to confront Bandar.

"The man you spilled coffee on," said Bandar, nodding in Roy's direction.

"I tell each man, I will give him more money if he reports anything unusual to me that happens during his watch. This one, he likes my money very much. He came to me at once."

"That's why it took him so long to return?" asked Syman.

"We had to prepare and then we followed you to here," said Bandar, pleased with himself.

The three prisoners were led below to the former accommodations. This time however, Bandar handcuffed all three together and to the bulkheads in such a way that they could not so much as scratch.

"I take no more chances with you meddling Americans," said Bandar, inspecting his handy work. "You will get me killed."

Osmid Bandar had unwittingly chosen the one method of restraint Syman could not overcome despite all his escape training. Because Syman could not bring his hands together, he could not free himself. Nor, could he touch any part of his two companions.

Except for a well guarded one hour respite each day, when they were fed and allowed to use a bathroom, Dexter, Karrie and Syman spent the next three maddeningly uncomfortable days traveling across the Atlantic on the Hana Maru lying on their backs, arms spread wide, hand cuffed to each other and the walls.

23

Monday morning, it felt good to be back in the office again. Except for some sniffles and a runny nose, Sumiko felt almost as good as new. The food poisoning or flu or whatever it was that had attacked her so viciously at the office Friday morning had subsided only to return with a vengeance that evening at home. Chills and fever, muscle and joint aches and hypersensitive skin that felt like it was burning had assailed her all night. By early morning, Sumiko felt so bad, she thought she would die and that scared her. She couldn't remember ever feeling so bad before. And then, just before dawn, as quickly as her illness had begun, it subsided, leaving her with only a mild cold.

Thinking about it now, Sumiko realized that whatever illness she'd had was really strange. It had all been so abrupt in its beginning, its end and its violence.

She'd left work midday Friday and gone straight to her doctor's office. Fortunately for Sumiko, her doctor, Ralph Akamada, was a close friend. They'd attended UCLA at the same time, he as a medical student, she as a budding computer scientist. They had dated for a while, but it didn't take them long to realize they were better friends than lovers and the relationship had cooled from a boil to a simmer. Still, they'd remained good friends over the years and curiously, they'd both settled in the South Bay area after college. Staying in touch had been easy.

When Sumiko called Ralph on Friday, she told him about the blood. He told her to come to his office immediately.

When she'd arrived, Ralph first asked her some questions about her activities during the previous few days. Sumiko told him she had just returned from another business trip to Japan.

As he examined her, she described her symptoms, relating the violence of the vomiting. He noted she had an elevated temperature and he puzzled over this for a moment. From the symptoms she described, he initially thought she had a garden variety stomach flu and that her violent retching had been the cause of her vomiting blood. But the elevated temperature was anomalous, more indicative of a bacterial infection than influenza. When people get the flu, their temperature initially goes down.

As he continued to examine her, he noticed small black spots under some of her fingernails near the cuticles. Sumiko was surprised when he pointed them out to her. He asked her if she had somehow pinched or struck her nails in a way that would have caused the minute hematomas. Not that she could remember. Sumiko suggested that carrying her luggage might have been the cause. Ralph admitted that it was a possibility, but then on a hunch he examined her retinas. Here, he also saw small blood spots. It was very unlikely carrying luggage would have caused bleeding there.

He asked Sumiko if she remembered any sudden changes in cabin pressure while flying. She told him she did not remember anything unusual about her recent flights and that since she flew the same flight to Japan for her company several times a year, she would have noticed.

Ralph knew that some toxins produced by bacterial food poisoning caused these types of bleeding and fever. He told Sumiko she had probable eaten some bad fish in Japan.

She'd laughed weakly and told him she had lived on fast food in Japan and hadn't eaten any fish while she was there. He'd laughed and said she was probably the only person who could go to Japan and not eat fish.

Again, he told her he didn't think she had anything to worry about. As far as he could tell, she most likely had a case of some type of food poisoning. He told her she needed to go home and get some rest. He also said, he would call her later to see how she was doing.

He took a culture of her throat and swabbed an agar dish with it, telling her he'd see if he could flush the little buggers out into the open.

He took a bottle of streptomycin pills from a drawer and told her to take two every six hours. If she had a bacterial infection, the pills would kill the critters.

Sumiko went home and did as her friend instructed, hoping he was right.

Unfortunately, now, Monday morning, Sumiko knew Dr. Ralph had been wrong about her being fine by one very terrible night. And the pills he'd given her had done little or nothing. Still, she decided to call Ralph later and let him know what had happened. Maybe the bug city he'd cultured from her throat would tell them what illness she'd caught. Knowing that might help her avoid it in the future.

Reaching her office, Sumiko surveyed her desk as she sat down. Seeing additional work needing her attention, her heart sank in dismay. Since she'd left Friday morning, more paper had found its way into her already overflowing In Basket. She still hadn't caught up with the work that had collected while she was in Japan.

After fretting a moment Sumiko laughed, remembering the old joke about documents in an In Basket breeding at night when there were no people around to watch. It was ridiculous and childish of course, but still, she laughed at the thought as she began sorting.

Although facing a mountain of paperwork, Sumiko realized she was really thankful to be back working. She would gladly do ten times as much paperwork to avoid having to go through such an ordeal a second time. She never wanted to be that sick again.

She began prioritizing documents creating three stacks in the middle of her desk. It took her twenty minutes before she'd decided the order in which she would tackle everything.

Knowing how to begin helped a lot and Sumiko worked diligently through several items in the first hour.

She was on and off the phone several times and more than one person said they were glad she was feeling better. She was surprised so many people knew she had been ill.

Having gotten a good start, around ten, Sumiko decided to go get some tea. She left her office and walked into the common office area where most of the people in her department worked.

As she walked through the larger office, she immediately noticed that only about half the people who worked in this area were at their desks. Sumiko wondered if there was a meeting that she didn't know about.

Seeing Kay Long, an office friend sitting at her desk, Sumiko walked over to her.

"Hi, Kay."

Kay glanced up and started. Then she said, "Hi, Sumiko. How are you feeling?"

"A lot better, today. Thanks."

"Good!" said Kay.

"Where is everybody? Is there a meeting I don't know about?"

Kay looked surprised by Sumiko's question.

"Don't you know?"

"Know what?" Sumiko asked.

"Since Friday, a bunch more people have come down with the same flu you had," said Kay. "The phone's been ringing off the hook all morning. Everyone's out sick."

"Oh, my god!" exclaimed Sumiko, shocked by this unexpected revelation. In a moment, she understood why the people she had spoken to that morning sounded so effusively glad to hear she was well.

"What ever it is, it's gone through the office like wildfire. You were just the first to get sick."

When Sumiko said nothing, Kay continued, "I guess I'm being selfish, but I'm really hoping I don't get it, because my mother just arrived from Grand Rapids for a visit. I don't know what I'll do if I get sick. She's only going to be here a few days."

Finding her voice again, Sumiko said, vehemently and without thinking, "I hope nobody else gets what I had! It's really nasty. I've never felt worse in my life."

Kay's face fell and Sumiko realized that she'd just said the wrong thing to her friend. Without meaning to, Sumiko had just filled her friend with the subtle dread of one waiting for disaster to strike.

"You're still okay, so you're probably not going to get it," said Sumiko, in a hollow attempt to undo the damage she'd done.

"Probably," said Kay. But, it was clear from her expression that she doubted her own assertion.

Forgetting completely about tea, Sumiko returned to her desk. She picked up the phone and called Ralph. As far as she could tell she was over her illness. There wasn't anything she needed from him, but, maybe the throat culture Ralph had taken could help him prescribe some better form of treatment for her office mates.

Sumiko heard Ralph's secretary answer, "Hello. This is Dr. Akamada's office. How may I help you?"

"Hello, Betty. This is Sumiko Fujita. Would you ask Dr. Akamada to call me when he has a free moment. It's important."

Knowing that Sumiko and the Doctor were good friends, there was a momentary pause as the secretary considered how much she should tell her. Then she said, "I'm sorry, Miss Fujita, but Dr. Akamada won't be in the office, today. He's ill with the flu."

Surprised, and more than a little concerned, Sumiko thanked the secretary and hung up. Then she dialed Ralph's home number

24

With the arrival of the Hana Maru, Dexter, Karrie, and Syman had been moved from the ship to the island, but until this moment little else had changed. Though nearly overwhelmed with fatigue from days of sitting with arms outstretched, cuffed to each other or a wall, all looked up when the door flew open. As they watched, Osmid Bandar, aka Sabir Hassan, was frog marched into the concrete block room, their prison since arriving at Ilhas Desertas the previous night, by a gun toting thug dressed in combat fatigues. Bearded and dark featured, with a maniacal glint in his eye, the thug kicked Bandar from behind sending him sprawling onto his face on the dirty concrete floor. Staring fearfully over his shoulder at his assailant, Osmid began to pick himself up, but stopped on his hands and knees, when the thug began screaming.

"Bandar, it is a good thing your usefulness to the Islamic Brotherhood is over. You are a clumsy fool and you have endangered our operation with your stupidity." Barely in control of his anger, flecks of spittle flew from his lips as he pronounced b's and c's, f's and p's. "For that you will die. I would kill you right now if the leader would permit it, but he will not allow killing on a holy day if it can wait. Lucky man, you. You get one more day of life to worry about how you die. Tomorrow I will kill you after I kill these infidels," he said, sweeping his assault rifle over Dexter, Karrie, and Syman. "It will take a very long painful time," said the maniac, "as I even the score between us. And, I will enjoy it! Ha!" The man was clearly insane with rage. He then stepped over to Bandar and kicked him in the face. With that, he turned on his heal and marched out of the cubicle. The door slammed shut and it was deathly still again.

The three friends looked from one to another and then back at the paunchy little man still on his hands and knees in front of them. Blood ran freely from his nose, and he wiped at it with his hand several times in a futile effort to stem the flow. Despite the blood, when he looked up, apprehension rather than fear showed on his face. Still, he was frozen in tense immobility like a cat cornered by a dog.

Dexter broke the silence, "How does it feel to be on the receiving end, scumbag?"

Osmid reddened perceptibly.

Dexter continued. "If I could get loose, I'd twist your head off your shoulders, right now!"

Osmid paled perceptibly.

With deep satisfaction, Dexter leered at Bandar, seeing he had succeeded in pushing his buttons.

"Dexter!" said Karrie, "Stop it! You frighten me with that kind of talk. And it doesn't accomplish anything."

Dexter made no reply.

Without taking his eyes off his fellow prisoners, Osmid got up and moved to the corner farthest from them, though it did little to increase the distance between them in a room only 15 feet square. He sat quietly on an empty wooden crate turned on its side against the wall and watched the others.

Their cell had been used as a store room for the temporary offices that had filled the rest of the concrete building during construction, but with the facility nearly complete, there was no longer any need for the offices. Consequently, the store room now contained only a few pieces of abandoned office furniture, several boxes, and some trash. Only the office on the other side of the door was still being used. However, today was a Moslem holy day and it was empty.

Osmid Bandar slowly surveyed their pathetic cell as he sat there considering what to do to save himself. He was nothing if not a survivor, but he couldn't remember having ever been in a more perilous situation. He knew when the brotherhood had finished with him, they would go after his immediate family, intent on killing everyone they could find. It was the oldest of humiliations and would thoroughly disgrace his memory. He realized if he lived through this he could never return to his beloved Pakistan. More importantly, he needed to contact his loved ones there and warn them to leave if they were to survive. He thought all this over for several minutes, under the stare of his three former prisoners, knowing that they were now his only hope. With that realization, he decided it was time to change sides. He screwed up his courage and spoke to them.

"We are in a very bad situation here."

"No thanks to you, right?" Dexter shot back.

"Originally, it is my fault, yes," said Osmid, trying to placate. "But it will not help us to fight each other anymore. It no longer matters to me what you have learned of the Brotherhood's activities. They are now my enemies as well. It is no longer in my best interest to protect them. It is now in my best interest to work with you to escape as quickly as possible."

"You really are a scumbag, aren't you, Hassan?" said Dexter, with utter disdain. "Not only are you vicious and ruthless, but you have no loyalty to your own people!"

Syman, who had listened silently, said, "Dexter, let the man speak."

"Why do we want to listen to this snake, Sy? He's not trustworthy."

"In most circumstances that would be true," said Syman, sounding like an expostulating university professor correcting an errant undergraduate, "but in our present predicament, we can assume that our mutual interests correspond sufficiently to allow us to work together toward escape."

Dexter looked at his sister and rolled his eyes as Syman blathered on, saying with thirty words, what might have been clearly stated with ten. It was one of the few things Syman Pons did that truly irritated Dexter and right now Dexter was in no mood for a lecture. Karrie gave Dexter a knowing smile. She deeply loved both her brother and Syman, but she would not get between them by taking sides. In this particular matter, she agreed with Syman, but she said nothing and just listened. She would speak her mind if the result was not to her liking.

When Syman was done with his admonition, Dexter looked at Osmid and said, "What possible reason is there to justify our helping you?"

"I still have the key to your handcuffs," Osmid said, with a sly expression."

"That's a little too convenient for me," said Dexter, scowling at Bandar.

"You seem to have something in mind Mr...? What is your name?" asked Syman, opening a dialogue.

Osmid considered his answer, deciding it no longer mattered if they knew his real name. In fact, it might help him in later negotiations he was already considering in the back of his mind. He would need a new home and what better place away from the Brotherhood, where his money could really do him some good, than the United States. He could help their country, his new country, stop the Brotherhood from carrying out their brutal plans. He had never liked what they had forced him to do. He had no fight with the USA. On the contrary, he had always liked the country. "Osmid Bandar is my name."

"Be careful, Syman," Dexter warned. "You're making a deal with the devil if you go along with this guy."

Syman ignored Dexter and considered the various possibilities. If Bandar had been planted to find out what they knew, they could take good advantage of him without telling him anything. In playing the game with him, at least they would get out of their handcuffs, which in itself, was a good enough justification to play along. Once the cuffs were off, if they could get past the outer office, they might actually get free.

Though unsure of Bandar, Syman was sure of something much more important to them. If they had any chance at all, they had a much better chance on their feet, than chained to a wall. If on the other hand, Dexter was wrong and Bandar really was running for his life, then they would take advantage of his honest willingness to help them all escape and so much the better.

Syman could not discuss all this with Dexter in front of Bandar, but he suspected his partner had also come to similar conclusions, and it was just because of his stubborn Anglo-Saxon nature that he continued to be so ill-tempered toward the man. Besides, if Dexter all of a sudden declared his eternal friendship, Bandar would certainly not believe him.

Dexter's irascibility aside, Syman knew the truth about Bandar's sympathies would come out before too long and then they would deal with the man accordingly. Either way, they would be no worse off than they were at present and Syman's arms hurt like hell.

"As I said, Mr. Bandar, what's on your mind?"

"You people have been drawn into a terrorist operation without your meaning to be and without realizing the scope of it."

"Yes," Syman replied, dryly.

"I was forced into working for my former employers against my will. I was ordered to perform certain services in locating and acquiring materials and supplies for their operation. If I had refused, they would have killed me and all my family. So, you see, I am as much a prisoner of these people as you are."

"Yeah, sure!" said Dexter. "You didn't have anything to do with our being here. Right?"

"Mr. Gordon, I have already told you, I am at fault for bringing you here, but my other choices were to kill you or to let you go, and then the Brotherhood would have killed me."

"You chose that we should die instead of you, that's all?" Dexter was incredulous. "And now you want us to trust you?"

"That is right, and you would have chosen to do the same if you were me, but now I choose to help us live, so please stop wasting time we will need to escape. I will do you no more harm and perhaps a great deal of good, but you will have to trust me, a little."

"Okay, say I trust you a little and don't kill you the minute I'm able. What can you do to get us out of here?"

"I know this island, and I know where we can hide until dark when we can call your rescue people to come pick us up."

Dexter looked at Syman and then back at Bandar.

"What makes you think we have a rescue plan, Mr. Bandar," Syman asked.

"There are several clues, Mr. Pons. First, you brought an American special forces satellite communications device with you aboard the ship. Second, you also brought a large quantity of military light armaments. You had enough for several people to use, all of it the best available. Third, you succeeded in boarding a moving ship at sea without being spotted. All this implies that you are extremely well trained. Probably, you are an American special forces commando. However, I am puzzled that you are alone. Regardless, if you are, as I suspect, a military person, then the military will have some plan for picking you up. That would explain the communication device and the weapons."

"How would you know what the best military weapons are, Bandar, unless you're military yourself?" asked Dexter.

"I am, among other things, Mr. Gordon, an arms dealer. It was in this capacity, that I was originally associated with the Brotherhood. But, I am not a military man."

"I told you he was a snake," Dexter said, with no hint of apology in his voice.

"Enough of this, Mr. Gordon. Someone must take a first step. Time is growing short and we must get going or we will lose any chance of escape. Colonel Ibrahim, the man who kicked me, is as likely as not to disregard the leaders wishes and come back at any minute and kill us. We have no time to waste. We must work together or we will certainly die here. Since it is obvious that your countrymen do not hold the lethal animosity toward me you do, then I must deal with you first. Will you give me your word, you will not kill me if I let you go?"

Dexter was taken aback at the turn of events. He didn't say anything for a moment. Then he said, "Bandar, I don't like you. I don't like what you've done to us. And I don't trust you as far as I can spit, but if you don't screw us again, I won't harm you."

"I understand your reasons, Mr. Gordon." With that he crossed the room and undid Karrie's cuffs first, then Syman's, and finally, Dexter's. The order in which he released them was lost on no one.

The sudden release from their restraints hurt like hell. At first all three swung and shook there arms gently to get the circulation going. As their limbs awoke an agony of tingling caused all three to gasp softly and moan quietly as feeling and muscle control returned in small stages. It took several minutes before the ability to use their arms approached something like normal. Osmid Bandar returned to his crate, where he sat quietly keeping a wary eye on Dexter the whole time.

Dexter was aware of Bandar's vigilance and said to him, "I gave you my word, Bandar. As long as you're square with us, you don't have anything to worry about."

Osmid nodded solemnly in acknowledgment. As Karrie, Dexter, and Syman gently rubbed feeling back into their tortured arms, Osmid spoke, "We are fortunate that my late associates do not think I am capable of tying my owns shoes. And because they believe you are securely handcuffed, they suppose there is no threat of escape. Also, they believe we are too far from anywhere for us to get away from the island and, therefore, they have neglected to post a guard in the adjoining room."

"Can you believe the luck? Let's get out of here," said Dexter.

"Yes, I think it's time to go," said Syman, walking to the door.

"Just a moment, Mr. Pons," said Osmid. "We must have a plan, but first I must tell you more about the island so you will understand what we should do."

"That's a good idea," said Karrie, still rubbing her arms slowly. "We didn't see much of it in the dark last night when they brought us in here."

"We are on one of the Ilhas Desertas islands belonging to Portugal. It has been leased to Libya for establishing a fishing and canning complex. The fishing operation is located around the island on the south side, where there is a small harbor. This facility is the fish canning plant and is located on the island's northwest coast. Its real purpose for being here has nothing at all to do with canning. In reality, it is a cover operation for a small missile launching site."

"Why does Libya want a missile launching site in the middle of the Atlantic Ocean?" Dexter asked, interrupting.

"The reason is complicated and I don't think we should waste time talking about that now. There will be time later when we are safely off the island." The truth was, what the Brotherhood intended to do with the island was Bandar's ace in the hole. If played correctly it would get him into the U. S. as a new citizen. But it needed to be played at the right time and that was not now. Osmid continued, "This island is one of the outer uninhabited Madeira islands. It has only one reliable water source, a small lake near the top of the mountain that occupies the center of the island. Having a reliable water source nearby was the reason given for putting the facility here on the northwest side of the island, but that is not really the important reason."

"Why are you telling us about the islands water source?" asked Syman.

"The island is desert most of the year. As you will soon see, there is little vegetation at this time. I am telling you about the water system because there is a large water pipe, that runs across the face of the mountain and will lead us to cover. The pipe itself will give us no cover, but we must follow it. It passes just behind this building on its way to a shallow valley, what a Mexican would call an arroyo, about one hundred meters away. It has been laid up the arroyo, which carries the overflow from the lake during heavy rains. Once we reach the arroyo, it will hide us for several hundred meters up the mountain. There is much vegetation in it."

"Why go up the mountain"? asked Dexter. "We want to head for the beach."

"They will send out men to find us when they discover we are gone. At first, we want to go up the mountain because they will expect us to go down to the harbor where we might try to steal a boat to escape. They will search the route to the harbor first, then the harbor area, then the coast. We will be on the mountain, where they would not expect us to be. When they do not find us on the coast, then they will search the mountain. At that time we will move to the coast."

"Good thinking," said Syman, nodding his head in agreement.

Osmid continued, "We climb the arroyo to the ridge above. From there we turn and follow the ridge to the quarry road. A few hundred meters beyond the quarry a trail descends to the coast. On that trail we will be out of sight of both the harbor and here. There are several good places to hide off that trail"

"It sounds like a good plan, Bandar," said Dexter, "but how do you know about the trail?"

"I have spent much time on this island working with the engineer and builder on the materials I needed to procure for them. In several instances they had to show me what was needed so I would get them the correct things. Ships are the only way on or off the island and there is only one a week because they do not want to bring attention to this place. In the last eight months I have been here on three separate visits, each time for a week. It never took more than a day or two to learn what was needed. I spent the rest of those weeks exploring this island because there is little else to do. I know this island well"

"Your familiarity should come in handy," said Syman.

"Yes," said Bandar continuing, "Now, we are about four hundred miles west of the African coast and about seventy miles from the nearest of the inhabited Madeira islands. As you can see, we are a long way from help. I can get us away from this facility, but can you get us away from the island?"

"That might be a problem without our gear, Syman said."

"That should not be a problem, Mr. Pons. Your gear is being kept in a closet in the office next to us. To get outside, we will have to go through the next office. There is no other way. It will be a small thing to gather your equipment as we pass."

"Great," said Dexter, with returning enthusiasm. "That's the best news yet."

"How long will it take for your people to pick us up from the time they hear from you?"

"That depends on how close they can come into shore," said Syman. "If we are on the beach, an hour or two would be a reasonable time, I should think."

"Now, I think, we are ready to go," said Bandar.

"Let's see if we can find some wire or a paper clip," Syman said as a distraction. When no one was looking, he removed the flat wire and one of the picks he had hidden in his belt. He palmed them. There was no percentage giving away trade secrets unnecessarily. He was surprised how easily it came back to him after all these years. Old skills are tenacious, he thought with a smile.

Karrie opened a drawer in a battered metal filing cabinet standing alone opposite the door. She found a few paper clips daisy chained together sitting in its bottom. "Here you go, Syman!" she said with glee, sounding like a kid in an Easter egg hunt coming upon the first egg. "I've found a bunch of them."

Syman realized it was the first time he had heard spontaneous joy in her voice since all this began.

Karrie carefully handed her prize to Syman. Syman disengaged one clip and began to unbend it. He then closed its end in the metal file drawer's top and bent the very end to 90 degrees. He unbent a second clip and walked over to the door. Leaning over in such a way that he blocked everyone's view, he quietly went to work on the lock mechanism in the doorknob. He was using his magician's tools, not the paper clips. They would have worked, too, but it would have taken him longer. And though switching tools was cumbersome, he wanted to keep his tools existence a secret until he was sure they could trust Bandar.

"Get ready everybody," he said, in a stage whisper and with that he turned the knob and opened the door a tiny bit. Syman put his eye to the crack and looked to see if there was anyone in the office. Seeing no one, he opened the door wider until he could see the room was empty.

Letting out a big sigh, he said, "We're okay!" and stepped into the empty office.

Dexter immediately followed Syman into the room, heading straight for the closet to get the weapons and other equipment. Syman walked to the office door and checked the hallway. It too was empty.

Dexter opened one duffel and looked inside. Then he handed it to Bandar. It held the communications gear and tools. He picked up a second bag. It contained the weapons. He removed a holstered nine millimeter automatic. He put the holstered gun on a utility belt that had two pouches full of extra 9 millimeter ammunition clips, one on each hip. He strapped on the belt. When the belt was secure, he unsnapped the flap of the right pouch and removed two clips, putting one in his front left pants pocket and the other in the gun. He removed a second gun and ammo belt and handed it to Karrie. She looked at it as if it were a poisonous snake.

"What am I suppose to do with this, Dexter?" she asked.

"You don't have to shoot it, Kar, but we need to spread the weight around. It's a lot for one person to carry up a mountain. And you never know, it might come in handy. You know how to shoot a revolver. It's almost the same thing."

Karrie shook her head and grimaced as Dexter helped her strap the belt, with its bulky cargo, around her waist. When it was secure, he reached over unsnapping its flap and pulled the gun from the holster.

"This is the safety," he said, showing her the button. He handed the gun to her and told her to work the safety a few times to get the feel of it. Karrie did as she was told frowning the entire time. Taking the gun back from her, he continued the lesson.

"Hold the gun out in front of you with both hands, like this and keep your feet planted wide," he said, showing her the correct stance. He pulled the slide back and released it. Aiming, he dry fired the gun. He handed her the gun a second time.

"When you have the right stance, look down the top of the barrel and squeeze the trigger, gently."

She again did as she was told pulling back the slide and releasing it. She took her stance, but the trigger wouldn't depress. She released the safety, which Dexter had reset. Taking her stance again, she aimed at the door knob and squeezed the trigger. The slide jumped forward with a loud 'clack'.

Dexter took the automatic from her and slapped a clip of ammunition in to the receiver, checked to see the mode switch was on single fire and set the safety.

"Here you go, Sis," Dexter said, handing the gun to her for the last time. "Remember to always start with the safety first and keep the barrel up until you're ready to take your stance. No stance, no shot—unless your hiding behind something or laying down."

"I don't think I like any of this, Dex," she said.

"Sorry, Kar, but were not making the rules right now."

"I know," she said, resignedly, as she fumbled with the holster, trying to get the heavy gun back in it.

The other two men had watched Dexter's abbreviated lesson, anxiously looking out the window and down the hall.

Dexter handed a silenced, Hoit Vortex long barreled, 6 millimeter machine pistol to each of the other two men, along with a belt of 100 round clips. A belt held six clips.

Finally, Dexter armed himself with a Coley Robins, 9 millimeter, scoped sniper's rifle. With its IR/light amplifying scope, silencer and flash suppresser, Dexter could reliably hit a beer can sized target, 3 out of 4 times, at three hundred yards, while giving no clue as to his location, night or day.

It was a hell of a lot of fire power for four people. Slinging the still heavy weapons duffel up onto his back, Dexter handed Syman's small pack to Karrie, which she slipped on easily. Dexter hoisted the last duffel containing the food and water onto Syman's back.

Syman groaned and said, "Thanks a lot," when he felt the weight. Dexter laughed and said, "Remember the day this all started, when I told you someday I'd find a suitably distasteful task for you to do. Well, this is it!"

"I should have known better than to agree to that deal," Syman said, smiling broadly as he slapped Dexter in the chest with the back of his hand. "Let's get going!"

With Bandar leading the way, the four people went out the back door of the building. A large pipe, about 4" in diameter, crossed diagonally to the right, leading to the valley. As he had told them, the pipe provided virtually no cover. Fortunately, it was the heat of the day, on a holiday and most of the construction work on the facility was complete, so there were few people outside. The majority of them were in their quarters resting out of the sun. Three men were working on a truck downhill from the office building, but they were too far away to pay any attention to the four people above them. In less than a minute, they crossed the intervening hundred meters and disappeared into the arroyo without incident. Looking downhill from their narrowed vantage point in the arroyo, they could clearly see the cream colored sand beach a mile or so down the mountain and the deep sapphire blue ocean with its greenish shallow water fringe along the shore. Happily, they could not see any of the canning facility.

Unfortunately, there was only a whisper of a breeze to stir the afternoon's heavy, hot, humid air and it was blowing across the mountain, never quite reaching into the shallow, trenchlike little valley. Rivulets of sweat ran down their skin and each of them was soaking wet within a few minutes. With the tropical sun beating down and with only occasional shade from the tallest shrubs in the ditch, it was hard going up the mountain. When they had traveled about half the distance to the ridge, where they would leave the stifling little valley, Dexter unzipped Syman's bag and took out a bottle of water and passed it around. They each consumed their share greedily with no pretense. It was damn little water considering what they had already lost, but they continued up the mountain side without complaint, tripping and back sliding, one step out of two as the angle of ascent increased with each step upward. After forty minutes of crushing effort, they reached the ridge. Leaving the arroyo, they hiked along the back side of the ridge completely out of sight from anyone who might be lower on the mountain. Having now reached the highest point in the climb, it was easier going. The ridge began to gently descend as they traveled laterally across the mountain toward the quarry road.

25

Yousef climbed to the lake early that morning, before it had gotten hot. He'd brought lamb and bread and yogurt to eat for the midday meal. He'd also brought water.

Twice a week, it was his job to climb the mountain, following the pipe to the lake. On the way, he checked to make sure the pipe, valves, and other equipment were in good condition. He also brought along four pounds of chlorination powder which he put in the dispenser next to the inlet pipe. The dispenser metered the antiseptic chlorine into the water before it started on its way to the storage tank at the facility. The trip downhill in the pipe guaranteed it was thoroughly dispersed and mixed before it reached the tank.

Two years before, with a new degree in hydraulic engineering, the Brotherhood had signed him on and brought him out to this island, where he and the first construction workers set to work. Originally, he'd been hired to build the system he now maintained. But Yousef was no longer satisfied with the situation as it now stood having gone from engineer to mechanic. And once again, he considered his predicament as he hiked back down the mountain along the pipe.

Reaching a particularly steep grade, the trail veered away from the little valley. Yousef followed the serpentine path. It led to a bluff which presented a spectacular view of the entire north side of the island and the surrounding ocean before turning back to the valley lower down the mountain.

Of late Yousef had taken to spending an hour or so eating and thinking at this spot while quietly sitting in the shade of an outcrop of rock enjoying the view. Today, the air was crystal clear and he could just make out another island 75 miles to the northeast. As he sat thinking, his attention was drawn downhill and to his left by the sound of people clambering up the valley. When he first became aware of them, they were about 100 feet below him on the mountain and having a difficult time of it. Their feet sent small avalanches of stones and debris down the valley with each step they took. Carefully peering over the edge, he watched as they followed the side trail away from the valley toward the quarry road. He wondered who they were and what they were doing. Yousef was going to hail them, when he saw they were carrying guns.

That was unusual. Only Colonel Ibrahim's security men carried guns on the island. The strangers were also carrying duffel bags on their backs. Yousef wondered about that for a minute. Why were they climbing the pipeline trail, carrying heavy packs, when they could have walked up, or for that matter, driven a truck up the quarry road? When they were closer, Yousef could see one of them was a woman.

Now he was sure there was something strange about these people. There were no women on the island. Suddenly it occurred to him that they might be a Jewish military unit, sent to the island to somehow sabotage the facility. They weren't exactly dressed like soldiers but Yousef knew Israel had women in their army. And Israel was the Brotherhood's arch enemy. Realizing that he might be in real danger, he hunkered down and waited until they had passed by. When he was sure they would not hear him, he began bounding down the trail toward the cannery. Yousef needed to tell Captain Ibrahim about the strangers before they did any damage. Fortunately, going down the mountain was much faster and easier than going up. If he didn't slow down, he could be at the facility in about 10 minutes.

Sweating profusely, they left the pipe and the sweltering valley behind. After a quarter hour of relatively easy hiking down a gentle slope, the four reached a dirt road just where it began winding its way around the far side of the mountain. The sun was still fierce and the air temperature was solidly in the 90's, but there was a little breeze on the road.

"We do not have far to go, now," said Osmid Bandar in encouragement. They had come abreast of one another, walking along in a relax manner on the road.

"This heat is giving me a headache," said Karrie, voicing her first complaint since beginning their trek up the mountain an hour before.

"There are several places where we can rest in the shade up ahead," continued Osmid.

"Where's the best place to hold up and sleep for a few hours?" asked Dexter.

Osmid considered that for a minute before responding, "The coolest and darkest place would be in a cave that was uncovered in the quarry."

"How big is it?" asked Syman intrigued.

"It is about 10 meters wide, I think."

"Are there any snakes or poisonous creatures on the island that might have crawled inside?" asked Karrie.

"There are scorpions, but no snakes," said Osmid. "The floor of the cave is stone, so we will see them if there are any. They hide in sand. That is how most people get stung. They sit on them in the sand."

"I'll remember that," said Karrie, none too reassured.

"Is their sting serious?" asked Syman.

"No, just painful."

"I need some shut eye," said Dexter. "I'm falling asleep on my feet."

"I guess we all need a little sleep," agreed Syman.

"Shouldn't we contact the sub," said Dexter, changing the subject abruptly.

"We can set up your equipment at the quarry," suggested Osmid.

"I need to get something out of your backpack, Kar," Syman said, as he stepped behind her. Karrie stopped walking, while Syman fished around in the sack. He took out the Sat-Link, removing it from its water proof pouch. He dialed Esmirelda.

Dexter laughed, when he saw the mobile phone.

Karrie asked, "What's so funny?"

"Syman's a true tech-renaissance man, definitely one of the first electronically enlightened human beings. He carries those gadgets with him everywhere."

"You can go anywhere and do anything if you have three things with you at all times: your credit cards, your mobile phone and your laptop. You'll be glad I brought them this time," Syman said, with a straight face. And then, he winked at Karrie.

"Hello, Syman," said the machine, via the phone.

"Hello, Essy. Did you give my message to John Claire?"

"Yes, Syman. He has been calling several times a day and is quite concerned for your safety. He told me to contact him the moment you called and I'm presently doing that."

"Hello, Syman?" Syman heard, as Claire came on the line. "Are you okay?"

"Yes John. We're all okay for now. Did you pick up Lufkin?"

"Yes. He's fine. Had the shit scared out of him, when he thought he was going to go through the prop on that freighter, but we picked him up."

"Glad to hear that," Syman said, sincerely.

"What happened to you?" asked Claire. "The sub stayed with the ship, right up to the island, but when you hadn't contacted us again, we began to think maybe they disposed of you all. We were worried."

"We're okay, John. I was taken prisoner and put in with Dexter and Karrie. They transferred us to the island last night, but we were able to escape about an hour ago with the help of one of the people here. Incidentally, we're bringing him with us so be prepared for four people. We're going to hide until dark."

"Okay," said Claire.

"Where is the sub?"

"It's patrolling around the island, waiting to hear from me."

"Good," said Syman, with evident relief in his voice. "We'll try to get to the beach tonight after dark, on the north side of the island. We can signal with a flashlight, let's say, two long and two short, if the sub can wait off shore. Or I can call you."

"Let's do both," said Claire. "Then we have some redundancy. I'll have the sub off the north shore after dark. When they see your signal, they'll launch a boat, whether they hear from me at that time or not. But be sure and call me, if you can."

"If we can't do either, what will you do?"

"We'll keep the boat on station and wait. I've still got the boarding team aboard the sub. They're preparing to extract you right now. We were going to hit the island tonight, if we hadn't heard from you. Their orders are to get you out of there or find out what happened. Now that I know you're okay, we'll hold. If we don't hear from you tonight by 4 a.m., your time, we're coming ashore and get you."

"That's good John, but, I think we can make it to the shore, without any problems. We'll talk to you later."

"Later, Syman."

Syman turned the phone off and wondered how much battery time was left. Enough to call later and now that wasn't absolutely necessary, in any case.

They walked on down the quarry road. Five minutes later they were in sight of the quarry, but before reaching it, they heard the sound of an approaching vehicle.

"Run for the cave, there in the face of the hill," Osmid yelled. He stabbed the air, frantically pointing toward a dark opening at the back of the wide gravel filled hole confronting them. While they were still a hundred feet from the cave opening, a large stake bodied truck roared around the bend in the road, they had just passed. And it was loaded with uniformed, armed men.

Running along stumbling, jumping over large rocks, and jinking around the larger holes in the quarry's floor, the four clambered carelessly past all obstacles in their headlong rush to reach the cave and get out of sight. But it was to no avail. Just as they reached the cave's entrance, shots began to ring off the surrounding rocks, zinging and whining, with dozens of metal fragments hissing around, as they chipped pieces off the stones. Dexter was the last one in and he caught a face full of blasted grit from the cave's wall near his head as he bent to pass through the opening.

"Goddamnit!" he said, loudly as he dumped his backpack to the floor of the cavern. His voice boomed in the small space.

"What's wrong?" Syman and Karrie replied, in unison, alarmed at Dexter's noisy expletive.

"I caught some ricochet in the face," he replied.

"Are you hurt?" asked Karrie, as she stepped in his direction.

"Stay back!" Dexter yelled at her to halt her movement toward the deadly doorway. "I'll be fine. Quick! We've got to return fire or they'll be all over us in a flash." Dexter had assumed command, his SEAL training naturally asserting itself. "Syman, get behind the edge of the entrance there and open up on them," Dexter ordered. "Bandar, you get on the other side. "You don't have to hit anything to begin with. Just discourage them from rushing us. We need a standoff to give us time to organize. Try to put out a slow steady fire to keep them away."

Syman dove for the far side of the opening. Leaning to his left, he fired several times in the general direction of the truck, which had pulled to a screeching halt about thirty yards from the cave on the opposite side of the quarry pit. Syman realized it was the first time he'd ever fired a gun at a human being. As he watched, the front right tire of the truck sagged and went flat, having been hit by one of his bullets.

Immediately after the first shots rang out from the cave entrance, the security force's disorganized actions turned into a frantic scramble for cover, wherever cover could be found just as Dexter had hoped. Laying on his stomach behind the pile of rubble just inside the opening, Dexter took aim at one of their less careful pursuers. The man was kneeling behind a rock that was too small to give him complete cover. Taking aim through his rifle's powerful scope, Dexter shot him in the ass. The man jumped up and then fell over when his seriously injured gluteus maximus refused to bear his weight.

"One down. Twelve to go," Dexter said, reporting the success to his companions. "We're in a hell of a spot here," Dexter continued, after shooting another security man in the chest when he stupidly stood up to fire like some kind of fearless Dirty Harry. "I probably just killed a second one. There'll be no mercy now. Syman, will the phone work through the rock?"

"It doesn't work very well when I pass under highway bridges, but..." Syman said. Then, he yelled, "Karrie, get the phone and try it. We could really use some help from that SEAL boarding team on the sub."

Karrie did as she was asked. "Who do I call?" she asked, during a lull in the shooting.

"Push the number 2, and then the speed dial button," he told her. "Essy will connect you."

"All I hear is a loud hum," she told him.

"Okay, it won't work in here," Syman concluded, "Put it away."

All the while, Dexter had been methodically shooting one man after another with the sniper's rifle. It was an extremely deadly weapon in the hands of a trained marksman like himself. The security men on the other hand, shooting into the dark cave, could see no one and had no idea of the effectiveness of their shots. They were at a distinct disadvantage.

"I've hit five of them. All the easy targets are down," Dexter said, without remorse. He knew it was a 'them or us situation' and he wasn't about to let 'them' win if he could possibly help it. "There are eight more, but they all have good cover. It will take some lucky shots to get them."

Syman and Osmid had been alternately firing single shots and short bursts, which had hit no one, but had held the security men in their places of refuge while Dexter nailed the more exposed men, one after another.

"Slow your firing rate," Dexter told his companions. "We have to conserve ammunition and they seem to have gotten the point and are going to stay back."

Colonel Ibrahim watched as bullets from the cave mouth quickly found their targets and cut his force to ribbons. In the first five minutes, he had lost five men.

"Stay the hell back from that hole in the ground," he screamed at his men in Arabic. He considered the situation. Although livid at having lost his prisoners and wanting desperately to get his hands on them, (so he could take his slow pleasure in killing them) Ibrahim realized he would have to put the Brotherhood's interests before his own desires for revenge. Forcing himself to think rationally, he asked himself, 'What is the objective here?' In answer he thought, 'These people endanger the mission. They know nothing he needed to know. They were creating havoc amidst his forces, but they were of no real value. Therefore, the priority was simply, dispose of them.'

Ibrahim could see he was not going to get at them as long as they were holed up in the cave. Then he realized that the very strength that now protected them could be used against them.

"Khalil!" he hollered. A solder behind the truck answered.

"Yes, sir."

Bring the explosives to me," Ibrahim ordered.

The security man looked at his superior and then at the mouth of the cave forty yards away. Then, he looked at a dead comrade lying on the ground ten feet away. He said a silent prayer and climbed onto the back of the truck, which was fortunately behind the cab, so he was not seen. Khalil removed an open wooden box of dynamite from the steel utility box bolted to the truck's bed. He also removed detonators and flash cord from a walled-off compartment in the steel box. He put the detonators and fusing on top of the dynamite sticks. With another silent prayer, he jumped off the truck's bed and sprinted toward Colonel Ibrahim, who was behind a huge boulder that was almost entirely out of view from the cave's entrance. Just as Khalil was about to reach the boulder, a single shot from the cave hit him in the leg. He flopped down on top of the explosives. Colonel Ibrahim, standing less than twenty feet away, nearly fainted with fright as the dynamite box hit the ground. Nothing happened. Taking a huge breath, Ibrahim crawled to Khalil and dragged him back behind the rock. Surprisingly, Ibrahim noted that lying on the ground, he drew no fire. Looking toward the cave he saw why. They were hidden by a slight rise of gravel that had been mounded up during quarry operations. When Khalil had been moved to safety behind the boulder, Ibrahim crawled back to the explosives and retrieved them. With dynamite in hand Colonel Ibrahim considered his next move. Originally, he had thought they could just toss some dynamite into the cave's entrance. He was now sure no one could get close enough which was too bad because one stick inside the confines of the cave would crush everything inside to pulp. Undaunted, he picked up the explosives box and began making his way up the side of the mountain, completely out of sight of the cave.

There was sporadic firing back and forth between Colonel Ibrahim's men and the people in the cave, but without any results.

Ibrahim climbed to a spot directly above the opening to the cave. Once in position, he began to methodically fuse and bury one stick of dynamite after another, until he'd placed the entire contents of the wooden box in the rocks and rubble on the side of the mountain. Taking one last long look at his handy work, he lit the end of the main fuse and ran like a scared rabbit across the face of the mountain, putting as much distance as possible between himself and the mountain side that he was about to bring down on the cave.

The opposition had stopped firing a few minutes before. There was a loud silence punctuated only by the cicadas shrill buzzings. Dexter rolled to the side and stood dusting himself off.

"We seemed to have discouraged a frontal assault," he said to the others. Syman and Osmid kept their crouched positions at opposite sides of the entrance, watching the limited field of view for movement.

"Why would they stop?" asked Syman. Then he continued, "They must be up to some mischief. I know I would be."

"They might have stopped for one of several reason," answered Dexter. "They may be bringing more men, or they may be preparing to storm the cave, although I doubt that."

"Only one of their men has been out of sight," said Syman. "I've been keeping track. I think it's that pissed off gentleman, who kicked Mr. Bandar in the face. He was behind that big boulder on the right, but I haven't seen him in a long time."

"That would be Colonel Ibrahim," said Osmid. "It is likely he has gone for reinforcements."

"How are we going to get out of here?" Karrie asked, point blank, voicing the problem no one else had wanted to confront so directly.

"That's the sixty-four-thousand dollar question, Sis."

"Mr. Bandar, is there a back entrance to this cave?" Syman asked.

"I do not think so, but I have never explored far back in this cave. When it was first opened, the construction foreman brought me in here to show me a stone pedestal further back in the cave. It is where he discovered the metal artifact you removed from the envelope. When he showed me the pedestal, he explained how he had found the gold plate locked in its top. He knew I dealt in artifacts. He sold the plate to me for its weight in gold, a very modest price, I suspect. It was all quite unique, very curious. I have no idea what the plate is or where it was made, but I was intrigued."

Syman and Dexter said nothing, but listened carefully to every word Osmid said.

"What are you taking about?" Karrie asked, impatiently. "What's this about a gold plate?"

"We'll explain later, Kar," answered Dexter, "when things are a little less hectic."

"I think we should search the back of this place to see if there is another way out of here," said Syman, definitively. "Look in the equipment duffel Mr. Bandar carried. There are at least three flashlights in it. There are extra batteries too, I believe. Dexter, why don't you and Karrie go back and see what you can find out. We'll hold the fort here, so to speak, and make sure no one comes in the entrance. If you hear shooting please come back, quickly."

"Good idea, Sy", said Dexter. As it turned out, there were four lights. Taking two, he and Karrie walked back into the mountain down the sloping tunnel. With light, Dexter could see the tunnel had been cut through the rock. It was obviously not natural. It had been made by men. Until that moment, Dexter had assumed the cave was a natural formation of some kind.

"This tunnel is man made," he said, to Karrie.

They came upon the stone pedestal Osmid had just told them about. They stopped to look at it. It had a metal, box like lid, hanging askew on a single metal strap the foreman had failed to cut. The flashlights showed a square recess cut into the top of the stone pedestal. Dexter attempted to quickly explain to Karrie about the metal plate having been in the same envelope with the other information he'd acquired at the bank. He concluded saying, "The metal plate was apparently put in this depression, and this box was strapped down over the top to protect it."

"This is bizarre, Dexter."

"Yeah, it sure is," he said, agreeing with her. "Come on, let's check the rest of this place and see if we can find a back door."

They continued walking down the tunnel until they came to a cave-in, where the rock roof of the tunnel had fractured and dropped a pile of stone and debris on to the floor, almost completely filling the tunnel. Dexter could see a small opening at the very top of the pile of rubble. He climbed up the face of the pile and shined his light into the hole. Through it he could see that the roof had fallen away for several feet beyond. He could also see the tunnel was otherwise undamaged on the other side of the fall. With surprise, he noticed a breeze of air was blowing past his head into the hole.

"It's clear about six feet beyond here, Kar and there's air blowing through this hole."

"It's spooky in here, Dexter. It reminds me of Huckleberry Finn, in that cave with the Indian chasing him," said Karrie.

Dexter chuckled and said, "Then that would make you, Becky Thatcher, right?"

As he climbed off the rock fall, a deep rumble reverberated down the tunnel from the direction of the entrance.

"Oh my God! What was that?" Karrie asked, in a nearly hysterical voice.

"Come on!" said Dexter, already running for the opening.

Karrie followed close on his heals, as they sprinted back up the tunnel. When they reached the opening, dust was billowing thickly, filling the tunnel.

"Syman. Bandar. Are you okay?" They could hear the two men hacking and coughing in the dust filled darkness. After a moment, Syman came out of the dust and into the light, like an apparition. He had his shirt pulled up over his mouth to filter the air.

"Where's Bandar?" asked Dexter.

"I don't know," said Syman, wiping his face and hands on his very dusty T-shirt.

Dexter lifted his own shirt over his mouth and went into the dust cloud after the missing man.

"Bandar, where are you?" he yelled, flashing the light around looking for the little man. His words sounded flat in his own ears, the dust somehow distorting and deadening his call. He heard Osmid coughing to one side. Like a blind man, Dexter navigated toward the sound with his hearing. After a moment, he stumbled into Bandar. Grabbing hold of him, he steered the disoriented man toward the back of the cave. When Dexter stumbled out of the dust holding Bandar, Syman got on his other side to help guide him further back into tunnel. Once out of the dust they could see there was blood mixed with dirt on Bandar's face. He'd been cut in the forehead and blood had dripped into his eyes. There was the same ghoulish mixture on his hands, so apparently, he had tried to rub them with disastrous results.

While Dexter settled Bandar, Syman located their equipment bags. With Karrie's help, the equipment was dragged further down the tunnel.

"There's some more water in with the food," said Syman.

Dexter took a grubby handkerchief out of his pocket and said, "We'll have to clean up Bandar before we do anything else."

Karrie knelt in front of Bandar, who was sitting on the tunnel's floor with his back to the wall. He looked dazed. She took a bottle of water from the food duffel, along with Dexter's handkerchief and began to gently wash Bandar's filthy face.

"What the hell happened?" Dexter asked Syman.

"Don't know, pardner. One minute, we're watching the banditoes and the next, there's a terrific roar and the entrance caves in on us."

"Well, now we know what they were up to."

"I think we are trapped in here now," said Osmid speaking his first coherent words since the cave-in.

"Maybe not," said Dexter. "There's another cave-in down the tunnel a ways, but air is blowing into a hole at the top of the debris pile. Through the hole, I could also see the tunnel continues intact on the other side of the fall, so, we may have another way out of here."

"Do you suppose we should try to dig our way out the entrance?" suggested Karrie.

"We can always do that as a last resort, but the bad guys might have a guard outside for a while to keep an eye on the cave entrance and make sure we don't rise from the dead. That's what I'd do in their position," said Dexter.

"Ultimately, our options are limited by the batteries in these flashlights we have," said Syman.

"Yeah, that's right," agreed Dexter, snapping off the large flashlight he was holding. That left them in the limited illumination from Karrie's small light.

"There are two simple ways that we can increase the time the lights will last," Syman instructed. "First, whenever possible we should try to use only one light at a time. Second, the batteries will last 3 or 4 times as long if they are only turned on for a few moments at a time while we memorize the surroundings and then turn them off. We'll stumble around a bit, but we can get around that way. A battery will give off more power in many small bursts than it will when turned on and used continuously. There's less internal heating."

"No use wasting this while we sit here doing nothing," Karrie said, turning off her little light as well.

"Before you do that, Kar, how about finding us something to eat and drink in that bag," Dexter suggested.

Karrie's light flicked back on, and she rummaged around in the food duffel, taking things out for them. They made an impromptu meal of food bars, crackers, a little dried meat, and some of fruit juice and water.

"I can't remember food ever tasting better," said Dexter, feeling stronger by the minute.

"Dex, you said you could see over the top of the other cave-in?" Syman asked.

"Yes, we can probably dig our way through in an hour or so."

"Mr. Bandar, are you up to a little digging?" Syman asked.

"I am ready. Let us get it done, quickly. I do not like this place," answered Osmid.

"I think you have just spoken for all of us," said Karrie.

With that, they gathered the equipment and walked down the tunnel and set to work. The digging was tough going, harder than they had first thought it would be. The smaller debris had cemented together the larger, requiring that they break the rubble apart chunk by chunk. It took them almost two hours, toiling in the dark most of the time, with a screw driver and prybar Syman had brought with him aboard the Hana Maru. Finally, the opening was large enough and Dexter wiggled through to the other side of the fall.

Wanting to hurry, but being forced to go slowly, they pushed the duffel bags through to Dexter, one at a time and then crawled through themselves. Finally, Syman rolled down the rubble and on to his feet, the last one through.

After a moment, Syman bowed formally, sweeping an arm in the direction of the dark tunnel and said, "Lead on, Mr. Gordon."

"Thanks a lot," said Dexter.

26

The tunnel continued unchanged about 50 yards on the other side of the fall. At this point the rough hewn walls and ceiling came to an abrupt end at what looked like a vault door. Swung back on its massive hinges, the open metal door was covered with multicolored streaks and stains from years of subterranean exposure, but was surprisingly free of any signs of corrosion. The door swung out toward the tunnel entrance and had been left wide open by the last people to occupy this odd place. The closing mechanism consisted of two comma shaped, cam like latches, designed to pull the door tight shut and secure it at the same time from the inside. Syman reached up and tried to move the top latch, but it wouldn't budge, even with a forceful pull. He tried to move the door, but it also was immovable. The smooth, gently sloping floor continued on unchanged except for a narrow rim that went completely around the tunnel and was designed to catch and seal the door when closed. On the other side of the door the character of the tunnel was completely transformed. The ceiling and walls were smooth, and in the poor light of a flashlight, could be seen to have been painted, although the color was unknowable under streaks and stains similar in nature to the ones on the door. There were also what looked like light fixtures, connected by pipes to the ceiling every ten feet or so as far as they could see down this new type of tunnel. Other than this, the tunnel was featureless.

"We seem to have stumbled into someone's bomb shelter," said Dexter, as he examined everything minutely with his flashlight.

"It looks like an abandoned military installation," said Syman, in partial agreement.

"It does," said Dexter, "but what country would build a place like this out here in the middle of the Atlantic Ocean?"

"That's a good question," said Syman, with several answers coming to mind, "but I don't think we have time to dwell on it right now."

"This place gives me the creeps," said Karrie.

With nothing to be gained by staring at the doorway, they continued walking.

Dexter said, "I think Syman's right and we're inside some type of abandoned military installation, maybe one the Nazis built during the second world war, so be careful of what you touch. There might be booby traps anywhere. The Germans often left boobytraps in their abandoned bunkers. And we have no idea what other type of hazards we might come across in here."

"That's presuming this place was built by the Germans," said Syman, thinking of the strange arrangement of pictographs he and Royce Aldrich had discovered on the gold plate just a few days before. He continued speaking his mind. "I don't think they did. They wouldn't have left a metal plate in a pedestal in the entrance tunnel to a place like this and there was no German on the plate that Royce and I could see.

"Regardless Syman, this place could be dangerous as hell no matter who built it."

"You're right, Dexter," said Syman. "We need to be careful."

"You were intrigued with the artifact, then?" Osmid Bandar interjected.

"Yes, with that and the plutonium on that list of yours," Syman replied, coldly.

"But, how could you know what was on the list?" Bandar wondered out loud, surprised. "It was in Arabic!"

"Yes, so my office comparitor discovered before providing us with a complete translation," answered Syman.

"That would explain it." Bandar was quiet for a moment and then he said, "So, you have known all along about the bomb the Brotherhood is assembling."

"Yeah! We discovered that just a few minutes before you arrived at our office," Dexter said, with evident anger in his voice.

"And you have notified your government?" Bandar continued, as understanding came to him. "And they put you aboard the ship, Mr. Pons?"

Syman gave Bandar a hard look.

"Look, Bandar," Dexter growled, "talking about this right now is beginning to piss me off! So, let's stow this discussion until we get out of here."

Osmid nodded without saying anything further. They continued on in silence. After walking perhaps a hundred yards, they came upon a single door on their left in the wall of the corridor. Dexter grabbed the handle and gave it a sharp tug. Nothing happened.

"Let's pry it open," he said, having failed to dislodge it.

"After what you just said about hazards a few minutes ago," Syman remonstrated, "I think we should do a little more investigating before we go forcing doors open. Let's keep going down this tunnel and see if we can find out what this place is before we start assaulting things."

"Maybe your right," said Dexter, not quite convinced, despite his own earlier admonition.

Leaving the door unmolested, they continued walking and within fifty feet came to a transverse hall that was identical to the one they were walking along, but the intersection was strange. The corners, which would normally have been square, were beveled to 45 degrees.

"It looks like a warehouse. Judging by these diagonal corners, they must have driven some kind of vehicles along these halls," said Dexter.

"That would also explain the smooth gentle slope of the entrance tunnel," said Syman, in agreement. "Let's split up and check this hall in both directions?"

"I don't think that's a great idea, Sy. This place looks like it might be 'muy grande' and we don't want to get separated and lost in here."

"I don't want us to separate, either," said Karrie.

Osmid said nothing, still smarting from Dexter's rebuke.

"Okay," said Syman. He lead the other three down the corridor to their left. About 10 yards from the first intersection, there was a second, created by a short corridor to the right about 10 feet long. It created a wide doorway beyond which yawned the unbounded blackness of a very large area. They entered the blackness cautiously, inspecting the floor as they went. The stone floor continued for about 12 feet before reaching a foot high curbing that disappeared into the darkness left and right. On the other side of the curb was an unvarying flat expanse of dirt floor that continued beyond the range of their lights. What their lights did reveal were walls 25 to 30 feet to either side, although they weren't really walls. Rather, they were the lower parts of an arched ceiling which rose to a similar height of 30 or so feet. The arched structure transferred the enormous weight of the mountain above to the sides, leaving an auditorium sized room with no supporting columns. The room resembled a 60 foot wide cylinder sliced in half and laid on its side. Though they could clearly see the walls, illuminated by their flashlights, the room's length was indeterminate with the far end disappearing in darkness. The chamber, it could hardly be called a room, was huge.

Hung from the ceiling suspended about 10 feet from the floor was a grid of cables and struts that carried what looked like long parallel light fixtures and pipes sprouting sprinkler heads every 8 or 10 feet. The array covered the entire area.

"This place is as big as an airplane hanger," said Syman.

"I visited some caverns in the Ozark mountains once, where they grew mushrooms under ground," said Karrie. "This place is sort of like it."

"We've discovered an underground mushroom farm with a bomb shelter door. Sounds like a new kind of really secure investment opportunity to me," said Dexter, introducing a little humor to their otherwise grim situation.

"Touché," said Syman, smiling. "It does look like some kind of garden or farm."

"Come on, Dexter. Be serious." said Karrie, condemning his comment.

"This would be an excellent place to grow things," said Osmid, "that the American DEA could not see with their spy satellites."

"Dexter, how much power and water would it take to make this place work?"

"I don't know, Sy. I'm not any kind of farmer. I don't think it would take much water. There's not much evaporation. If you were going to light it enough to grow plants on the other hand. Let's see. One thousand watts of sunlight per square meter is normal," said Dexter, thinking like the engineer he was, "60 feet wide, say the plants would grow at one third the normal intensity with the lights on 24 hours per day. That's 50 watts per square foot times 60 feet. Three thousand watts per lineal foot of this room. How long would you say this room is, Sy?"

"About two hundred feet, I should think," said Syman, just barely able to discern the opposite end of the chamber in the beam from his powerful flash light.

"Wow!" said Dexter, as the realization dawned. "If you used incandescent bulbs, it would take something like 600,000 watts of electricity to light this place. But of course, if you used fluorescent bulbs, which is what those look like," Dexter said pointing his flashlight at the nearest part of the grid hanging from the ceiling, "you could cut the power needed by probably a factor of six to say about a hundred thousand watts. But, that's still one hell of a lot of energy in an area this size..."

"And the heat from that much lighting would be enormous," said Syman, completing Dexter's thought, now sure Dexter had gotten the original point of his question.

"That means there must be a huge ventilation system to keep this place cool," Dexter continued.

"Why are you two talking about all of this technical nonsense?" asked Karrie, interrupting. "We're trapped in a cave on an island somewhere in the middle of the Atlantic ocean, hundreds of feet inside a mountain where we might die and you're talking about watts and ventilation."

"It's not technical nonsense, Kar. What Syman was trying to point out is that this place must have large vents to the outside, somewhere. Watts are a rough measure of heat and the heat from lighting this chamber would require a lot of cool air to keep the chamber from overheating. If we can find one of those vents, maybe we can get out of here."

"Oh. Sorry," said Karrie, abashed at having rebuked Syman and Dexter. She realized she should have had a little more faith in them. They hadn't been wasting time on unnecessary chatter.

Syman walked to the curb. Stooping down, he picked up a hand full of soil. It was powdery dry and ran through his fingers like dry sand. Turning around, he shined his light up above the doorway they had just come through.

"Look at this, Dex," he said.

There, high above the doorway, at the top of the wall, was a large vent about six feet in diameter.

"The arched shape of the ceiling would funnel all the hot air directly into that vent," said Dexter. "It's a perfect design."

"Let's see if we can find an air inlet for this place," suggested Syman.

They left the chamber and explored along the corridor, carefully scrutinizing everything as they went. To their surprise, they found a series of identical chambers, eight in all, side by side. Then, instead of ending, the corridor became a downward sloping ramp to the right that curved back toward the far ends of the eight chambers. To the left at this corner, they also found a doorway to a stairwell which went down. Unsure about which way to go, they decided to walk down the ramp instead of taking the stairs. After a minute's walk the sloping corridor took another right hand turn. They were now forty feet lower in the mountain but headed in the opposite direction. As the four walked along, they again came to another set of eight short side tunnels which led into eight more arch roofed chambers positioned directly under the first eight chambers one level above them. As they continued to follow the corridor, it brought them to yet another right hand corner and another down sloping ramp. Here, they also found another doorway opening on a stairwell. It was the same stairwell but from here it went up to the level above and down to, as yet, unknown areas.

"In an installation this big there should be air inlets at the bottom and top levels. Which should we look for?" asked Syman.

"When Bandar's buddies didn't know where we were, going up made sense," said Dexter, focusing on the crucial consideration. "We would have been on the mountain, where they wouldn't have expected to find us. But now they figure we're dead and no longer a problem, so there's no advantage in going up anymore. Down is closer to the beach."

"I don't care where we go," said Karrie. "Just get us out of here."

"Mr. Bandar?" asked Syman. "What do you say?"

"I do not know which way is better. I will go where you decide," said Bandar.

"I think Dexter's reasoning is sound. We should go down," concluded Syman.

"Okay. Let's get going, then," said Dexter, this time turning to the stairs. He led them down and they came to another doorway.

Leaving the stairwell they found yet another level of arch roofed chambers. After exploring this third level, they began to understand the layout of the underground warren.

Climbing down the stairs, checking each doorway they came to, they found more layers of the eight chambers, all directly under the first. The stairs descended deeper and the corridor continued to loop around and around the eight-chambered levels in an enormous helix. Like a huge coil spring around the outside of the chambered levels, down the corridor went, connecting everything together, providing a vehicle road.

They inspected several more levels down and found no variation, but on the tenth, eleventh, and twelfth levels, they found the chambers were full of endless shelving, miles of it, filling every chamber from floor to ceiling.

If full, the twenty-four chambers, would have formed an enormous storage area of some kind, but there was no indication of what had been stored there. There was nothing on the selves except the thick omnipresent layer of fine dust that covered every flat surface in the place.

On the thirteenth level, they found the chambers were full of very large coolers or refrigerator freezers with thick insulated doors. These chambers had catwalked second and third story levels filling each chamber floor to ceiling.

"We need to find the heat exchangers for all this refrigeration, Dex," said Syman, after searching behind the nearby ground level units. They could see there were large insulated pipes for carrying the refrigerant to and from the boxes.

"I'm way ahead of you, pal," said Dexter. "The main pipes go into the wall over here in this corner, but I don't see any access to them after that."

Syman walked over to look around, but he also found nothing.

"Have you noticed that all the metal in this place is the same, Dex? The doors, pipes, catwalks, and any other metal we've come across, looks like it's stainless steel," said Syman.

"Yes, I noticed, but I'm too tired and hungry to give a damn about what kind of metal they used in this place. Besides, I have a headache. All I really want is to get the hell out of here and safely aboard that sub you said is waiting for us. I feel like I could sleep for a week."

"You're getting grumpy, Amigo," said Syman, but he did not pursue the subject of the metal. Instead, he decided he would find a small piece of the stuff to take back with him. He wanted to check the alloy in the metallurgical lab at TMI, when they got home—if they got home, he thought grimly.

He turned his attention back to the refrigeration piping. "If we could follow these pipes, they would probably lead us to the nearest outside vent." He said this to himself as much as to Dexter.

"Yeah, well, there's nothing here."

"Have you seen the large metal panels at the corners at each level, Dex?"

"Yes. I noticed them."

" I suspect they give access to the ventilation system and that the builders ran all the electrical cables, water piping, and any other mechanical systems, like these refrigerant pipes, through the ventilation ducts. That way, they only had to excavated once for everything."

"That makes sense," agreed Dexter, "but there are panels at every corner. There must be four separate ducts."

"Probably. And I should think they'd be cross connected as well."

"They'd have to be, if they're the main ventilation ducts," said Dexter. "Let's open up the panel nearest to where the pipes go into the wall and have a look. Maybe we'll see where they go."

Syman nodded wordlessly.

Dexter lead the way through the corridor, heading for the corner where the refrigeration pipes disappeared into the wall. They found a large metal panel in the wall, right where they expected it to be. They examined it carefully looking for a way to open it. There were no fasteners visible.

"Time for exercising Pons' first law of facility," said Syman, trying to keep their spirits up. Stepping behind Osmid, he opened the pack on Bandar's back and removed the large screw driver they'd used earlier to enlarge the hole through the rubble in the entrance tunnel.

"So, what is Pons' first law of facility?" asked Dexter, taking the bait with a chuckle. He knew his partner was making this up as he went along.

"When faced with an unknown obstacle, try the first thing that comes to mind," he said, holding up the screw driver.

They all laughed at that.

"And, if that doesn't work, we can try Gordon's first law of persuasion."

"And what might that be?" asked Syman, now playing the straight man.

"Try using explosives," said Dexter.

They all laughed again and then Syman began prying at the crack along the bottom of the metal panel. The panel lifted slightly and Syman was able to get the screw driver under the lower left corner. Dexter worked at the other corner using the prybar. After a few moments of concerted effort the bottom edge popped away from the wall about an inch. In unison, both men grabbed the bottom edge and pulled. With a grating sound the panel pivoted, going up and back like an old fashioned garage door. Using their largest flashlight, Dexter and Syman peered into the yawning black opening. Just as they'd suspected, there was a large bottomless, well like shaft with a myriad of pipes and wires and other unidentifiable conduits traversing up and down.

At floor level, the two large coolant pipes from the refrigerators entered the shaft through the opposite wall where they immediately turned downward, disappearing into the depths beyond the range of their light. A few feet lower, they could see where the horizontal ventilation shaft for the next lower level of chambers joined the vertical shaft's side.

"This is one hell of a hole, Sy," said Dexter, moving back from the opening.

Then Osmid and Karrie looked cautiously into the shaft while Syman held the flash light.

Syman thought he saw a sharp reflection far down the shaft. He removed binoculars from Osmid's pack and looked carefully. He wasn't sure, but far down he thought he could see the pipes disappear into water.

"Dex, get me one of those small cans of juice, will you."

Dexter did as he was asked but wondered at the strange request. Syman handed the light to Osmid, who was standing next to him.

"Hold this for me, please, right here."

Taking the juice can, he handed the binoculars to Karrie. With his head near the opening, he looked carefully at his watch and dropped the can into the shaft. They all listened intently for what seemed like a long time and then, there was a faint but unmistakable splash.

"Four seconds," said Syman. "Earth's gravity provides a 32 foot per second acceleration. Times 4 seconds, that equals a speed of 128 feet per second at the end of 4 seconds. The average of 0 feet per second at the beginning and 128 feet per second after four seconds gives an overall average speed of 64 feet per second, times the four seconds. That's a drop of about 256 feet. And also, there's apparently water at the bottom of the shaft, which may or may not be good for us. Either way, my little experiment provides us with some significant information."

"What do you mean significant? How so?" asked Dexter.

"The refrigerant pipes go out of sight into the water. If the machinery rooms for this place are in the bottom chambers, it's unlikely we'll find the way out we're looking for through a refrigeration heat exchanger vent. It's probably under water."

"We still might find a lower ventilation opening, Sy," Dexter countered. "It's unlikely they'd put the two types of vents close together. The fresh air vent would pull the heat from the heat exchangers back inside. That would be very bad engineering and the people who build this place were good engineers."

"Yes, that's just my point, Dex. Heat rises. They'd put the fresh air vent below the heat exchanger's vent. If the heat exchanger vent is below the water, then, they're both probably below the water." After a moment he continued, "I could be wrong, but I don't think either vent is our ticket out of here."

"Well, we still need to check. We might get lucky," said Dexter.

"Gentleman," said Osmid speaking for the first time in a long while, "whatever we do, we should do quickly. My light is nearly gone."

"There are some more batteries in your pack," Syman told him. "But you are right. We need to get going."

Karrie unzipped Osmid's pack and searched for batteries. She found only one. Removing it, she zipped up the duffel and then handed him the one battery.

"Here you go," she said. "It's the last one, that size"

Osmid took out one of the exhausted batteries in his small light and replaced it with the new one. He turned it on. It produced a dull glow, lighting his way ahead only a few feet.

"It is better than nothing," he said, with a frown.

They headed for the nearest stairway to continue their search for a ventilation duct or some other way to the outside. By now, they'd been underground for more than six hours. They were tired, and the replacement batteries were disappearing at an alarming rate. Knowing this was frightening and depressing. They walked on as fast as they could.

Also knowing how important it was to keep their morale up, Dexter forced himself to start a discussion to get their minds off their predicament

"Who would ever thought an installation like this could exist out here on this desert island in the middle of the Atlantic Ocean?"

"I'm still wondering who built this place and why," said Syman.

The conversation got no further because in the next lower level the chambers again changed dramatically. Every chamber was divided into what appeared to be eight apartments or office suites. Mirror image suites were built four on one side of a chamber and four on the other with each suite composed of 6 rooms. The area for a suite measured about 28 by 50 feet at the floor. With a wide walk down the center of each chamber there was good access for each of a chamber's eight suites. Upon close examination, they found that each suite of rooms had one room with stone work tables. And that one of the stone tables in each suite had a large sink cut into it. There were also what looked like cooking stoves made from the same ubiquitous metal found everywhere else in the facility. On this slim evidence, they decided the rooms were probably kitchens and concluding this, they decided the suites were probably living quarters, although they would have served well for other purposes.

The other ground floor rooms in the suites were plain, bare and empty.

The second floor areas, which were smaller due to the arch of the roof, appeared to be about 20 by 50 feet. In each suite, the second story rooms were divided into four modest sized rooms eight or ten feet square, separated by what they concluded were bathroom areas. However, the bathroom areas were not quite like any bathrooms they had ever seen before. They were much too large, each having a pool with a fountain at its center, and large raised planters full of dusty soil positioned randomly around theses area which were open to the arched ceilings. At first, they thought these rooms were gardens, but the unique shape of toilets placed in secluded corners of these large upper rooms unmistakably identified the room's function.

Surprisingly, though covered in the same fine gray dust that covered everything in this underground facility, illuminated only with dim flashlights and devoid of all color and vegetation, these once splendid garden baths still suggested a faint aura of beauty and comfort.

"These bathrooms must have been very elegant and soothing," said Karrie, imagining what one might have looked like clean, well lit and full of lush vegetation and pretty things.

· "Speaking of bathrooms," said Osmid with embarrassment, "I am in need. If you will excuse me, I will go to the next apartment..."

"Now that you mention it, Bandar, we should make hay while the sun shines."

Osmid had no idea what Dexter was talking about. "You misunderstand me, Mr. Gordon," he stammered, now clearly embarrassed, "I need to use the toilet in the next apartment." Bobbing his head once in a strange little nod, he turned and scurried down the stairs.

"We'll meet you down stairs in five minutes, Kar," Dexter said, unabashed. "Come on, Sy. Let's go find our own privies. Holler if you need anything, Sis."

Karrie silently blessed her brother. She had needed a john for an hour and had not wanted to say anything or be the one to slow them down.

They reassembled in the hall between the apartments a few minutes later.

"This is a perfect engineering design," Dexter said, again. "By putting the chambers directly over each other, the stress is greatly reduced, with all the rock in the upper chambers having been excavated. All that weight has been removed and the weight that remains is transferred to the columns of stone between adjacent chambers. It's brilliant. I've never seen anything like it, have you, Sy?"

"No I haven't," Syman answered. After a moment, he said, "There is something that's bothering me, though."

"What's that?" asked Dexter.

"When Bandar used the word apartment, it came to me that these are set up as family quarters. Each level could comfortably house four, maybe five-hundred people in family groups of say four to eight people using this type of accommodation.

A military installation wouldn't be built like this place. A military installation would probably have barracks and a cafeteria. And no military would ever allow dependents in a place like this."

Syman then addressed Bandar. "Mr. Bandar, is there something you haven't told us? Did your former associates possibly build this place?"

"There is no possibility of that, Mr. Pons," Osmid said, with certainty. "We have had a difficult time just bringing in the materials to build what you saw on the surface. This place would require enormous amounts of materials and there are a lot of things in here I have never seen before."

"Perhaps, they have another buyer, you don't know about," suggested Dexter.

"You give the Islamic Brotherhood too much credit. They will create great trouble for the world if they succeed with their plans, but they are not capable of building a place like this," said Bandar. "They can only destroy, not build."

"This place is so very intriguing," said Syman. "I only wish we could explore it properly, but getting out of here alive will have to satisfy us for the time being."

"You've got that right," said Karrie, not at all taken with their surroundings. "Home and a hot bath for me. I never want to see this place again."

They continued exploring, going down four more levels. All were apartment filled chambers identical to the first. The sixth apartment level down however, was flooded and water blocked any further descent.

Syman dipped his finger in the water and then tasted it.

"We seem to have reached the island's water table," he said. "It's brackish. You can taste a little salt in it."

"Syman! Should you be putting that in your mouth?" asked Karrie, with a worried tone. "It might make you sick and we're in no position to get you help."

"I don't think it will hurt me, darling. And in any event, we need to get out of here in the next few hours, before the flash light batteries are all used up. If we don't succeed by then, it won't matter anyway. What we need right now, most of all, is information that might help us get out of here, and knowing if this is fresh water or salt might be important to us."

Karrie made no reply.

Dexter said, "What I don't understand is, why is there water in here? The people who were sophisticated enough to build this place would have known better than to build below the sea level. I mean, we're on an island in the middle of an ocean. They would have had to run huge pumps constantly to keep the lower areas dry. It doesn't make sense from an engineering point of view. It would take too much energy and the maintenance would be a nightmare."

"Good points," said Syman, giving Dexter's comments serious consideration. "Speaking of energy, where did they get the power to run this place? We haven't seen any generators or other equipment." After a moments consideration, he continued, "For the sake of argument, let's say you're wrong and it is all under water. That would explain it."

"No way, Sy. They just wouldn't put their machinery rooms below the natural sea level. It doesn't make sense. If the pumps stopped for any reason, they'd flood and that would be it for this place."

"Perhaps the island has sunk a little since this place was built," suggested Karrie.

"It's unlikely this island has subsided that much," Syman said. "If hypothetically, there is say only one more level below us, it still would have had to sink at least 20 feet. That's a lot."

"Maybe the water level has risen," she persisted.

"The sea level hasn't risen 20 feet in the ten thousand years, since the last ice age was over. No, you're probable right about the island settling, although it's hard to imagine it happening in the last fifty years," Syman concluded.

"What's fifty years got to do with anything?" Dexter asked.

"The technology to build this place has only existed for the last fifty or sixty years," answered Syman. "Only since the second World War."

"Yeah, I guess you're right," agreed Dexter, understanding.

"Perhaps the machinery rooms are not below, but above the level where we entered," said Osmid.

"Maybe," said Dexter. "I know I'd never build below sea level. It's bad engineering and we know these people were good engineers. There's some other explanation."

"Well, regardless, we haven't found any equipment rooms or other outlets down here, so it looks like we have to go back up," said Syman.

"Oh, god!" said Karrie, sounding utterly exasperated. "Where are the elevators?"

"We're...let's see..?" said Dexter, still considering the flooded corridor in front of them. "Nine farm levels, three storage levels, one reefer level, and six living quarter levels down. That's nineteen levels total, times about 40 feet, seven-hundred-sixty feet. That would put us just about at sea level and that would explain the flooding."

"It also fits with the brackishness of the water," said Syman. "The fresh water on most islands floats on the heavier salt water. As more fresh water is drawn off, the remaining water becomes saltier. It's a big problem on many islands around the world. Ground water on most ocean islands is a little brackish."

"Do we really have to climb all the way back up? I'm so tired."

"The alternative is dying, right here," said Dexter.

"He's right, Karrie," said Syman in a soft voice. "We have to go back up and try to find another way out because there's no way out down here."

"Of course," said Karrie, feeling foolish at her outburst. "What time is it?"

Dexter and Syman looked at their watches simultaneously.

"It's just after eleven P.M.," Said Syman, whose watch had been automatically adjusted for time zone changes by signals it received from the global positioning satellite system.

"My Rolex says it's eight P.M. It's still on eastern standard time," said Dexter, adjusting his five-thousand dollar watch to Syman's.

"You really should get rid of that obsolete piece of junk and get yourself a decent timepiece," said Syman, smiling.

141

Dexter scowled at him and then said, good naturedly, "Screw you, Syman." After a moment, Dexter continued, "It will take us about an hour to climb back up the stairs to the level where we started if we take it slow and steady. We only have till four AM before they send in the SEAL recovery team. That gives us about five hours to get out of here and warn off a futile rescue attempt."

"Judging by the rate we're using the flash light batteries," said Karrie, "we'll be lucky to have that much more light."

It was obvious they were all feeling depressed by their lack of success. And it was beginning to take its toll, along with the lack of sleep or proper food and the high level of stress they'd been coping with the last several days. Despite the humorous jibes, they were becoming listless and sluggish, and their pace had slowed.

Well aware of his own waning energy, Dexter decided to push them forward and said, "Let's get back up to our starting point, and then we can use an hour to eat and maybe take a short nap.

We're all going to be very beat by the time we get there, but it gives us an immediate goal and that should help. And if we can stay with the time table, it will still leave us three hours to find a way out before the cavalry arrives."

There were appreciative sounds from the other three.

"Is it not possible, to climb the stairs in the dark?" asked Osmid, making his first suggestion since their entrapment. "We would gain an hour of light that way. We know we won't get lost in a stairway."

"That's a good idea, Mr. Bandar," said Syman. "But, we should probably flash one light every few seconds, so we don't get too disoriented. That will still significantly decrease our battery use."

With that, they proceeded to the dark stairwell and the wearying climb. As it turned out, with only a few rest stops, they made the climb in fifty minutes. To the foot sore and exhausted climbers however, it felt like hours had passed.

27

Having eaten and rested, they felt stronger and more hopeful.

"I hate napping," said Karrie. "I always feel like my brain is full of crud after a nap."

Syman walked over to Karrie and touched her face gently before kissing her.

"I'm sorry you're in this mess with us, Karrie."

"Me too," she said putting her chin on his shoulder as his arms encircled her." It's just, for the first time in my life, I've found a person who makes me feel complete and I don't want to lose you. I love you so much and I want to live a long happy life with you and now everything is in danger. We might die in this hole in the ground," she said, as she began to quietly sob. Syman held her tight. He could feel her body shudder silently as she let go.

"I can't guarantee we won't die, Karrie," he said, quietly, "but we still have a good chance of finding our way out of here."

Karrie made no reply. After a few moments her sobbing slowed and she nestled against him.

Dexter came over to them and said, "Sorry to intrude, but if we're going to make it out of here, we better get going. We only have about three hours until the SEAL team comes ashore."

Karrie and Syman separated and again reached for their packs.

"We know the stairwell we climbed doesn't go up any further," Dexter began, "but we also know there have to be areas above us because there are ventilation ducts above this level. You guys go check the stairs at the other three corners and see if one of them continues up."

"What are you going to do?" asked Karrie.

"I want to check something else out."

No longer afraid of getting lost, they split up, each person going in a different direction in search of a stairwell. After five minutes, Osmid, Karrie and Syman were back and each had found a dead end.

"Where's Dex?" asked Karrie, sounding a little worried.

"I'm here," they heard him say from the dark entrance corridor.

Syman flashed his light toward the voice, spotting Dexter as he walked toward them in the bright beam.

"Turn that damn thing off, will you. It's hurting my eyes. God, I must be turning into a troll."

"Stop being grumpy, Dexter," Karrie ordered, playfully.

"Did you find anything?" Dexter asked.

"No, we didn't find anything," said Syman. "The stairs all go down from this level. Where'd you go?"

"I went back to that door, we passed in the tunnel, when we first arrived. I pried it open. It's another stairway and it goes up."

"Great!" said Syman. "I was beginning to think we had run out of options."

"Not yet," Dexter said, smiling at them all broadly. "Let's get going. We don't have much time."

"Do you really think we have a chance of getting out of here, Dex?" Karrie asked, sounding forlorn.

"Well, I climbed the stairs a way and there's a detectable draft going up. Apparently the air is going somewhere. It's a good indication there's an outlet somewhere above us."

Once again, the four exhausted people shouldered their backpacks and headed back up the entrance tunnel to the door they'd by-passed just before embarking on their futile search of the lower regions of the installation eight hours earlier. They'd now been trapped underground for more than ten hours. Their clothes were ragged and filthy. Their spirits as well as their bodies were weakening.

At the doorway, Syman stopped and wet a forefinger in his mouth using the age old method to test the direction of the air. He felt a cooling breeze on the tunnel side of his erect finger.

"It's too bad we didn't check this door first," said Dexter.

"Well," said Syman, "we didn't want to blow ourselves up by accident."

With Osmid in the lead this time, they began to climb this new set of stairs. They must have climbed about a hundred feet when the stairs delivered them into a large arched chamber similar in shape to the many with which they were already familiar, but this one was not as large, only twenty feet or so in diameter. They shined their largest flash light down its length. Just a few feet in front of them, they saw a cavernous opening in the floor surrounded by a simple railing. An assortment of pipes, cables and wires extended up from the opening about a foot before turning to run along the floor deeper into the chamber. Skirting the hole, they followed these service lines for twenty-five yards until they came upon what looked like a large room occupying most of the chamber's floor at that point. Upon closer inspection, Dexter and Syman determined that the room was not a room, but rather the housing for an enormous blower.

"I think we're getting warmer," said Dexter, feeling truly encouraged for the first time in many hours.

"Yes, I believe we are," said Syman, feeling similarly heartened by their discovery. "This is the blower for the ventilation system. We should be close to a vent to the outside now."

"Oh, goood!" said Osmid, clapping his hands together like a happy child.

Karrie give Syman a big hug and laughed. "Finally," she said.

"We're not out yet," said Dexter, "but now I think we have a fighting chance."

Syman climbed inside the enormous machine, wiggling through its large blades. "You think there's a chance of this thing starting up while we're in here?" Syman asked Dexter, who was right behind him.

"Hell no! This thing hasn't turned in years," Dexter said with certainty as he laid his full body weight against a blade. It felt like it was welded in place. "Besides, it would need lots of power to run and there is no power in this place."

"Let's hope," said Syman.

"These must be the reduction gears in here," Dexter continued, patting a large metal housing that surrounded the center of the shaft on which the two enormous propeller's were mounted. "And that must be the driveshaft," he said, pointing at a large metal pipe that was connected to the reduction gear housing at a right angle. "The power must come from a motor in a room on the other side of the wall."

"I wonder why they didn't put the motor in here?" Syman said.

"Probably to keep it cleaner," answered Dexter.

"That makes sense," said Syman, inspecting the blower's large exhaust ducts. With his flash light, Syman could see that the two exhaust ducts first went through the back wall of the blower room at floor level and then curved straight up. He clambered into one of the ducts, stretching as far as he could to shine his light up the 6 foot diameter pipe he found rising above him. Dexter climbed up beside him.

"What do you think?" Dexter asked.

They could see the pipes were identical, except for a five inch pipe and a one inch cable or rod that traveled up the inside of the left duct. Syman did his wet finger routine again.

"I can feel a breeze going up this duct. What do you think?"

"Unfortunately," said Dexter, with disappointment, "I think the vent is up there. Why couldn't they just drill straight out the side of the mountain? Sometimes, I think engineers are just a little too smart for their own or anyone else's good." After a moment's pause he continued, "How the hell are we going to get up there?"

"I don't know, Dex. You're the mountain climber. You tell me."

"Shit Syman, maybe I could make it and I say maybe, because I'm not in very good shape right now, but how are you three going to do it? Actually you could probably make it too, but Karrie and Bandar? I don't think so. And we can forget about bringing the equipment."

Syman said nothing. Instead, he continued looking back and forth from one duct to another with his flash light. He studied the sides of each duct, carefully looking for hand holds or climbing points. In the duct that contained no pipes, there was absolutely nothing. It was smooth and it looked like it went straight up about sixty or eighty feet, where it turned horizontally. In the other duct, there were the two pipes and their mounting brackets attaching the pipes to the duct wall about every ten feet. That was it.

"You think you could you climb that small pipe, Dex?"

Dexter took the light from Syman and carefully examined the pipes and the duct. "Probably, but that still doesn't get you guys up there."

"No, it doesn't, but if there's no exit, we wouldn't need to. But we need good intel on what's up there before we can make that decision. You can get that. Then we can act accordingly."

"Okay Sy, but, before I climb all the way up there, let's look around the rest of the chamber. Maybe there's some other way out of here."

"Sure, Dex."

They retreated back through the fan blades. After explaining the situation to Karrie and Osmid, all four methodically searched the rest of the chamber. They found another open shaft in the floor with the same type of railing around it, about the same distance from the blower but on the other side of the housing at the far end of the chamber. There was an assortment of wires and pipes coming across the floor from that shaft as well.

"These openings must be the tops of the exhaust shafts for all the chambers," said Dexter. "These two shafts would be cross tied all the way to the bottom of the installation. Horizontal cross ducts would make good ventilation manifolds for each level of chambers. There are probably two shafts, with the same design, leading to vents below the chambers for inlet air, the ones we think are flooded."

All the pipes, wires, and cables, except the two going up the inside of the blower duct, converged next to the blower, where as one bundle, they went through the curved chamber wall into the motor room. Next to this was a stout metal connecting door to the motor room which was closed. Aside from these few things, the chamber was bare. After ten minutes of searching, they found nothing else.

"This whole chamber must be the plenum," Dexter explained, "a collection area for the blower. There'd be some kind of whirlwind in here if that thing were running."

Syman decided to try the door to what they thought would be the motor room. He walked over to it. Putting his shoulder to the door, he pushed as hard as he could, but to no effect. It wouldn't move.

"Dex. Let's see if we can force this thing open."

Dexter applied his not inconsiderable strength to the task along side Syman. Still, the door would not move.

"Hells, bells!" Dexter said, in frustration. "It's no good."

"Sy, hold the latch open."

Syman pulled the latch sideways.

"No, from the other side, so you're not in front of the door," Dexter instructed."Yeah, that's good."

Dexter backed up and then took a running leap at the door, hitting the heavy metal door a terrific blow with both feet next to the latch. It was like kicking a brick wall. Badly jarred, Dexter barely landed on his feet after bouncing off the door.

Angry at the door's stubborn refusal to open, Dexter snapped, "Bandar, bring the tools over here."

Osmid quickly complied. Dexter removed the prybar he'd used on the metal access panel hours before. After several minutes of fruitless effort, Dexter said,"To hell with it!" He handed the bar to Syman.

Syman shrugged and gave Dexter a quizzical look, as if to say, 'Oh, well. ' Instead, he said, "You want to give it up?"

"Maybe. I'm not sure, Sy." He stood before the door for a minute scrutinizing it thoughtfully and then said, "We want to look on the other side of this door, but do we really need to?"

"What do you mean?" queried Syman.

"We're pretty sure, we already know what's in the room."

"Yes," said Syman. "We know the drive motor or what ever passes for the drive motor is in the room because we can see the reduction gears are being driven by a shaft from there."

"Right," said Dexter. "We can see that all these pipes and stuff go into that space as well. There are power cables and some insulated pipes that probably carry coolant for the blower motor and some wires, probably some control wires or sensors or things like that. I don't see much else going in there through this wall. I don't think we need to get in there. It's probably a dead end. What do you think."

"I don't know Dex, maybe you're right," said Syman, "but the last door we bypassed turned out to be the one we should have gone through."

"Yeah, that's true, but then our getting out of here at all is one big crapshoot. We're bound to make some mistakes along the way. But, in this case, because of the draft, we know for sure there's an outlet up those ducts. So, as much as I hate to admit it, Sy, I think I'm going to have to climb that damn pipe if we're going to get out of here."

"Yup, I guess you are."

"Whatever you decide to do," said Karrie, "you better do it quickly. My light is just about gone and there are no more batteries. When Mr. Bandar's light goes, that will be it for the small lights."

"How about the larger batteries?" Dexter asked.

"We only have two more of those."

"We're out of time, Dex. You better get to it," said Syman.

"Okay. Give me one of the large lights, the one with the weak batteries," said Dexter. "Take the weak batteries out and put the new batteries in it."

Syman quickly changed batteries.

"You're going to have to sit down here, inside the blower and listen up the duct and your going to have to do it in the dark. If you sit still, you won't need any light down here. "Now that he had a plan, Dexter was all action. "I need both of those shoulder straps from your little back pack, Sy. I want to have a safety belt if I need one. They're nylon. They should support my weight."

Karrie unsnapped both straps and snapped them together, creating a four foot long harness for Dexter. Dexter looped the harness over one shoulder across his chest so it was handy but not in his way. He drank some water and then put the bottle in one front pocket and the flash light in the other. He didn't like the feel of the two bulky objects, but he had to bring them and there was no time to come up with a better way to do it.

"I'll let you know what I find by yelling down the duct, so keep your ears up," Dexter said, as he slipped through the fans blades. One by one, they followed him inside the massive blower.

Dexter took hold of the smaller pipe with both hands and began pulling himself up the duct. He was able to wrap his feet around it as he went and he quickly climbed to the third bracket without stopping. At this point, he stood on the bracket with his left foot and rested for a minute. "The old muscles ain't what they used to be," he yelled, down the pipe to the others.

"Turn your light on now, Dex. I want to save this one. It's getting dimmer," said Syman.

Syman's voice sounded very close in the duct. With nothing to absorb it and nowhere else to go, sound carried extremely well. Dexter reached down and turned on the light. Just enough light escaped his pocket to see up.

"Sorry to leave you in the dark. I'll be back soon," Dexter said continuing his rope like climb. He stopped again after another two brackets.

"Be careful, Dex," Karrie said.

"I will, don't worry," he reassured her. He climbed another length of pipe, past the next support bracket. Again, he rested. Dexter was surprised how difficult it was climbing this simple pipe, and he was surprised when he began to get a cramp in his right biceps as he pulled himself up the next section of the pipe. Once more, standing on one foot, he held on with his left arm and shook out the cramp.

"I'm almost there folks," he hollered down to his companions. "Just one more section to go."

Breathing deeply from the unaccustomed exertion, Dexter shimmied up the last ten feet using only his left arm and his feet because the cramp had come back with a vengeance. At the top, he pulled himself into the horizontal duct and rested for several seconds.

"I made it," he said, loudly.

"That's great. We'll be waiting to hear from you," said Syman.

Dexter lay still for a few moments. He felt very weary. Days of confinement and lack of food and proper rest had taken their toll on him. He lacked his normal reserve of energy. As he lay there trying to gather his strength, he felt like he was going to pass out. Blackness crept up to the edges of his awareness as spasms of fatigue washed through his exhausted body. He wanted to sleep more than he could remember wanting anything in a long time. "Can't sleep. Got to go on. If I sleep now, I'll die in here. Karrie, Syman, they'll die in here," he said to himself.

With a massive effort, Dexter picked himself up from the cool floor of the ventilation duct and stood to his feet. He shook his head and slapped his face several times, forcing wakefulness back into his weary brain.

Taking the brightly shining flashlight from his pocket, he walked forward. Dexter went only twenty feet before the duct, along with its twin, opened into a small chamber. This chamber was unlike any other Dexter had seen inside the mountain up till then. Rather than having an arched roof this area was square cut into the native rock and resembled the rough entrance tunnel.

Dexter shined the light around. Fifteen feet in front of him was the bent and corroded remains of a heavy metal screen tangled in a large rock fall that rose from the floor to what would have been the ceiling before the collapse. It was similar to the cave-in at the entrance tunnel except there was more small debris and dirt.

Dexter examined the metal screening closely. It was made from the same metal as the doors and access panels and other metal objects they'd come across. He picked up a small fragment. He saw that the metal wasn't rusted in the way iron or steel would have rusted. Rather, it had corroded and pitted and turned to an odd grayish white powder where it had been in contact with the soil. Elsewhere, it just looked stained or maybe tarnished would have been a better description.

Not sure why, Dexter pocketed the fragment. Whatever metal it was, it was an unusual alloy. Dexter was sure of that.

He decided the screen must be the remains of the ventilation outlet screen and that the mountain side must have collapsed into the vent opening destroying the screen.

Although frustrated to see the vent had collapsed, he was glad to know they had finally found a place where they might at least dig their way to freedom without having to face armed men on the outside. Unfortunately, the problem with digging their way out was time. Dexter looked at his watch. It said 3:20. They had only forty minutes to get to the open air with the telephone to stop the rescue team from coming ashore in a futile attempt to find them. Otherwise, a lot of people were going to get hurt for nothing. So near and yet so far.

Dexter felt frustrated, but he refused to waste time dwelling on a problem he could do nothing about. They weren't out of here yet. He needed to stay focused on that until they were.

Dexter examined the rest of the rock fall carefully. He clambered up to the top of the rubble pile looking for an opening to the outside. He found none, but he did feel a strong breeze blowing past him into a two inch wide crack in the rock above his head. He'd found the opening that was venting the installation, but it was too small to climb through. Well, they'd just have to dig. Dexter shined the light around the chamber. He looked back at the wall through which the ventilation ducts entered and saw there was a door just like the one in the blower chamber below.

"Well, what'd you know?" he said, to himself. "There must be a stairway up to here, after all."

Looking around further, he noticed that the pipes he'd climbed turned right after they entered the room. They then went straight into a small three foot diameter tunnel that lead away from the room at a right angle to the ventilation ducts. Dexter climbed down from the rock pile and walked to the small tunnel. Kneeling down, he shined his light into it. The small tunnel angled down away from him and about twenty feet in, Dexter could see it was full of water.

"Shit!" He could not even begin to imagine what the purpose of this smaller tunnel was. He only knew it was not a way out.

Turning away, he went to the door. He was leery of the door. It was probably jammed like the other one. Grabbing the handle, he tried to slide the latch to the side. It didn't move. He banged it with his hand a couple of times. Grudgingly, the latch moved, little by little. When it cleared the strike plate, the door popped open about a quarter of an inch. Dexter put his shoulder to the door and pushed. It opened a couple of inches, but it was scraping the floor. He pushed again and the door opened another two inches and stuck fast."Damn!" he said to himself. He tried to get his head and arm through the opening, but his head was just a little too big. He pushed again, harder, but the door only moved a fraction of an inch. Frustrated, he sat down in front of the door. Leaning back on his arms, he reared back with both legs and slammed them into the bottom of the door with every ounce of his strength. There was a loud crunch and the door hesitated for just an instant before slamming back against the wall. Dexter sat up from his extended position. There had been a stone wedged under the door which he'd pulverized.

"Thank God," he said. Picking himself up, he dusted off his back side which was covered with fine, dry dirt. As he had thought, there was a dark stairwell just like the others he had trudged up and down for the last several hours. He climbed down it, round and round, until he arrived in what he could tell was the motor room on the other side of the wall from the blower chamber. Dexter walked over to its troublesome door and examined it with his light. From here, he could see why it would not open. Over the years, the weight of the arched wall-ceiling of the chamber had cracked the rock over the doorway, deforming the doorjamb, causing it to settle onto the top of the door. The weight had forced the latch side of the door to the floor, pinning it shut. The damn thing might be holding up tons of weight. No wonder it wouldn't open from the other side. "Oh, we puny mortals," said Dexter, with a wry laugh.

He stood there thinking about his predicament. What he needed, he realized, was some real power to open the damn door.

Until then, Dexter had not allowed himself to honestly consider the problem of getting his companions up the ventilation ducts. Instead, he had tried to obey the premier survival principle: Deal with only one problem at a time, whenever possible.

No longer able to avoid the truth, Dexter had to admit to himself that his companions could never climb the pipe, especially with the equipment they had. He had to open the door, somehow.

As he stood looking at the door, Dexter thought about the tools available to him and knew they were hopelessly inadequate for the task. Then, it came to him. They did have one thing with them that might do the job—gunpowder! With the idea rapidly taking shape in his mind, he knew just what to do. He turned and ran back up the stairs to the vent chamber. Without stopping, he carefully walked back into the duct.

"Hey!" he hollered down the duct. There was a moment before a sleepy confusion of voices responded with, "What'd you find?" and "We were beginning to get worried," all being spoken at the same time. Dexter saw a dim light come on at the bottom of the duct.

"I think, I've found a way out of here. There's a stairway up to here from the motor room, but the door we tried to open has the weight of the wall sitting on it."

"We can climb up the pipe, just like you did," said Karrie.

"Maybe you could," said Dexter, with doubt in his voice, "and maybe you'll have to, if it comes to that, but I have an idea I think will open the door."

"Great," said Syman. "What are we going to do?"

"Okay, here's the plan. You're going to have to work fast, because there's not much light left. You're going to build an explosive package to blow the door open."

"Okay," Said Syman, thoughtfully. "How do we do that?"

"There's a small roll of silver duct tape in with the tools, right?"

Osmid climbed out through the fan and retrieved the tool bag. He opened it and took out the roll of tape and handed it to Syman.

"We've got it," said Syman.

"Now, you're going to need two empty juice cans," said Dexter.

"Right," said Syman. He turned to Karrie and asked her to bring two cans of juice.

"You'll also need all the bullets we have, except for five 9 millimeter rounds for the sniper rifle. You're going to use those to set the package off from across the chamber."

Thinking about it, he amended his previous instructions and said, "Keep ten rounds, instead of five, just in case."

"Okay," said Syman. Then he said to Bandar, "please bring all of our equipment in here."

Osmid followed Karrie through the fan blades and returned a few moments later with the first of the duffel bag packs.

Dexter continued, "You'll need to dry the inside of the juice cans. Then take the pliers and gently wiggle each bullet out of the brass casing and dump the powder into one of the cans."

"Hold on, Buddy. We need to get the cans ready. Should we cut the whole top out of the cans?" Syman called up the duct.

"No. You don't want to remove the tops. They provide a pretty good pressure stop. As the powder begins to burn, the tops will hold the hot gases inside the can for a faction of a second longer. The pressure and the increase in temperature will back flash through the rest of the powder that much faster."

"How do we dry the insides of the cans?" asked Karrie.

Dexter hesitated a moment to think about the problem, before he replied, "If there are only a few drops of moisture in the cans, I guess it won't make too much difference. As long as most of the powder is dry. A little moisture might actually boost the power of the explosion, but too much will slow the powder's burning."

"The cans are empty. Now what?" Syman asked.

"Now, take apart all the rounds and dump the powder in the cans."

The three people set up an impromptu assembly operation, with Osmid handing the rounds to Syman, while holding the flashlight on Syman's hands. Syman gently pried the bullets apart, as fast as he could, handing them on to Karrie, who then carefully emptied them, first into one can and then the other. It was a slow and tedious business and it took the better part of an hour to fill both cans. Surprisingly, when they were done, they still had a clip and a half of 6 millimeter rounds and the ten 9 millimeter rounds for the sniper rifle.

"We're done," said Karrie, finally. "Now what?"

There was no reply from Dexter.

"Dexter!" Karrie shouted up the duct.

In response, they heard some coughing and a groggy, "What?"

"Are you okay, Dex?" Syman asked in a loud voice.

"Sorry folks. I guess I fell asleep."

"Might as well, pal. You gotta take it where you find it," Syman said to his tired friend. "That's what we did while you were up there looking around. What's next? The cans are full of powder."

Dexter had to think for a moment to comprehend what Syman was talking about. Then he said, "Tape the two cans top to top, so the drinking openings are facing each other. That way, the blast wave will travel from the first can to the second."

"Understood," said Syman.

"Now tape around the rims completely."

Karrie held the cans while Syman wrapped tape around them.

"We've got it, Dex."

"Al'right, how much light have you guys got?"

"Bandar's and Karrie's lights are out," said Syman. "We're down to what's left of the weak batteries you left us with."

"Okay, we're finished just in the nick of time," said Dexter. "Here's what you've got to do and you have to do it just the way I tell you. Take the package and the tape out to the door. Tape it to the jam right at the latch. How much tape is left?"

"A lot. Probably twenty, thirty feet," answered Syman.

"Good," said Dexter. "After that, you need to take something heavy, made from metal and tape it on the outside of the explosive package as a tamper. When the explosives go off, they'll push against the tamper increasing the power of the blast against the door."

Syman considered their inventory of possessions and asked, "How about one of the machine pistols?"

"Not enough mass," said Dexter, who had also been thinking about what to use. "Here's what will work. Take all the bullets and put them in a bag of some kind. Use a shirt sleeve tied off at both ends and tape it over the explosives. Can you do that?"

"We can do that, Dex," said Syman.

Dexter realized that the lead bullets were the perfect thing to use for a tamper, being extremely dense. And they would conform tightly to the cans, maximizing the effect of the powder. But, he also realized, he had just told them, in effect, to build a very efficient, very powerful Claymore mine-like anti-personnel device. The damn thing would be incredibly dangerous when it went off. Spraying hundreds of pieces of lead in all directions, it would rip into every thing in the chamber like a nest of hornets gone insane.

The only protection from being hit was distance. The further away the shooter was the less likely he'd stop a piece of flying shrapnel.

It took him only a moment to decide he'd have to be the one to detonate the device. For one thing, he was the best shot. He could hit it from the greatest distance. Second, he was the only one who knew precisely where to hit the explosives buried under all that lead shot. Third and most important, was his unwillingness to subject his sister or his best friend to that kind of danger. He knew Bandar couldn't do it. So that left him. .

Dexter was the expert. He was the retired Navy SEAL. He was the one trained to handle this sort of thing.

"I'm coming down," Dexter shouted down the duct.

"Say what?" asked Syman.

"I said, I'm coming down. I'm the only one who can set the thing off safely."

"Okay," was all Syman said. He knew better than to argue with Dexter about it.

Dexter started climbing down the duct. About half way, he heard a loud ripping sound. He realized they were preparing the tamper from someone's shirt sleeve.

"You'll have to take all the equipment to the stairway," he instructed loudly, standing on a pipe bracket.

Climbing down was much easier and quicker than climbing up had been. So much so, that fatigued as he was, Dexter got careless and nearly lost his grip twenty feet from the bottom. He reminded himself that breaking something like a leg would not be a good idea right then and he slowed his descent. He could now see that Karrie and Osmid Bandar were shifting the equipment duffels back out through the blower's blades to the chamber. When Dexter reached the floor, he found Syman tying a knot in the sleeve torn from Dexter's discarded sixty dollar dress shirt. Syman had filled it with the lead bullets, as per instruction.

"Where's the device?" he asked, Syman.

Syman reached between his legs, where he had been keeping it, so no one would inadvertently step on the delicate tin can assembly in the dark. He handed it to Dexter, who inspected it minutely in the still strong light of his flash light.

"Nice job," he said. "Are you done with the tamper?"

"Yes, just finished," said Syman. "Let's go install it."

They slipped through the blades with their precious bundles. Going to the motor room door, they taped their jury rigged explosive assembly to the space between the latch and the jam. Using the rest of the tape, they secured the tamper, leaving the bottom inch of the device exposed so Dexter would have a clear shot at it.

Finally, they walked the ninety odd feet to the stairwell opening.

"Have you got all the equipment in the stairwell?" Dexter asked.

"We've got everything," said Karrie, still puffing from the exertion.

"You all get down in the stairway. I don't want you to catch any shrapnel or ricocheting fragments. This thing is dangerous as hell and there's going to be metal flying all over the place."

"What about you, Dexter?" Karrie asked, with concern in her voice

"I'll be all right, Sis," he lied, knowing full well what he was about to do might very likely get him badly hurt. Then he had an idea. "Bring the duffel bags up here and lay them across the floor just above the top step, like sand bags, sideways. I'll hide behind them. It'll give me some good cover."

When everything had been prepared, Dexter banished the others down the stairs.

"Sit down and cover your ears. It's going to be loud in here." Dexter laid the food duffel over the sniper scope of the rifle, which allowed him to still sight the rifle. The rifle was nestled on top of one of the other packs to give him a little elevation off the floor. The rest of his body was down in the stairway. He test sighted the scope and saw that the flashlight gave him enough light to use the night sight. In its green glow he could clearly see the bottom of the can ninety feet away.

"Is everyone ready?" he hollered, down the stairs.

"We're ready," said Syman.

"Here goes," said Dexter, as he let out his breath and squeezed the trigger. The rifle barked and Dexter saw a bright spark just below the can where the bullet plowed a furrow in the metal door.

"I missed," he said loudly so no one would move. "Here we go again." He again let out his breath and squeezed the trigger.

There was a deafening roar and concussion that made the air bounce violently. Hundreds of flying projectiles splattered and rattled off the stone walls of the chamber. Then it was silent. The chamber was now full of a thick cloud of dust and smoke that obscured Dexter's view of the door. The acrid smell of the burned powder was nearly overwhelming.

"Everybody okay?" Dexter asked.

"Something hit the back of my hand and it hurts like hell," Syman said, trudging up the stairs to Dexter where he held the back of his hand under the light. Karrie came running up the stairs just behind Syman to see what had happened to him. The back of his left hand had a nasty red welt that had already begun to swell, but the skin had not been cut.

Dexter took a good look at it and said, "You're lucky. You must have caught that on the third or forth bounce. If you'd gotten hit on the first you'd have a hole there instead of that welt." Then he turned to his sister, worried and asked, "How are you, Karrie?"

"I'm okay. I felt some grit hit me, but that's all."

"Thank God!" said Dexter. Then, he said, "Bandar, you okay?"

He shined his light down the shaft to find him. They all froze in shock. Osmid Bandar lay crumpled on the stairs with a surprised expression on his face, eyes wide open, dead.

"Holy shit!" said Dexter, climbing down to Bandar. Turning the body, Dexter saw blood dripping from where a bullet had punched a neat hole in the back of Bandar's neck. Osmid had been sitting with his head bent forward, down the stairway, facing away from the blast. The projectile had burrowed into Bandar's brain through the small space at the juncture between his spine and skull. It was a one in a million chance that a piece of shrapnel would strike that exact spot. Still, it had happened and Bandar was dead. Confronted with that stark reality, Dexter was appalled at the danger that had passed so close to them. He turned and went back up the stairs, where Karrie was quietly crying. Syman and Dexter left her alone while they gathered the equipment.

After a few minutes, the dust and smoke thinned to a tolerable level.

"Come on. There's nothing we can do for him," said Syman, as he gently led Karrie away toward the motor room door.

When they got to the door, they found it folded in half laying inside room. The head jamb, above the doorway, was hanging down about two inches and some of the rock above it had fallen out of the wall and was laying in the doorway.

"I didn't realize how powerful this thing would be in this enclosed space," said Dexter, inspecting his handy work. "I really over did it."

Syman could hear the deep doubt in Dexter's voice.

"Well, it worked Dex, and that's all that matters, right now. Desperate times require desperate measures and the truth is, if Bandar had left us alone, he wouldn't have been in here. I know that sounds cold as hell, but it's his own fault, not yours."

"Yeah, I guess so, Syman, but you misunderstand me. What's bothering me, is that I could have killed you or Karrie."

"But, you didn't and now we can get out of here."

Dexter did not reply.

Turning away, Syman saw a small metal chard lying on the stone floor. He picked it up and put it in his pocket. It would do for the sample he wanted to take with him.

Exhausted, Dexter, Karrie and Syman hoisted the equipment one more time and slowly climbed what they hoped was the last set of stairs on their way to the outside world.

When they reached the vent chamber, Dexter said, "There isn't actually an opening to the outside, except a large crack in the rock that's acting like a chimney. The air going up it is creating the draft we noticed." He shined their last working flashlight on the rubble pile in the entrance of the vent chamber.

"The vent opening has collapsed like the entrance tunnel, but we can probably dig our way out."

"Probably is the operative word in that statement," said a gloomy Syman, when he saw the large pile of dirt and rock blocking the outlet.

Dexter looked at his watch. "It's 4:30. The rescue team should be ashore by now."

"Unfortunately, it's too late to stop them," said Syman. "I hope no one gets killed on our account."

Dexter had already settled that problem in his own mind and he'd dealt with enough depressing things in the last week for a life time. He didn't have the energy to think about someone dying needlessly on their account. Instead, he changed the subject.

"Karrie, there's only room for two people to dig at a time. Syman and I can start, but I'm hungry as a horse. Could you fix up something to eat?"

"Sure," she said, sounding cheerful, but there were streaks of light colored skin showing, where tears had run down her dirt covered face and muddy smudges, where she had wiped her face with her hands.

Dexter handed her the light after rummaging in the tools for the prybar and screw driver. With tools in hand, Syman and Dexter set to work at the top of the rock fall. They worked steadily, as fast as they could, on the uppermost 3 feet of the pile, knowing from their earlier experience that they needed to clear a wide area at the beginning to counter the inevitable narrowing that would occur as they dug further into the fall. Almost before they had begun, Karrie called a halt and presented them with a meager fare of cold canned meat, crackers and fruit juice. There was only one can of juice for each person.

"That's the end of the juice," she said, wistfully wishing she could have another. She did not want any canned meat. It disgusted her, even as hungry as she was. "We still have some water."

As if reading her mind, Dexter handed his juice back to her and said, "I'd actually prefer water right now. All the sugar we've consumed since yesterday is bad for our health."

For a moment, they looked at one another, thinking about what Dexter had just said. Then as one, the three of them broke into laughter, struck by the ironic absurdity of his pronouncement in the light of their current predicament.

While Dexter and Syman ate their meager rations, Karrie climbed the debris pile and worked alone digging at the newly started hole. As she worked, the flash light flickered and dimmed perceptibly.

"Damn! There's less than an hour left to the batteries, when it starts doing that," said Dexter. He turned the light off. Karrie stopped working.

"I can't see," she said.

"I know," he said.

The men gulped their food and switched places with Karrie. This left her with nothing to do except sit alone and watch, holding the flash light for them.

Refreshed and strengthened by their meal, the men redoubled their efforts and attacked the debris with a will. The one bright spot in their otherwise grim situation was the stiff breeze that flowed over them on its way to the outside world through the large crack just above them in the roof of the tunnel. It continuously vacuumed away the copious dust they stirred into the air.

"I think this tunnel and the entrance tunnel were both purposely blown shut with explosives," Syman told Dexter during one of their short breaks."

"What makes you think that?"

"Well, the condition of the rest of the facility is excellent. We didn't find a single rock fall or cave-in anywhere else in the place. The rock of this mountain seems to be very durable and stable. With the exception of the motor room door, we didn't see any subsidence or shifting. Did either of you see cracks anywhere else? The only problems are at the entrances to this place."

"I didn't," said Karrie.

Dexter said, "Maybe you're on to something. If the builders had wanted to save it, they would have closed it."

"That's what I think," said Syman. "The only thing I don't understand is the metal plate left in the stone pedestal at the entrance."

Dexter shrugged, "Oh well, what the hell, Sy. There have to be some mysteries left in life. Besides," he said, laughing, "it'll give you something to think about while you dig.".

"Screw you, Dexter," said Syman, also laughing.

They resumed digging. They dug like dogs, pushing the loose debris out between their legs or along their sides every few moments. It was the only way they could work in the confined space. The second man then reached in and pulled the debris out the rest of the way. It was miserable work, and they were both achingly aware that there might be tens of feet to dig through. If that were the case, both men knew they were going to die long before they could dig their way out through this miserable hole.

Their flash light lasted exactly 47 minutes, more. Karrie had been turning it on for a few moments and then turning it off, in an effort to stretch its life. Finally, it dimmed to a useless dull glow and went out completely.

"The light's gone," Karrie reported.

"What was that?" Dexter asked, as he backed out of the hole.

"She said the light's gone," answered Syman.

"Well, that shouldn't matter much," he said, no longer able to see his companions. "It's dark as a coal sack in there. Even when there was light, you couldn't see a damn thing."

But Dexter was wrong. The little light the flashlight had provided had been a great help. They didn't need much light to see well enough to work efficiently. With the light completely gone, it was much more difficult to dig.

"It's your turn in the hole, Sy."

"Let me take a turn," Karrie demanded, as she stumbled toward them in the dark. She found Syman when he said, "You might have to later, Kar, but not just yet."

Syman turned from her and stumbled up the rubble in the blackness.

"Ouch!" he yelled, kneeling on a sharp rock. Guided only by touch, he found the prybar and began to pick away at the face of the hole.

They went along like that for several minutes with Syman digging and Dexter fumbling on the pile trying to find the debris Syman was raking back toward to opening. The truth was, progress had slowed to a pitiful rate in the absence of even a minimum of light.

The darkness closed in on them irresistibly eroding their hope. After an hour in the dark, Karrie had again started to cry softly. When Dexter took over digging, Syman found his way to her guided by her small sounds.

He put his arms around her and held her gently. "We'll be okay, Darling. I'm sure we're almost through." He told her this, not at all sure they were almost through.

Overwhelmed and discouraged by the seemingly unending onslaught of problems, Syman considered using his ace in the hole, their last available light source. They might only be inches from freedom. He dearly hoped they were only inches from freedom. Having some light would speed up the digging and it would certainly lift their spirits. It couldn't be much further to the outside, or could it? After days of fear and stress, physical abuse, lack of rest and sustenance, their spirits were finally flagging with the absence of light. In his present shape, Syman knew better than to completely trust his own judgment, but they truly might be only inches from freedom.

Syman decided there was no point in waiting. "Where's my little backpack, Karrie."

"I'm not sure," Karrie replied.

"Help me find the pack, Kar. I want to get my laptop."

"Your laptop, Syman! It has batteries! We can put them in the flash light!" Karrie"s voice was buoyant with renewed hope.

"They won't fit," said Syman, "but I can turn on the computer and the screen will give us a little light."

"I left it over here somewhere," she said, as she moved away from him, cautiously stepping in what she thought was the direction of the large duct openings where she had set up her ersatz kitchen two hours earlier. When she found an equipment duffel with her foot, she knelt down on her knees and began crawling back and forth feeling each bag. She could see absolutely nothing in the pitch-black room, but her hands told her what she needed to know. As she moved further to the left, her attention was drawn by a shimmering oval of light.

"Aeh!" she barked, frightened by the sudden appearance of the apparition. "Syman, come here!"

"What's wrong," he responded, having heard her exclamation.

"There's a light over here!"

Syman moved toward her as fast as he could in the darkness. "Say something so I can find you," he instructed.

"Say something like..." She stopped, when she felt Syman brush her arm with his outstretched hand. "Do you see it."

"No."

"Down here near the floor," she instructed him.

Syman knelt down and scanned the blackness. There on his left, he saw it too, a gentle shimmering oval of bright light. At first, he had trouble focusing on it. There was no frame of reference to relate it to. His mind flip it this way and that, as he tried to make sense of what his eyes saw. Curious, he crawled on his hands and knees toward the light, but carefully, so he wouldn't take a flier down one of the ventilation ducts he knew must be near by. He was doubly careful as he approached the strange light because he suspected he was seeing a reflection of a previously unnoticed light source coming from inside one of the ducts. It didn't make sense, but it was the only explanation that came to mind. Feeling with his hands out in front of him, he came upon a down sloping floor. He felt carefully along the change in the floor. It didn't feel like one of the ventilation ducts. For one thing, there was a much smaller opening in the wall than he remembered. For another, the curve of the floor was wrong. What he saw, as opposed to what he remembered seeing, just didn't make any sense.

"Karrie, see if you can find my computer, please."

Karrie resumed her search for the small back pack. After a minute, she located Syman's bag. "Here you go," she said, handing him the heavy little machine.

Syman fumbled with the waterproof bag that protected it until he located the zipper. Taking the laptop out, he quickly opened it, activating the screen. It glowed brightly in the darkness, clearly illuminating the back of the ventilation chamber.

Now that Syman could once more see, he immediately understood the mysterious light. He found himself gazing down the small water filled tunnel he'd noticed when they'd first entered the vent chamber. He'd puzzled over its purpose at the time, but nothing had come to mind. Full of water, it had been beyond their ability to explore and he had turned his full attention back to Dexter. Now focusing a newly critical eye on the tunnel, he saw it was only three feet across and that it ran at a right angle to the larger ventilation ducts, conveying the five inch pipe Dexter had climbed, away from the vent chamber and down into the water.

In a flash of instant understanding, Syman realized the five inch pipe was the water intake pipe for the installation and the light they saw was sunlight streaming into the lake Osmid Bandar had described to them. To test this, he crawled down the tunnel to the water and tasted it. It was fresh with no hint of salt.

"I think you've solved our problems, Karrie," he said, without preamble. "That's sunlight coming through the water of the lake Bandar described to us. Actually, I suspect it's not a natural lake, but rather a reservoir for this place. That big pipe is the water intake for this installation."

"Are you sure, Syman?"

"No, I'm not absolutely sure, but it covers all the known facts and it is fresh water."

"Oh, Syman!" she said, ecstatic with happiness at the prospect of finally escaping their underground tomb.

"Dexter!" Syman yelled. "Karrie has found an easier way out of here."

Dexter backed out of the hole, surprised and pleased to see the light from the computer when he emerged. Still, he had grit in his teeth, he was frustrated by his slow progress and he was in no mood for one of Syman's brilliant ideas.

"What are you talking about? Let me guess. Karrie's suddenly become Alice in Wonderland and we're getting out of here through the computer's screen in lieu of a looking glass?" he retorted, sarcastically.

"No," said Syman, ignoring Dexter's foul humor. "Come take a look at this."

Sourly, Dexter complied. When he reached Karrie and Syman, he looked down at them and said, "Okay, now what?"

"Look in there," said Syman, pointing to the tunnel.

"Yeah, so what? It's a water filled tunnel."

"Yes, it is," said Syman, patiently, "but it's more than that. Look from down here."

Dexter knelt on sore knees, as Syman closed the laptop.

"Well, I'll be stripped and dipped!" said Dexter in astonishment, seeing the sunlight coming through the far end of the water filled tunnel.

"Yes, that's just about, what I had in mind," said Syman, laughing.

"Fantastic!" exclaimed Dexter, his demeanor completely transformed. "I was beginning to feel like a goddamn mole! How come we didn't see that, when we looked before?"

"The sun hadn't risen when we first got in here. It was still dark outside," explained Syman.

"Of course," said Dexter, and then after a moments reflection asked, "How are we going to go about this?"

"I guess we strip and dip," said Syman, with a big smile, laughing.

"We can't take all our equipment out of here, through that sewer pipe," said Dexter, seriously. "It would be too dangerous. The bags would hold air and try to float us back up the pipe. One of us might get stuck in there."

"We only need the telephone," said Syman.

"It's a good thing you brought it, because there's no way we'd get that SEAL satellite phone out of here. Its carrybag would float like a balloon."

"How about the laptop?" Syman asked.

"If it's carried in just its water proof pouch and there's no air in it, you might get it out of here But carry it separately from the phone. If it's a problem, you'll have to dump it."

"Okay," said Syman.

"I think we should bring the sniper rifle and one handgun," Dexter continued, "just in case. We still have eight rounds for the rifle and a clip and a half of six millimeter rounds for the handgun."

"I still have this, Dexter," said Karrie, handing him the nine millimeter pistol, she'd been carrying on her utility belt the whole time. "It still has the bullets you put in it."

"Wow, okay. We sure have a lot of stuff for not bringing any equipment," Dexter said. "We'll have to divide it up between us, so it doesn't float or sink one of us."

"We should bring some water, too," said Syman, practically.

Dexter looked at the pile of things they deemed essential, wondering how to pack it through the water filled tunnel. It looked to be about thirty feet long, but he knew distances were distorted under water. He didn't want one of them to drown. He dumped the remaining food supplies from its duffel pack and then picked up a full water bottle, and rolled it in the empty pack. He carried the pack down into the tunnel far enough to push it under water to test its buoyancy. It ballooned with air.

He decided to put the firearms in it. Wrapped tightly, the pack just might attain neutral buoyancy.

"We'll put all the metal in the pack along with the water. If we wrap it tight, it shouldn't float too much and it shouldn't sink and drag me to the bottom, either," Dexter said, having decided to be the one to haul it through the tunnel.

"We can use that other almost empty water bottle to adjust its buoyancy by filling or emptying it."

"Good idea," said Syman.

Dexter prepared the duffel bag by adjusting the buoyancy until it was just right. When he had finished, he said,"You carry the computer, Sy, in that little back pack you have for it. Karrie, you bring the phone in one of your pants pockets. You can dump the pouches on your utility belt, but keep the

162

holster." A few minutes later they were ready.

Dexter carefully inspected everything and then said, "I hope that water tight pouch you brought the phone in is really water tight or we'll have a long swim back to the good ol' USA."

"We'll know in a few minutes," said Syman, and then after a moment he asked, "Kar, are you up to this?"

"I'm more than up to it, Syman. In fact, I wish you guys would get going. I hate it in here. Give me the phone."

Syman handed Karrie the Sat-Link which when folded in half in its water proof, form fitting, zippered pouch was about the size of a man's wallet. Karrie stuffed the phone into the front pocket of her jeans without fanfare.

"Let's get out of here!" she said.

"Who goes first?" asked Syman.

"I think I should," said Karrie.

"It might be dangerous, Kar. Shouldn't Dexter or I go first to make sure it's okay?"

"Darling, I'll have you know, I was California women's all state swimming champion in high school." She punctuated her declaration with a mischievous little flounce. "Where do you think I got this great body?"

"Amazing!" Syman said in reply.

"Pull yourself along the pipe with both hands and don't stop for anything," Dexter instructed.

"See you outside," Karrie said. She paused only a moment to give her brother a peck on the cheek and Syman a lingering kiss. Then without hesitation, she crawled into the tunnel. Once in the water, she pulled herself head first down the tunnel, hand over hand along the pipe, blocking the sunlight for several seconds before clearing the far end and disappearing toward the surface and the light.

"God, she swims underwater like a fish," said Syman, admiringly. "I didn't know that."

"Our family is full of all kinds of unrevealed talents, Sy," Dexter said, kidding his friend. "And now that you're going to be part of it, who knows. The sky's the limit."

"Come on, Dexter. Let's get the hell out of here!" Then, he asked, "You ready?" before closing the computer and dousing their only useful source of light.

"I'm a lot more than ready!" said Dexter.

With that, Syman carefully closed and zipped the machine in its water proof pouch. Then he wrapped it tightly in his small nylon back pack to remove any air.

"See you top side, pal," he said and then with less grace than Karrie, he crawled down the pipe into the water.

A few moments later when Dexter could see Syman was clear, he followed dragging the bulky equipment pack along with one hand while pulling himself forward along the pipe with the other. When he'd cleared the end of the tunnel, his lungs were aching, and he swam with all his strength for the surface where he burst into the life giving air seconds later.

He found Karrie and Syman treading water together in an embrace of celebration and joyful uncontrolled laughter.

"God, it feels great to be out of there! Hey you two! Help me get this heavy goddamn bag ashore, will you?"

28

Having eaten as much as he wanted, Dexter pushed his plate away, deciding to dispense with civilities. He was fed up with the run around they'd been given since coming aboard. He wanted answers and he wanted them now. He looked the submarine's Captain directly in the eye, "Captain, there are two things I would like to discuss with you," he said, without preamble. "First, I would like to radio John Claire at the Defense Intelligence Agency. Second, we would like to know where you are taking us?"

Dexter, Karrie, and Syman had been taken aboard the submarine early the previous morning. Their journey from the lake to the submarine had been accomplished without incident, although they'd had to wait until that night to rendezvous with the boat from the submarine on the east side of the island.

Since coming aboard, none of the crew would answer any of their questions and the Captain had refused to talk to them. But now, thirty hours later, the Captain had suddenly invited them to share a meal with him in the officer's stateroom.

Taking his time, Captain Henebry stirred his fork in the muddy brown puddle of apple sauce on his plate as he considered Dexter's question. Normally tight lipped, he allowed himself to be distracted for a moment thinking about how he loved the pork chops but detested the apple sauce. For some unfathomable reason they were always served together aboard the Los Angeles. He made a mental note to look into the matter. Finally, he answered Dexter.

"I've been ordered to deliver you and your party to the Navy base at Rota, Spain. I've also been ordered to maintain radio silence, unless a situation arises, Commander Gordon," he said, using Dexter's rank, addressing him as a senior officer to a junior with the obvious intention of putting Dexter in his place.

Completely uncowed, Dexter immediately asked, "Why Rota, Spain, Captain, and what exactly do you mean by a situation?"

Captain Henebry was not used to being questioned so directly by a person of lesser rank under any circumstances and certainly never by anyone aboard his submarine. He especially did not like being so treated by this retired Navy

SEAL. Still, orders were orders and he had been ordered by no less than COMSUBLANT, who had been ordered by the Secretary of the Navy to extend every courtesy to his guests.

"Well," he thought, bristling, "there is courtesy and there is Courtesy." He wished he knew more about what was going on. Then, at least, he could have the satisfaction of giving this upstart SEAL as little information as possible with a clear conscience.

"I have been ordered to bring you to our base at Rota where you will be transferred to the carrier, Tarawa. Mr. Claire will be meeting you there."

"I'm not sure I understand our being transferred to the Tarawa, Captain?"

Allowing his displeasure at being questioned to show in the tone of his answer, the Captain said, "Commander, I was not told why, I am to deliver you to the Tarawa."

Captain Henebry's answer told Dexter more than he realized. Dexter now knew the Captain had little or no idea why he'd been required to follow the Hana Maru across the Atlantic this past week, ready to pick them up at a moment's notice. So, Dexter decided, there was no point in further antagonizing the man by badgering him with questions he obviously could not answer. Anyway, what Dexter really wanted, was to talk with John Claire right away, but he realized, he'd just have to wait.

"What is our ETA for Rota, Sir?"

Henebry looked at his watch and said, "We'll be coming along side the Tarawa in about two hours, Commander."

Then, changing the subject, he asked, "How's the food, folks? We pride ourselves on having the best chow in the Navy." He looked at Karrie for a response.

"I don't know how they like it, Captain, but it tastes heavenly to me," she answered, giving their host her warmest smile, "specially after the last several days."

"I've been talking with the President all week about the implications of this thing," John Claire said to Dexter and Syman. They were seated at a table in the empty Ward Room of the aircraft carrier Tarawa. "And to say the least, he's very concerned with the situation. A thorough analysis by experts of the list you gave us points to these people building at least one and possibly two nuclear devices and the missiles needed to deliver them."

"That's no news, John. Syman and I deduced that much and told you so when we first gave you the document," said Dexter.

"Yes, well, your deductions needed a little more proof to back them up before we could be sure we had a real National Security problem. Since then, we've done a little hard science and a lot of investigating. Bandar told you the group is the Islamic Brotherhood?" Claire asked, abruptly changing the conversation's direction. "We've been thinking we were dealing with the Libyans."

"He told us the Libyans were leasing the island for a fishing and cannery operation," said Syman. "And, he told us that we were dealing with a terrorist organization called the Islamic Brotherhood. He also said the fish cannery was a cover for a missile launching site, but we saw no evidence of that. We were too intent on getting away."

"If we're dealing with the Islamic Brotherhood," said Claire, somberly, "then, we're dealing with a particular vicious bunch of extremists."

Well, that's what he told us," said Dexter, "but Bandar could have been lying to us."

"While you were being held," said Claire, "a sniffer plane scanned the Hana Maru and the island for radioactives, but we found no unusual radiation. We also scanned Nalut and we're pretty sure we've found the plutonium there. We continued to watch the Hana Maru and it just off loaded a cargo of non-nuclear materials in Tripoli. They're being trucked, as we speak, to the base in Nalut, Libya, so we think they may not be done working on the devices. If so, we still have time..."

"John," said Dexter, cutting him off, "this is all very interesting, and we're glad you've found the bombs, but let's cut to the chase here. Syman and I want to know why we're on the Tarawa with you instead of on a jet back to the U.S.?"

Claire looked from Dexter to Syman and back again. "I've been with the President, as I've said, and he's very concerned. We discussed options. They're limited."

"What does that have to do with us?" Syman asked.

"It's been decided that the U.S. should take the bombs away from the Libyans, but secretly. Because of the possibility of an international incident, the president wants us to mount a black operation and remove the bombs without tipping our hand while maintaining complete deniability for the United States, if we can," said Claire.

"Are you using the pronouns 'we' and 'us' broadly, John," Syman asked, with rising suspicion, "or are you including Dexter and me in a more personal way?"

"I'm including you, Dexter, and myself," Claire answered without dissimulation.

"Why do I feel like I'm about to get washed behind my ears without my permission?" Dexter said, sarcastically.

"I think it's probably time you fill us in on all the ugly details, John," Syman said, frowning.

"It's really rather straight forward," Claire explained. "The President wants us to take a small team into Nalut, where we're now pretty sure they've been building the devices and take them."

"Keeping in mind, 'the best laid plans' and all that, John, you know damn well an operation of this type is never straight forward," Dexter remonstrated.

"Never is too strong a judgment, Dex," said Claire, by way of denial. "In this case, because Nalut is way the hell and gone out in the middle of the desert, miles from the nearest military base, the plan is very straight forward. We have the SEAL team with us here and we're having six more ADARTs flown from Kirkland onto the Tarawa. The Tarawa is scheduled to traverse the Mediterranean and the Suez Canal on a re-supply mission to our forward positioning base at Diego Garcia in the Indian Ocean. As it transit's the coast of Libya, we'll fly the 'DARTs off the Tarawa and head for Nalut. Once there, we grab the bomb cores and leave."

"Why doesn't the President just send in our quick response force?" Dexter asked. "A couple of thousand men would guarantee success."

"Because of all the political fallout," said Claire, "things like an international incident, invading a sovereign nation and all that. He wants to maintain deniability until we have the devices in our possession."

"Why are Syman and I included in this? We're civilians."

"You were civilians, until yesterday, but you're both reservists and your country calls. As of midnight, last night, you were both returned to active duty by order of the President for the duration of the crisis."

"He can't do that to us," said Dexter, indignantly.

"Well Dex, actually, under the special threat section of the War Powers Act, he can," said Claire, bracing for an angry outburst.

"There are a lot of things the government can do that most people don't realize," said Syman, thinking of his own earlier experiences and dealings with the U.S. government concerning his encryption work. "The politicians, and specially our presidents, have been very busy since the last World War, enacting all kinds of contingency legislation that abrogates a citizen's constitutional rights when it's deemed necessary. You'd be appalled by the truth, Dexter. And you, John,should be ashamed of yourself for being party to this sort of procedure."

"You both have a right to be angry, but you're not going to be forced to help. You have to volunteer. I'm in," continued Claire, "because I don't want some nutty terrorists nuking Chicago or Washington or New York or Tel Aviv or Paris, killing hundreds of thousands or maybe millions of innocent people because I didn't take them out when I had the opportunity. I might get killed on this operation, but if I don't do something, there's a good chance these bastards might kill me and my family while we're home asleep in our beds. We only live a couple of miles from the Capitol." He paused for a moment. Then he continued, "As I said, if we're dealing with the Islamic Brotherhood, then we're dealing with a pretty nasty group and I'd much rather deal with them on our terms than on their terms.

"Dexter and Syman sat quietly, each thinking his own thoughts about the effects of a nuclear bomb on New York City, sixty mile west of their own little beach community of Lordship.

"Why are we being included?" Syman asked, again.

"You're being included for several reasons," explained Claire. "First, you both are already fully aware of the situation. Second, you, Syman, are the highest ranking officer, and you received nuclear device handling training when you were in the Air Force.

Dexter, you are included because you are a highly trained SEAL, experienced in black ops. Incidentally, you're the highest ranking SEAL as well."

"Who happens to be completely out of shape!" Dexter shot back.

"You're obviously not completely out of shape, Dex," Claire countered, "and besides, you won't have to do a whole lot of running around. Your job is to direct the younger men."

"So you say," said Dexter. "That just shows there's a lot you don't know about leading a SEAL team, leading being the operative word. You lead by example. You don't sit back and tell the men what to do."

"See what a good choice you are, Dex!" said Claire, gently kidding his old friend. "You've already focused on the key problem of your new command."

"My command?" said Dexter, incredulously. "I thought you said Syman was senior?"

"He is, but you two will share command responsibilities. The SEALs will be more comfortable taking their orders from a SEAL commander, than from an Air Force colonel."

"We're being shellacked again, Sy," said Dexter,

"Do you mean as in our being hosed down with the thick varnish like slime exuded by gutless politicians, Dexter?" Syman asked. "Or do you mean as in our being defeated, overcome, and violated by an incompetent bunch of bureaucrats as they hand us the shitty end of the stick?" Every word dripped with sarcasm.

"Both," said Dexter, giving John Claire a withering look.

"If we decide to go, when's the operation scheduled for departure?" Syman asked.

"Four AM, tomorrow."

The six ADARTs rolled off the Tarawa, one after the other, five of the six laden with two men, their equipment and weapons, the sixth carrying only Master Chief Lufkin. His backseat, which originally had been slated to carry

John Claire, had been reassigned to carry the shielded container needed to safely convey any nuclear materials found, back to the ship. When the load calculations had been done, it was determined that the six ultralights did not have sufficient capacity to carry twelve men and the lead container. One man had to stay behind and Claire, who had never been in the military was the obvious choice. The little help he might bring to the operation was in the form of knowledge and that, Gordon and Pons decided, could be provided as readily over the radio as in person.

Traversing the Mediterranean northeast of Tunisia and north of Libya, just outside the gulf of Sidra, the Tarawa would be in range of the ADARTs for about twelve hours. It was plenty of time to fly to Nalut, capture the bomb cores and return.

Syman, with Dexter as his backseater, headed the flight up on a course, first to the southwest into a relatively barren area of Tunisia and then to the southeast, out across the wastes of the Sahara desert into Libya. This flight path would bring them to the source waters of a 12 mile long underground water tunnel, known locally as a qanat that began in the low mountains of the Jabal Nafusah, southeast of Nalut. At this time of year, it carried only an inch or two of water and would provide a perfect highway. It was reasoned that the settlement's end of the qanat would be heavily guarded, but the approach from the mountain's end of the tunnel would have little protection.

Ironically, they would actually have to fly around Nalut, to the north, to get to the qanat, but the isolation of the area around the headwaters was perfect for the operation. It would provide the team with a place to secretly transition their 'DARTs into the three wheeled, fast attack vehicles that would carry them swiftly through the underground irrigation tunnel to their destination at the other end. The complete surprise that would result justified their somewhat indirect approach. And the qanat would hide them and protect their flanks and rear during the assault.

From reconnaissance over-flights, it had been determined that there was a powerful radioactive source in the vicinity of the oasis. Because maintaining surprise was of paramount importance, the spy plane could not approach close enough to pinpoint its exact position. But pictures taken at the same time showed there was some type of industrial operation located just inside the qanat's tunnel. Its presence was evidenced by large mounds of debris and rock recently excavated and dumped just outside the water tunnel entrance and by the busy traffic in and out of the tunnel itself.

In the same photographs, the adobe type desert earth colored dwellings of the settlement's five hundred odd inhabitants and the verdant green fields of rice, wheat and date palms that surrounded them could also clearly be seen. Sadly, Nalut was reminiscent of a thousand other pathetic, lonely little outposts spread widely across the continent's desert northlands.

One hour and fifteen minutes after leaving the Tarawa, they crossed the silvery line of surf cascading on to the desolate beaches of the Tunisian coast. Cutting across the southeast corner of Tunisia, they arrowed for a point of nondescript desert about eighty miles inland where they changed their line of travel to bring them across the border frontier into Libya, about twenty-five miles from the mountains where they were going to land.

Built mostly from composite plastic and with all metal parts heavily covered with radar absorbent or dispersive coatings, the small aircraft returned virtually no radar reflection. Not incidentally, their point of entry to Libya had been chosen for its lack of radar coverage, positioned as it was, on a straight line to nowhere, way out in the wastes of the Sahara desert, one-hundred-fifty miles southwest of Libya's capitol, Tripoli.

They anticipated no trouble when they entered Libya thirty minutes later and there was none. At one-hundred-fifty miles per hour, they skimmed over the desert only fifty feet above the sandy landscape. They were right on schedule and if nothing turned them from their course, would arrive at their destination in ten minutes.

"Remind me to get a mental health checkup, Sy, when we get back to the States," Dexter said, over their intercom connection. "I must be nuts to have agreed to be part of this. I'm in no shape to spend a day trying to steal a nuclear bomb."

Syman laughed and said, "Quit bitching, Dexter. We'll leave the heavy lifting to the youngsters."

"That might work with you fly-boys, but it won't pass muster with us amphibians."

"How long to our ETA, Dex?"

Dexter typed the latitude and longitude from the GPS indicator into Syman's laptop and then did the math. After a moment, he said, "Four minutes."

They could see the outline of low hills against the brightening eastern dawn sky ten miles in front of them. A few sparse lights twinkled about the same distance to the south in Nalut. As they neared the hills, they climbed to gain sufficient elevation to surmount them. With this increase in height, they could clearly discern the line of vertical well like shafts that rose from the qanat as it crossed the barren landscape and wound its way up under an old dry river bed to its head waters and springs. The large black dots of the qanat's access shaft openings showed every thousand yards or so, leading them directly to the qanat's open end. With surprising swiftness, they came upon the yawning funnel of the manmade water tunnel. A slim dark stain of quietly running water was clearly visible as it started its twelve mile trip to Nalut.

"We're here," said Pons, breaking communications silence.

Using the laser communications gear built into their ADARTs, the members of the flight could communicate using invisible beams of ultraviolet light instead of broadcasting radio waves all over the area giving away their presence. It worked well as long as they were in sight of each other, as was the case now. "We can land on that ledge of rock above the qanat's entrance. Follow me in at thirty second intervals. When you get on the ground, roll out to the south side of the opening. Stay away from the edge and that big field of boulders to the north. Count off," Pons ordered.

"Two, aye."

"Three aye."

Pons and Gordon listened as the pilots acknowledged their understanding, until at last they heard Master Chief Lufkin's gravelly voice say, "Six aye."

Pons dropped the 'DART in a wide sweep and lined up perfectly on the ridge top. Seconds later, they were rolling over its surprisingly smooth surface as they taxied down a natural ramp-like rock formation that brought them to the large bowl shaped area at the mouth of the qanat. Pons stopped as close to the qanat as he could to leave room for the other five. Three minutes later, like clock work, Chief Lufkin brought his plane to a halt, last in line, and shut down his motor.

The perfect peace of the place was stunning to the men's senses after their noisy hundred minute ride. The trickle of the water running across the rock in its 2700 year old trough and an occasional gust of mountain wind were the only sounds to intrude on the silence of the new day. Though cool now, the men could feel the growing heat of the day building as they stood in the morning sun.

The team gathered and Gordon took over command for the ground assault.

"Prepare your weapons first, " he said, wasting no words. "You all know the drill. Then we need to reconfigure the 'DARTs. Finally, if you're hungry, eat something. If you need to relieve yourself, do it now. We don't want anything to distract us between now and when we arrive back at the ship. It should take us about thirty minutes to do these things and then it's into the tunnel. Any questions?" There were no questions, and after a moment, Gordon said, "Let's move."

The knot of men exploded into action as they ran back to their machines and began preparing their weapons. In ten minutes, all six ADARTs were coming apart and being fitted back together again as three wheeled ground vehicles. The wings and control surfaces were dismounted and stowed in a purpose built compartment in the bottom of the frame where they would be protected and where their weight would help lower the vehicle's center of gravity. The large fan-like propellers were also dismounted and folded to be stored with the wing sections. Two wheels were installed in the front to steer and brake the machine. The third larger nose wheel was attached at the rear of the machine and connected to the motor via a drive shaft to propel the car.

Although switching wheels, two to the front and one to the back took time, it made the ground vehicle configuration three times more stable when turning and braking than the tricycle landing gear arrangement of the 'DARTs. As ground assault vehicles, it was the best design and the time lost was worth the gain in maneuverability.

Pons and Gordon struggled to keep up with the other two man teams, watching them to double check the reconfiguration procedure. When Master Chief Lufkin saw they were having difficulty, he came over.

"I could use a little help puttin' my 'DART together," he said to Gordon and Pons, as he neared. Then holding them aloft, he said, "Only got two hands. Better with four."

"We could use a little help ourselves," said Gordon, "This contraption is a new issue I'm not familiar with."

"That's not surprising, Commander. We're only the second unit to ever deploy 'DARTs on a mission. They're still warm from the box. In fact, technically, Colonel Pons there and I were the first men ever to fly 'em into action,"

"No one told me that!" said Pons, indignantly, now realizing he'd been 'guinea pigged,' without his knowledge or consent.

"You musta' been volunteered, Colonel," Lufkin said, with a short laugh.

"They did that to me?" Pons asked, truly shocked.

"Must've," said, the Chief. "I thought you knew or I woulda tol' ya."

Pons shook his head in disbelief. He was going to raise hell with somebody when they got back home.

When their vehicle was reassembled, Gordon helped Lufkin with his.

As Pons stood watching the SEALs work, he marveled at the quickness of the transformation of the ADARTs to ground vehicles. He had never been what one might consider a heavy mechanic of any sort, although he was excellent with lighter weight mechanical assemblies such as clocks, locks and the type used to animate the Servidor robots TMI was presently developing.

"Everyone's ready, Sy," Dexter said, distracting Pons from his musings.

"Let's inspect everything, just to make sure nothing's been overlooked."

Although Pons hated management with a passion, he was ironically, very good at it. He rarely failed to meet his goals.

Pons and Gordon inspected each two man team and vehicle carefully. Everything was in order. The SEALs were obviously very fastidious about details. Pons liked that and was pleasantly surprised, but Gordon had known what to expect. He knew just how good United States SEALs really were at what they did. They were the best soldiers on earth, bar none.

"Everything looks ship shape," said Pons, nodding his assent. "I think we're ready."

"Mount up, men," said Gordon. "Let's roll!"

173

29

The six 'DARTs reconfigured as ground vehicles were lined up facing down the sloping rock floor toward the cave-like opening of the qanat at the end of the funneling side walls. About eight feet high and ten feet wide, the gaping opening to the water tunnel swallowed the six small vehicles as they rolled inside.

Sitting in the front tandem driver seat, Gordon could clearly see the carved rock of the walls as it flashed past at about fifteen miles an hour. Though irregular and rough, the contours of the walls and ceiling were softened by a fine coating of yellow-brown sand that covered every little horizontal niche. The floor, by contrast, had been polished smooth from almost three millennia of water and sand flowing over it. Although there was now only a trickle of water running in the gutter-like depression in the center of the tunnel, Dexter noted that the walls widened and became smoother as they neared the floor. This was clear evidence that great quantities of water had washed through the qanat for considerable periods of time in the past. It occurred to Gordon that a good thunder shower in the mountains, where they had just entered the tunnel, might quickly fill the qanat floor to ceiling and drown them all like sewer rats. The realization left him feeling uneasy, but he consoled himself with the knowledge that there had been no rain predicted for the desert in the mission's weather briefing.

With the ceiling only inches from their heads, their relatively slow speed seemed much faster. It reminded Gordon of sledding face first down a snow covered hill. The nearness of the ground always made it seem much faster than it actually was.

Focusing once more on reality, he looked down the tunnel, and another much less pleasant image came to mind. The bright headlights illuminated the tunnel for a hundred feet or more, but the limited scope of Gordon's field of view and lack of background perspective gave him the impression they were in fact traveling down the inside of a large sewer pipe. The similarity was complete even to the trickle of water at the center of the rounded floor. The false impression that they were trapped made Gordon feel uneasy, but he clamped down on his imagination and forced his mind to banish his fears.

Every few moments, the back center wheel of the cart was shoved to one side or the other by the water worn rut in the center of the rock floor. Each time this happened, Dexter had to instantly adjust the steering to compensate for the small change in the cart's direction. It was annoying and it denied him any chance to relax. The continual tense vigilance required to keep the vehicle centered in the narrow tunnel caused a muscle to knot in the middle of his back.

"Why can you never find a parking space when you need one?" he said, over the intercom to Syman in an attempt at humor. There was no reply. Then he said, "This place looks like the inside of a sewer pipe."

"Um-ha," Syman grunted in reply, preoccupied with his own thoughts. His attention was also focused on seeing down the tunnel ahead but by looking over Dexter's left shoulder without cracking his skull as they bounced along.

In one more attempt at lightening his mood, Dexter said, "Maybe we should have just dumped a few thousand gallons of drain cleaner into the opening and flushed."

Still, Syman didn't laugh.

Dexter thought, the road to Hell couldn't be too much different from this place. Syman's probably as uneasy as I am.

Dexter's thoughts were diverted when the com-link clicked and he heard Petty Officer First Class Dean, the driver of the next cart behind them say, "Commander Gordon, we need to back off a little. The dust and the spray are reeking havoc back here. We're running blind and I've almost plowed into you several times."

Moments later, a roll call of agreement began, unbidden.

"Three aye."

"Four aye."

"Five aye."

"Six aye.".

"Sounds like we have a consensus for that decision, gentlemen," said Gordon, pushing the transmit button on his com-link to reply. "Spread out as far as necessary, but keep up. We don't want to bump into each other, but we don't want anyone left behind, either."

There was no reply to his order, which did not surprise him. He knew, as SEALs, they had been trained to speak only when necessary. 'No unnecessary chatter,' was a rule that had been endlessly repeated to them by their instructors, along with, 'Unnecessary talk gets men killed.' Gordon could still clearly remember his special forces instructors screaming these admonitions at anyone foolish enough to have spoken out of hand during his own training.

After a few moments, Gordon added, "Master Chief Lufkin, you sing out if you have any problems back there."

"Aye, aye, Commander," Lufkin replied and silence once again descended on the com-link circuit as the carts rolled toward the oasis of Nalut still eleven odd miles ahead down the qanat.

They rolled along without incident for a couple of miles. Bright white wells of light flashed past overhead every 500 yards or so as they rolled through small enlargements in the qanat's tunnel where spiraling stairways had been carved up the raw rock walls to allow the builders access to the life giving air above and to provide a way to remove the rock from the tunnel. When they arrived at the next lightwell, Gordon saw a pile of rock in the middle of the tunnel floor. He slowed the cart and came to a halt just before running into the rubble. "Shit," he said, under his breath. The sensitive interphone, nevertheless conveyed his expletive to Pons.

Looking up, they could see where a portion of the wall of the lightwell had crumbled down the shaft.

"Gentlemen," said Pons, pressing his com-link's transmit button. "We have a blockage in the tunnel."

Gordon and Pons dismounted from their cart to inspect the obstruction. The other carts rolled to a halt, one behind the other and the men sat waiting patiently to hear their officer's assessment

"We'll need to clear some debris from the floor up here, men," Gordon said, while pressing the transmit button on the com-link unit hanging from his belt.

Allowing himself to be momentarily distracted, he tried to imagine the ultraviolet light being pulsed from his com-unit's tiny laser emitters as they flooded the tunnel with intense flashes of invisible high frequency light, carrying his voice to the other com-link units. Unable to sense the pulses of light he knew were there, he turned his full attention back to the problem at hand.

The men were now gathering around the pile of rocks in the middle of the tunnel.

"Let's clear the road," Gordon said, in friendly command.

The men, beginning with Gordon and Pons, picked up the stones and carried them up the nearby stairway to dispose of them. About twenty feet up the steps, they placed the stones on the steps, using them as the only available dump site. Like a well ordered procession of ants, the line of men climbed up and down the stairway to dump their loads. In ten minutes, they had removed the debris and were rolling again. Forty minutes later, Dexter was getting anxious, expecting to see something down the tunnel. He did not want them to be seen, headlights blazing down the qanat, giving away their only real tactical advantage, the element of surprise.

"We ought to be getting close."

"I'm wondering if we've taken a wrong turn somewhere, but of course that's not possible," Syman replied.

"An hour ago I would have agreed with you, but now, I'm not so sure. Let's stop at the next light well, and reconnoiter."

"Seems like the logical thing to do," agreed Syman.

"We're going to do a recon at the next stairway, men. Be advised,"

They rolled along to the next opening and stopped. The other vehicles again halted behind them. Turning, Syman glanced back at the string of headlights in the tunnel behind them. It reminded him of a traffic jam he'd been in recently in the Holland tunnel under the Hudson River between New York and New Jersey. The tunnel's lights had gone out and the traffic had come to an abrupt halt. Then too, all he had seen behind him was a string of headlights stretching away in the dark.

"Let's go topside and have a look," said Dexter, interrupting Syman's thoughts.

Gordon keyed his com-link unit, "Petty Officer Charles!" he said. "Please bring the periscope up here."

There was immediate movement three carts back as one of its riders dismounted and opened the equipment locker on the side of the vehicle. Gordon and Pons watched the backlit silhouette of the man as he removed something long and narrow. Moments later he had sprinted up the tunnel to Gordon and Pons.

"We want to have a look, Chief," said Gordon. "Please set it up."

The Chief removed an olive drab and sand colored tube from the bag in which it had been zipped. It had a right angled eyepiece at one end and a large glass lens at the other. He draped the bag over Pons' and Gordon's cart and then ran up the stairway with Gordon and Pons close on his heels. As they neared the top, the intense desert sun made them squint their dazzled eyes. The pressure of its heat stunned them. They stopped climbing just before exposing themselves above ground. The Chief extended the lens end of the tube above the rim of the opening and scanned in a full circle before coming to a halt. Looking in the same direction they'd been traveling underground, he said, "It looks like we're clear, Commander."

"Let me have a look, Mr. Charles," said Gordon.

The periscope was handed to him and the Chief carefully climbed down the stairway past them, where he knelt to wait.

Gordon did the same thing as the Chief, checking their perimeter all the way around, coming back to his starting point.

Framed clearly in the strong amplifying optics of the device, Gordon could see seemingly featureless desert stretching away everywhere, except in either directions along the line of the tunnel, where he could see a faint track worn into the surface of the landscape. The barrenness of the place was startling and frightening, even to someone familiar with the most desolate of California's vast waste places. Gordon was struck by the feeling of utter emptiness. Only in the direction they were traveling was there a sign of life. Downhill from their position, off in the bright shimmering distance was the isolated desert settlement of Nalut. Gordon adjusted the laser range finder on the 'scope and saw the number 3090 displayed by the instrument's LED counter. He subtracted 1760, (the number of yards in a mile), in his head and came up with 1330. From earlier days, he remembered that 1320 yards was three quarters of a mile. Pretty close.

"We're one and three quarter miles from Nalut," he told his companions. Then he handed the instrument to Pons, who handled the instrument with less confidence and no familiarity.

"Your turn, Colonel Pons," he said as he followed the Chief's example and climbed down to give Pons room.

Pons stood up unsteadily as he put the instrument to his eye. He fiddled with the focus knob trying to look in the direction of Nalut. Balancing at the top of the precipitous circular stairway while trying to get the unfamiliar instrument to work properly Pons began to sway. Gordon reached up and grabbed his belt to steady his friend. Still, Pons felt very unsteady with nothing to hold onto. He lowered the 'scope and handed it to Gordon.

"To hell with that thing," he said, disgustedly. On his hands and knees he climbed the last few stairs and peered cautiously over the rim. Off in the distance, he saw Nalut sitting amidst the shimmering waves of heat floating up from the sand. He could see green fields surrounding the town's tawny mud colored buildings. Palm trees dotted Nalut right to the edge of the fields. Where the greenness stopped, he could see evidence of old dried up fields that were no longer irrigated. He could also clearly see that this garden town in the middle of the Sahara desert had once encompassed a huge area, just as Esmirelda, his desk top comparitor had told them a week before during her abbreviated geography lesson. Listening to the machine describe the place while sitting in the sumptuous comfort of his office at TMI, Nalut and the qanat had seemed somehow quaint and romantic. But now, peering over the edge of a hole in the sweltering desert and being confronted with the stark reality of the place, Pons wondered to himself, (not putting too fine a point on it), 'Just what the hell am I doing out here in the middle of the Sahara Desert?' Of course, rationally, he knew very well what he was doing there. Nevertheless, that didn't reduce the sharp feeling of unreality he was experiencing at that moment.

Reminding himself that precious time was slipping away, he struggled to concentrate once again on the scene before him. To his left, he could just make out the ragged line of a road leading northeast across the desert toward Tripoli.

"I think I see the road to Tripoli, but I don't see any traffic," Pons said.

"I saw it too," Gordon replied. "Do you see any military around?"

"I don't see any movement of any kind."

"You better let me back up there, Sy" Gordon said.

They switched places again.

Gordon climbed to the top, where Pons had been, now sure they would not be spotted by anyone nearby. He held the scope up and adjusted it and looked carefully over the ancient desert town spread out below him. He took in the green fields where he could see people stooped over working in the morning coolness. He carefully scanned the road, right to the gated wall of the town. He looked minutely for military or police, but saw none. He noticed there was a large helicopter sitting out in a courtyard-like area, just on the other side of the town's wall. It looked like the qanat passed right under the courtyard, but he wasn't sure, because his field of view was blocked by the town's wall and some buildings that backed up to the wall just to the left of the courtyard. He looked at the helo and saw the words 'Cargo Malta' painted on the side in two foot high letters.

"There's a large 'copter with the name 'Cargo Malta' painted on it. What do you suppose it's doing out here in the middle of nowhere?"

The question was rhetorical, but Pons seemed not to notice, answering offhandedly in his peculiarly literal way, "They must ferry a lot of personnel and material back and forth to here. It seems like a logical way to do it."

Annoyed by Pons' needless observation, Gordon glanced at his friend, and saw that he was staring fixedly, down the stairway, lost in thought.

Unknown to Gordon, Pons was busy searching his mind. The name 'Cargo Malta' seemed somehow familiar, but try as he might, he could not remember where he had heard it before.

Gordon turned his attention back to searching the town, "There's a pond on the far side of the town just inside the wall. That's where the qanat must come out."

Pons climbed up beside Gordon and peered over the lip of the stairs trying to see the things Gordon had described.

"They obviously walled in their water source to protect themselves," said Pons, knowingly. "Water out here is life itself and many dry land cultures walled in or hid their wells. Water in the desert is power."

"It surely must be, considering how much work they did digging this tunnel," said Gordon. "And to think they did it all by hand. What could have possessed them to go to all the trouble?"

"Essy said the climate has been getting drier since the last ice age. I would guess that when they saw their old water source drying up, they decided to bury it, to conserve and protect it from evaporation. There was probably a river at one time in that ditch over there," said Pons, pointing to a spot behind them, where the track along the line of the qanat dipped out of sight into a shallow wandering trench that more or less paralleled the qanat. Beyond that point the track reappeared only to disappear again further away into the same trench, where both disappeared behind a low rise slightly up hill of their position.

"They must have been nuts!" said Gordon, with conviction. "Why would anyone want to live way to hell and gone, out here in this wasteland?"

"You have to imagine what this place must have looked like six or eight thousand years ago," said Pons, ignoring Gordon's comments, "when that ditch was a wide stream flowing with clear, clean water. When men probably first settled here during the last ice age, North Africa was a very different place. There's actually a petrified forest out in the middle of the Sahara about 400 miles southeast of here. There were probably trees all over the place around here.

Listening to Pons with half an ear, Gordon began to imagine what the broad plain below would have looked like, when it was green and lush with miles of cultivated fields and a bustling community of happy farm families to tend them.

Grudgingly, he said, "Maybe it wouldn't have been too bad if there was more water out here."

"Well, I think we've seen all we need to," said Gordon, concluding their recon. He turned and began climbing back down the stairs toward the men waiting below. When the three men reached the bottom, they gathered the others for an impromptu planning session.

"Nalut is one and three quarter miles further down this tunnel, gentlemen," said Gordon. "We'll drive another mile at speed with the head lights on and then we'll stop. We don't know what we'll find at the end of this tunnel, so we need to send a scouting party ahead on foot to guide us. I'll lead that group and I want the men who aren't driving, one from each team to accompany me. That will give us a five man recon squad. The drivers will fix light sticks to the back of their vehicles and follow on, if and when they get the signal from the recon squad. Just exactly what we do at the end of this tunnel will depend on what we find when we get there. Any questions?" Gordon asked.

There were none.

After a moment, Gordon ordered, "Let's go!"

The men returned to their vehicles and the caravan proceeded down the qanat. About five minutes later, just past the last light well before reaching Nalut, Gordon brought his cart to halt and shut off the headlight. The rest of the drivers did likewise as they came up from behind.

"Okay, men," said Gordon in a 'no nonsense' tone of voice over his com-link. "We need our rifles. Two of you bring grenade launchers. One man, bring the C-4 pack. The last man and I will bring extra ammo clips for all of us. Everyone wear your night vision equipment and bring water and an extra flash light. If we get cut off from the vehicles, we'll have about ten hours in the sun out here in the desert before dehydration starts killing us.

Now, for you men with the vehicles. As soon as we know what we're facing, we'll let you know. Getting the hell out of here, in one piece, with the bomb cores is a must if we're to succeed with our mission, to say nothing of living to fight another day." There was just a hint of ironic humor in Gordon's voice, but the subject matter he was discussing was deadly serious and none of the man laughed.

"Over flights indicate a large amount of earth and rock was recently dumped just outside the town's wall. Also, a radioactive source was detected in the vicinity of the tunnel's entrance, so we're expecting to find an industrial facility underground near there. The terrorists thought they could build the bombs underground and not be observed. Fortunately, they have no knowledge of how sensitive our detection equipment really is." Gordon paused for a moment and then continued, "Now, if the tunnel is blocked completely and there is no way to get the vehicles out, then the drivers are to turn the 'DARTs around in that lightwell we just passed. That way, we can make a hasty retreat through the qanat when we've got what we came for. We'll have the advantages of surprise and confusion. They won't know we came in through the water tunnel if we're careful in our approach. On the other hand, if the way is clear and we can drive out this end, it will allow us a faster, if more exposed escape. After we've got the bombs, if we get separated, each team is to drive out into the desert, find a safe place and change their 'DART back to flying mode for the return to the ship. We'll keep in touch via radio if we get separated. Everybody goes back. We don't leave anyone behind, dead or alive. Understood?"

There was a chorus of, "Yes, Sir."

"During our recon at the stair back there, we didn't see any military or police personnel. That doesn't mean there aren't any, but there's probably not a large protecting force in the town. Nevertheless, don't take anything for granted. Keep a sharp eye on each other's back. Remember what our instructor's told us in training, 'It's the unexpected that will get you killed!' That's the truth, so watch very carefully as you move. Any questions? Count off and reply!" Gordon finally ordered.

"Two! No questions, Sir," came back immediately over the com-link.

"Three! No questions, Sir."

"Four! No...

The men reported in order, until Gordon heard the final, "Six! No questions, Sir."

30

Dexter paused in silence for a moment to think if there was something he was forgetting. He keyed his com-link, "Seaman Aboulli, I read in your file your family emigrated to the U.S. from Tunisia when your were a child and that you know the local dialect spoken around these parts. Is that true?"

There was a moment of silence on the open com-link and then Aboulli replied, "Yes Sir. I speak the local dialect. In fact, we flew over the little town where I was born on the way here, Commander."

Dexter could just make out a slight wobble in Seaman Aboulli's English, apparently a last remnant from his first language.

After a moments pause, Seaman Aboulli continued, "When it was decided to go into Libya a few days ago, I was transferred to this SEAL group from my group with Central Command because of my familiarity with the language."

"I'm glad to hear that. We'll need your help if we run into any locals and we need to talk. Are you the driver of your vehicle?"

"No, Sir. Petty Officer Ramirez is driver, right now."

"Okay. Before you come forward, go to six, Master Chief Lufkin, and get the radiation detector from him and bring it with you."

"Aye, Sir," Aboulli replied.

Three minutes went by before the men gathered around Dexter and Syman.

Just before leaving, Dexter turned to Syman and said quietly, "If there's no way out, we'll let you know." If we can't exit through this end of the tunnel, we'll have to go up that shaft to get to the town."

Syman nodded his understanding

"I'll test the com-link every 100 yards or so. When we get out of line of sight, they won't work, so I'll leave a man at those points along the way with their com-links on, set to relay messages. This is only a recon. We're not going into the town until we know how to get out of here. If it's clear, I'll let you know and then you can bring the 'DARTS along. We'll meet you at the end."

"Okay," said Syman. "Holler when you need us."

With that, Dexter stepped off down the tunnel at the head of the recon group. They walked along quietly, shining their flashlights on the tunnel floor. Except for small rocks, sand and other occasional debris, the tunnel was clear and they walked along easily.

Dexter tested the com-link at intervals of about a minute. Four minutes from the vehicles, the signal had grown weak. He walked a man back up the tunnel fifty yards and left him as a relay. Three minutes more walking and he had to leave another man. The dark tunnel would be spooky as hell for the men, alone at their relay points, but each man had a flashlight to push back the darkness. Gordon kept up a steady flow of chatter between himself and the men with the vehicles to keep the men's minds occupied.

When they'd walked along for ten minutes they began to hear small noises coming down the tunnel. At that point, Dexter and the two men with him put on their night vision visors. Turning off their flashlights, they opened a single cold light stick. They put it in a reflector backed holder that directed its light down and kept it from shining directly into their visors. The visors did their job well, amplifying the available light thousands of times. Through their visors the tunnel was brightly lit in hues of cathode ray tube green, allowing them to advance the last 200 yards, in what to the unaided eye would have been all but total darkness.

Finally, they saw a bright circle of light. Gordon sighed a breath of relief, seeing the way out was near at hand. He removed his visor. The outline of the tunnel showed itself in reflected light from the opening, but it was still dark in the tunnel without the light amplification equipment. Dexter took a small spyglass like monocular from a pocket and walked another hundred feet down the tunnel toward the opening. Bright sunlight streaming in the open end of the tunnel backlit the scene in stark silhouette making it difficult to see. The sunlight washed out most of the details and cast long shadows down the tunnel in Gordon's direction. Nevertheless, poor as the viewing conditions were, Gordon could see some significant things.

The tunnel had been greatly enlarged just inside the exit. It was now wide enough to drive a large truck through with room to spare. There were lights hung from the ceiling and they illuminated the entrance and two side tunnels on the right. He saw a pipe-railed concrete stairway on the left side of the tunnel giving access to what looked like a loading dock. As he watched, a loaded fork lift entered the tunnel through a large doorway on the left side of the tunnel just beyond the stairs. A squad of men with rifles at the ready ran along side the forklift in escort.

What, he wondered, was so important that it required an armed escort? In his mind's eye, he recalled the Cargo Malta helicopter they had seen. He decided instantly that the fork lift must be carrying a nuclear device to the aircraft.

"We may have arrived just in the nick of time, men." Dexter quickly described the scene before him over his com-link. His words were instantly relayed back along the tunnel to the men waiting with the 'DARTs.

"Colonel Pons, bring the vehicles. There is no time to lose."

After a moments hesitation Gordon heard, "Roger that. We're on the way."

Pons keyed his com-link, "You heard Commander Gordon, men. Let's move."

Almost as one, the file of vehicles moved quickly ahead toward Nalut, slowing only to scoop up the relays on the way. Three minutes later the vehicles reached Gordon's forward position.

"Here's the situation," Gordon said with no preamble, "There's a loaded forklift carrying something, probably a nuclear device, to a large helicopter with the name Cargo Malta just outside the tunnel's entrance. The forklift is accompanied by a squad of ten soldiers carrying rifles. I didn't see any heavy fire power. So, one, two, three, and four are going to drive through the facility at the mouth of the tunnel without stopping and take the forklift away from them. Five and six, I want you to stop at the mouths of the two side tunnels and set up a rear guard. There may be a large number of men inside here somewhere. If there is, you'll have to keep them bottled up. Our only advantage is that they won't be expecting us."

Gordon heard faint clicking sounds of weapons being readied." Remember men, 'It's the unexpected that gets you hurt,' so stay focused. Let's go."

Gordon worked the action on his weapon as Pons piloted them toward the tunnel's exit.

"Not too fast, Sy," Gordon admonished him, "We don't know what to expect."

"I'll slow us down when we're through the complex and almost in the sun."

"Still a fighter jock at heart, aye Pons?"

"You betcha, pardner."

A few moments later, they rolled out into a fierce blast of hot sunlight. As they emerged, they immediately saw they were too late. The helicopter was already lifting away to the northeast, engines straining with an earsplitting whine and the enormous rotor whop-whopping its booming concussive thump half a dozen times a second.

Over the cockpit's edge Dexter began firing carefully aimed shots up at the airborne machine. The gunner/rider of each of the 'DARTs did likewise as soon as they exited the tunnel.

The guard squad, momentarily startled by the surprise attack, dropped to the ground. Laying prone, the guards began shooting at the 'DARTs. Almost as quickly, the SEALs realized it was hopeless trying to knock the big 'copter down. Instead, they began firing at the prone defensive force. Although out in the open, the SEALs were protected by the Kevlar fabric skin of their 'DART's cockpits. Their cover gave them a distinct advantage and they proceeded to carefully pick off the defenders. When three of the guards had been shot, the rest ran for cover dragging their fallen comrades behind a nearby truck. Realizing there was no longer anything to protect and therefore, no point in getting themselves killed, the guards stopped firing at the SEALs and disappeared into the building behind their sheltering truck.

With the sudden quiet, Gordon's attention was drawn back to the tunnel, where from the sound of the gunfire, he could tell a serious situation had developed.

"Seaman Levine," he barked into his com-link microphone, "follow us back into the tunnel. Five and Six need our help."

"Aye, Commander," Levine replied.

"Five, Six! We're on our way!"

"Aye, One," said Master Chief Lufkin. "We could sure use a little help right now. We seem to have stirred up the hornets nest. It looks like we got us a barracks here in this side tunnel."

"Hang on, Chief. We'll be right there."

"Levine! Do you have some C4?" Gordon asked.

"Yes, Sir," the seaman replied

"Bring it to me when we get inside."

"Sy, stop just back from the side tunnel. I want to do the same thing to these guys that was done to us on the island. I want to bottle them up with a cave-in."

"Good idea, Dex," Syman agreed. "You're not only cute, but you're obviously educable, too, having learned from your recent past."

"Shut the hell up, Sy. This is serious," he rebuked his partner, but there was laughter in his voice.

The two 'DARTs came to a halt just before reaching the line of fire from the side tunnel where Five and Six had positioned themselves. Gordon keyed his com-link again, "Levine, hurry up and bring me the C4 and then you and Sykes cover our ass. We don't have any idea who might shoot us from those other doorways there up the tunnel."

Levine was already running up to him carrying the explosives as Gordon finished his instructions through the com-link. The seaman handed a brick of C4 and a small package of detonators to Gordon and nodded before turning away to join his teammate in establishing a covering position.

Shots whistled out of the now dark side tunnel and splattered on the opposite wall of the main tunnel. Ricocheting lead, rock fragments and dust filled the air of the intersection. It was a very dangerous place.

Chief Lufkin lay on his belly at the near corner of the intersection with his weapon aimed down the side tunnel. Every time he saw a sliver of light from a door opening or any other movement he squeezed off a round to dissuade the trapped garrison soldiers from trying to advance toward the main tunnel. Five Team, Petty Officer Harlon and Seaman Olszewski were similarly positioned across the side tunnel's mouth, one kneeling and one prone. The three kept up a sizzling continuous barrage guaranteed to discourage even the most stout hearted. So far, they were successful. With their night vision equipment they could quite clearly see the garrison soldier's every movement and there were now eleven of the garrison laying on the floor dead or wounded. The tunnel was thick with the acrid smoke of the gunfire, the air almost too foul to breath. Nevertheless, several men from the garrison had made it about half the fifty yard distance to the intersection before they were pinned down behind pallets of supplies and miscellaneous equipment sitting along the side of the tunnel. For their part, the SEALs were equally determined. Despite the gloom, every time a garrison soldier tried to advance, he drew the combined fire of the three SEALs.

The grim nature of the battle was clearly evident. Some canned goods on one of the nearest pallets were leaking their contents onto the dark floor where it mixed with the blood of the dead soldier sprawled half hidden behind it. The cans had proven to be insufficient cover when Seamen Olszewski had fired a burst though them to stop the man's advance.

"We're going to blow this tunnel closed, men," Gordon said, in a loud voice. "I've got to stand where you are, Master Chief."

Chief Lufkin jumped up and moved aside. Gordon took half the C4 and formed it into a long thin rope of explosive. Reaching around the corner as far as he could, he wadded it in behind a pipe that circled over the top of the side tunnel. He threw the other half of the C4 to Petty Officer Harlon, who did everything the same way. Gordon then unrolled some prima cord and tossed the loose end to Harlon. Both men wrapped the prima cord under the pipe next to the plastic, leaving extra cord to loop along the floor. Finally, Gordon inserted a detonator into the end of the prima cord. A mini timer was mounted directly to the detonator.

"Okay, everybody. Turn your vehicles around and bug out! Sy, I'll hold them off and arm the timer when you've got the cart ready."

Pons waited for the others to turn and go. Then he pushed the vehicle backwards like a man moving a large motorcycle. Back in the driver's seat, he revved the 'DART's engine.

"Okay, Dex!" he shouted.

A furious fusillade had begun issuing from the tunnel when the garrison soldiers realized explosives were being placed at the mouth to their tunnel. As best as he could, Gordon had returned fire to keep them back. On Syman's signal, he fired one last spray side to side, set the timer for 15 seconds and then running, vaulted over the cockpit's edge onto the rear seat. The moment he hit the seat, he shouted, "Go!"

Pons took off down the tunnel toward air, light and freedom. Just as they reached the entrance there was an enormous explosion behind them. The blast wave hit them in the back like the kick from a Missouri mule.

186

"Oh my god," Gordon gasped, catching his breath. "I guess I overdid it, again."

"You could say that," said Syman, chiding his friend before smiling broadly. "Maybe I'm wrong and you're not so educable, Commander Gordon. Didn't you learn anything about blowing things up underground on that island?"

"Screw you, Syman." Gordon said, laughing. "We survived, didn't we?"

"Yes. Both times," Pons said, teasing his friend. When Gordon didn't respond, Pons asked, "What now, Fearless Leader?"

"Well, for one thing," Gordon said, without missing a beat, "you should call the carrier and tell them to keep an eye on that helo in case it's carrying a nuke. And when the dust clears from the tunnel, we'll have to go back inside and look around."

Pons immediately took out the Sat-Link and called the special number that had been set up to connect them directly to the carrier communications center.

Gordon paused a moment while Pons placed the call and talked with the Captain of the Tarawa. Staring off in the distance, eyes unfocused, Gordon collected his thoughts. Then he keyed his com-link.

"Seaman Levine, did you and Seaman Sykes encounter any resistance from the areas further in the tunnel?"

"Negative, Commander," Levine replied.

"You see anyone?"

"Negative, Sir,"

"Okay men, as soon as the dust clears, we've got to go back inside and investigate the rest of the place. Two, Three, and Five, you maintain positions out here. So far, we don't seem to be drawing the locals, but keep a sharp eye and report any change in status, immediately. Four and Six, you follow Colonel Pons and me inside. Acknowledge by count," Gordon ordered.

"Two, aye, Three, aye...Six, aye."

"Let's go," Gordon said, seeing the tunnel was clear.

Two, Three, and Five waited for One, Four, and Six to reenter the tunnel. Two, Three and Five then positioned theirs vehicles in a semicircle in front of the opening in a protective cordon ready for fight or flight.

When Gordon and Pons reached the intersection again, the scene was havoc. The roof of the side tunnel had caved in and blocked it from floor to ceiling, just as they had intended. It also blocked almost all of the main tunnel as well, but there was a sliver of an opening far up on the right of the pile of rubble.

"We'll need to bring the radiation detector, Chief," Pons said to Lufkin, handing him the device.

"Aye, Sir."

"We'll need our night vision equipment, flashlights, and light arms,"

Gordon directed. "Mr. Ramirez," Gordon said to Seaman Aboulli's teammate. "Stay here and stand relay. Keep a tight eye on things and call if you need us. Although I think it highly unlikely, I don't want any of the garrison soldiers digging out and catching us unaware. Don't hesitate to call us. Okay?"

"Yes, Sir," replied Petty Officer Ramirez.

"Seaman Aboulli," Gordon commanded, "you come with us in case we find someone in here we need to talk to."

"Aye, Sir," the seaman said in response.

Gordon keyed his com-link, "How are you men outside doing? Any activity?"

"Negative, Commander," came the nearly instantaneous reply.

"Okay, everyone, stay focused. It really is the unexpected you have to watch out for," concluded Gordon.

With that, Gordon proceeded to climb the rubble and wiggle through to the other side followed by Pons, Chief Lufkin, and Seaman Aboulli.

Some of the lights were still on further in the tunnel. That surprised them, but it made their investigation much easier.

"Should we check the other side tunnel on the right or should we check the area where the fork lift came from first?" Asked Gordon, as if taking a vote.

"If you think that fork lift loaded a nuclear device aboard the helicopter, then we should first concentrate on the smallest area with the largest likelihood of yielding information, if not another nuclear device," Pons said, as they walked up the tunnel.

"Makes sense," said Gordon, "let's do it that way."

"Aboulli and I could check out the other areas, Commander," suggested Master Chief Lufkin.

Gordon thought about that for a moment and then said, "I don't want to split our force until we know more about what's going on in here."

"Yes, Sir."

As they came up to the doorway where the fork lift had exited, they brought their weapons up and prepared themselves for action. A large garage-like door had been rolled up on tracks suspended from the ceiling. Through the doorway was a short tunnel about 12 feet long which opened into a large room that had been excavated from the rock. There were rough stone pillars about every ten feet that went on in ranks across the open space. The rock pillars had been left to support the enormous weight of the roof above. The bare rock, including the pillars had been painted bright white to reflect the light from the long rows of fluorescent fixtures attached to the ceiling. The room was cavernous with a 12 foot high ceiling and an area about 100 feet square. It was full of machine tools, work tables, and open areas strewn with materials and parts. It looked like the inside of a large factory.

They stopped and listened intently. The place was silent as a tomb. There was no noise, no activity.

"Spread out and let's check this place out," Gordon ordered in a loud whisper.

They crept away toward the sides of the area and then advanced carefully, quietly, step by step. It took about four minutes to reach the far end of the space. They found no one. Coming together once again, Pons was the first to speak.

"I think I walked past the area where they assembled the device. Chief, I need the radiation detector."

Lufkin handed it to him. Pons quickly walked toward the center of the area to an open space with a cradle like stand in the middle. The stand was surrounded by electronic testing equipment of various types and a hand tool covered workbench, but the object that most drew their attention was an open lead lined box sitting on the floor next to it. Pons took the radiation detector and held it to the box. The LED counter raced upward as he approached indicating that it was radioactive.

"Damn!" said Pons, emphatically. "Stay away from that container," he instructed the other men. "In fact," he said, picking up a stout broom leaning against a nearby rock pillar, "I think I'll close it." He handed the detector back to Lufkin and with both hands, used the broom handle to flip the box's heavy lid shut.

"The material they're using is hot as hell," Pons explained, "which indicates that it's very concentrated and its high concentration indicates that it's not a very sophisticated device. I suspect they bought their fissile material on the Russian black market. It was probably an early model Russian bomb core."

"What makes you think that, Sy."

"In the early years of their nuclear program, the Russians built unsophisticated devices using a much more concentrated form of plutonium, but they were always dangerous to handle, much more radioactive. In fact, the United States did the same thing at first, but then our scientists realized we could make more bombs with less concentrated plutonium if we made them more sophisticated. Since the plutonium was the most expensive and difficult material in the bombs, it made a lot of sense."

Skipping over Syman's impromptu history lesson on atomic bomb development, Gordon said, "Syman, Bandar's list said the uranium was acquired in the United States. He wouldn't have bought a Russian bomb core in the United States."

"Why not?" asked Pons. "The U.S. is the perfect place for a Russian to peddle a pilfered nuclear bomb core. The U.S. is the center for all kinds of world commerce and the Russian underworld has deep ties and connections in our country."

"Yeah, so?" replied Gordon skeptically.

"Well, just because the deal was made in the United States doesn't necessarily mean the core was ever there.

"That's possible," said Gordon.

"It doesn't appear there are any other devices in here. I think they only have one device." said Pons. He scanned the immediate area again and then said, "Let's look around carefully and see what else we can find. I'll take this area. Dex, see if you can find anything resembling an office in here."

With that, the men turned away from the assembly area and began inspecting everything they came upon. Pons walked to a tool box unit full of drawers. He opened one drawer after another, looking carefully at the contents of each. When he'd finished that, he began inspecting a work table covered with more electronic testing equipment. It was then that he noticed that all the electronic equipment was manufactured by Kyoto Electronics Limited. Kyoto Electronics was located in Kyoto, Japan, just as its name suggested to anyone who took a moment to think about it. The company's products had a reputation for being some of the finest quality testing equipment made on the planet, right up there with Hewlett Packard, Digital Equipment and Hughes Electronics.

As Pons thought about this, his photographic memory brought forth a picture in his mind. The last place he'd seen the name Kyoto Electronics was on a list of names of companies that were subsidiaries of Hinode Worldwide. Here was Hinode, once again lurking behind the scene. Pons had first taken note of Hinode when Dexter and Karrie had been shanghaied into the back of a Carrier Services Limited truck and then onto the ship, Hana Maru. Both vehicles belonged to subsidiaries of Hinode Worldwide Ltd. of Tokyo, Japan. It was a funny coincidence and Syman, always suspicious of coincidences, had decided to do a little more research on Hinode. His digging had generated the list of Hinode subsidiaries. The coincidence was just a little too convenient.

As he considered this, another association clicked into place in his brain. He walked back to the tool box and saw that all the tools and other equipment were made by Japanese companies. This fact, in and of itself, might not have been significant, but it only took a moment's thought to verify that everything in this room had been manufactured by a Hinode Worldwide subsidiary.

A dark realization formed in Pons' mind and he now saw a pattern of involvement more malevolent than anything he'd previously considered. He now knew the terrorists and the Libyans were not working alone and that the Japanese were somehow involved.

Syman knew that Japan imported enormous quantities of oil from all the middle east oil producers. He made a mental note to check on Libya's contribution to the total. He suspected he would find an awful lot of Libyan crude was being carried in Hinode bottoms.As he considered this, one more name swam into his awareness. Cargo Malta was also on the list of Hinode companies. Now he knew why finding the Cargo Malta helicopter in Nalut had troubled him, when he'd first seen it.

With this realization, Syman Pons was certain he'd uncovered a very dark secret. Hinode Worldwide, Japan's largest industrial company, was deeply involved in a conspiracy that threatened the United Stated of America and the consequences of that could only be described as ominous. What they were involved with here might have international ramifications as serious as the Cuban missile crisis.

Pons called to Gordon, "Dex, I think I've discovered something important."

Gordon quickly made his way to Pons.

"What is it, Sy?"

The other two men were converging on Pons, as well.

"I think the Japanese might be involved with this business." Pons quickly explained everything to Gordon. The other two men listened intently but said nothing.

Summing up his facts Pons said, "First we have the trucking company that owned that container they kept you in. Then, there's the Hana Maru. Now we find a helicopter owned by a Hinode subsidiary ferrying supplies out here in the middle of nowhere, and all this equipment was made by other Hinode subsidiaries."

"Hot damn! That's just too many coincidences to be random. I think you're on to something, Sy."

Pons turned to the other men, "Did you find anything interesting?" he asked.

"No sir," said Chief Lufkin.

"I didn't either, sir," said Seamen Aboulli, "but now that you mention it, everything I've seen in this place is Japanese."

"Did you find an office, Dex?"

"No, there's no office."

"We've seen everything of value in here, I think," said Pons.

"In that case," said Gordon, "let's have a look at that other side tunnel."

With that, the four men withdrew back into the main tunnel.

"Ramirez. Anything to report?" Gordon asked over the com-link.

"No, Sir. Everything's quiet, so far," the SEAL replied.

"We're going to investigate the other side tunnel,"

"Aye, Sir," replied Ramirez.

With Gordon in the lead, the four men headed straight up the tunnel to the other side shaft. Twenty feet down the tunnel on the left side was a large steel double door. It opened into a humming machine room. The room was a cavern carved in the rock. It contained a generator, large fuel tanks, air conditioning equipment, water piping and all the mechanical systems needed to make living underground possible. Ducts, pipes and wires entered the chamber from many different places. The men spread out and carefully searched the space, but they found nothing of importance.

They continued down the side tunnel where they next found a large storeroom behind another set of double steel doors. There were boxes of food, clothing and paper goods, but again they found nothing of significance, except that everything in the place was Japanese.

"It looks like our friends from Hinode may be provisioning this place," said Pons, as he looked around the room.

Directly across from the storeroom they found a large dining mess full of long chaired tables. It too was empty. Adjacent to it was the kitchen.

"Looks like nobody's home in here either," said Master Chief Lufkin. He walked over to a large refrigerator door and yanked it open. Inside he saw a small man huddled against a stack of cardboard boxes. The man was wearing a traditional white chef's uniform and he had wrapped himself with half a dozen cloth vegetable sacks to no avail. Shivering violently, he looked up at Lufkin with frightened eyes.

"I've found a man hiding here in this reefer, Commander," he yelled to Gordon. "I think he's the cook."

Master Chief Lufkin waved the huddled little man from his crouched position inside the walk-in refrigerator. The cook stumbled over the threshold, too stiff with cold to lift his feet very high. Lufkin shot out a big beefy hand and caught him before he tumbled onto the stone floor of the kitchen.

Gordon, Pons, and Seaman Aboulli gathered with Lufkin round the man.

"Aboulli, try talking to him," Gordon ordered.

Seaman Aboulli spoke to the man in the clipped guttural tones of his childhood language. The half frozen cook looked at him with surprise but said nothing through his clenched teeth.

Then after a moment of uncontrollable shivering the little man answered with a few guttural exclamations of his own.

Aboulli translated. "The man says he's the cook."

"Okay," said Gordon. "Ask him if there are any more people down this side tunnel."

Seaman Aboulli complied with Gordon's request.

The cook croaked again, this time a little longer.

"He says there haven't been any people in the hospital since the Japanese doctors left."

Gordon and Pons looked at each other for a moment, wondering at the significance of this new information.

Pons asked, "What hospital?"

Aboulli queried the dark little Arab again. After a minute of banter between the two, Aboulli began explaining, "He says there were a lot of Japanese doctors here until a few months ago. They were here for a couple of years before the Japanese machine people. He says it was a strange sort of hospital. When his wife was sick the doctors refused to help her. There were no people in the hospital, only a lot of animals, mostly monkeys and rats. He knows, because they made him prepare food for the monkeys in the kitchen."

"What in the hell is he talking about?" Gordon exclaimed.

Forsaking military formality for a moment, Pons said, "Hold on, Dex. I want to find out more about this hospital."

"Mr. Aboulli, ask the man to show us where the hospital is."

Aboulli did as asked and the Arab led them toward the door of the dining mess and into the side tunnel. Once in the tunnel, he turned left and walked 75 yards to the end of the tunnel and yet another set of large steel double doors. He pointed and spoke to Seaman Aboulli.

Pons tried to open the doors but they were locked.

"Syman, be careful," Gordon admonished his friend. "We don't know if this guy is really a cook. He might be leading us into a trap."

"That thought had occurred to me," said Pons, "but I think it's important we investigate this hospital if hospital there be."

"Master Chief, shoot the lock off the right door," commanded Gordon.

"Just a moment, please, Commander Gordon," said Pons, returning to formal military speak. "I would like to try something first."

With pick in hand, Pons proceeded to work on the door. It took but a few moments before the door clicked open. They saw only darkness on the other side.

Gordon took out his flashlight and approached the doorway warily. He shined his light in and quickly looked around. The bright beam revealed what looked like a dark uninhabited medical laboratory. Seeing no one, he found a panel of light switches next to the door and switched one. A long row of fluorescent lights flickered to life on the right side of the space. The area resembled the other large space they'd inspected. Gordon switched on the rest of the lights. In a few moments it was daylight bright in the underground room.

Aside from the ubiquitous rock pillars supporting the ceiling and the bright white enamel paint, there were rows of large animal cages ranked all around the available wall space. There were also several freestanding rows of the same size cages at the back. In front of these were hundreds of smaller cages, (apparently for the rats the cook had told them about), stacked ten high, also in long rows parallel to the larger freestanding cages.

All the cages sat atop low raised concrete platforms. There were drains in the middle of the platforms and curbs at their edges to facilitate cleaning the cages. There were also rubber hoses coiled on wall hangers at strategic places near the cages and connected to a piping system hung from the ceiling to provide water.

Each cage had a plastic holder on its front and each of these held an index card with Japanese writing in bold strokes of black magic marker.

All the cages were empty but the air held the smell of a veterinarian's office, with pungent spicy chemical smells riding atop the smell of animal waste and strong detergent. Having been closed and unused for a long time, the fetid air in the space was unpleasant.

To the left and right of the door were large stainless steel worktables covered with medical equipment and instruments. The room looked vaguely like a morgue and in fact, one table had gutters along its edges which emptied into a sink next to it. It obviously was an autopsy table.

The tables further back toward the cages were mostly bare except along the left wall. There, several tables held lab equipment. As the men fanned out to inspect the room, Pons walked toward the equipment laden tables. As he got closer he recognized an autoclave sterilizer, a centrifuge, and a microscope amidst a bewildering assortment of complicated machines and fixtures. He took his time and looked carefully at everything and tried to understand what had been going on here.

Beside the tables were several cabinets and five freezers. He proceeded to methodically open and inspect each of these, beginning with the cabinets. The cabinets contained lab equipment. Glassware, electrical and mechanical apparatus, tubes, spools of wire and other pieces of lab equipment were neatly stored inside. Two cabinets contained bottles of chemicals. Another contained only racks of clean test tubes. The last contained boxes of latex surgical gloves, paper towels and several neatly folded piles of green surgical uniforms.

Again he saw that everything was of Japanese origin. He could feel anger rise in himself at the realization. With an effort he reined in his emotions and concentrated his attention back on his inspection.

Pons was now almost sure the lab had been used for biotech research of some kind and the implications of that were truly frightening, considering that these same people may have just finished building a nuclear bomb. With that in mind, he approached the freezers with trepidation. For a moment he considered omitting the freezers from his inspection. The idea of opening a Pandora's box full of biological weapons made his blood run cold. Nevertheless, after a moment's hesitation, he steeled himself and opened the first of the freezers. It was empty. The inside was clean and dry. The machine was not running. A wave of relief swept over him, but it was short lived. There were four more freezers and all were turned on. Gingerly, he opened them one after another, but aside from a thin coat of ice on their metal walls, they also contained nothing.

Dexter walked over from the other side of the room.

"Find anything?" he asked his friend.

"I think they may have been doing biological weapons research in here,

Dex," he said without preamble.

"Shit, I hope not," Gordon said, smiling grimly, "My mother would be very disappointed if I caught something wandering around in here I wasn't born with."

Pons didn't laugh and Gordon's attempt at humor fell flat, because they both knew how close to the truth it might be.

Gordon turned and walked over to the last table. Sitting on it was some type of rectangular appliance. It was painted mud brown and Gordon could hear the quiet sounds of a fan coming from its rear. An orange light glowed through a half inch diameter plastic lens set in the box's metal front and there was a chrome handle with a keyed lock set into its lidded top. Gordon casually tried to open it. The spring loaded top rose easily to his touch.

Inside were a half dozen frost covered stoppered test tubes. The appliance was a miniature freezer.

"I think I've found something here," Gordon said.

Pons, who had not yet inspected this last table, walked over quickly and looked at Gordon's discovery.

"Don't touch that, Dex," Pons sternly commanded his friend, seeing he was about to pick one of the tubes from its place.

Gordon froze and then drew his hand back.

"I guess it might not be smart to handle those with bare hands, ay?"

Pons shook his head but made no reply. Holding a finger up to indicate his desire for an undisturbed moment, he rubbed the skin around his mouth with his thumb and forefinger as he thought about what to do next. He looked toward the cabinets he'd just inspected. Walking to the third cabinet in line, he opened it, bent over and removed a large stainless steel Thermos he'd seen just a few moments before. He then walked to the cabinet at the far end and took out a box of latex surgical gloves and a roll of the Japanese paper towels.

Seeing the Japanese writing on the wrapper again made him angry. The idea that the Japanese and some terrorist organization were making nuclear and biological weapons together here in this underground bunker was nearly unthinkable. Again, he suppressed his thoughts. Now was not the time to think about it.

As he walked back to the table Pons put on a pair of the gloves. Then he put a second pair on over the first. Thus equipped, Pons reached into the small freezer and removed one of the test tubes he'd just told his friend not to touch.

"Do as I say not as I do, right Sy," Dexter chided his friend.

"I want to bring these with us for testing, Dex. They may be lethal, so we have to try to keep them from leaking, but we have severe space constraints." As Pons explained he pushed the tube into a finger of another new unused latex glove. Then he took the finger gloved test tube and pushed it into a finger of a second glove, double wrapping it.

"See if you can find some wire in one of those cabinets over there, Dex. We need twist ties to keep these gloves shut."

Gordon quickly began searching for wire in the cabinets.

"How much do you need?" he asked.

"There are six to wrap, so I guess we'll need about three feet."

After a fruitless search for the right kind of wire, he decided they could use some twine he'd found instead. He broke off a foot of the string and held it out to Pons.

"You tie," said Pons, refusing the proffered twine.

Pons had four of the six test tubes double bagged in latex gloves and Gordon gingerly began tying them shut. When all six were bagged, Pons then wrapped each one in a generous padding of paper towel. Finally, he unscrewed the top of the stainless steel Thermos container and carefully pushed the little paper bundles inside using extra towels to fill all the space inside the Thermos.

"Well, I'm not sure I'd want to Fedex this thing back to the U. S." Pons said, with sardonic humor, "but it will have to do."

"You carry it," Gordon said, with his own sardonic comment.

Pons looked at his friend and chuckled.

"Now what?" Gordon asked.

"Did you find anything else interesting in here?"

"No, it's a dry hole."

"I wouldn't exactly call it that," Pons said to Gordon, holding out the now closed Thermos.

"Stop trying to pawn that damn thing off on me, Syman," Gordon chided his friend, "You're the one who packed it. You carry it."

They both laughed as they stripped off their gloves.

"Well Mr. Wizard, I think it's probably time we mount up and get the hell out of Dodge."

"Yes, I think you might be right," said Pons.

They walked to the door where Seaman Aboulli and Master Chief Lufkin were waiting with the cook, having toured the rest of the facility without finding anything of significance.

"It's time to go gentlemen," Gordon said.

The five men headed back toward the main tunnel, bypassing the mess hall and kitchen, amidst protests from the now less frightened cook.

"He says he wants to get his clothes from the kitchen," Seaman Aboulli translated.

They stopped a few yards past the mess hall doorway.

"Ask him if there's another military or police garrison here in Nalut," Gordon instructed, ignoring the man's concerns about his property. Aboulli asked the cook a question. The cook answered. Aboulli asked him another. Again the cook answered. This went on for a minute and then Aboulli turned to Gordon and Pons.

"He said except for the soldiers living here underground, there are no other military people around Nalut, but he says the town has two policeman. He also said there's a border patrol unit of soldiers in Dehibato, about ten miles west of here at the highway border crossing to Tunisia. They're the nearest soldiers."

"Why would this guy tell us all this?" Gordon asked out loud.

"Sir, I asked him that. He said he hates the soldiers and the government. They forced him to close his little restaurant and come here to cook. At first he didn't want to do it, but they beat him and raped his wife and daughter and told him worse would happen if he continued to refuse. He said he'd do anything to get rid of Kadafi and his cutthroats."

"Poor bastard," said Gordon, feeling sorry for the man. "Tell him to go into the kitchen and stay there for ten minutes and not to come out until we've gone. And tell him we're sorry about his family."

Gordon had been looking at Pons while he said this and Pons had nodded his agreement.

Aboulli translated Gordon's words. The cook's eyes widened when he heard what Gordon had said and then he bowed repeatedly before scurrying toward the kitchen.

The four Americans headed in the opposite direction with no less vigor for the hole in the rubble pile in the main tunnel and freedom.

Upon reaching the sunlight again, Gordon and Pons conferred on their next course of action.

The 'DART's were still drawn up in a tight defensive semicircle. The hunkered down men vigilantly scanned the open area surrounding the outflow from the qanat. Nothing had changed during the thirty minutes they'd been investigating the rest of the underground facility.

"All's quiet, Colonel Pons," said Petty Officer Harlon, Five Team's leader, as Gordon and Pons approached. "There's been no activity since the firefight."

"Good," said Pons, meaning it wholeheartedly.

Pons went to their 'DART. He put the Thermos with its dreaded cargo in a side pouch next to his seat. Then he retrieved his laptop computer and the SatLink phone and connected them together with a small cable. Dialing the special military interface number he'd been given, the mobile phone connected directly to the aircraft carrier Tarawa's combat information center via a Pegasus geosynchronous communication satellite stationed in space 22,000 miles above them.

"This is Colonel Pons. I want to speak with the Captain and John Claire."

"Aye, Sir. He's right here," said the sailor aboard the Tarawa. Pons realized they had been standing by waiting for him to call again.

A moment later, he heard the Captain's voice.

"What's your status, Colonel Pons?" the Captain asked.

"We're still at the objective. We've been here a half an hour, but we're ready to return. We need your position. My computer is up and ready to download your GPS information."

"Roger that. Just a moment," the Captain replied.

"A helicopter took off just as we got here and we believe it might be carrying the nukes they were making. Do you see it?"

"We're tracking it, Syman," said John Claire, speaking for the first time.

"Good," said Pons. "We've also found some evidence of biologicals here. We're bringing along some samples to be checked."

"By biologicals, do you mean as in weapons?" asked Claire.

"Affirmative," said Pons.

A map scrolled onto the computer's screen. It showed an X about one hundred miles off the coast of Libya in the Mediterranean half way between the island of Malta and Tripoli, the Capitol of Libya. It was flanked with the ship's numerical co-ordinates.

"We're still on the ground and in ground mode. We're going to drive toward Jadu on the road and then out into the desert, south of the Jabal Nafusah hills, where we'll find a secluded place to reconfigure the 'DART's to their flying mode. That should take about an hour and a half. With that in mind, can you project a vector that will bring us home."

"Give us a minute, Colonel Pons" said the Captain.

His voice was tinny and difficult to hear, coming as it was from the small speaker of the laptop. Bright sunlight made it difficult to see the screen. Pons tried adjusting the screen to shield it from the glare of the now fierce sun beating down on them. As he watched, the screen scrolled another copy of the same map with the present position of the carrier and the projected position of the carrier for the rendezvous. It also showed a dashed line beginning at a point in the desert northeast of Nalut on the far side of the Jabal Nafusah hills. The line entered the Mediterranean just south of the coastal town of Misratah, extending straight out about ten miles before turning due north toward the carrier.

"That position assumes you drive 15 miles out of town in forty-five minutes, you reconfigure in forty-five minutes, you fly at nominal cruising speed and you cross the coast right at the east end of the Gulf of Sidra on your return flight."

"I have it here on my screen, Captain," said Pons. "I hate going between Tripoli and Bengazi. With their two largest air bases in those cities, we're taking quite a risk."

"I understand your concern, Colonel, but it can't be helped. With the 'DART's stealth capabilities, if you fly low and fast, you should be all right. We've got a P-3 in the air and there's still no unusual air activity anywhere over Libya. You said you've been at the facility a little over half an hour. They must know something's going on there by now, but they still haven't sent any planes up."

"Yes, and that worries me," said Pons. "I guess we better get moving before they do."

"Look, we'll keep an eye on you with the P-3. If we can't see you, they can't see you. The P-3's radar is better than their ground radar. If we see you, we'll holler loud and clear. We'll also send escort aircraft if there's trouble. We can have a Harrier over you guys in 19 minutes and a couple of gunships in half an hour and they're standing by, right now. If we see them move in your direction, we'll come running, right away."

"I hope it doesn't come to that," said Pons wearily. "We'll call you when we're in the air."

"Roger that Colonel," said the Captain.

"We'll see you soon," said John Claire.

"Okay, we're outa here," said Pons.

He put the computer in suspend mode, disconnected the SatLink, and quickly put both away in their carrying cases.

"Let's go, Dex."

"You bet," Gordon replied. "Let's get rolling, men," he said to the waiting team.

All six 'DARTs lined up single file. They quickly wound their way through the deserted streets past the ancient sun bleached houses of Nalut before turning onto the road to Jadu. Traveling through the town, they saw no one and wondered where the people were. They did pass three skinny dogs sleeping together in the shade of a side street but not another living soul. Gordon and Pons discussed it.

"Maybe they just stay indoors during the heat of the day," suggested Gordon. "But then, we did see people working out in the fields."

"Maybe, they heard the gunfire and are hiding," concluded Pons.

"That's more likely," agreed Gordon.

Pons reached down beside his left leg and checked the stainless steel Thermos to make sure it was still securely in the cockpit's side pouch where he'd put it. It was still there.

The road to Jadu was the same road they had scouted earlier from the qanat's stairway. It wound up into the Jabal Nafusah hills north of Nalut, the same hills where the qanat had its source, but the road trended away from the line of the qanat. They followed the road until it reach the crest of the hilly range. At that point they turned off the road which continued on east north east toward Jadu. They headed due east down into the Gharyan basin of the Sahara. They drove the 'DARTs carefully along a sheep track that dropped steeply toward the shimmering desolate flats far below. Now well into the heat of the day, the land rippled and wavered in the distance. The dry heat was so intense it evaporated perspiration the moment it appeared on the skin and the charcoal gray color of the 'DART's Kevlar fabric, which made it so difficult to see at night, now made the small enclosed cockpit insufferably hot.

"What do you suppose God was thinking the day he created this place?" Gordon asked, by way of comment, expecting no answer from Pons. The scene before them was more desolate and forbidding than anything Gordon had ever seen in the worst deserts of California. Far to the southeast low corrugated sand dunes rippled away to the horizon. Gordon realized those sand dunes marked the true beginning of the trackless wastes of the Sahara, and he was very glad they were going in the opposite direction.

They rolled downhill slowly, bumping and sliding all the way. After twenty five minutes, the track turned back on itself and became extremely rocky for several hundred yards. It was too rocky for the 'DARTs and they had to abandon it and head straight down hill. Finally, just before they reached the bottom, they found themselves on a steep bluff, the last shoulder of the foothills above the flat immensity of the Gharyan Plain. From the bluff, the descent was too steep to head directly downhill. Instead, Gordon turned to the left, following the edge of the bluff. From his elevated position, he could see that half a mile to the north east the descending bluff blended seamlessly with the Gharyan's flat plain. Gordon relaxed a little, seeing the last of the way down would be relatively easy.

Like a line of marching ants, the 'DARTs descended, one behind the other, rolling along the edge of the bluff.

"One!" Gordon and Pons heard Master Chief Lufkin's loud agitated voice yell over the com-link." Five just went over the edge. The bluff let go and they're rollin' down the hill!"

Gordon stopped instantly. They both strained to look back over their right shoulders to see Five Team's 'DART roll over and over down the steep hill toward the bottom. Horrified, the SEALs watched helplessly as their mates were slammed around like rag dolls, still strapped into their machine. When the vehicle reached the bottom, it stopped on it side and lay motionless. There wasn't a sound and there was no movement from Petty Officer Harlon or Seaman Olszewski.

A moment later, Gordon gunned the engine and had them speeding down the remainder of the bluff, recklessly ignoring the danger. At the bottom, he hauled the 'DART around and roared back toward Five team and their overturned vehicle.

For Pons, who was presently riding as the passenger, there was nothing he could do and time telescoped, slowing everything down to a crawl. Although it was only a minute before they rolled to a stop along side the battered 'DART, it had seemed to take much longer to reach it.

Pons and Gordon were out in a moment and beside the 'DART inspecting the motionless men. The other 'DARTs rolled up, one right after the other and as each machine came to a halt, the occupants quickly jumped out and ran over to help.

"Let's roll it onto its wheels," Gordon commanded, when there were enough men for the task.

"Gently!" he yelled. "We don't won't to hurt them anymore than they already are."

Petty Officer Ramirez, the team's medical corpsman, took control of handling the injured men.

"Hold the Petty Officer's head so it doesn't move if you can, Master Chief," Ramirez ordered, as the others gently brought the 'DART onto its sprung wheels once again. Petty Officer Ramirez held Seaman Olszewski's head in a similar fashion.

"Aboulli, take over for me here," Ramirez said, firmly. "Sirs," he said, turning to Pons and Gordon, "I have to check their vital signs, and then we need to strap them down on some kind of stretchers. We have to immobilize their heads. If they have any neck injuries, we want to try and minimize any further damage, and we got a long way to go before we're home, alotta bumps, if you know what I mean."

"Understood, Mr. Ramirez," said Gordon.

"Could we use their stowed wing sections for stretcher frames?" Pons asked him.

Ramirez was thoughtfully silent for a moment and then said, "Yeah, we could use the wings, but then how are we going to fly their 'DART outa here? We can't fly their machine without the wings, if it will still fly, and we don't have any extra cargo capacity in the other 'DARTs. They're each carrying two men now."

"One problem at a time, Mr. Ramirez," said Pons gently, without a hint of criticism in his voice. "You have enough on your plate, right now, dealing with the injured. We'll get the wings ready."

"Aye, Sir," said the Petty Officer before turning back to the injured men.

"Sykes, Levine!" Gordon ordered quietly. "Remove the wings from Five Team's 'DART and rig them as stretchers."

The two men began their task immediately, worrying the wings from their stowage compartment at the bottom rear of the 'DART's frame.

Petty Officer Ramirez directed as the rest of the men gently removed Petty Officer Harlon and Seaman Olszewski from their seats.

Harlon had begun to moan, although his eyes were still rolled up in his head. His right arm twitched erratically. Ramirez wasn't sure what the significance of that was yet and so he strapped the man's arm to his side to restrain further movement while he looked him over.

Seaman Olszewski hadn't made a sound or moved a muscle, although his breathing was regular.

The two men were laid gently on the sand in the shade of the nearest 'DART and Ramirez got down to the business of a thorough examination.

He checked each man's pulse and blood pressure using a miniaturized electronic instrument he carried in his medical bag. It had a cuff just like the standard instrument a doctor would use to take someone's blood pressure, but there the similarity ended. The inflation bulb was built into the cuff and was pumped by squeezing with two fingers. Readings were shown on an LED screen, also built into the body of the cuff. It told him the patients pulse, blood pressure, and temperature.

He quickly determined neither man had problems in those areas. When he'd finished that, he examined their eyes, ears, noses, and inside their mouths. Again, he found no gross injuries to either man and that surprised him. Other than some bruises and a few cuts there was no sign of the massive head and facial trauma normally associated with a vehicle accident. He decided it was probably due to their rolling sideways down the hill rather than being slammed into something head on. Still, the fact that they were unconscious was ominous. Ramirez suspected they both had internal head injuries, which could be serious as hell. But until they woke up and began describing their symptoms, could be given a CAT scan, or died, Petty Officer Ramirez had no way of knowing what their true conditions were.

31

Master Chief Lufkin shook his head. "We ain't got the extra cargo capacity or space in the other five 'DARTs to carry Harlon and Olszewski strapped to them wings, Colonel. And there ain't no way we're gonna get this mother into the air again unless we pick her up and carry her."

Gordon and Pons stood with him looking at the wrecked carcass of the 'DART in which Chief Petty Officer Harlon and Seaman Olszewski had rolled down the bluff.

An idea along the lines of picking the wreck up and carrying it had already formed in Pons' mind.

"Chief, when you and I flew onto the Hana Maru, you told me about several different vehicle configurations of the ADART. It's suppose to convert to all sorts of other vehicles useful for combat."

"Yeah, that's right, Colonel. You and I went over that before the mission."

"Well, now I think it's time for a practical demonstration of the 'DART's versatility."

"What do ya have in mind?" Lufkin asked.

"One of the configurations you told me about was a hovercraft. You said it was intended to allow a fast assault group to carry heavier fire power to a battle, if I remember correctly," said Pons.

"That's right."

"Master Chief, would it be possible to reconfigure the vehicles we have here into a hovercraft?"

"Sure, we could do that," said Lufkin, "it only takes four 'DARTs to make a hover vehicle, Colonel. We got five and a wreck."

"Would a hovercraft have the cargo capacity to carry us all?" Pons queried the Master Chief.

"Well, let's see," said Lufkin, pausing to think about his answer. "A hovercraft's gross lift's about 8600 pounds. A 'DART configured for flight's gotta be less than 740 pounds max gross weight. Each of our six was just under that when we took off this morning. Now, if we got six machines we git..." Lufkin had to stop talking and close his eyes to do the multiplication in his head.

"4440 pounds," said Pons, after a moment.

"Yeah, that's the load. Now, subtract 4440 from 8600 and that leaves..." Again the Master Chief began torturous calculations.

"4160 pounds," said Pons, almost instantly, "in excess cargo capacity, just over two tons."

"Yeah, that sounds about right. I'll take your word on the numbers, Colonel, I can't do 'em, fast in my head."

"Does the gross weight of the 'DARTs include the weight of the passengers, Chief?" Gordon asked.

Yeah. That includes the passengers, cargo, fuel, everything, Commander," said the Chief.

"The next question is, can we load the hovercraft with the two extra 'DARTs."

"We know we got the lift capacity, Colonel. We just figured that."

"Right. But I mean, is there enough space to fit both vehicles and the men," Pons asked.

Lufkin was quiet for a moment, while he thought about it. "It might be a tight squeeze, but I think it'll do'er." After a pause, he added, "We could leave the wreck here, if we have to."

"We could, if we absolutely have to, Chief, but we're supposed to bring out anything we bring in," said Gordon.

Lufkin nodded.

"What is the forward speed of the hover configuration?" Pons then asked him.

"It'll go just over 45 knots, Colonel"

"How's it work?" Gordon asked.

The Chief explained, "Two motors are used to maintain the air cushion, and two motors are used to move it and steer it."

"One more question, Master Chief," said Pons, "Can the machine travel over water?"

"Sure, Colonel. The whole reason for the hovercraft's ta git the 'DARTs and some serious equipment ashore fast during amphibious insertions."

"Will it float?" asked Gordon.

"The four emergency flotation collars'll float her in a calm sea, if you don't have cargo, but you'd be takin' a hell of a chance. You might not be able to git the motors started again because they'd probably git soaked. You ain't supposed to shut her down over the water. Besides, she'll hover on only one motor, as long as you tarp off the other propeller duct. Won't have much clearance when you git ashore. Probably be draggin' the skirt, but she'll fly."

"If you think it'll work, Chief," said Pons "then make it so. It's too goddamn hot to stay here."

"Aye, Aye, Colonel," said Lufkin with a sharp salute before turning away to carry out this new order.

Gordon and Pons walked back over to where Petty officer Ramirez was working on the two injured men.

"How are they, Mr. Ramirez?" Gordon asked.

Petty Officer Harlon and Seaman Olszewski were now each strapped to one wing section of their 'DART. Neither man had regained consciousness, although Harlon moaned from time to time.

"I don't know how they are, Sir," replied the Petty Officer with a hint of nervousness in his voice, "but, I've done as much as I can for them."

Gordon wanted to know the full extent of their injuries, but he didn't want to badger the corpsman. "Let us know if there's anything we can do for the men."

"The best thing we can do for them now is get them back aboard the Tarawa, where there's a real doctor."

"We're working on that, Mr. Ramirez."

"As far as I can tell, Sir, they both have severe concussion from having their heads slammed back and forth inside their 'DART and I think Chief Harlon's arm is broken. He may have got it outside the vehicle when it rolled down hill. It's begun to swell badly."

Gordon and Pons looked more closely at the man. Knowing what to look for now, they both saw that Harlon's sleeve had been cut to his shoulder to accommodate a bloated arm and that the wrist and elbow were strapped to his body.

"They may have some internal injuries, but I can't tell without them being awake to tell me what they feel."

"You're doing a fine job under bad circumstances," Gordon said to the corpsman, trying to encourage him. It was obvious that Ramirez was a little rattled.

"We're going to configure to a hovercraft, Mr. Ramirez," said Pons, "and when we do you'll have to get them situated aboard."

"Yes, Sir," said Petty Officer Ramirez.

Gordon and Pons turned their attention back to the now very busy Chief Lufkin and the rest of the SEALs who were working furiously to change four of the 'DARTs into a hovercraft.

All the possible vehicle configurations of the 'Air Deliverable And Recoverable Tranporter' system were basically prestressed tensile pipe structures using carbon fiber composite pipe for the framework, carbon fiber fabric for the body panels, and carbon fiber wires for stressing the tensile structures.

The motor, propellers and wheels, all modular and light enough for just one man to lift, were mounted where needed to make the 'DART roll, hover or fly.

It was an innovative system, allowing both maximum flexibility and minimum assembly times.

The Kevlar fabric coverings from the wings and cockpits had been rolled and set to the side while the fixed composite pipe frames that made up the rigid floor sections of the four vehicles were joined together with the adjustable pipe sections that had comprised the upper framework of the cockpits and the frame roots for the wings.

Laid out on the ground next to the rolls of fabric were the dozens of carbon filament stays used to tension each finished frame.

The assembly was an amazing thing to watch. The connecting system used to put the 'DARTs together was similar to that used by Tinker Toys except every joint and connection used a Marstan pin to secure it.

As Gordon and Pons watched, the eight wing frames were first joined in pairs, root to root, then out-rigged, like a drop leaf on a table, one from each edge of the strong central floor frame to increase the square footage of the float frame. Two of the motors were mounted side by side in the center of the two forward frames so their propellers turned parallel to the ground. Mounted thus, their props would blow air straight down through a fabric cowling and under the float frame creating the air cushion on which the machine hovered. The other two motors were mounted as they had been when configured as ultralite aircraft propulsion on pipe mountings with their propellers facing to the rear. Two of the ultralites' vertical stabilizers with their rudders were mounted just behind the propellers to steer the craft.

Half assembled, the bare ribbed framework looked a little like the skeleton of a beached whale, sitting there on the bright white sand of the Sahara Desert. Unable to help in any meaningful way, Gordon and Pons continued to watch as the SEALs finished assembling the framework and began installing the fabric skin that would keep the air trapped under the machine. Finally, the individual flotation collars were zipped together end to end and attached to the outer edge of the float frame to provide the skirt that contained the air cushion under the hovercraft. Over water the inflated flotation collar would also give the vehicle some buoyancy if the motors had to be shut down.

Master Chief Lufkin, sweating rivulets, walked over to Gordon and Pons.

"It's incredible, Master Chief," Pons said. "In less than an hour, you've turned those four ground vehicles into a hovercraft!"

"Yes, Sir," said the Master Chief, before changing the subject to what he needed to discuss. "We need to load the other 'DARTs, Colonel, before we inflate the skirt."

"What did you have in mind, Chief?" Pons asked.

"We can roll the good one on first, down the center, up front. Then we can pick up the wreck and carry it aboard and lash it to the deck behind the first. That would keep the load centered and balanced," said the Chief.

Pons was thoughtful for a moment and then asked. "How fast do you think the machine will go?"

"Normally, forty-five knots without a head wind, unloaded, but we've got a good load, so we'll probably go about forty knots," answered the chief.

Pons did a conversion calculation in his head using 1.15 miles per hour for one knot. "That's about forty-six miles per hour, Chief."

"Yes, Sir," said the Chief.

"Would it be possible, Chief, to one; put the wreck forward; two; reconfigure the one remaining 'DART to an ultralite without wings and three; lash it to the rear deck, and use its motor to add thrust to the other two?"

Now it was the Chief's turn to think for a moment.

"I don't see why that wouldn't work, Colonel. We'd hafta have one of the men control the motor, but the extra power would probably add ten, fifteen knots to our speed. We'd really be flyin' then," Lufkin said, with enthusiasm.

"That would put our speed somewhere between fifty-five and sixty miles per hour on the level," said Gordon, doing his own calculations. "And that would take more than an hour off the return trip,"

"If you think it will work, Master Chief," said Pons, "then make it so."

"Aye, aye, Sir," said the chief.

Walking to the wreck, Lufkin called the other SEALs to help carry the crumpled vehicle onto the front deck of the hovercraft, where they lashed it down securely. Lufkin then ordered Sykes and Levine to reconfigure the remaining 'DART, Gordon's and Pons' as it turned out, back to a wingless airplane, before lashing it to the pipe frame of the rear deck.

While Sykes and Levine did that, the rest of the men worked with Lufkin on the last step of the assembly procedure, connecting the mechanical and electronic controls.

Seeing it was nearly time to move out, Pons and Gordon climbed aboard the hovercraft. Pons, until then, had not realized that Gordon's and his 'DART had been the one set aside to provide extra thrust. When he reached it, he checked the pouch to see that the Thermos was still intact. He then connected the Sat Link and the computer again to call the Tarawa with an update on their change in status. He related everything that had happened and told the Captain, they would follow the same basic course they had intended to fly across the desert, east of the Jabal Nafusah Hills. In the hovercraft, it would take much longer, but they had no other choice. Flying back to the Tarawa in the ultralites at a speed of 150 knots, it would have taken just over an hour. But, returning in the hovercraft traveling at only 50 to 60 miles per hour would take 3 to 4 times as long to reach the Tarawa's projected position 200 miles away. And that was assuming they could travel at best speed over flat unobstructed terrain. Pons knew of course that although the ground of the Gharyan Basin appeared flat on the topographical map on the computer screen, there would be obstacles that would slow them down in the first hundred odd miles traveling over land. He had no notion of what to expect over the water.

"We'll travel east north east to the wadi Sawlajjin," said Pons, explaining their new plans to the Tarawa's Captain and John Claire. "There should be a road or trail along the wadi. If there's not, we'll use the dry river bed for our road."

"There are three small settlements along the wadi," said Claire, when Pons paused. "Mizdah, Shumaykh, and Bir al Malfa."

"Yeah, I see them," said Pons. "Mizdah is the only one on a major road and it's the first one we come to. That may work to our advantage. By the time the Libyans find out were we are, we'll be gone. After that, they'll have a hell of a time getting to us on the ground."

"The wadi twists and turns a lot, Syman," said Claire. "That usually indicates rough terrain."

"I noticed that, too, John, but what choice do we have? We've got to cross the country somewhere." There was dead air for a moment.

"We'll try to get a better map to you, Sy."

"Roger, that," said Pons. "We're ready to go. Anything else?"

"Not right now," said Claire. "Call us in half an hour for the map."

"Will do. Pons, out," he said, breaking the connection.

Pons looked up from putting the phone and computer away. It was quiet and all the men were looking at him expectantly from their new places aboard the hover vehicle.

Master Chief Lufkin was just then carefully inspecting the helm and control panel at the center front of the craft. The helm consisted of a cockpit cowling complete with control panel and clear plastic wind screen from one of the reconfigured 'DART's. The controls consisted of a joy stick, which moved the rudders to turn the machine, two throttles to control the fans that inflated the skirt, two throttles to control the vehicles forward speed, four on/off controls, and four small dials that controlled the pitch angles of the propellers. The control panel also held temperature, pressure, and amperage meters, a forward air speed indicator, a compass, and a GPS locator.

"We're ship shape and ready to go, Colonel," Lufkin said, over his shoulder.

Pons looked quickly left to right, front and back. At the front corners of the craft were the two lift fans with the helm in the center. Behind that, six men sat cross legged on the deck, three to a side, holding onto the low pipe side rails that kept people from stepping off the floor frame and onto the fabric covered float frame extensions. Just inboard of them were the two injured men strapped to their stretchers. Between the injured men, at the center of the hovercraft, sat the wreck. At the rear corners of the floor frame, with Gordon's and Pons' de-winged 'DART between them, were the two pipestand mounted propulsion motors with their fifty inch propellers.

Standing on either side of their wingless aircraft at the rear of the hovercraft, Pons and Gordon stood surveying their new command.

"It's a pretty tight fit, Sy."

Pons nodded without saying anything.

"You and Commander Gordon sit in the 'DART,'" Lufkin said, seeing them standing there. "One of you will have to control its thrust."

"Very good, Chief," said Pons. "Let's get under way."

"What's the coarse, Sir?"

Pons looked at Gordon, who said, "Head east south east, Chief, for that opening between those two hills, there."

The Chief looked where Gordon was pointing and said, "Aye, Aye." A moment later he added, "We need a com check. We won't be able to hear each other once the engines are running."

Gordon and Pons climbed into their 'DART.

"One, test," said Pons, when they were settled.

"Two, test."

"Three, test."

"Four, test."

"Okay," said the Chief. "Time to git the hell outta here!"

The two fan engines spooled up, one right after the other, quickly inflating the skirt and lifting the frame of the machine two feet above the ground. The bottom of the air cushion skirt showed a clearance of about four inches. When the two propulsion units started, the machine picked up forward speed as it moved smoothly toward the distant pass through the hills at the far edge of the flat sandy Gharyan plain. As they watched, mesmerized, the hovercraft rode over rocks, plants and the rough terrain with ease.

"I keep expecting to feel us bump over something," said Gordon.

"Me, too," said Pons. "I've never been on a hovercraft, before."

"Colonel. Let's try bringing your unit on line and see what this baby will do."

"Okay, Chief," said Pons. He started the 'DART's engine and ran it up. He could feel the little plane straining against its lashings. "I've got her at ninety percent." The hovercraft increased its speed significantly with the 'DART's additional thrust.

"We're really moving along now, Colonel. The airspeed indicator's right at fifty knots!"

"Mine shows about the same, Chief. That means we're doing about fifty-eight miles per hour. Does it feel stable?" Pons asked.

"Solid as a rock, Colonel," replied the Chief.

They streaked across the sizzling sand of the Gharyan plain at nearly sixty miles per hour for a quarter hour. The furnace hot air assaulted them but cooled not at all as it swept over the self propelled land sailer and its tired, sweaty passengers. Adding to their misery, grit and bugs smashed relentlessly against the men's faces. Sweat running backward painted thin lines in the dark grime plastered to there skin. Without their flying goggles, they would have quickly been blinded by their own dripping sweat and the onslaught of flying debris thrown up by the crafts headlong rush.

Everywhere heat waves shimmered over the desiccated landscape blurring the wavering edges of anything more than a few hundred yards away. The ferocious heat pressed down on the exposed men. Sweating profusely, the heat sapped their strength though not their resolve.

The white noise of the passing air and the thrumming roar of the three propellers made it impossible to talk without using their com-links and so the men sat silently, each with his own thoughts and fears, watching the desert flash by in the blinding light of the midday Saharan sun.

As time passed, the rocky hills at the edges of the plain drew together funneling them into a shallow, irregular, boulder strewn river canyon and the ground took on a decided tilt to the east as they began their descent to the Mediterranean along the wadi Sawlajjin. During the next quarter hour, the river's banks became bluffs and then the bluffs became towering perpendicular faces ever narrowing, until the way was too constricted to turn the sixteen by thirty foot machine around.

When they had first entered the wadi, Pons had shut down the 'DART's motor at the Chief's behest slowing them significantly. Now, after several more miles of travel, their speed had dropped to a crawl, just over walking speed.

"We may have made a mistake traveling down this wadi, Chief," Pons said to him over the com link.

"Yeah, may be, Colonel," said Lufkin, "but, how far da we hafta go in this canyon?"

"I don't know. We obviously don't have a very good topo map for this area, but judging by the one we have, we've got three or four miles to go before we reach the settlement of Mizdah."

"If the canyon don't close in no more, we'll get her through."

Moments after saying this, rounding a slight bend, the Chief was forced to reverse the pitch on the propellers bringing the machine to an abrupt halt. There before them was a huge boulder sitting against the canyon's left wall, blocking their way.

"I guess I spoke too soon, Colonel," said the Chief.

"Set her down, Master Chief," said Gordon.

The Master Chief did as he was ordered and the machine settled unevenly, its inflated skirt astride a partially exposed rock dike running diagonally across the wadi's floor.

Grabbing the low rail, Gordon jumped down from the machine, vaulting over the soft wing extensions onto the sand.

He walked to the boulder and looked it over carefully. He got down on his hands and knees and crawled out of sight behind it. When he reappeared, he was shaking his head and there was a frown on his face.

"We've got a real problem here, folks," he said. "At first I thought we could just blow the goddamn thing up, but we might bring the wall behind it down and really block the way. Syman, let's let the men get down for a few minutes while we figure out what to do."

"Let's take five, Gentlemen," said Pons, into his com-link.

The men uncoiled from their positions and jumped down onto the sand in much the same way Gordon had done, vaulting over the soft sides of the hovercraft.

"Mr. Charles," Gordon said, to Chief Petty Officer Charles, the group's demolition expert, "I think we have need of your specialty."

Chief Charles quickly walked to Gordon. Syman and Chief Lufkin followed to inspect the enormous rock blocking their path.

"How can we dispose of this thing, Chief?" Gordon asked.

Chief Charles did the same type of inspection as Gordon and then said, "We can serialize it, Sir."

Gordon, Pons and Chief Lufkin stood there expectantly waiting for Chief Charles to explain.

"This boulder is a sedimentary rock, a type of shale. It will split quite readily along the layers that were built up as it was laid down a million years ago or whenever. Although this thing is real big, we can use timed charges to slice it apart, kind of like the way you slice fried potatoes. It will come apart in large thin plates. Once we've sliced it, then we can blow up the individual plates into smaller pieces the HC will go over."

"What about the canyon wall?" Gordon asked.

"It won't hardly touch the canyon wall, Sir. Our charges will be placed to project their force along the grain lines of the rock, beginning with the layers farthest from the wall. The charges farthest out go off milliseconds before the charges nearer the canyon wall. As each charge goes off, it blows off the next layer and then the next and so on until the last charges next to the wall go off. By then, most of the rock will have already been blown away."

"This sounds similar to the method used to demolish buildings in a city, when there are things nearby they don't want to be damaged," said Pons.

"Yes, Sir, Colonel. That's exactly the method I'm talking about using."

"Won't it take a lot of time?" Gordon asked.

"It'll take some time, yes, Sir," said the Chief.

"How much time, Mr. Charles?" Gordon asked.

The Chief paused a moment before speaking. "If Dean and Sykes and Levine help me, we can probably do it in about an hour."

"It sounds too complicated to do in an hour, Chief," said Gordon.

"Well, I can't promise it won't take a little longer, Commander, but it's really not very difficult with the sophisticated explosives we have with us. The detonation cords tying the charges together control the timing. We don't use big charges. We use several small charges around the rock on the same cleavage line timed by the det cords to go off at about the same instant. You'll be surprised to see how easy it cleaves that big bastard. Like I said, it'll slice it like a potato and blow the slices downhill into the center of the canyon. Serializing is a slick operation, Commander."

Gordon and Pons looked at each other for a moment. Pons nodded and then Gordon looked at the Chief.

"Chief, get to work. If more men are needed or would speed things up, then use them."

"Aye, aye, Commander," said the Chief.

"Sykes! Levine! Bring all the demo supplies over here," Chief Charles hollered. "We're gonna dice this son of a bitch!"

Chief Charles signaled his teammate Petty Officer First Class Dean and Seaman Aboulli to come help as well. The five SEALs set to work rolling plastic explosives into pencil thin strands, about a hundred-fifty feet all told. Three inch pieces were duct-taped along carefully identified single layers in the shale. In this way, Chief Charles placed six explosive charges, one every thirty degrees around the rock for each cleavage plane he wanted to split. Timed properly, a ring of six charges would go off at the same instant slicing that layer of shale from the rock. To accomplish this, the Chief connected the charges of adjacent layers with slow speed detonation cord. Six separate detonation cords connected each line of charges from front to back. The det cords resembled the longitude lines of the earth.

Just over forty minutes later, Chief Petty Officer Charles pushed a plunger to set off the explosives. In a fraction of a second, all fifty odd rings of charges went off, one right after another, dismantling the boulder in the blink of an eye.

Like a stack of poker chips kicked by an angry child, the massive boulder jumped away from the canyon wall, dismantled into dozens of large plates and rubble which sprawled downhill across the canyon in a low irregular mound.

"I wouldn't have believed it possible if I hadn't seen it with my own eyes," said Pons to the men. "A really fine job, Gentlemen." And then, "Chief Lufkin, can we get over that?"

"I think we gotta get rid of that one big one on the right, there. Tipped up like that it might tear the skirt."

"Okay, do it," said Pons.

The men set another small charge to blow the obstruction out of the way. Five minutes later it disintegrated with a muffled whump and a cloud of dust, leaving a low area in the rubble.

"I wanna fly her over unloaded, Commander."

"Right, Chief," replied Gordon.

Lufkin fired up the hovercraft's engines and slowly slid it forward over the remains of the boulder with no trouble. On the other side, he turned and gave the thumbs up to the team.

"Let's mount up, men," commanded Gordon.

In a minute, everyone had resumed his previous place and they got under way once again

32

After surmounting the boulder the way became rockier and the grade became steeper. There were several tight places, but no more impassable blockages. Twice the men had to dismount to assist in getting the machine over high rocks and once they had to hold the machine back going down a steep grade in the narrow defile, the reverse thrust from the engines being too imprecise for control. Holding on to keep the machine away from the walls, they guided the vehicle inch by inch through the hundred yard long trouble spot. A half mile further on, the canyon widened, the grade leveled and the walls lowered to bluffs as the river once more became a dry trace across the desert.

From this new perspective Pons could see they had just passed through a transition zone in the hills. The river dropped very quickly from its original height to a lower plain. Pons wondered idly if the Gharyan Plain was a plateau. He didn't know for sure, but what he did know was that the gorge they had just passed through was the result of a sharp drop in elevation. The steeper grade had caused fast moving water born gravels to scour the canyon into the bedrock.

As he pondered the geology along their route, his thoughts were interrupted by Master Chief Lufkin's voice over the com-link, "Colonel! We hava problem."

"What's up, Master Chief?" Pons inquired.

"We only traveled about thirty miles in three hours. We're gonna run outta fuel before we get back."

"How much fuel have we got?"

"We're just about dry on the fans. They been doing most of the work. There's probably thirty minutes of fuel left in 'em."

"How much do we have for the other motors, Chief?" Gordon asked.

"They've got maybe an hour's worth, Commander. If we transfer the fuel from the wreck and from your 'DART, we'll have about a' hour and a half with all four runnin'."

"Very good, Master Chief. Commander Gordon and I will need a minute to consider this new problem," said Pons.

"Yes, Sir," said the Chief.

The hovercraft was moving along at a good rate as they spoke, the wadi having once again become relatively flat, wide and unobstructed. But with another 70 unknown miles of land and 100 miles of sea still left to cross, they had a big problem on their hands.

"I hadn't thought about fuel, Dex," said Pons, over the intercom, sounding a little surprised. "I'd just assumed we had plenty, but of course, that was if we had flown the 'DARTs back. This heavy monster is really running through the go juice, and it never occurred to me."

"It occurred to me, but I assumed Chief Lufkin had the situation in hand."

"Actually," said Pons, "if we'd hadn't been delayed, we'd probably have had just about enough, with the transferred fuel. Under those conditions the Chief would have hit the mark."

"Oh, well." said Gordon. "Now, what?"

"I was kind of hoping you'd have one of your bright ideas," said Pons.

"Sorry, Sy, but I don't have a gas station in my bag of tricks, just now." Gordon said, sounding a little tired.

Pons was silent for a while and then said, "Maybe that's it!"

"Maybe, what's it?" Gordon asked.

"Maybe, we can find some gas in Mizdah," replied Pons, with mounting excitement in his voice. Then with a more cautious tone, he keyed the com link, "Chief, what kind of fuel do we need for the engines?"

"They use av-gas, Colonel," the Chief answered.

"We were thinking of looking in the little town up ahead for some gasoline, Chief."

"Won't work, Colonel. Sorry. Octane isn't high enough. They'd knock themselves to pieces in twenty minutes."

"Well, it was a thought," Pons concluded. The com-link fell silent.

Gordon and Pons sat perplexed, hot, tired and a little discouraged. Not knowing what else to do, Syman did the most natural thing that came to mind. He turned to the computer. He knew the computer couldn't solve their present problem, but being at a total loss, it would at least help him think. He' turned it on to look at the pathetic map he'd downloaded from the ship. He now knew it was an almost worthless representation of the area. He decided he needed to contact the ship again. They'd said they'd have a better map for him when he called again. He should have done it two and a half hours ago, but in the canyon he'd been unable to connect to the satellite, because of the high rock walls. He wondered if he should take the time, just then, considering their pending fuel shortage. He began to consider if there was some way the Tarawa could get fuel to them. As he thought about it, he tentatively decided it was their best option. They'd probably have to hold up somewhere around here until nightfall, when a helicopter could bring them fuel. The thought of sitting in the desert heat another eight hours was not comforting, but there didn't appear to be any better solutions available. He was just about to discuss the idea with Dexter, when his eyes came to rest on a little tilted T symbol representing the crossed runways of an airport next to Mizdah.

"We may have a solution close at hand," said Pons to Gordon.

"What's up?" Gordon was immediately alert.

"There's an airport in Mizdah!" said Pons, sounding a little triumphant.

"How do you know that? Does it show on that crummy map."

"Yes."

"I don't think we can trust it. It didn't show the canyon."

"The only other option I can think of is to call for fuel from the Tarawa. If we do that, we'll have to wait until dark."

Gordon said nothing while he considered that.

"We're going to run out of fuel on the lift fans soon, Sy. Why don't we set her down and transfer the fuel."

"Right. Master Chief," Pons said over the com link, "Find a way out of the wadi on the northwest side and set her down. We need to transfer the fuel."

"You got that right, Colonel, and none too soon," Then the chief added. "Colonel, start your engine and leave it idling. I'll need your help gettin' her outta here."

"Roger that," said Pons.

The hovercraft slowed, but continued traveling several hundred yards before coming to a gently sloping bank on the north side. Chief Lufkin turned the machine slightly to the left. "Give her all you got, Colonel, and then shut it down when we're over the hump." Pons opened the throttle of the 'DART wide. Chief Lufkin gunned the other two engines and the hovercraft wafted up the bank of the wadi and onto the sandy flat above. Once on top Pons shut down the 'DART's engine as instructed. The Chief brought the machine to a halt and then settled it gently to the earth. When the engines fell silent the men stood and stretched, savoring the pleasure of release and the freedom of movement.

"Sykes, Levine!" the Master Chief called rising from the helm's seat. "Transfer the av-gas from the wreck to the fan engine tanks."

"Aye, Sir," they replied in unison and immediately set about the task. The tank module was removed from its mountings in the damaged vehicle. The two men carried it to the first of the fan engines and balanced it on the pipe mounting that held the fan in its place. Its rubber fuel line was inserted into the fan's fuel fill pipe and its shut off valve was opened. When half the wreck's fuel was transferred, they performed the same operation with the second fan engine. It took about ten minutes, adding about seven gallons of fuel to each of the fans.

Chief Lufkin walked back to Gordon and Pons. "How much fuel do you have in your 'DART? he asked.

"We've got just over half a tank, probably about eleven gallons," replied Pons. Then he said, "Master Chief, we're thinking about going after more fuel at the airport in Mizdah. They'd have av-gas there with the right octane for our engines."

"I didn't know you was talking about getting hold of fuel from a' airport. I thought you was thinking of getting regular gas from ground vehicles, Colonel."

"Originally, Chief, I was. But then I noticed there was an airport of some kind shown on the map outside Mizdah."

"What the hell kind of airport they gonna have out here in the desert?" Lufkin asked, forgetting himself for a moment. "We may just find an empty landing strip and no fuel, Colonel."

"That's a possibility, Chief," said Pons, not taking offense at the Chief's lapse of military decorum. "But we think it's worth checking out. Mizdah is an oil field service center. We may just get lucky."

"The only other option," said Gordon, joining the conversation, "is to wait till dark and try to get the carrier to fly us some fuel out here."

"According to the GPS locator in our 'DART," continued Pons, changing the subject abruptly, "we're about two miles from Mizdah. See those oil well pumps over there? It should be just around the other side of those rocks."

He pointed ahead and to the right at a low craggy hill on the south side of the wadi a mile further down the dry river. The wadi continued on curving gently to the south behind the hill. It curved back into sight far out on the plain, five or so miles away. From their elevated vantage point in the shimmering air of the desert, they could see dirt tracks amidst dozens of oil well pumps methodically heaving up and down heedless of the intense midday heat. Away to the north, past the oil field, a tiny vehicle crept along, apparently in the direction of the as yet unseen town of Mizdah. Beyond that, they could also just make out the dark edge of the distant Mediterranean, some sixty odd miles away.

As the Chief scanned the immense horizon spread before them, he said, "I hope you're right about that fuel, Sirs, cause it don't look like we're gonna find nowhere around here to hide until dark."

"It's time to get moving again, Chief," said Pons. "The airport is north of Mizdah. It looks like it's about half a mile outside of town on our side of the river. If we stay on this side of the wadi, it should more or less bring us right to it. I want to explain to the men before we get going."

"Aye, aye, Colonel," said the Chief.

Pons walked over to the men. "Men, we think we've located an airport in Mizdah, the next little settlement along the wadi. We're going to try to shanghai enough av-gas there to get us back to the ship, which means we need enough to fill our tanks. We don't know that we'll find what we need there, but the only other option is to hide out here somewhere in this desert and wait for the Tarawa to fly us some when it's dark. Commander Gordon and I think it's worth the risk to investigate. Does anyone have any other ideas?"

There was silence from the six tired SEALs staring back at him as they continued to listen attentively.

"Check your weapons again, men," Pons instructed. "Keep alert and don't hesitate to sing out if you see something." He turned to the Chief who had been listening with Gordon at the rear of the machine and said, "Let's get going, Chief."

The Chief nodded and walked to the helm as the men rechecked their weapons. Pons and Gordon climbed back in the 'DART.

"Com check," said Chief Lufkin, when he was once again settled at the controls.

"One, test," said Gordon.

"Two, test..."

Gordon now sat in the front pilot's seat of the 'DART. Pons, sitting in the back, called the Tarawa to appraise them of the situation.

"We were in a deep canyon for the last couple of hours and I couldn't get line of sight on the satellite," he informed them.

As he spoke, the 'DART elevated and began moving along the sandy bank of the wadi with increasing speed.

"We've been sweating bullets here, Sy," said John Claire, sounding clearly relieved.

"We're low on fuel and we're going to try and get some from the airport at Mizdah. We're about two miles out and closing fast."

"Crank her up, Commander," Pons heard, as the Chief's order overrode the com link.

Gordon started the 'DART and immediately ran it up to maximum. The hovercraft jumped ahead in response. They were again doing close to sixty miles per hour.

"John, I need you to download that other map, if you've got it ready."

"It's ready. Here it comes," said Claire.

As Syman watched, a much better quality topographical map scrolled onto his screen.

"Why didn't we get this map to begin with?" Pons asked, with anger in his voice.

"It's the topo map from our Tomahawk cruise missile's terrain following guidance system, Colonel Pons," said the Captain of the Tarawa. "They're the most accurate maps in the world, but they're classified. I had to get permission from the Pentagon to release it to you. The maps you were given for the mission are adequate to get you in and out of Libya flying the 'DARTs. No one considered you might try to return on the ground."

Pons immediately saw the airport in much more detail. There were little squares representing buildings around two parallel runways. He also saw the contour lines of another large deep wadi entering from the west.

Instantly, Pons yelled a warning into his com link. "Chief! Slow us down! We've got a large wadi across our path joining this one from the west!."

"Roger that, Colonel. Shut your engine down to idle, Commander."

"Aye, Chief," said Gordon, as he throttled back in unison with the Chief.

Heeding Pons' warning, the Chief immediately reversed the pitch on the main propellers bringing the hovercraft to a complete halt and not a moment too soon. There before them yawned a deep, wide, rocky ditch that would have wrecked them a moment after coming upon it at their previous speed.

"Damn, Colonel! I'm sure glad you warned me or we'd be dead now."

"Sorry, Chief. I would have warned you sooner, but I just now received a new map. We won't get caught like that again."

"Yes, Sir," replied Lufkin, relief evident in his voice.

"Can we cross it here, Chief?" Pons asked. "Or should we go to the west to find a better place?"

"I think we can get across here, Colonel."

With no hesitation the Master Chief crabbed the machine diagonally down the steep bank of the hidden wadi, by reversing the pitch of the propellers and using more power on the uphill engine. Pons marveled at the maneuver. It showed what a virtuoso the Chief was at operating the hovercraft.

They traveled two-hundred yards left to the west along the dry wadi searching for the lowest slope in the bank on the other side. Finding what he wanted, the Chief aimed the big machine up the bank, and gunned both main engines, commanding Gordon to do the same with the 'DART. The vehicle moved ponderously up the incline slowing as it went. Near the top with all three engines roaring at full blast, the hovercraft came to a halt and sat trembling, straining to travel the last few feet uphill. When it began sliding back, Chief Lufkin barked over the com link, "You men are gonna hav'ta get out and push this son of a bitch. Quick!"

As one, the six men vaulted over the skirt and began hauling on the hovercraft with all their might. At first, their assistance only halted the accelerating backward slide and then almost imperceptibly the machine began inching up the slope. In a few seconds it was moving faster as the six men overcame the combined inertia and weight of the two ton vehicle. Twenty seconds later the machine wallowed over the top of the embankment, dragging them along as fast as they could run. The Chief immediately brought the craft to a standstill, ordering Gordon to shut down the 'DART's engine as he reversed the pitch of the propellers on the main engines. Then, reducing power to the fans, he settled the machine down on the sand so the breathless soldiers could clamber aboard. A few moments later the hovercraft resumed its journey toward the airport. It had all happened so fast. The men were back aboard and the dangerous obstruction was behind them in less than a minute with Pons narrating the entire episode to the ship as it occurred.

"Sure glad we got that map to you when we did," said John Claire.

"So am I," said Pons, and then, "The airport's in sight. I'll let you know how we do after our raid. You may still have to bring us some fuel if we don't find any."

"I'll set it up, right away, Colonel Pons," said the Tarawa's Captain. "We'll be waiting to hear from you."

Pons broke the connection, closed the computer and put the gear in the side pouch, next to the thermos.

They had traveled around the hill that had blocked Mizdah from their sight and were fast closing on the airport. He now saw the buildings marked on the map. There was a large corrugated metal building with a curved roof, like an oversized Quonset hut. There was no end wall to the building and Pons assumed it was probably a hanger. Across the two potholed macadam runways and a cracked concrete taxiway from the hanger sat a wrecked DC-3, down on one crumpled wing tip, the landing gear on that side only partially extended. Both the engine mounts, festooned with disconnected pipes and wires, sat exposed to the weather, the engines having long been removed from the stout old aircraft's wings. Also on the far side of the runways, east of the DC-3, were two long low buildings that looked like barracks. As they got closer Pons could see the windows were without glass and the siding was askew in several places. Clearly, they were also long abandoned and unused. He saw a large faded sign written in Italian. It occurred to him that the buildings were probably built by the Italian army to protect the airfield during the war.

Glancing east, he could also now see the town laid out before them a half mile away. Three roads met at the edge of the town where a bridge crossed over the Wadi Sawlajjin as it passed the town. Pons could also see there was a walled courtyard with a well just inside the town's gate only a few yards from the dry wadi. Water would, of course, have been the reason the three roads met at this particular spot along the river. Hence the well and hence the original town.

As the hovercraft came even with the open end of the hanger, Pons could barely see inside because of the harsh glare of the desert sun. Inside its shaded recesses he could just discern the outline of a modern two engine aircraft.

"Let's have a look in the hanger, Chief," said Pons.

The Chief turned and looked over his shoulder in Pons direction.

"Over there, Colonel?" the Chief asked, pointing at the metal building.

"Right, Chief."

The machine drifted right up to the cavernous open end of the building and hovered motionlessly.

"Face her out and set her down, Chief. Idle the engines."

"Aye, aye, Colonel."

"Let's see if we can find some fuel men," Gordon ordered.

"There's a combat field tester and some plastic tubing in the tool kit of your 'DART, Commander. It'll tell you if it's gas and what the octane rating is."

"Will miracles never cease, Chief. Just the right tool, when you need it. This must be the new Navy," said Gordon, his comment laden with sarcasm.

"Yes Sir," said the Master Chief, with a laugh. "Must be."

"Three, you check the drums at the back of the building." Gordon pointed to a pile of steel drums along the rear wall of the hanger.

"Two, you run around back and see what you can find."

"Sy, let's check out this plane and see what's in her tanks."

Pons said nothing, but hopped down from the hovercraft and ran over to the hangered plane with Gordon. It took only a moment to open the wing fuel tanks and inventory the fuel. Both tanks were nearly empty.

"Shit!" said Gordon, angrily. "There aren't ten gallons of fuel all together."

"Ten gallons is ten gallons, Dex."

"I suppose it's better than nothing, but not much," retorted Gordon. "This plane can hold sixty gallons of fuel when it's full and that's what I was hoping for."

"Let's see what they have back there," said Pons, walking toward the drums along the rear wall. The two men of Three Team were unscrewing caps as fast as they could, sniffing each drum for the distinctive aroma of gasoline. As Gordon and Pons reached them, Chief Petty Officer Charles turned toward them and spoke, "I think I've got a barrel of gasoline, here."

Gordon handed him his tester. The Chief collected a sample of the fluid from the barrel using the plastic tubing. He held the tubing toward the opening of the hanger and the light.

"It looks clean, Commander."

Then he emptied the sample into the tester and watched, waiting for the tester to work. After thirty seconds he read the scale.

"It's only 86 octane, Commander. And there's lead in it."

"Regular gasoline. Damn! That won't do us any good, Chief. keep looking."

Gordon and Pons started opening barrels as well. They found two more barrels of regular gasoline, two barrels of kerosene, several of different weights of motor oil and grease, but no aviation fuel.

"There's no av-gas in here," said Gordon, telling the others what they already knew. The men were walking toward the front of the hanger, when Seaman Levine hollered to them from a door at the rear corner of the hanger,

"We think we've found some fuel in back, Commander."

Gordon turned and ran for the door followed by Pons and Three Team. Behind the hanger was a large steel tank up on a stand about eight feet off the ground. Fifty feet of hose was coiled on a hook attached to an antique meter with a padlocked shutoff valve. Black tire marks on the concrete apron next to it told of years of aircraft filling in its shadow.

"Hot damn! It looks like you found the motherlode. Why didn't you guys come get us sooner?" Gordon demanded.

"We had a heck of a time getting a sample to test. I had to boost Levine up so he could climb on top of the tank."

"We got 106 octane av-gas in this tank here, Commander."

"Good going, men," said Gordon sincerely.

Gordon stepped through the door of the hanger and keyed his com link. "Master Chief, bring the machine around back. We've found the Holy Grail!"

"Aye, aye, Commander."

The hovercraft immediately rose and floated around the side of the hanger. Moments later, the machine settled next to the fuel depot.

"Sykes, Levine, you handle the refueling. The rest of you men, set up a perimeter around the hanger so we can see if anyone is coming in our direction."

The SEALs, weapons in hand, scattered to the compass points.

Seaman Levine hit the padlock twice with a large hammer before it popped open, allowing them to begin filling all the nearly dry fuel tanks on the hovercraft. Including the tank of the damage 'DART the six tanks swallowed 108 gallons.

"We only had about 20 minutes fuel left, Commander," said Chief Lufkin. "We cut it pretty close."

"Chief, do we have enough extra load capacity to bring a couple of 55 gallon drums of extra fuel with us?" Pons asked.

"Sure, Colonel. We got plenty of lift capacity. We just ain't got much room aboard."

"What do you think, Commander Gordon?" Pons asked formally.

"If we can, then let's do it!"

After ten minutes of sweaty, messy work emptying regular gas from two barrels and refilling them aboard the hovercraft, it was time to go.

"Levine, there's some rubber hose in the hanger next to the door. Cut off about ten feet so we have a siphon for transferring the extra fuel."

"Aye, aye, Commander."

When this last task was done, everyone loaded aboard the hovercraft and they once more moved off toward the Wadi Sawlajjin.

33

The most direct route back to the Wadi Sawlajjin would have followed the road from the airport to the bridge over the wadi just outside the town's gate a half mile away. To avoid coming anywhere near the town Chief Lufkin steered a course diagonally to the northeast over the scrubby desert toward a point about a mile east of Mizdah. Having dropped several hundred feet in altitude from the truly desolate fringe of the Sahara to the slightly less arid Mediterranean coastal rim was evidenced in the increase in desert flora. The hovercraft rode down acres of gray-green bush that sprouted sporadically in response to the region's miserly six or so inches of rain a year. The increase in rain was also apparent in the slight corrugation of the land created by countless shallow washes that flowed into the Wadi Sawlajjin with runoff from the infrequent but violent storms. The many washes gave the ground a rolling appearance with a few hundred or so yards between alluvial low spots. As a consequence the hovercraft's gentle rising and falling was not unlike that of a sailboat running with a following sea.

"How's it handling, Chief?" Gordon asked.

"It's okay, Commander."

"We're going to run along side the wadi like this rather than down in it," said Gordon.

"I was kinda hopin' you'd tell me ta do that. It'd be a lot easier and faster if we do. It'll beat the skirt up pretty bad, but we'll make some time." And then, after a moment the Chief asked, "Any more of those hidden valleys gonna come in from the side?"

"The country's pretty flat, Chief," said Pons. "In fact, a road from Mizdah crosses to this side on the bridge outside of town and it follows the wadi for about forty miles. After forty miles the wadi gets swampy and heads for the coast and the road veers off to the northwest toward Tripoli."

"We actually want you to run this thing down the highway, Chief" Gordon said. "Can you do that?"

"If there are no poles or trees or nothin' we can go like a bat outta hell down a road."

"Then let's do it Chief," said Gordon.

A few minutes later, again nearing the Wadi Sawlajjin, they came upon the highway. It was anything but a good highway by American standards, being little more than a graded gravel track only just wide enough for two vehicles to pass in opposite directions. For a hovercraft, however, it was as fine a surface as any that could be hoped for stretching away toward the horizon straight as an arrow's flight.

Gliding almost without friction over the level unobstructed flat surface with all three engines running flat out, Master Chief Lufkin felt like a man reborn after the four previous confined and tortuous hours.

"My air speed indicator reads right at 60 knots, Chief," said Gordon. "That's about seventy miles an hour!"

"Mine, too," replied Lufkin, with laughter in his voice. "You said this road goes forty miles or so before we get to the swamp, Colonel?"

"That's right, Chief, and then there's about ten miles of swamp before we reach the sea."

"This here's great! We're really gonna make some time, now."

"At this speed it feels like a magic carpet ride," said Pons. Then with a note of doubt in his voice, "The hovercraft will go over a swamp, won't it, Chief?"

"She'll fly over anything that's flat, Colonel. Unless there's trees, we got no problems."

"It's unlikely there'll be many trees, Chief."

"Good! If that's the case, then we're home free."

The hovercraft roared along the road like a speeding tornado, blasting dust, stones and plants in all directions.

The heavy bright light and heat of the midday laid on them, squeezing them down into themselves. The onrushing air helped to cool them a little, flash evaporating the sweat from their clothing and skin. It was now noon, no time for human beings to be traveling across the desert. Unfortunately, they had no choice. They could not hunker down and wait for the cooler evening to arrive. By what ever means, they had to get their injured comrades back to the ship as quickly as possible because the conditions of both men were getting worse.

Petty Officer Harlon was semi-comatose, moaning in pain and struggling weakly against his restraints. His arm had swollen to a grotesque size turning purple, black and was giving him a great deal of pain. Petty Officer Ramirez gave him morphine, but it was a poor substitute for proper treatment.

For his part, Seaman Olszewski was faring no better. His breathing had become shallow and his pulse weak as time went on. He had not regained consciousness and Ramirez suspected Olszewski had serious head injuries.

About ten miles out from Mizdah, the twin engine airplane that had been in the hanger overtook them from behind.

"We've got company," said Petty Officer Dean, who had been sitting facing backward on watch.

Everybody swiveled around to find the intruder. It flew low and parallel to them, three heads visible through its windows. The plane circled them several times, easily keeping pace with the ground bound hovercraft. Staying several hundred yards away it reconnoitered them like a bird of prey.

"They better not have any weapons or we're sitting ducks out here," said Gordon. "We probably should have disabled that damn plane when we had the chance." Scanning the plane with his monocular, Gordon saw nothing threatening at the moment. "I don't see any weapons."

"No doubt they've reported our position to the authorities," replied Pons.

"Yeah, probably."

Just then the plane swerved over the hovercraft and a cascade of round objects fell from the plane.

Gordon, who had been watching the plane like a hawk, yelled, "Hard to port, Chief, we're being bombed!"

The Chief reacted instantly steering the machine diagonally off the road. Incredulously, they watched as a rain of rocks and a short section of heavy steel pipe smashed into the road just ahead of where they would have been. Everyone except Pons and Chief Lufkin started shooting at the plane with their rifles. Seeing it was having no effect, Gordon hollered, "Dean! Break out a Blowdart and knock them down."

Petty Officer Dean opened a long olive drab fiberglass case and removed one of its four hand held bazooka like, surface to air missile launchers. He and Petty Officer Charles quickly removed the end caps revealing aluminum foil dust membranes. He pushed the release lever forward unlocking the missile from its transport latches and arming the weapon. Flipping up the sighting reticle, he lifted the launcher to his shoulder and stood up. Petty Officer Charles, kneeling behind him, legs wide spread, held Dean firmly around the waist to steady his partner on the bobbing vehicle.

As the two men prepared to fire the missile the plane wavered, its wings waggling once before turning away and fleeing from the hovercraft.

After glancing over his shoulder, Charles hollered, "Clear behind." Petty Officer Dean fired. The flaming missile squirted from the launcher faster than the eye could follow. It traveled about five hundred yards toward the aircraft and then abruptly dove into the ground, exploding with a muffled 'phump' and a little spume of sand.

"Must've been a bad arrow, Mr. Dean," said Gordon, over the com-link.

"Yes, Sir," replied Dean, replacing the spent launcher back in its case next to its three still potent siblings.

Though the missile had come nowhere near its intended target, it had been enough to drive the plane away. Having cheated death once, the plane disappeared over the horizon and did not return.

"Cat's out of the bag, men. Keep a sharp eye," Gordon ordered over the com-link.

Alone again in the desert, they continued down the road at top speed. Fifteen minutes later, surmounting a low rise, they saw the turn off to Shumaykh ahead. They also saw it was occupied by a tank and a six by six truck loaded with soldiers. It looked as if the tank and truck had been waiting for them to arrive. Spotting the hovercraft on the road, the tank immediately fired a round straight at them. There was now no doubt they had been waiting for the Americans.

"Hang on!" Chief Lufkin yelled, as he pushed the stick hard to port. The shell only missed them by feet, continuing past a thousand yards before exploding harmlessly over the rise behind them. The speeding machine vaulted off the road into the scrubby wastes away from the wadi. In moments, the hovercraft was even with the tank and troop carrier, passing them several hundred yards out in the scrub. The tank's deadly turret swiveled to keep them in its sights. Again the tank bucked as it fired. The round went in front of the hovercraft, the gunner having led his target too much. This time the exploding shell went off very close to the hovercraft causing it to rock dangerously. If the hovercraft nosed into the sand at the speed they were traveling the machine would disintegrate.

"That was too goddamn close for comfort," Gordon said to Pons. "We don't have anything we can stop that tank with, so we'll have to outrun it."

"Chief," said Gordon, "Give her all she's got. We have to outrun them."

The truck bolted down the road in parallel pursuit to the hovercraft, though still several hundred yards away, while the tank gave chase cross country. Almost immediately, the tank began falling behind, not quite able to keep up with the flying machine over such rough country.

Now past the Libyans, and still off road out in the scrub, the Americans were throwing up such a terrific cloud of dust, they were invisible to their pursuers. Nevertheless, another round crossed their bow from behind, but it was obvious the tank's gunner could no longer see them well enough to sight the enormous cannon accurately.

"Commander, these bushes are slowin' us down and I hafta to keep changing course so the tank don't get an accurate fix on us and that's slowing us down, too. We're only able to do about thirty knots relative ta the road. I don' know if we can outrun 'em at this speed. I don't know how fast that tank'll go, but that six by six they got the troops on can make forty-five knots on the road, easy."

"Can we get back on the road, Chief?" asked Pons. "We could probably outrun them, there."

"Not yet, Colonel. We can't outrun that gun. If we get back on the road, that tank gunner'll send a round right down the pipe inta our ass. And that's why we gotta keep changing course, so he can't do that."

"How about using a Blowdart on it?" Pons asked.

"Won't even scratch a tank, Sy," said Gordon. "It was designed to damage the aluminum skin of an aircraft, and some times it hardly does that."

"Can we use one against the truck?"

"That's a possibility, but we need to deal with the tank first."

At just that moment a chance small arms round whapped the Kevlar fabric of their cockpit.

"You might want to rethink that last statement, Dex," Pons said to his friend with a raised eye brow and a grim smile.

"Yeah, maybe," said Gordon, with his own grim smile.

The two men were silent for a minute, each trying to think of some way to stop the tank, but hoping they could simply out run it. If they stayed out in the bush they just might do it. With all the dust thrown up by the air cushion, they could not see their adversaries behind them, which gave them a little security. Unfortunately, that security was becoming more ephemeral by the moment with each small arms round that pelted the hovercraft.

The six men out on the deck next to the rails were gathered around the two wounded men on their stretchers. They were trying to stretch their portable Kevlar foxholes, (Kevlar fabric sheets), with bungee cords on the railing nearest the Libyans in an effort to fend off the increasing number of bullets. As they worked, the six by six came into view nearby. Having also followed them into the bush, it surprised the Americans appearing only a hundred feet away and nearly even with the hovercraft.

Sykes and Levine opened up with their M-16's as their mates wrestled the Kevlar sheets in the furious air stream. A Libyan tumbled from the back of the truck, one of Levine's shots finding its mark.

Seeing one of their men shot so infuriated the Libyans, they retaliated by throwing a wall of lead at the fleeing hovercraft, shots striking almost every vertical surface.

Since most surfaces were made of Kevlar in one form or another there was little damage. But a bullet cracked Chief Lufkin's windscreen and Seaman Aboulli took a glancing round to the skin of his left upper arm.

"Damn, that smarts," he said as he pulled back from the rail, feeling the wound with his hand. Ramirez, who was Aboulli's fireteam mate as well as the mission's corpsman, quickly took a look at his arm.

"Shouldn't have let the generals know you speak a foreign language, Aboulli," Ramirez said, when he saw it was only a flesh wound. "Then you wouldn't be out here getting shot up." He smiled crookedly at the young seaman, who had so recently become his teammate and his friend, as he put antiseptic cream and a gauze pad over the wound.

The seaman twitched slightly from the pain Ramirez caused him by touching the wound.

Now sure that his wound wasn't serious, Aboulli said with a laugh, "Thanks, a lot, Ramirez. Did anyone ever tell you you're a pain in the ass!"

"Yeah, my mother tells me that whenever she sees me."

Encountering the truck full of Libyan soldiers off road, Chief Lufkin continued to steer the machine further to the west away from the highway hoping to find rougher terrain in an attempt to shake both the tank and the truck. By weaving back and forth Lufkin was able to deny the tank's gunner a fixed target, but it kept bringing the hovercraft near the searching truck. Easily able to pace the hovercraft, the truck lacked the firepower to quickly destroy it. Nevertheless, the Libyans attacked when the Americans again loomed into view through the gloom of dust thrown out by the hovercraft. Hoping to hit something vital, the Libyans again fired a fierce volley of bullets.

This time, they scored a bullseye as pieces flew off the starboard propeller and a strong vibration rattled through the frame of the hovercraft.

"We've taken a hit in the starboard propeller," said Petty Officer Dean, over the com-link.

"Roger that, goddamn it!" Everyone heard Chief Lufkin's reply as the right engine idled down and the rudders canted a little to the left to counteract the uneven thrust. As the engine slowed, so did the hovercraft.

A cheer sounding much like a tribal war cry broke out in the back of the troop carrier when the Libyans realized they had scored a serious hit, slowing their adversaries down. Like mad dogs sensing the kill, they redoubled their shooting, sending another fierce fusillade of metal toward the wounded hovercraft.

The SEALs returned fire with a vengeance to keep them at bay.

"Break out another Blowdart, Mr. Dean," Gordon hollered.

"It's time to get shut of these bastards before they do some real damage!"

"Aye, aye, Commander," said Dean, as he and Charles went to work readying a missile.

Then, another shell was fired from the tank when its crew saw it was gaining on the hovercraft. This one exploded near the left side rear of the hovercraft, but fortunately to no effect.

Instead of standing, Dean knelt in deference to the opposing fire from the nearing truck.

"Clear behind," yelled Charles, ducking.

Petty Officer Dean fired the missile. It flew across the intervening hundred feet in a moment. Flying just above the ground, it disappeared under the truck. It missed the body of the truck entirely, but it hit the outboard set of dual tires, blowing them to tatters with a flash. The damaged wheel caused the speeding troop carrier to career wildly to the right away from the hovercraft. It rolled over, pitching the Libyan soldiers in all directions.

The Americans on their injured hovercraft flew on, leaving the Libyan riflemen to their fate and glad to be rid of them.

Still, there was no respite. Another shell arched over the hovercraft. It went way beyond them, having apparently been fired as an angry, poorly aimed retaliatory strike, but it did serve to remind the Americans the fight wasn't over.

Traveling now on only two engines, and still slowed by thickets of wiry brush, they lumbered along at only twenty knots in serious danger from the now fast advancing tank.

"We still got a real problem with that tank, Commander," Chief Lufkin said over the com-link. "If it catches us, it can drive right over us if one of them damn treads touches our stern. And that's if it doesn't just blow us to hell, first."

"Roger, that, Chief. I've got an idea how to get rid of the tank now that the truck is gone."

"I sure hope so, Commander, because we're goin' as fast as we can and at this speed, he'll catch up to us in about five minutes."

"Let's get one of those barrels of av-gas to the stern, men," said Gordon. "Chief, this is what I want you to do. When I tell you, I want you to bring us to a stop as fast as you can. We're going to drop a booby trapped barrel of gasoline off the back and detonate it with a radio controlled charge when the tank gets near it."

"How you gonna see it, Commander, with all the dust?"

"The moment it's on the ground, I want you to get us the hell out of here as fast as you can, but perpendicular to our line of travel. The dust should hide the barrel and us from the tank crew until they're right on top of it when I'll set it off. We should have about ten, fifteen seconds head start when we get back aboard."

"It'll be pretty goddamn risky, Commander, if it don't stop 'em. We'll be giving up our cover and they'll be right on top of us then."

"That's true Chief, but I can't think of any other way to take out that tank. We don't have any other weapons powerful enough to stop them."

"Aye, Commander. Let me know when you're ready to stop."

"Chief Charles, we need your special skills to rig the barrel."

"Aye, Sir." Chief Charles immediately set to work making a small charge of C-4 with a radio controlled detonator. He then attached the whole package to the top of the barrel of av-gas with some duct tape

"We're ready, Commander," said Chief Petty Officer Charles.

"Set her down, Master Chief," Gordon ordered, "and then get her back in the air as soon as I tell you. We'll hop aboard her on the fly."

While Pons and the Chief controlled the hovercraft, the six SEALs and Gordon grabbed the four hundred pound barrel of av-gas and quickly manhandled it to the ground, leaving it standing on end in the sand.

"Let's go, Chief!" Gordon hollered.

The hovercraft lifted as the men scrambled aboard. They moved off diagonally as fast as they could go. As the hovercraft came around to a perpendicular heading, Gordon could just make out the silhouette of the charging tank through the dust not ten seconds behind them.

Just before the behemoth ran down the barrel of av-gas, its cannon began turning in their direction, but it was too late. With the tank not ten feet from the gasoline, Gordon fired the charge and the speeding war machine was engulfed in an enormous fiery explosion. As they watched, from five-hundred feet away, the thirty ton monster was flipped into the air and turned over by the force of the blast. Rammed into the desert sand, its massive cannon barrel was ripped from the turret as the tank came to rest upside down. Laying like a turtle on its back, its flat featureless belly and treads to the sky, the fire coated wreck billowed gouts of oily black smoke amidst bright leaping walls of red and yellow flame. Explosions rocked the tank every few seconds as the cannon's rounds cooked off in the fierce heat of the burning gasoline. Pausing to inspect their handiwork, the strong smell of gasoline mixed with burnt flesh wafted across the intervening distance on the hot wind. Master Chief Lufkin got them moving again after a few moments.

Watching the wrecked tank recede from view, the Americans, both elated and shocked, rode away from their victory in silence.

After a minute of travel, Gordon broke the silence. "Chief, as soon as you think we're a safe distance away, we've got to stop and replace the bad prop with the one from Harlon and Olszewzki's 'DART.

Lufkin brought the hovercraft to a halt a couple of miles further on, setting it down out in the bush away from the road. Behind them they could still see the thick, though lessening, black smoke rising high into the desert sky from the burning tank. The sight gave them no pleasure.

It took them only six minutes to switch the propellers and they were once more on their way. Seeing no one, they regained the highway and their breathtaking former speed. As they flew along, the men ate some of their rations and drank as much water as they could, having been denied any during the previous hour. In the desert heat, sweating as they were, their thirst had been voracious.

Ramirez tried to pour a little water into the mouths of the injured men, but without much success. It had now been five hours since Harlon and Olszewski had last had a drink that morning at the head waters of the qanat. In there injured state, they needed fluids even more than their tired thirsty comrades, but without IV's Ramirez was powerless to help them.

Considering all the shooting, it was amazing that the hovercraft had not sustained more damage. Discussing it, Pons and Gordon decided it was probably because the Libyans had a very difficult time aiming from the back of the moving truck. Still, it was surprising some stray rounds hadn't hit the fuel barrels or one of the engines. The first scenario would have been an unmitigated disaster. The second heartbreaking, though probably bearable. For their good fortune, all aboard were heartily thankful

34

After traveling an uneventful half hour, the hovercraft reached the end of the road where it joined the coast highway. Across the intersection on the far side of the highway was a field of sedgy plants with reeds edging a shallow pond into which ran the wadi. Skirting the wetland, the coast highway continued on to the northeast toward Tripoli, Libya's capitol city.

Gordon looked carefully in all directions with the monocular. He saw no one to the right, left, or behind them and was surprised. He had expected the coast highway to be busy with traffic. The coast highway was Libya's main highway. Main highways are busy places, therefore, he'd expected it to be busy, but he was wrong about this. He had also expected to run into some kind of trouble here, but there was none.

Relieved that the way was open, it bothered him that his assumptions had been so far from the truth. He reminded himself to be wary of this type of stereotypical thinking. North Africa was not the United States.

They proceeded across the road into the swamp. It was here that the wadi changed into a shallow water filled channel running through sand flats and boggy marsh. Chief Lufkin steered the craft along side the channel, staying on the land as much as possible. Traveling at forty knots, it was not long before the sand flats disappeared giving way to an enormous grass covered marsh.

Occasional areas of tall plants and trees forced them over the water, but for the most part, they traveled over the marsh grass covered flats.

The cool greenness of the marsh after hours in the monotonous yellow-brown oven like desert was a welcomed change for their tired eyes. The sight of verdant trees, bushes, and marsh teeming with birds and buzzing insects, all of which fled the approach of their roaring hovercraft, surprised them and lifted their spirits.

As with the empty highway, the enormous green wetland caught Gordon off guard. Again thinking in a stereotypical way, he said, "I didn't realize there could be a place like this with all these birds along the North African coast."

"This marsh is undoubtedly part of the north/south flyway system used by migrating birds flying between Africa to Europe," said Pons.

Hearing this exquisite beginning to a tutorial, Gordon realized, too late, he should not have given Pons such an open ended opportunity to lecture. He braced for one of Syman's pedantic monologues. Surprisingly, Syman said nothing else and they continued to ride along in silence.

In fifteen minutes they had left the coast's swampy fringe behind, quickly skimming across the narrow white sand beach and onto the Mediterranean sea toward the Tarawa.

"Crank'er up, Colonel," Lufkin said over the com-link as the machine settled on the water. Pons complied and the hovercraft accelerated, skimming over the sea's calm surface at seventy miles per hour.

Pons called the Tarawa with their present status. Those aboard ship were relieved to learn they were so close and on their way home.

"I have two birds in the air on standby, Colonel Pons," said the Tarawa's captain. "If you need help, they'll come running. You're a little over a hundred miles away. They can be over you in about twelve minutes if need be. We're running flank speed straight toward you at thirty five knots. Adding our speed to yours, we should meet in about an hour."

"That's great, Captain," replied Pons, truly relived. "Harlon and Olszewski are in rough shape and need attention and we're all pretty tired. It'll be a relief to be aboard again."

"I could send a chopper to pick up the injured men," said the Captain.

"I don't think it would save us enough time to make it worth it, Captain. By the time we completed a midair stretcher transfer, we could be along side where everyone would be safe."

"It's your call, Colonel," said the Captain.

"Let's keep going the way we are. We'll see you soon."

He put the phone in the storage pouch and fingered the com-link. He gave the Chief a course correction to bring them onto the exact heading for the Tarawa and then settled back to enjoy what he hoped would be a refreshing, uneventful ride back to the aircraft carrier.

They'd only ridden along ten minutes when Seaman Levine called out, "Bogey at four o'clock."

All eyes swiveled to the east southeast. Just above the horizon a jet was skimming the surface. Approaching like a wraith from hell, the thirty ton fighter roared overhead, rocking the hovercraft with its violent wake. The noise was deafening and the sudden nearness of the hostile war machine was unnerving even to the battle hardened SEALs.

Passing them, the fighter healed over hard to the south with its wingtip nearly in the water as it turned to line up again on the hovercraft. As it approached for a second pass, machine gun bullets stitched the water straight toward them.

"Syman, call for cover!" Gordon yelled. "Chief, take what ever evasive action you can!

In a moment, every weapon aboard was spitting lead at the attacker.

At the last possible second, Chief Lufkin swung the machine to starboard just as the bullet track reached them. The oncoming aircraft stapled a line of shots straight across the back of the hovercraft, the fifty caliber rounds easily punching holes through their Kevlar armor.

As Pons lifted the phone to call the aircraft carrier, the SatLink exploded from his hand. Plastic and electronic parts peppered him and a large hole appeared next to him in the Kevlar fabric of the cockpit's side.

"Shit!" Pons yelled, shaking his stinging hand. "That turd nearly took my hand off!"

"Are you okay, Sy?" Gordon asked, instantly.

With a calmer, but still angry voice, Pons said, "I'm okay, but he shot the phone, Dex. We're on our own, unless the Tarawa sees him on their radar."

"Great!" said Gordon, sarcastically. "What can we do against that monster? He's going ten times faster than we are and with his guns he can stand off a thousand yards and shoot us to pieces."

The adrenaline coursing through Pons sped up his thinking. Time telescoped as his immense intellect considered possibilities, one image after another past through his mind like slides through a projector gone wild. Dozens of ideas flashed passed in seconds before he settled on a plan. With a maniacal smile, the cool fighter pilot in him surfaced, ready once again to face an airborne adversary.

"We knew this was a possibility we might have to face, Dex," said Pons with steel in his voice. "I have an idea."

"Yeah, well, I'm glad to hear that, because just now, I'm fresh out of ideas. What da ya wanado?"

"As officers our first duty is to do what we can to protect our men, agreed?" asked Pons.

"Agreed," said Gordon.

"We can't do that on this raft of a vehicle."

"Which means?" Gordon asked.

"We fly our 'DART away from the hovercraft drawing the jet with us," said Pons.

"Committing suicide in the process, right? Great plan, Sy!" said Gordon, sarcastically.

"We take the Blowdarts with us and we shoot the jet down," said Pons, ignoring Gordon's comments.

"Your plan has two big problems, Sy. First, this hovercraft is no aircraft carrier. We can't fly the 'DART off this thing and as you can see, we're out in the middle of the Med with no runway in sight."

As they spoke, the Libyan jet again streaked by, overtaking them from the rear this time. Once again everyone opened up on the low flying jet as Chief Lufkin hollered to Pons, "Full reverse Colonel!"

Pons instantly reversed the DART's prop angle, fiercely straining its lashings. Simultaneously, Lufkin threw the helm hard to port and reversed the port engine, causing the machine to pivot sharply to the left.

Caught off guard by the hovercraft's wild maneuver, the jet's attack missed them completely.

"And the second thing," said Gordon, continuing, "the Blowdarts might work against a helicopter or a small plane, but they won't touch that thing."

"Taking your objections in reverse order," said Pons, "a Blowdart or even a rock for that matter, will stop that jet if it goes into the engine duct. And I can fly this 'DART off this hovercraft if we're moving when I do it."

"Your nuts, Pons! Did anyone ever tell you that?"

"Be that as it may, Dex, we better do something and fast or we're mulch. You and I can do it, together."

In a moment, Gordon made up his mind and called to the other men on the com-link, "Help Colonel Pons and me get this 'DART ready to fly."

Several of the SEALs looked over and inspected their officers.

"Let's go!" shouted Gordon, when he saw the men balk.

Pons climbed out of the cockpit of the 'DART and ran to Chief Lufkin carrying the Thermos full of test tubes.

"Whatever happens, Chief, get these back to John Claire on the Tarawa."

"Did you say you're gonna try ta fly the 'DART off this thing, Colonel?"

"With your help, Chief," replied Pons, without hesitation.

"When we're ready, you just go straight and fast and I'll fly it off."

"Yes, Sir. Whatever you say," said the Chief with doubt in his voice.

Gordon and the SEALs were already busy working on the 'DART when Pons returned.

"We'll have to get the Chief to bring us to a stop for a moment, so we can put the wings in place," said Gordon, "or the wind'll blow us overboard with them."

After hurriedly removing the wings from their storage compartment in the bottom of the 'DART's frame, they prepared for another pass from the Libyan jet. It wasn't long in coming.

Flying in from the port, the jet opened up on them, and again sent a line of bullets through the hovercraft. Fortunately, due to the craft's insubstantial nature and good luck, nothing vital was hit.

The moment the plane was past, Gordon ordered the Chief to shut the engines down. The hovercraft coasted to a near standstill as every man aboard wrestled with one wing or the other in a furious effort to assemble the 'DART. The moment both wings were securely fastened, which took just under a minute, Gordon shouted, "Go!" and the Chief again throttled the engines to maximum power.

"Here he comes again!" Lufkin yelled into the com-link.

Everyone braced for the deadly machine gun fire from the fighter. To their surprise, the jet flew past them this time without firing a shot. It was just the break they needed.

"I think he's doing recon on us. He's probably wondering what kind of strange things we're doing or maybe he thinks we've been damaged," said Pons, over the com-link.

"Put the two Blowdarts in the aft cockpit," Gordon ordered.

A moment later Petty Officer Dean said, "Commander! One missile was damaged by a round from the jet."

"It's a good thing the round didn't hit the warhead or we'd be dead. Toss it over the side and put the other one in the 'DART."

"Aye, Sir."

Dean did as ordered and then returned to fastening and tightening all the connections with the rest of the team getting the little plane ready to fly.

When they'd finished, Pons got in the pilot's seat and Gordon squeezed in next to the one remaining Blowdart.

"You know how to fire a Blowdart, Dex?"

"Yes," Gordon replied. "You get us in front of him and I'll take him down."

Pons spoke over the com-link, "Levine and Sykes, snub this rope I've tied to the floor frame of the 'DART to the frame of the wreck. You're going to hang on and help me fly her off. Hold her in position like a kite. Pay out rope as we gain altitude. Tell me when we're clear, and I'll release the rope from my end. Be sure to keep the rope out of the HC's propellers. The rest of you have to unlash the 'DART and hold her until I tell you to let go."

There was a flurry of movement as the men took their assigned positions. Awe showed on the faces of some of them, inspired by the nearly impossible takeoff being attempted by their officers. All of them, as experienced pilots, clearly understood the difficulties involved.

"Chief, after the Libyan's next pass, hold her straight and level, and go as fast as you can on your two engines. At forty knots, we should be able to lift and back straight up until we're away from your props."

"Aye, aye, Colonel. Good luck."

By then the jet had once again lined up on the hovercraft. This time, however, before it got anywhere close to the Americans, it loosed one of the two missiles it was carrying at them. The missile, traveling at over two thousand miles an hour, arrowed straight for them faster than the eye could follow. In seconds it was upon them and unbelievably, in a horrific hot flash, it boomed past just over head, skipping away like a stone over the water and was gone.

"Shiiit!" said Gordon, to Pons on intercom. "If we'd been in the air..."

Pons slowed their 'DART's engine.

"Unlash us!" he ordered the men, who instantly scrambled to comply. The hovercraft slowed to just over forty knots with the loss of the extra thrust from Pons' and Gordon's 'DART.

"Hold us steady, men," he ordered, as he increased the throttle and pulled back on the stick. The 'DART wavered and then trembling like a new butterfly unfurling its wings for its first flight, rose into the air, four feet, six feet, then ten feet. Levine and Sykes, struggled with the rope tether, trying not to hold the plane down without letting its wings drift back into the hovercraft deadly propellers.

Pons had been right. It was exactly like flying a very large kite, but in a gale force wind near power lines. It was also a very near thing. As it rose, the 'DART's frail wings only cleared the hovercraft's spinning props by inches.

Finally, Chief Petty Officer Charles said, "You're clear, Colonel. Good hunting!"

"Roger, that," said Pons, as he struggled to keep the 'DART airborne.

"Cut us loose, Dex!" Pons yelled.

Gordon yanked the end of the rope, releasing the slipknot tied to the "DART's frame. In the blink of an eye, the rope unwound with a zing and disappeared though the hole in the floor.

Now free, the 'DART rose abruptly as Pons throttled up the engine. Healing to the left, the little craft broke free of the turbulent air over the hovercraft and sailed away.

"Hot damn! Yahoo! Yeah! Right on!" The SEALs went wild cheering their officers on with raised arm salutes and hoots of admiration at their successful takeoff.

"Go get that big basta'd, Colonel!" Chief Lufkin hollered, over the com-link.

"We'll do what we can, men," Pons said, modestly, not wanting to tempt fate with arrogance, just then.

Moments later, the speeding Libyan jet roared in again in its relentless harassment. Seeing the tiny plane separate from the hovercraft gave its surprised pilot a moment of doubt. He turned off his original heading, deciding to pass by, instead of directly over, the air cushion vehicle.

Pons flew due east away from the hovercraft and the approaching jet at about one-hundred and fifty knots, the 'DART's top speed.

Seeing this new target, the Libyan slowed his machine from the four-hundred knots he'd maintained since coming upon the hovercraft, to two-hundred-thirty knots, just above the big plane's stall speed. Even at this perilously slow speed, he was still traveling eighty knots faster than the ridiculous craft in front of him and as a consequence, he caught up with the

American craft and was past it in a few seconds.

Scowling through the jet's clear plastic canopy, he waved a balled fist as he flew past. He now saw there were two men in the little airplane. What a silly toy it was! Savoring feelings of absolute power, he considered how he would knock the flimsy American bird from the sky. He decided he had three options.

He could fire his last remaining missile at it, but he doubted if it would lock on such a small target. He'd noticed it had almost no radar reflection, even as close as it was. That was odd, but he didn't dwell on it. Using the missile on so small a target was like stepping on an ant. There was no challenge in it. He decided he'd use the missile later on the hovercraft, when he was done tormenting its unfortunate crew.

His second option was shooting the two Americans to pieces with his machine gun. He liked the challenge in this method. It would take some skill to fly slow enough and hit so small a target.

There was a third option, which he was unsure of because it contravened everything he'd been taught in flight school about flying too close to another aircraft. He could try to physically knock them down by ramming them or perhaps clipping them with the tip of his wing. There was a tremendous element of excitement in this idea. In his mind's eye he envisioned his jet sweeping down upon them like a bird of prey, slamming them into the water. Flying only a hundred feet above the water, that's exactly what would happen if any part of his jet hit the ultralite.

He began a wide sweeping turn to bring him back for his attack. Taking his time, he wondered why the little aircraft was running away from the other machine. He suspected the two Americans were the leaders fleeing to save themselves from the certain destruction they knew would come to the hovercraft. He'd heard in training that American leaders were cowards and that they abandoned their men when there was danger. It appeared that what he'd been told was right, but these cowards weren't going to get away.

Like a cat playing with a mouse, he decided he'd begin by putting a few rounds in them, just to see their reaction. He hated cowards and he wanted these cowards to be afraid, very afraid, when he finally killed them.

Pons and Gordon watched as the Libyan jet roared past. The wake from the big jet shook the 'DART violently as they flew through it. They watched as the jet swept around to line up on them.

Gordon began positioning the Blowdart.

"Looks like the opportunity we need," said Pons. "He coming head on, straight for us."

"Turn us forty-five degrees to port, Sy, so I can shoot this thing at him without burning your hair off."

"Roger, that ol' buddy," Pons said, turning the 'DART onto the requested heading.

As the two aircraft closed on each other, the Libyan opened up on them with his machine gun. The big slugs flashed across the sky, intermittent tracers lighting their track. Pons and Gordon watched as they came closer and closer, but they could do nothing. Pons had to wait until Gordon took his shot before evading, and Gordon had to wait to fire the small missile until the big machine was right on top of them.

Seeing the convergence of the bullet stream and the 'DART was only a moment away, Pons turned their tiny airplane the moment Gordon fired the missile. The missile flew hot and straight for the jet fighter. From their position, it looked like the Blowdart was going right into the engine intake.

Taken completely by surprise, the Libyan stopped firing and froze until the last second before impact, when he twitched his stick slightly to the right. The big warbird had only just waggled, when the missile reached him. Unbelievably, the waggle, though moving the engine intake just a foot to the side, was enough. Missing the air intake by only inches, the Blowdart brushed the engine, tearing off a fin as it passed.

Banking steeply to the right to avoid the onrushing jet, Gordon and Pons watched with disbelief as their missile glanced off, flying into the water a half mile further on.

"We've got problems now, Pardner," said Gordon.

Pons said nothing, as he considered his options. He immediately began climbing as fast as the 'DART would go.

"We need to get our friend there above the Tarawa's radar horizon," he explained. "They'll send those jets when they see him on their scopes."

"It's a long shot, Sy, but I guess it's the best we can do under the circumstances."

"Oh, I wouldn't say that. We still have one more good option left, but I want the Tarawa's jets to cover us from here on because we won't be able to do much more when I'm finished with our next move."

"What are you up to, Sy?" Gordon asked, with a worried tone in his voice.

"Well, as you so accurately observed, earlier, I'm nuts. I've decided to take out that jet with a midair collision."

"You really are nuts if you think you can play chicken with that fighter and win!" Gordon retorted.

"Do you feel up to a nice refreshing swim?" Pons asked his companion.

"We'll die if we bail out from this height, Sy. You can't be serious."

"Oh, I'm serious, all right. But we're not going to bail out up here. We'll only be fifty to a hundred feet above the water when we fall out of our seats."

"When we fall out of our seats?" Gordon repeated sounding shocked.

"That's right," said Pons.

"Do I have a choice?" Gordon asked, sarcastically.

"Not if you want to live," said Pons, deadly serious.

"This maneuver is obviously not in the training manual!" Gordon said.

Pons ignored this last sarcastic comment, instead concentrating fiercely on the business at hand. The Libyan was once again sweeping around in a wide arc to line up on them. Once again bullets arched across the sky at them as they continued struggling upward for altitude. This time however, no longer constrained to fly an unchanging course, Pons took advantage of the 'DART's innate ability to do intricate aerial acrobatics, putting the little plane through several strenuous maneuvers to evade the jet's attacks while gaining a little altitude with each one. When they'd reached two thousand feet, where he was sure the Tarawa's radar would pick up the Libyan jet, Pons abruptly snapped the 'DART to the left, initiating a corkscrewing dive toward the sea. With the Libyan dogging their every move, anxiously awaiting his opportunity to destroy them, Pons hoped the Tarawa would not be long in sending their jets.

"Unfasten your seat harness, Dex and hang on until we're upside down. Then let go. I'm going to do a barrel roll at the bottom of this dive. At the top of the roll, the 'DART will add almost two-hundred knots speed to the collision. The Libyan will also be going something like two-hundred knots. Unable to stop, he'll fly into the 'DART a few second after we drop away."

"You're really going to try to splash that jet with a collision, Sy?"

"That's right, Amigo. Here we go!"

"Maybe you really are nuts, Syman. I know I am, to go along with a crazy stunt like this." As he said this, Gordon hurriedly unbuckled his harness and shrugged it off. Nuts or not, he knew he didn't want to get tangled in it when he dropped from the aircraft.

"Chief Lufkin!" Pons said, over the com-link, "We're going to knock the jet down in a few moments, but we'll end up in the water. Come pick us up."

"Aye, aye, Colonel," replied the Master Chief. "We'll be there ASAP. Give'em hell."

Now just a speck in the distance, Gordon glanced toward the hovercraft, which had been angling away as fast as it could travel. It abruptly changed course heading back toward them.

Finding the little American plane a more difficult target than before, the Libyan twisted and turned the jet to get in position behind it. He marveled as the American jinked his kite like little machine left and right, turning and twisting, up two thousand feet before healing over in a graceful corkscrewing dive toward the sea. After several sweeping turns the little plane pulled out into a straight dive and continued seaward.

For the stalking jet pilot, it was exactly the move he had been waiting for. Keeping a wary eye ahead for another missile shot from the little craft, he followed the ultralite down intending to pull out on top of the Americans, forcing them into the sea.

To keep the pressure up on the way down, the Libyan fired short machine gun bursts at the Americans, putting several shots into the wings and one into the vertical stabilizer. Surprisingly, his hits seemed to have no effect on the little plane. Nearing the bottom of their dive, he stopped firing, knowing it no longer mattered. In a few moments the Americans and their absurd little airplane would be no more.

"Get ready, Dex!" said Pons, just before putting the 'DART into the tight little climb that would turn them upside down. At the bottom of their dive, traveling at nearly two hundred knots, the fierce strain of their sudden reversal nearly tore the wings off the little ultralite.

"Bail out!" He yelled, just as the centrifugal force from the loop disappeared. A moment later, he glanced over his shoulder, to reassured himself Gordon had dropped free before launching himself into the void. As he dropped the hundred odd feet toward the water, he inverted his position to feet first and watched, mesmerized in horror, as the enormous jet fighter, which had been closer than he'd realized, swept under the upside down ultralite, missing it completely, nearly hitting him instead.

Stunned by the nearness and the noise of the enormous, fast moving war plane, Pons nevertheless watched with rapt attention as his laptop, which had apparently slipped from the storage pouch, was sucked into the big jet's voracious air intake as it flashed by just yards above him. The roar of the jet engine was deafening and its hot exhaust caused Pons to turn his face away. He looked down just as Gordon, also feet first, arrowed into the water. A moment later he hit the water. It was not a soft landing.

Hitting the water wrong would have had the same effect as hitting the ground from a hundred feet up. Fortunately, both men entered feet first and instantly found themselves twenty feet under water. Though stunned by the brutal landing, they struggled to surface as quickly as possible. Gordon popped to the surface first. Shaking the water from his face in an effort to clear his vision, he looked around wildly for his friend.

"Are you okay, Sy?" he yelled toward the head that popped to the surface near by. Hearing no reply, he began swimming in his friend's direction. As he neared him, he hollered again. Then he saw that Pons was looking in the direction of the receding jet. It came to him that the jet was still in the air. As he focused on it he also noticed that it was trailing thick black oily smoke.

"Did it work?" he hollered at Pons again.

"He missed the 'DART completely."

"Shit!" said Gordon, sputtering sea water in angry frustration

"But, I saw my laptop go into the air intake. No mistake about that."

As he said it, they heard the throaty roar from the retreating jet fighter stop and as they watched, they saw the jet disappear behind a wave and then reappear as it cartwheeled over the surface of the sea. A moment later, it disappeared again. A load slapping noise came over the water a few seconds later and then there was silence.

"That's it," said Pons, grimly. Gordon shook his head up and down once and said, "Yeah, that's it."

Now that the danger was gone, both men were too tired to waste anymore energy talking. They needed all their strength just to tread water until the approaching hovercraft picked them up.

35

Syman put the report down on the desk. He turned and looked out the French doors behind him. What he saw was a perfect spring day with a vivid blue sky and a few puffy white clouds off in the distance. The new leaves on the tree just outside the doors wavered slightly in the gentle breeze. The afternoon sun slanted in from the west brightening the room and giving its wood paneling a golden hue. Feeling its warmth on his face, Syman sat up and arched his back, yawning and stretching at the same time.

A week had past since their return from Nalut. Syman and Dexter had been office bound the entire time working through the problems that had appeared during their unexpected ten day absence. To Syman, the seemingly endless details had become irksome. Needing a break, he rose from his chair and walked to the coffee pot on the sideboard next to the wall. He poured himself a steaming cup and returned to his desk.

Management bored Syman and when he was forced to do it, he usually became sleepy in the afternoon. When he was working in the plant or in the development lab he never got sleepy. He loved research and he loved the work that TMI did — everything except the management. Their products, improving their performance, getting them to market, creating new products, all of this thrilled Syman. He never felt sleepy when dealing with these things.

He wondered how Dexter was doing in his office next door. Syman considered inviting him for a cup of coffee. He decided against it, recognizing this for the diversion it was. Just because he wasn't in the mood to do more paper work wasn't an acceptable reason to disturb his partner. He marveled at how childish his thinking could be sometimes when he had to face doing a task he didn't particularly like. He was pondering this when the phone rang interrupting his thoughts.

After a moment, Esmirelda said, "Royce Aldrich is on the phone, Syman."

"Ah, excellent! Just the diversion I need," Syman said, instantly forgetting his self recriminatory observation of a few moments before.

"Royce, glad you called. How are you doing and how is the work on the plate going?"

"I'm doing very well, Sy. And the work on the plate is really moving along.

The comparitor you sent me is worth a whole classroom of graduate student's help and the results so far are astonishing. That's why I called, to tell you what I've found."

"I'm all ears," said Syman, feeling not the least bit guilty about abandoning the office work on the desk in front of him.

"I'll start by saying that if the artifact is real, it may be one of the most important discoveries in archaeology."

Syman was taken aback by Royce's bold assertion. Having seen where it had been discovered at the mouth of the tunnel to the underground facility, Syman could not imagine what Royce was about to tell him.

"Is Dex around? He'll want to hear this, too."

"Okay. Just a minute." Syman adressed his comparitor, "Essy, would you ask Mr. Gordon to join our conversation, please."

A moment later, Dexter came on the phone.

"Hi, Royce."

"Hi, Dex."

"What's up?" Dexter asked.

"I wanted to tell you guys what I've discovered about the metal plate you asked me to examine. If it's real, it's one of the most important finds in the history of archaeology. It might be the most important, but only if it's real."

"You're not serious, right Royce? You're pulling our legs?"

"No. I'm serious", said Royce, sounding a little miffed at the tone of Dexter's question.

"Sorry, Royce," said Dexter abashed. "I didn't mean to insult you. It's just that until a moment ago I'd been reading about production delays. You caught me flat footed. It's a far piece of mental real estate between the two subjects."

"It happens, Royce," said Syman, getting Dex off the hook, "that since I gave you the artifact, we've had an opportunity to actually see where it was originally found."

"That's great! Any chance I might be able to see the place?"

"I don't think so. Not right now, anyway."

"Why not?"

Syman and Dexter proceeded to tell Royce all the details of their run-in with Osmid Bandar and the circumstances of the last three weeks. Now it was Royce's turn to be astonished.

"This is nuts! You say an extremist terrorist group has a nuclear bomb and the government sent you guys to get it?"

"They sent a special forces group with Syman and me in command. We're both reservist with a lot of time in the service. In fact, we met in the Persian Gulf during the war."

"You two are amazing," said Royce. "First you hand me what might be the most important archaeological find in history and then you go off chasing after terrorists to take a nuclear bomb away from them. I don't know which is more incredible." After a moment, he continued. "Do you think they'll find the bomb?"

"There's no way to tell, but our Government is working overtime, right now, trying."

"The idea of terrorists having a nuclear bomb is the stuff nightmares are made of. It gives me chills just thinking about it. You involved in it still?"

"No," said Syman.

There was silence on the line for a long moment.

"Well, let's see," said Royce, changing the subject back to archaeology. "Tell me more about this underground facility you were in."

They spent several minutes describing every detail they could remember to Royce.

"The plate was found locked in a hollow in the top of a three foot high rock pedestal," said Syman.

"Yes," said Dexter. "It was kind of like a podium or music stand. But it was all rock and about a foot and a half square. It was sticking up right in the middle of the entrance tunnel. There was a metal cover, like a hood, with metal straps that held it in place. The workman who originally found it used metal shears to cut the straps to see what was under the top. That's where the plate was found."

"You saw this pedestal?"

"Yes, we both looked it over."

"It was obviously placed there to be found," said Royce.

"We've told you just about everything we know. Now it's your turn. What were you going to tell us?"

"What you've just told me lends a great deal of credence to what the plate reveals about itself. The upper half of the plate is a pictorial dictionary specifically designed to make its fifteen thousand pages of nonpictorial writing quickly and easily readable by whomever found it."

"Did you say fifteen thousand pages?" Dexter was incredulous.

"Yes," said Royce, "six quarters of the plate's surface is covered with microscopic text; the two quarters on the lower half of the front of the plate and the four quarters on the back of the plate. Each quarter is composed of twenty-five of those small shiny squares, five by five. You both are familiar with that aspect of the plate. When each of those shiny little squares is viewed under a microscope, it resolves to four squares each of twenty-five smaller squares. Each of these smallest squares is a micro-page of text. It's like a box within a box within a box.

By studying the pictorial dictionary on the top half of the front of the plate, the reader can quickly learn the language used in the text.

The comparitor has already translated the entire fifteen thousand pages and

I've read the first thousand pages. What those pages tell, if true, will change our entire understanding of history."

"Royce our curiosity is killing us. What does the damn thing say?" Dexter asked, impatiently.

"The plate indicates that the earth was peopled by civilized men 500,000 years ago and just as they reached a technological level a little more advanced than our own, the Earth was hit by a comet. Supposedly, it killed almost everything larger than an insect on the planet."

"Now, you're pulling our legs, right?" Dexter said.

"No, I'm not," said Royce continuing, "and the underground facility you just told me about will probably prove the plate to be genuine.

"How can you know the date from that far back in history?" asked Syman. "There are no commonly known reference points in time."

"The people who made the plate put an ingenious radioactive clock on the plate. Above the square with the sun and moon, there's no gold plating inside the little inscribed moon. If you look closely you'll see that tiny area is gray instead of gold, but it's so small that you don't notice the color difference. The square below it explains that the gray metal showing is a mixture of uranium isotopes 232, 235, and 238 rather than the base metal, which incidentally is pure platinum. By measuring the isotopes and comparing their test percentages to the original values inscribed on the plate when it was made, it's easy to calculate the age accurately using the half life values for each isotope. They also listed the percent values for radioactive isotopes for the spot of gold covering the disk of the tiny sun inscribed next to it. It was specially prepared with radioactive gold isotopes. And as if that weren't enough, they also listed the original amounts of the radioactive isotopes for the platinum base metal of the plate. This gives triple redundancy for the dating."

"You know how to do those tests, Royce?" Dexter asked, sounding surprised.

"No, Dex, I don't. I enlisted the help of a friend, Lorraine Beck, to do the measurements. She's a chemistry professor here at Yale and she does most of the physical tests and dating for me on my other work.

I've been having my doubts about the dating test accuracy, but now that you guys have actually seen a shelter, I'm beginning to think maybe they're right.

Anyway, the plate says the facility where the plate was left protected a number of people from the comet strike and the resultant disaster for a generation while the planet's climate restabilized."

"If this is true, Royce, its significance is staggering!" said Syman.

"When I called, I wasn't anything like convinced that the plate was a genuine artifact. Still, it's so provocative that I hoped it was. The people who made it were incredibly ingenious, but it's almost too perfect to be real. The truth is, I've been waiting for the other shoe to drop ever since I began translating it. Until now, I've been thinking it was all just too fantastic to believe, but since you've both seen the shelter it describes we can probably go forward on the assumption that what it says is true."

There was silence on the line for several moments as the three men contemplated the possibility.

"Now that you've told me where the artifact was found, some of the other things it says make more sense. It says that each shelter held 3125 people selected for their skills, knowledge and..."

"What do you mean each shelter?" Syman asked, interrupting Royce.

"That's one of the other things I really couldn't believe. The artifact says there were originally twenty-five shelters around the world. It says they were spread over the widest area to increase the chances of survival for the largest number of people. Three were destroyed when the comet hit the Earth. And there's a map showing all the locations. I looked at it, but at the time I didn't take it seriously. I guess I better look at it again. It's hard to believe something as big as you described this place to be could remain hidden until now."

"If you had seen how deep underground it is, you'd understand," said Dexter.

Royce continued, "It says they began tracking the comet during its first pass through the inner solar system nine years before the strike. It broke apart as it rounded the sun and they discovered it would probably strike the earth when it returned the next time. This gave them almost a decade to prepare the shelters it describes.

The plate states unequivocally that the comet hit the earth and the people survived in the shelters for many years after that, until the earth's climate settled down again.

You have to understand, when I read all this I started thinking hoax—big time hoax. I don't know of any large scale extinctions 500,000 years ago."

"If memory serves," said Syman, "one of the recent ice age periods started about that long ago. Maybe a comet strike initiated a planet wide cooling period that led to the ice age and maybe the ice age masked the extinctions."

"Maybe," said Royce.

"Or maybe they preserved enough of the Earth's flora and fauna in the shelters, that there weren't many extinctions," said Syman. "I don't know enough about the science to know if that's possible, but that might be one theory worth checking out."

"You just might have something there, Sy," agreed Royce.

"Can we get together this weekend? I really want to take some time and look carefully at what you've got."

"Sure. Why don't you and Dex come here Saturday and I'll show you everything."

"Sounds good to me," said Dexter. "I want to see that map."

"How's 10 AM?" Syman suggested.

"Perfect," said Royce.

"See you Saturday, then," said Syman.

Royce hung up.

With Dexter still on the line Syman said, "Absolutely amazing!"

"Yeah, I guess you could say that," Dexter said, in what was for him a masterpiece of understatement.

They were both silent and then Syman said, "How're you coming with the backlog?"

"I'll be finished by the end of day. How about you?"

"About the same," said Syman, as an idea came to him. "Since we're both still on the phone, why don't we call John Claire? I want to hear how the spooks are doing with their efforts at locating the bomb."

"Yeah. I do, too. And I want to find out what that bio-crud we brought back is."

"Essy, Please call John Claire," Syman instructed the comparitor.

"Yes, Syman." There were clicks on the line as the comparitor made the connection and then they heard John Claire answer, "Hello?"

"John, it's Syman Pons."

"Hi, Syman."

"Dex is on the line, too."

"Hi, Dex."

"Yo, John. We're calling to see how you bureaucrats are faring with the great snark hunt?"

"Well, to tell you the truth, not very well, yet, but there are one hell of a lot of noses being ground down looking, right now."

"Aboard the Tarawa," Dexter continued, "the last thing we'd heard was that the carrier's radar had lost the helicopter over Algeria."

"We think it landed there," said Claire. "Israel has a man on the ground there and he's checking it out."

"You told the Israelis?" Syman asked.

"Yes and every other friendly government and agency on the planet. We've got to find that bomb and quickly."

"You might as well put it on the evening news," said Dexter.

"Actually, the President is considering doing just that hoping it will flush the bastards into the open, but it'll probably make our job harder. They'll probably just go deeper underground."

"What'd you find in those test tubes we brought back with us from Nalut?" Dexter asked, abruptly changing the subject.

"Funny you should ask that. I just got off the phone with a Major Hunt, the liaison officer with the Army's biological weapons outfit USAMRID. They tested that stuff you found and apparently it's some kind of flu vaccine."

"Damn!" said an excited Dexter. "We nearly got killed over some flu vaccine!"

"Technically, Dex, finding those test tubes was an unexpected bonus," said Claire.

"Some bonus!"

"Well, at least we know it's not a biological weapon," said Syman.

"It's a goddamn strange place to be storing flu vaccine!" said Dexter, with finality.

"That's true," agreed Claire, "but that's what the man said it was, some type of flu vaccine."

"Dexter's right," said Syman. "It was definitely a curious place to find it. The middle of the Sahara Dessert doesn't strike me as a place one is likely to catch influenza."

"Seems like the trip to Nalut was a big waste of time."

"It was certainly no waste of time, Dex." said Claire. "Because of what you guys did, we now know absolutely that there is at least one bomb. Just the knowledge that it exists is a big help in preparing a defense against its possible use. It's much better than being blind sided when a city is destroyed."

"I suppose," said Dexter, unmollified.

"What have you found out about Hinode?" Syman asked. "Is there some connection there?"

"We began checking into that, Syman, but we got a call from higher up. They told us not to rock the boat on that." Claire, sounded a bit sheepish.

"Don't rock the boat?" said Dexter, his voice rising. "What is that supposed to mean? It looked like Hinode was involved up to its hairline with the Islamic Brotherhood in its effort to build an atomic bomb."

"Listen, guys. That's all I know right now. We were ordered to lay off that line of investigation, so we did."

"You were ordered to lay off?" Dexter asked, still sounding incredulous and now disgusted as well. "By whom?"

"I can't tell you," said Claire.

"You can't, John, or you won't?" Syman asked.

There was silence on the line for a moment. "You guys are putting me in a hell of a spot," said Claire, defensively. "I could lose my job for telling you about this."

"You can work for us if you lose your job," said Syman.

"We could have lost our lives, last week!" said Dexter. "You owe us an answer."

"Someone on the Senate intelligence oversight committee called and said we were upsetting some very powerful friends in Japan and we needed to stop it."

"This smells like politics, and it smells very bad," said Syman.

"Yeah, I know Syman, but my hands are tied. I have to do what I'm told."

"I think you've been living in Washington too long, John," said Dexter. "It's beginning to corrupt your thinking."

"That's not fair, Dexter!" said Claire, defensively.

"The hell it's not. Just remember, your real friends tell you the truth when they see you making bad decisions, no matter what."

"I concur, John," said Syman.

There was a pregnant pause on the phone and then Claire said, "I'll call you if anything happens," and he hung up.

After a moment, Syman asked, "You think we were a little too harsh with him?"

"No, I don't. We put a hell of a lot on the line for the country and now the politicians are defecating on our effort. They're also endangering the lives of a lot of people. Their meddling really pisses me off."

"Well, I feel the same way, but what can we do about it?"

"I don't know," said Dexter, thinking.

"You want a cup of coffee? I just made some."

"Sure, that'd be good."

Dropping the phone receiver onto its cradle, Dexter got up from his desk and walked through the connecting door to Syman's office. Syman was pouring hot, fresh black coffee into a bright red mug with the words "ROCKET FUEL" stenciled on it in bold letters. He handed it to Dexter. It was one of a set Karrie had given him. Each one had something amusing printed on it. Syman's said "LIQUID AMBITION." They sat down with their coffee at Syman's desk.

"I think there's a serious connection between Hinode and the terrorists," said Syman, with certainty.

"Yeah, I do, too. Hinode had its name all over everything."

"You know, Dex, I think we should investigate Hinode ourselves."

"We could do that. What do you have in mind?"

"Hinode's main office in the United States is in New York City. What I'm thinking is, that you and I take a little sojourn into Manhattan this afternoon and pay them a visit."

"We can do that, but what do you expect to find?"

"Well, fortune does favor the pro-active," said Syman, with a sly grin.

"And..." said Dexter, waiting.

"I was thinking along the lines of letting ourselves into their office and then maybe doing a little creative computer hacking. People put the damnedest things into their computers these days."

Dexter smiled, and said, "It sounds a bit larcenous to me, pardner,"

"Quite so, old schlub, but it's the quickest way I know to maybe find out what the bastards are really up do."

"Do you have anything vital on your desk?" Dexter asked.

"No. I took care of all the important things, first."

"Good!" said Dexter, with relish. "Let's go after these people and see what we can find out about them

36

Sumiko awoke panting. Breathless, she felt as if she were drowning. Her lungs were full of fluid. She coughed violently to clear them, but it didn't help. She swung her legs out of bed and sat up. Beating on her chest between her breasts, Sumiko leaned forward and coughed again and again trying to dislodge the fluid. Her efforts were in vain. Try as she might, she couldn't get a satisfying breath of air into her lungs and panic was hovering at the edge of her self-control.

It occurred to Sumiko as she sat there gasping that she may have developed bronchitis or pneumonia from the remnant of the horrid illness she'd contracted when she'd returned from Japan two weeks before. A sniffly, irritating little cold had stubbornly clung to her since then. It had annoyed her and sapped her vitality in small ways and it had kept Sumiko from feeling completely well. All this went through Sumiko's mind in a moment and the idea that she might be getting seriously ill again made her angry.

Sitting up helped her catch her breath. After a few minutes the coughing stopped. Still, Sumiko could feel she was really sick. Her head throbbed with pain and she had a fever. Her mouth felt like it was full of talc and she could feel a distinct soreness at the base of her tongue deep in her throat. She had a strong unpleasant taste in her mouth and the smell of her breath was disgusting.

Sumiko glanced at the clock. It said 5:40. It was too early to call Ralph.

She rose slowly to her feet, and headed for the bathroom. With one hand, she turned on the light. With the other, she turned on the water. Filling a cup, she swished a little water around her mouth. She spit it into the white porcelain sink. It was tinted pink with blood. Alarmed, Sumiko realized she needed to see a doctor right away. She decided she'd better get herself to the hospital rather than wait for Ralph to wake up

37

Dexter and Syman were surprised when they discovered that Hinode's U.S. headquarters' office occupied the entire thirty-third floor of the Empire State Building.

Driving into Manhattan in Dexter's Jeep took just over an hour, but finding a place to park took another half hour. Fifteen minutes after that, Dexter and Syman stepped out of a crowded elevator into an empty vestibule on the thirty-third floor. The lights shown brightly but there was no one around, not a soul. Syman looked at his watch. It said 4:38.

Dressed in attractive, conservative business attire, Dexter and Syman looked like the business executives they were, ordinary in every way, even to the slim charcoal gray briefcase Syman was carrying. However, the case, like the men, was anything but ordinary. Within it was the brand new, state of the art, portable comparitor with which Syman had replaced his old, and now destroyed laptop. With it Syman and Dexter would have no trouble searching through Hinode's computers and recording anything they found of interest.

"At this time of day I would expect to find a lot people bustling around finishing up and getting ready to go home," said Syman, as they approached the elegant double glass doored entrance of Hinode Worldwide's United States headquarters office.

"You'd think so, wouldn't you," agreed Dexter.

It was their intention to first reconnoiter Hinode's offices just before closing time. They wanted to familiarize themselves with the physical layout. To do this they would introduce themselves to the receptionist and say they'd just happened to be in the building on other business. They would explain that they hoped to establish a first contact between TMI and Hinode that might lead to a bit of business. With a little luck, they would be allowed to speak to someone for a few minutes out of courtesy and then be shown the door.

A few minutes inside the offices would be enough for them. Then they would return in a few hours, when the office was empty, and let themselves in to do their little computer search of Hinode's records.

As Syman approached the doors he could see a large empty desk sitting astride Hinode's entrance foyer. It was the receptionist's desk and it was curious that it too was empty at this time of day. He gave the left door handle a firm tug. It didn't move. He leaned close to the door to read a small printed card taped to the other side.

It said: "The offices of Hinode Worldwide will be temporarily closed for alterations and cleaning until Monday morning. Please forgive us for the inconvenience. Thank you."

"They're closed," Syman said, with surprise.

"Good," said Dexter. "Now we won't have to come back later." After a moment, he asked Syman, "You're sure you can pick the lock?"

Syman looked carefully at the polished brass lock on the doors.

"I think so."

Syman removed an eyeglass case from inside his jacket. Up ending it, he shook out a flat wire and a pick. With Dexter standing next to him to screen the procedure from anyone who might happen along, Syman proceeded to open the door. It took him longer than he liked, but finally the flat wire rotated down and they heard a satisfying snap as the bolt drew back.

Syman opened the door tentatively and held it that way without entering for a full minute. When no alarm sounded, they stepped into the headquarters foyer of Hinode Worldwide. Syman relocked the door behind them and they headed toward the inner offices, where they could work unseen with a couple of the firm's computers. They quickly walked past the receptionist's desk to another set of double doors, ornate with carved oak panels. There was no lock and Dexter and Syman were through the doors in a moment.

Entering the next room, their attention was instantly drawn to a large mechanical device about the size of a refrigerator, sitting on a six wheel piano dolly in the middle of this inner office. Squat and massive, the bulk of the machine was a large sphere, festooned with wiring and small tubes, sitting atop three pipe legs, mounted to a stout metal cabinet. It resembled a short ugly water tower, the type to be found outside any small town on the American great plains. The remains of a wooden crate lay in a heap on the floor behind it.

Dexter and Syman knew immediately that they had found the bomb.

"Well, that didn't take long," said Dexter, contemptuously.

Syman said nothing, as he stood there gazing at it.

After a moment, Syman began to recover from the shock of their discovery. He leaned close, focusing his attention on a low ominous hum issuing from the bomb. Without hesitation he reached toward the handle on the cabinet door as Dexter watched.

"Hey, don't open that!" Dexter yelled. But Dexter's warning was too late. Syman had already pulled the cabinet open to inspect the maze of wires and equipment crammed into it, suspecting they might have a bigger problem on their hands than Dexter realized.

Inside, there was a lighted numerical counter ticking off seconds. It blinked each time the number changed 17:46, 17:45, 17:44, 17:43...

"Holy shit!" said Dexter, realization coming to him. "It's going to go off!"

"Not if we can disarm it," said Syman.

He set the briefcase on the floor next to the cabinet and opened it. Taking out the Sat-Link, he handed it to Dexter. "Call John Claire and explain the situation to him. We've got to warn him in case we can't shut this thing down." After inspecting the electronics of the bomb for a moment, he said, "Dex, get me a parallel cable from one of these computers so I can connect the comparitor to the bomb's computer controller."

Dexter quickly walked behind the nearest desk to get behind its computer. Pinching the phone between his ear and shoulder to free both hands, he proceeded to unscrew the cable connecting the PC to its printer. Thirty seconds later he handed it to Syman, who was busy configuring the comparitor.

Syman took the cable and then on second thought handed one end back to Dexter saying, "Plug this end into the comparitor while I plug my end into the bomb."

"Any chance we could set this thing off if we tamper with it?" Dexter asked, sounding a little hesitant.

"I'm not sure if we can disarm it safely," said Syman, truthfully, "But what I am sure of, is that this thing is definitely going to explode in sixteen minutes and some odd seconds. Our only chance is that we try to shut it down."

"Damn!" said Dexter, with conviction.

Syman ran an interrogative program to find the programming language used by the bomb's builders. The results were unsuccessful. The comparitor was unable to interface with the bomb's controller, but Syman kept at it.

Dexter, who had been trying to contact John Claire on the Sat-Link suddenly heard him on the line.

"Hello. Claire here."

"John, it's Dexter Gordon. Syman and I have located the bomb and..."

"How in the hell'd you do that?" replied Claire, sounding very surprised by the revelation.

Dexter continued. "John, I don't have time to explain. You have to listen to me. The bomb is in the Hinode Worldwide office on the thirty-third floor of the Empire State Building in New York City..."

"How did it get there?"

Dexter again ignored Claire's question, "The bomb is armed and it's going to go off in about fifteen minutes. You need to know that in case Syman and I can't disarm it."

"Is this a joke, Dexter?"

"This is no joke, John. If New York goes up, at least you'll know what happened here."

"Dexter.."

"I've got to get off and see what I can do to help Syman." Dexter said, leaning over to look at the timer's display, "but, before I do, I'll give you the exact amount of time left. Do you have a watch?"

"Go ahead," said Claire.

"On my mark," Dexter said, cueing Claire, "It will be fifteen minutes and ten seconds. Mark!"

"Got it, Dex."

"I'll call you if we get the damn thing disarmed."

"After I talk to the President, I'll see if I can get some tech help for you guys, but there's not much time."

"Tell me about it!" Gordon retorted. "Still, Syman's had some nuke training in the Air Force, so we'll see what we can do."

"Good luck," said Claire, and disconnected.

While Dexter had been talking with Claire, Syman had been furiously trying every query and entry program he could think of in an effort to discover the language the builder's had used in the bomb's controller. The effort was without result. The comparitor for all its power was useless until it could find the right language to talk to the bomb's computerized brain.

Syman rolled his shoulders in an effort to adjust the now damp shirt under his suit jacket. He was sweating heavily and the shirt was clinging to his skin and it itched. It was distracting him and now was not the time to be distracted. He quickly shrugged the jacket off.

"What can I do to help?" Dexter asked, frustrated that he didn't already know the answer to his own question.

"Nothing," said Syman. After a moment he glanced up at Dexter and said, "Look around and see if you can find some tools. I'm not having any luck interfacing the controller. We may have to dismantle some part of the bomb to shut it down."

Dexter immediately began rummaging through the desks nearest him gathering anything he found that he thought might be useful. In the first four desks he found a contraption for removing staples from a document, a pair of large scissors and two letter openers. In the last desk he found a small brass hammer, whose handle contained a set of diminishing screwdrivers, one inside the other and another pair of scissors.

"How are you doing?" he called to Syman.

"Still not in," said Syman, without looking up.

Dexter walked quickly over to Syman and set the pathetic load of implements next to his partner on the floor. He glanced at the timer. It said 10:22.

"We've only got ten more minutes Sy."

"Give me another two minutes. After that we'll have to try dismantling something."

"Whatever you think. I'm in way over my head messing with an atomic bomb."

Dexter would not have been reassured if he could have read Syman's mind as he thought silently to himself, "So am I, pardner. So am I."

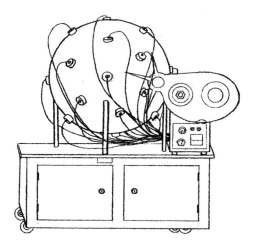

Dexter looked hard at the Medusa like bomb and asked Syman, "What are all these wires for?"

"Which ones are you talking about?" Syman answered absently without looking up.

"These wires that connect to the things that look like spark plugs all around the sphere at the top," said Dexter, stepping close and pointing.

Syman glanced up to see what Dexter was talking about. "Those wires carry the electric charges that detonate the high explosives that compress the plutonium to its critical mass so the fission process begins," explained Syman, unable to keep from giving a somewhat pedantic description even at such a perilous time.

"You mean," said Dexter, "if those wires can't carry electricity to the high explosives, then the bomb can't be set off."

"Yes," Syman said.

Dexter grabbed a pair of scissors and quickly cut one of the thirty odd wires leading to the detonators.

"Don't do that!" Syman yelled. "You might set it off!"

But Syman's admonition was too late.

Realizing he might have just made a big mistake, Dexter stood frozen, still holding the cut ends of the wire he'd just severed. Nothing happened.

The immobile men both sprang into action, now knowing they could cut the detonator's wires without consequence. Syman snatched up the other pair of scissors and the two men cut wires as fast as they could.

When they were done Syman said, "Sometimes I can be a little too bright for my own good."

"Is this thing safe now?"

"Well, I don't think this damn thing could ever be called safe, but it won't go off in..." Syman looked at the counter, "in nine minutes, if that's what you mean."

"Yeah, that's what I mean." After a moment's thought, Dexter asked, "Why didn't we cut the detonator's wires in the first place?"

"I thought the bomb's builders might have bobby-trapped the bomb to keep anyone from doing just that."

"Good reason."

Both men stood there just looking at the machine, feeling slack as the tension of the situation eased.

"We've got to call John and tell him," said Dexter.

"Right," said Syman.

He picked up the Sat-Link and pushed the redial button.

In a few moments John Claire's distinctive voice came on the line.

"Hello."

"John, it's Syman."

"Syman, how are you doing?"

"We've disarmed the bomb!"

"Good!" said Claire. "But we may have an even bigger problem on our hands."

"What do you mean an even bigger problem?" Syman asked. Dexter looked over at Syman, who motioned to him to come close to the phone, so he could listen to the conversation, too.

"While I was on the phone telling the President you two had found the bomb and that it was armed, we were interrupted by a call from NORAD. A Russian missile sub in the Atlantic transiting a little east of that island where you guys were picked up just launched two missiles at the United States. The first one is aimed at New York City and will arrive about the same time that bomb would have gone off. The second was launched five minutes after that toward Washington."

"That's incredible!" said Dexter.

"I don't think incredible even begins to cover it," said Claire, sounding glum.

Although shocked by Claire's revelation, Syman's mind instead fastened on the coincidence in the timing of the first missile's arrival over New York at the same time the bomb should have exploded. That coincidence was just a little too convenient to be unrelated to the bomb they had just disarmed and it tweaked Syman's mental alarm bell. He also considered the coincidence of the missiles being launched near the Ilhas Desertas Islands. That too was just too improbable to be a coincidence and Syman suspected there was something important going on that they didn't understand. It took him a moment to figure it out.

Osmid Bandar had told them the island's fishing complex existed to provide cover for a missile launching base being built by the Islamic Brotherhood. He'd also indicated the situation on the island was more complex than that, but he had died before he could explain further.

When Dexter and Syman had returned from Nalut, it had been assumed the bomb might eventually arrive at Ilhas Desertas and a radiation sensing sniffer plane had been flying over the island every night since to keep an eye on the place.

In light of the day's events and with the bomb sitting just feet from him, Syman was now sure the real purpose for the missile launching base had never been to deliver any weapons. Too large and fragile to fit into a missile, the warhead had been delivered to New York days before any missile would arrive. The missiles, Syman now realized, were just a feint intended to alert the United States to the fact that it was being attacked. Syman was now sure they were involved in something much more sinister than just a simple terrorist attack with a small nuclear bomb.

"John, how sensitive is the resolving power of the tracking system that picked up the launch?" Syman asked.

"Syman, at a time like this, who cares?" Claire shot back, sounding exasperated with the seemingly irrelevant question.

"Trust me, John, it's important. I think there's more going on here than we know."

"Shit! I don't know, Syman," said Claire, still sounding exasperated. "Why does it matter? Maybe a few miles."

"I don't think it was the Russian missile sub that launched those missiles, John. I think the people who put this bomb here in New York launched those missiles from the island. They're just taking advantage of the passing submarine's close proximity. They want the President to think that the Russian submarine launched the missiles."

"Why would they do that?" Claire asked.

"To trick the U.S. into starting a nuclear war with the Russians. I think the missiles were launched by the Islamic Brotherhood from Ilhas Desertas in cahoots with the Japanese."

"And how would they know when a Russian missile submarine would be passing close to the island?"

"These days, anything's for sale in the what's left of the old Soviet Union, John."

"Yeah, that's true," Claire said, now giving Syman's theory serious consideration.

"Think about it, John. If the U.S. and Russia get into a nuclear exchange and devastate each other, and of course, Europe as well, then the Arabs and the Japs can pick up the pieces when it's all over."

"I don't know, Syman. Maybe Islamic extremists would do something like this. They really hate us, but that's a pretty goddamn sinister accusation to be making against the Japanese. We can't be sure their involved in this thing."

"John, there's a nuclear bomb sitting ten feet away from Dexter and me and it would have destroyed New York City a few minutes from now if we hadn't accidentally found it. It's sitting in Hinode Worldwide's Headquarters office and Hinode is Japan's largest industrial company. It looks pretty suspicious to me, but I could be wrong. If the Japanese aren't involved, so be it.

Still, you need to call the President and tell him to call off a counterstrike. Don't let him launch any missiles! He'll be going after the wrong people. There are no war heads on those missiles!"

There was silence on the other end of the line for what seemed like a long time.

"Okay, let me get this straight. You think the bomb was supposed to explode when the first missile arrived over New York to prove to the President that the Russians had attacked us?"

"That's right," said Syman.

"And there's a second bomb in Washington somewhere set to go off when the second missile gets here."

"No, John. There's no second bomb. And there's no warhead in the second missile either, because there doesn't need to be. The only purpose of the second missile is to pressure the President into making a snap decision to retaliate on the Russians. The idea is that by the time the second missile reaches Washington, a counterstrike will already be on its way."

"But you've disarmed the bomb," said Claire. "There won't be an explosion in New York, so the President won't need to retaliate."

"The President won't be willing to sit and wait to see what happens to New York," replied Syman. "No politician would take a chance like that. He'll have to fire because he doesn't know there's no warhead on those missiles. And he won't ever know unless you tell him!"

Syman glanced at the counter. It said 7:41. That gave them just seven minutes at the outside to stop the President from starting the final world war on the planet and then only that long if he decided to wait until the last minute to launch.

With rising desperation, Syman said, "John. Hurry! Call him now. There's only seven minutes left and the policy is hit them sooner rather than later! If he launches a retaliatory strike, we're all going to die."

Claire hesitated only a moment more before conceding, "Okay, Syman, but I hope to God you're right. I'll call him and see if he'll listen."

The phone clicked as Claire hung up.

Dexter shook his head and said, "What a mess."

Syman quickly disconnected the comparitor and went to the nearest desk. With uncharacteristic violence he swept the top of the desk clean with his free arm. Everything on it went flying onto the floor. Dexter was momentarily taken aback by Syman's actions.

"I need a phone line, Dex. Quick!"

"What are you doing, Syman?"

"What I'm Not Doing is waiting for John Claire to convince the President to stop a retaliatory strike against Russia," Syman replied with vehemence.

"What's that supposed to mean?" Dexter asked, as he handed Syman the end of a telephone line. Syman plug it into the jack on the comparitor. In a moment he was on the Internet.

"I'm going to shut down the launch," Syman said. His sharp glance transfixed Dexter for an instant. Dexter had never seen such a fierce expression on Syman's face. Syman's look was pure steel.

"You're what?" Dexter said, though he well understood Syman's perfectly clear declaration and its unspoken implications.

Turning away, Syman made no reply. He began typing furiously. Then he stopped abruptly to wait for a reply to his request.

When the screen said: Welcome to Lawrence Livermore National Laboratory, Syman worked his way to a command that allowed him to access the system as administrator. He worked through an account the government had assigned him for use when updating work on his encryption software, which he'd used less and less in the last couple of years.

From there he accessed the Defense Department's network via Brookhaven Lab's Secure Advanced Military Systems Architecture Program, SAMSAP, a project that he had helped design in conjunction with the original implementation of his encryption program on the military's numerous and varied computerized weapons systems. From Brookhaven's computer, Syman accessed Taurus, the ultra secret super computer located at the Sandia Laboratory facility in Santa Fe, New Mexico that ran the command and control systems and software testing program that periodically tested all U.S. military nuclear weapons computer systems. This too Syman had helped create to run tests of his encryption program after it had been installed on the military's nuclear weapons systems. Once he had gained access to Taurus Syman proceeded to use a Taurus test subroutine to work his way to a connection with the United States Missile Command and Control Computers located under

Cheyenne Mountain. The screen read SysckLev2.

To this point Syman's hacking had been relatively simple and straight forward. He'd made this same set of connections dozens of times in the past to do maintenance work on his encryption programming. At this point however, he was stepping off into unknown territory. Syman typed in the command to change directory to level 1.

A password request appeared on the screen. Syman swallowed involuntarily and typed "PWDN,TY!"

In a moment the screen lit up with a long menu list of functions available to him. He scanned the list, hesitating every few seconds to decipher options such as: fbsystem\bus\reboot.data\nulplus\acs. and: gam\perspex\rps\fo9.

Names such as these meant absolutely nothing to him. Undaunted, he continued to read down the somewhat bewildering list looking for something that was familiar. His persistence paid off when he came across: launch\abort launch\sys.adm

Syman opened the program. A frightening warning message came up forbidding unauthorized use. He ignored it. Again, a password was needed and again, he used his PWDN,TY! entry key. Another menu appeared with a list of files such as: systest.adm, clckstck.set, and instruc.doc. This list was a little less abstruse. He read quickly down the list until he came to the file "football.exe."

The briefcase the president has near him at all times to initiate a nuclear missile launch came to mind. It was known euphemistically as the Football. Syman opened football.exe and immediately a window came up on the comparitor's screen with two words in button format. The first said: LAUNCH and next to it the second said: ABORT.

"Bingo!" said Syman, in triumph.

"That figures," said Dexter cynically. "They had to make it real simple for a politician to be able to run it." He'd been watching everything Syman was doing from over his shoulder.

Below the buttons were the words: "Time till LAUNCH" and under them was a bright red digital counter. With disbelief, they both saw the counter was at twelve seconds and counting backwards.

"Holy shit!" said Dexter, in alarm.

"There's nothing holy here," said Syman, with anger in his voice. Without hesitation he clicked on the abort button on his screen and a moment later the bright red digital numbers turned green and changed to 00:00.

Again, without hesitation Syman went back to the menu screen and initiated the systest program, knowing once it was started it would be impossible to stop and would effectively keep the launch procedure from being initiated until the automatic systems test had been performed. Since he had not specified an alternate backup launch procedure first, there was simply no way a launch could be initiated for several minutes while the complex internal housekeeping and maintenance program was running. Syman knew he had frozen the nation's nuclear missile force for a good fifteen minutes.

The abort signal which would appear to be from the President would cause all forces to stand down immediately. Seeing a systems test program being run, the land, sea and air keepers of the country's nuclear weapons would assume they had just gone through a very real simulation of the launch procedure.

"That should do it," said a relieved Syman Pons. "By the time the system can be reprogrammed for a launch, the President will know the missiles didn't explode."

"I can't believe you just did that, Syman! I'm very glad you stopped the launch, but you and I may be forced to enjoy our continued existence from behind bars."

"Oh, I don't think the government will put the two men who just averted the worst disaster in human history in jail," Syman said, with a smile. "Right now, only the President, the admirals and the generals know how close the world has come to Armageddon.

If they were to try to prosecute us, the truth would get out and they'd all be looking for new jobs in a month."

For once, Syman Pons was completely wrong in his assumption. He and Dexter had just averted what would have been only the third worst disaster in human history. The second, still unknown to them, was developing all around the world at that exact moment, while mankind's single greatest catastrophe had already occurred, half a million years in the past

38

Thirty-six days had past since Sumiko Fujita returned to the United States from Japan after attending a business conference. Now she was dead.

Kioro Itara's genetically engineered horror had done exactly what it had been created to do. It had indiscriminately and inexpensively killed a perfectly healthy innocent human being, but not before she had spread the disease to hundreds of others.

Thirty-one, and in excellent physical condition when she had been infected with the disease, Sumiko's strong immune system had kept her alive for several days longer than the malnourished, the ill, the old, and millions of others with weaker immune systems. Many of them had not even survived the first stage of the disease.

On the day she died, more than five-hundred-seventy million people around the world had contracted the disease. Within ten weeks, every human being on the planet would be exposed. Exempting only the Japanese inoculated by Kioro Itara, this gave the rest of the human race approximately 100 more days to live.

39

Karrie and Syman lay back on the couch to watch the news together in his study. Relaxing contentedly against his chest, Karrie loved the feeling of his arms around her. She could feel his breath on the back of her neck. She felt warm and loved and supremely safe and she never wanted it to end.

It had been three weeks since their return to the United States and three days since they had been able to spend some time together. Busy as they both were, Karrie had still taken time to again do some serious thinking. Nearly dying had brought those things that were truly important to Karrie into clear focus. Now, there was absolutely no doubt in her mind. She wanted to marry Syman, have a family with him and share her life with him.

She looked down at her wrists, one then the other, then at Syman's clasped hands resting on her stomach. The abrasions and severe bruising from their days of being handcuffed together had nearly disappeared. She shivered slightly, remembering some of the fearful experiences they'd been through.

Syman's attention was distracted from the TV by her slight shudder, "Are you cold, Kar? I can light a fire or something."

"No, that's all right," she replied, "I just had a slight chill.

I'm really quite comfortable laying here with your arms around me."

They listened to the familiar strident music announce the evening news.

"Good evening," said the news anchor.

"History's deadliest epidemic is ripping through countries around the world tonight, its devastating death toll so far more than a million people."

Syman and Karrie listened intently, taken aback by what they were hearing. Neither had heard the news for several days and they were not prepared for what they'd just heard.

"Since the mysterious disease now being called New Plague was identified last month by the Center For Disease Control in Atlanta, cases have been reported in one-hundred-eleven countries around the world, including the United States. The disease is highly communicable and the spread of infection has been greatly enhanced by the swift movement of modern transportation. As a consequence, the greatest number of cases are being reported in larger urban areas. Outlying and rural areas are reporting fewer cases at this time.

The disease, which first appears as a virulent and aggressive flu lasting a few days to a week, subsides only to reappear two to three weeks later, in a second fatal stage.

So far, there is no effective treatment for the disease and with a mortality rate of 100%, contracting New Plague is an automatic death sentence, making it history's most dangerous disease. Millions more people are expected to die in the next several weeks."

Syman sat forward, becoming very concerned when he heard the word 'flu.' He'd been informed by TMI's production manager, just yesterday, that an unusually high number of people were out sick causing TMI some problems and that fully one fifth of the people working at TMI had come down with flu in the last month. The symptoms of the New Plague sounded suspiciously similar to the illness afflicting TMI's work force, though as far as Syman knew, no one had died.

"Health care workers appear to be contracting the disease at an alarming rate and many medical facilities are reporting high absenteeism among their staffs.

Panic is sweeping countries around the globe as concern over the Plague deepens.

The President has pledged the full resources of the United States to work on a cure for the Plague. He has also ordered that an electronic forum be set up to link together as many world leaders as possible to allow them to discuss ways to minimize its spread.

It is hoped that this commitment by the United States will spur cooperation among all nations and encourage them to put their differences aside and work together against the onslaught of this vicious disease."

"My God, this is ghastly!" said Karrie.

"Here at home, the President is considering a nationwide declaration of marshal law to quell an increasing number of riots in Los Angeles, Detroit, Baltimore, New York, and several other cities and to reduce the amount of movement within the country in an effort to slow the spread of infection.

Leaders from both the House and Senate have been in contact with the President, but already, some members from both houses of Congress have decried the move as premature and unconstitutional.

Governor Hastings of Utah reports there are no cases in his state and says categorically that he will not enforce Marshall law."

The phone on the table next to Syman rang. He picked it up.

"Hello?"

"It's me, Sy," said Dexter. "Turn on the news. There's something you need to hear."

"Karrie and I are watching it. You're talking about this Plague. Right?"

"Yes."

"I'd heard something about an epidemic the day before yesterday," said Syman, "but I had no idea it was this serious. Yesterday, George Wydra, our production manager mentioned to me that a lot of people were out sick with flu. Do you think it's the plague?"

"I don't know," said Dexter. "I hope to God it's not. There's no treatment, no cure."

"Yes, we just heard that."

"I think we should consider shutting TMI down for a few days until we see what transpires," Dexter suggested. "We've already got a lot of people out sick. If nothing else, it will lessen the spread of flu among the rest of our people."

"I think that's a good idea."

Syman paused for a moment and then asked, "How much cash does the company have available, right now?"

"Well, I don't know exactly, off hand. Why?"

"This is a hell of a thing that's going on right now. If we close down, our people might get the impression their on their own, that we're bailing out on them when the going is just getting rough. I want to pay everyone, while we're shut down. Can we do that?"

"We have some reserves, Syman. But, the amount of money we'll need to do that will depend on the length of the shutdown."

"Naturally," said Syman. "Check into it first thing in the morning. If I have to, I'll put up some of my shares as collateral for a loan. I want our people to know we're not abandoning them to face this thing alone. Full pay for the duration."

"Right," said Dexter in agreement. "I'll do the same thing if necessary. That's a good idea. I know I wouldn't want to feel like I'd been laid off in the middle of this thing."

"Karrie's here with me," Syman said, changing the subject and the mood abruptly. "She said to tell you she's going to stay here tonight, so you won't be worried about her."

"I said nothing of the kind, Syman Pons!" Dexter heard Karrie say loudly in the background. And then he heard Syman say "Ouch! That hurt!" as he laughed.

"Good!" said Karrie, also laughing.

40

To keep you all abreast of current developments," said the quiet wavering tenor voice of Kioro Itara, their unseen leader, "I will begin by reviewing our recent efforts. To this, I will add some relevant new information.

As you are all aware, six months ago, the biological products division of Hinode released a rejuvenated strain of the 1918 influenza that killed some 20 million people worldwide around the time of the First World War. Releasing this influenza strain, here in Japan, was the opening salvo in our effort to cleanse the Earth. This was done to compel our citizens to participate in a gratuitous nationwide influenza vaccination program sponsored by Hinode. Under the guise of this vaccination program, every citizen of Japan also unknowingly received a vaccination to protect them against the effects of our biological weapon. Vaccinating our citizens against the effects of the weapon had always been our real goal and why we released the influenza in the first place.

Because of the exceptionally efficient work done by all of you, the ruse worked and none of our countrymen, other than those few we knew would stand in our way, have contracted the disease.

I am pleased to tell you, the same cannot be said for the rest of the world. The 100% effectiveness of our biological weapon in killing everyone not so vaccinated, will quickly bring us our long sought success and you are all to be congratulated for your fine work.

Unfortunately, I am sad to say, there is one glaring mistake in the execution of our plans; that of our ally's failure to initiate a nuclear war in the countries comprising the industrial west. It was intended that Russia, Western Europe and the United States would be devastated, so they could not oppose us."

All eyes in the room momentarily averted to glance at Colonel Ibrahim sitting stiffly, silently in a chair at the midpoint of the conference table.

"As it turns out, his failure to destroy their industrial and medical infrastructure is proving to be less of a threat than we originally feared.

We know from our sources around the world that only one of the industrialized nations Colonel Ibrahim was suppose to cripple, the United States, has been successful in creating a vaccine, though several others are also trying. It is an insignificant effort by the American Center for Disease Control, and so far, it is of no real consequence.

Because of the rapid spread of our organism, most of the world's non-Japanese people will be dead long before the Americans can produce even a million doses of their vaccine.

Again, fortunately for us, the Americans are greedy, arrogant and selfish by nature, lacking as they do, Japan's Samurai tradition of service and self sacrifice. Because of this, their politicians will use the first available vaccine on themselves, their families and friends. They will not vaccinate many of their armed force's people and certainly none of the great rabble of their citizens. This, of course, is to our advantage, because when we arrive in North American to repopulate the land, there will be only those few people left to deal with. Only the weakest and the worst of their people will remain and we will be able to hunt them down for sport, like deer. Remembering their treatment of our solders all across the Pacific during the Second World War, this should be a particularly satisfying revenge."

The men in the room could hear the fervent pleasure in their leader's voice as he talked of hunting down and killing the last Americans.

While Kioro Itara continued to speak, a panel of the wall facing Colonel Ibrahim slid into the ceiling and a trim distinguished looking Japanese gentleman dressed in an expensive, perfectly tailored business suit and wearing black leather gloves entered the conference room. He walked around the seated conferees and stood directly behind Colonel Ibrahim. A slight glint of perspiration appeared on Colonel Ibrahim's forehead as the leader continued to address the meeting from the speakers placed around the room. Colonel Ibrahim glanced nervously at the camera that sat on the table at the head where it normally scanned back and forth in accordance with Kioro Itara's attention. Presently, the camera had come to an unwavering rest on Colonel Ibrahim and the Colonel did not like its unblinking attention one bit. Nor did he like having the, now unseen, stranger standing behind his chair.

"Although no setbacks will likely result from the Colonel's ineptitude," continued Kioro Itara, "it is still incumbent on me to enforce the proper discipline for such a grave failure. But before I do, I would like to make you all aware, along with Colonel Ibrahim, of one more significant fact, which he probably already suspects, knowing as he does that some of his personnel are now, even as we speak, becoming ill with the disease. And it is that our supposed allies, Colonel Ibrahim, his associates, his countrymen and his religious cohorts, never actually received vaccinations against our weapon. They did received a flu shot, but that was all."

All eyes were now on Colonel Ibrahim and he began looking frantically from one face to another hoping to find support from someone. The other ten men in the room, all oriental, stared back coldly, without expression or compassion.

As comprehension of the Kioro Itara's utter duplicity came to Colonel Ibrahim, his face darkened menacingly and he turned to face the camera. Pointing his finger at the camera, he yelled,

"Itara! You have planned to betray us from the very beginning!"

"Of course Colonel," said Kioro Itara in his quiet and calm old man's voice. "Did you really think that after going to the trouble of cleansing the Earth of all those others, who are not Japanese, I would leave you and your Islamic hoards alive to create havoc in my new world? You were very naive to think that I would even consider the possibility."

In a fury, Colonel Ibrahim leaned forward to rise from his chair.

Unbidden, the stranger grabbed the Colonel by the hair to restrain him. In the same instant, he produced a thin four inch long dagger. Placing its point in Colonel Ibrahim's ear canal, he pushed it in up to the hilt before Colonel Ibrahim's face had time to register the shock of what had just occurred. In a last moment of understanding, a look of angry surprise froze on Colonel Ibrahim's features as he died

41

Syman walked through the connecting door to Dexter's office with fresh coffee for both of them. They'd been hammering together a shutdown plan for TMI since their arrival two hours before. Syman glanced at his watch. It said 8:30. Dexter, typing on his comparitor, was just totaling up the figures they'd developed that morning.

"We have just over 11,000 employees on the payroll, Sy, with an average aggregate employee cost of about 13.2 million dollars a week or about 53 million for the projected month-long shutdown. The aggregate cost includes their pay, benefits, the matching social security we have to pay Uncle Sam for each of them and so forth.

We have fixed expenses, property, building and aircraft maintenance, loan obligations, taxes and retirement matching funds payments of 2.8 million times four weeks, 11.2 million.

And we have a 24 cents per share stock dividend to pay in two weeks on 85 million shares. But since you and I own 45 million of those shares we only have to pay on the 40 million outstanding shares." Dexter did the math on his comparitor's screen. "It comes out to 9.6 mil. There are some other incidentals amounting to about two million for the month." Dexter was quiet for a moment as he added the totals. "It comes to 75.8 million bucks for the month."

He closed his eyes for a moment. Something vague was nagging at the edge of his mind. Then it came to him. "Oh, yeah. We're going to have to pay penalties to our suppliers for taking deliveries of the parts they supply to us late, or more accurately, for not taking delivery of any parts for the month."

"George," Dexter said addressing the comparitor, "look at all our supplier's contracts and then add up all the late acceptance penalties for a 28 day month."

"Yes, Dexter." A few seconds later George said, "the total for all 783 suppliers using current projections is $4,209,337.40."

Dexter added 4.2 million to the other figures. "It comes out to a nice round 80 million dollars for the month. It's a little more than I used to make on my paper route in Shell Beach, but we can handle it."

"What's our cash on hand?" Syman asked him.

"George, what's our cash reserve this morning to the nearest million dollars?"

"It will be a moment while I query the bank's computers, Dexter."

Dexter said nothing in reply, waiting for the machine's answer.

"We presently have 116 million dollars available to us at this time in cash and readily convertible instruments," George informed them.

"How much are the outstanding receivables we can expect in the next month?" Syman asked.

"Is that a 28 or 31 day month, Syman?" George asked.

"28 day month," said Syman.

There was a thirty second silence while the comparitor did the calculations that would have taken a human accounting department of a hundred people a week to perform.

"Based on an analysis of past payment histories for all customers, we can expect to receive approximately 173 million dollars in the next 28 days. 89 million is earmarked for immediate payment to our suppliers for that period leaving an overage of 84 million dollars."

"We can just bank that 89 million for the parts and supplies, until we start up again," said Dexter. "And the 84 million will cover our expenses for the month.

"Well, it looks like were not in too bad shape to take a month off or even six weeks if need be," said Syman.

"If our people are contracting this damn plague I just hope we aren't closing the doors of TMI for good."

"There's always that chance I guess, Dex. Who knows? You or I or maybe both of us will contract the disease. There's no guarantee that we won't."

"I suppose," said Dexter, looking grim. "We'll need to call a special meeting of the Board of Directors to inform them of the shutdown."

"As soon as possible, I think," said Syman.

"This evening will be the earliest opportunity. Most of them will be busy now."

"George, call all the Directors and inform them that there will be a special meeting tonight at 7:30."

"Yes, Syman."

"We're going to need to make a public announcement. When the public finds out TMI is shutting down for a month they'll freak if we don't explain. And it's going to play hob with our stock valuation."

"To hell with our stock valuation, Dex. If something isn't done to stop this plague there won't be enough people left alive in the country to have a stock market."

"Boy, I sure hope you're wrong about that, Sy."

"Me too."

Dexter addressed George. "Call Marie Bonetti in Public Relations. Tell her I want to meet with her in my office as soon as possible."

Speaking to Syman again, he said, "I'll have her prepare a press statement of some kind."

"That's a good idea. I guess we're done with this for now. I'll make a video address to the employees at lunch. That should give us enough time this afternoon to close the plant down. I'll be in my office working on the address if you need me."

Dexter nodded and Syman walked back to his office.

"...because of the severity of the epidemic," said a somber faced Syman Pons into the camera mounted in Esmirelda's cabinet, "we believe it will be in everyone's best interest to close TMI for one month, thereby reducing the risk of transmission and the consequent spread of the disease.

In the last month one fifth of our people have been absent due to illness. The majority of them have reported having some type of influenza. To date, no one has died and there is no proof that anyone working at TMI has contracted the so called New Plague, nevertheless, prudence dictates that we take some serious precautions to help ourselves if we can.

Mr. Gordon and I have reviewed the situation and have decided that a one month shutdown will give us a clearer indication of what we, as a company, are facing.

During the shutdown all employees will receive their full pay and benefits. Wage payments for the month will be made to you in advance. Your checks are being prepared as we speak and your supervisors will give them to you before you leave today.

At a time of unknown danger such as this it is fitting that each of you are home with your families.

In closing I'd like to say may God keep and protect you and your loved ones from this horrible disease.

Syman pressed the space bar under his hand on the comparitor's keyboard and the camera turned off.

42

The phone on the bedside table bleated incessantly. Dexter awoke to its pleading sound feeling like there was glue in his brain. Through one squinted eye, he could see a blurry red 3:14 on his alarm clock. He shook his head in an attempt to clear it. It didn't help. Rocking up on his elbow, he stretched to pick up the phone.

"Hello," he said, sluggishly.

"It's me, Dex." It was Syman.

"What's wrong?"

"Nothing's wrong, but I just received a call from the White House chief of staff, Richard McCaffrey. The President has asked that you and I meet him in the White House for breakfast at 8:00 AM."

"I'm really tired, Sy and I'm in no mood for a joke." Dexter sounded angry in a sleepy sort of way.

"I'm not joking, Dexter."

"Why didn't you call earlier?"

"I would have called you earlier, but McCaffrey only called me a few minutes ago. He said an important matter has just come to the President's attention tonight, and that the President wants us to handle it for him, but he wouldn't tell me what 'it' was."

"This is pretty weird, Sy."

"McCaffrey also said to be at the White House by 7:45 and to pack a bag, because it might take a few days."

"This is really weird, Sy. Are we being arrested or something?"

"No. I don't think so. I'll meet you at the hanger at 6:00. We can fly N273 down in an hour. That should give us enough time."

Dexter changed the subject and asked, "Where's Karrie? Is she with you?"

"No. She should be home with you. Why?"

"I want her to know where we're going just in case there's any monkey business. You might be wrong about them arresting us. I don't like the sound of that 'bring a bag for a few nights.' Sounds suspicious to me."

"Well, you don't need to worry about that. I've cued Esmirelda to release the entire story about the missiles and the bomb to the news services if she doesn't hear from you or me for seventy-two hours as insurance, just in case we're disappeared. I also sent a copy of the entire story to my lawyer and another person as a backup."

"A lot of good that will do us if they kill us."

"Dex, I seriously doubt the government would do anything like that."

"Yeah, right. That's why you took the precautions you did."

"Well, one can never be too careful," said Syman wryly.

"Uh, huh. I'll see you at...What time did you say?"

"Six."

"Six, right. Bye." Dexter hung up the phone, none too gently. In sixty seconds, he was fast asleep again.

Syman called the night maintenance mechanic at TMI's hanger. Along with the plant's security people, he and eleven co-workers tending TMI's fleet of aircraft were a few of the people still working at the plant.

TMI's aircraft were too vulnerable to leave abandoned for a month in an empty hanger at Bridgeport's airport. Because the maintenance people met few people during a work shift, it was decided to have those who wanted to work do so on a reduced schedule during the shutdown.

"Good morning. This is Mr. Pons. Who am I speaking to please?" He was familiar with all the people who took care of TMI's fleet of aircraft, but he didn't know who was working tonight.

"Hello, Mr. Pons. This is Sam Baroni."

"Hi, Sam," said Syman. "I need to use N273. Would you please ready the aircraft for a six o'clock take off."

"Sure thing, Mr. Pons," said Baroni.

The 300 mile flight to Washington's National airport took just half an hour. With Syman flying the executive jet, Dexter sat in the co-pilot's seat more as super cargo than as co-pilot. Dexter had flown the exact same route to Washington the day he'd gone to see John Claire and in the very same aircraft, but this morning, it was Syman's passionate love affair with all things airborne that decided who was in which seat. And that was fine with Dexter. This early in the morning, he'd rather just sit quietly and enjoy the fresh coffee they'd brought with them and the spectacular vistas of the Atlantic coast passing under them twenty thousand feet below.

The President rose from his chair as Syman and Dexter were escorted into the room. He walked to them and extended his hand to each man in turn and said, "Gentlemen, I've very much been looking forward to meeting you both. In addition to what I've read in the press about TMI and your phenomenal success, John Claire has told me a bit about each of you and your recent service to our country and I must say, I'm impressed. Still, there is no substitute for getting to know a person face to face."

Dexter said, "Thank you, Mr. President."

Then the president looked at Syman.

With just the hint of a smile Syman nodded slightly, and asked, "What can we help you with, Sir?"

"Right to the point, ay Mr. Pons? John did say you fellows didn't waste much time."

"As the most powerful leader on earth," said Syman, "we understand how valuable your time is."

The President was silent for a moment. He looked appraisingly at Syman wondering if he was being patronized and concluded that Syman meant just what he'd said, no more, no less.

"Before I explain why I've called you here, let's go into the other room. We can discuss it over breakfast, which I've been informed is ready."

The three men walked through the White House to the dining room. Sitting down, they were immediately served from large plates of piping hot food; eggs, bacon, sausages, pancakes with real maple syrup, accompanied by their choice of fresh fruit slices, juice and steaming cups of fresh coffee.

All three men were hungry and without pretension, they dug in to their excellent repast. They said little of importance as they ate, discussing instead light subjects of the President's choosing. Thoroughly enjoying themselves, Syman and Dexter waited patiently for the President to bring up the real purpose of their visit. As their elegant gold rimmed china coffee cups were filled for the second time Dexter said, "This was a meal fit for...well, a President!" They all laughed.

"Yes, the food is first class. We have an excellent staff here at the White House, good people all."

The President became introspective for a moment as if composing himself and said, "Mr. Gordon, Mr. Pons, some extremely important information has come to my attention in the last few hours. It relates directly to the business of the nuclear bomb you discovered and disarmed and the missile attack on our country last week."

Dexter and Syman both steeled themselves for the worst, knowing there was every possibility they would shortly find themselves behind bars on charges of treason for shutting down the United State's nuclear missile force. Dexter looked around the room nervously expecting the Secret Service people to rush into the room to arrest them or something, but nothing happened. Similar thoughts occurred to Syman, but he was struck by the oddness of the situation. If they were going to be arrested, why would the President invite them for breakfast.

"First of all," the President continued, "I want to thank you both for the spectacular service you performed for the nation and the world. Thanks to your efforts a massive tragedy has been averted. Millions of lives have been saved by your quick thinking and actions. The United States and the world owe you both a debt that can never be repaid. Your selfless actions are in the best tradition of our country's finest patriots. And as you both know, I personally owe you an incalculable debt for stopping me from attacking an innocent Russia."

Dexter and Syman glanced at each other for a second and then turned their attention back to their host.

The moment was not lost on the President.

"As I said, some very important information has just come to me. It also concerns this brutal plague epidemic that is killing so many people. And it is directly because of the heroic efforts you have recently expended on behalf of your country, that this information has come into my possession."

Syman and Dexter looked at each other again, still not understanding what the President was driving at.

The President said directly, "Because of your efforts, we have also discovered the source of the plague and a cure!"

"We don't quite follow you, Mr. President?" said Dexter.

"I'm talking about the mysterious test tubes you and Mr. Pons brought back from that terrorist base in Libya. They contain a vaccine for the plague."

"John Claire said they contained a vaccine for influenza."

"Yes, Mr. Pons. That's true, but for some reason a vaccine for the plague was mixed with the flu vaccine. It took the people at CDC and USAMRID a little while to figure out there was a second vaccine and then it took them a little while longer to figure out what the second vaccine did. It appears that Hinode biologically engineered the plague at that base in Libya."

"We've suspected that the Japanese were in league with the Islamic Brotherhood ever since our return," Dexter informed the President. "We told John Claire about our suspicions and he began to check them out, but the last time we spoke with him, he told us that someone high up in the government had ordered him to lay off that line of investigation."

"Yes, so I've heard" said the President with a frown, "and that person is now in jail. It's a small matter of some bribes."

"Is the Japanese government involved?" Syman asked.

"No," said the President. "We're sure the government is not involved. Hinode has been operating without their knowledge."

"We thought that Hinode might be a front operation for the Japanese government," said Dexter. "How can you be sure the Japanese are telling you the truth?"

"We can be sure the government is not involved because the only people in

Japan who have the plague are the politicians and top government people. Aside from them, not a single person in Japan has contracted the plague."

"That is a rather suspicious circumstance," observed Syman.

"Yes, rather," said the President. "Ironically, we think that the terrorists have been double crossed, because the plague is rampant in Libya and a lot of other Islamic populations around the world."

The President fell silent for a moment. He looked intently at Syman and Dexter and then continued, "The crux of the matter is, that last night the Japanese Ambassador made a formal request for assistance from the United State in dealing with the disease. He informed me that along with the top government officials, the Emperor has also contracted the plague and is dying. If the Emperor has the plague, then we can be sure the government is not involved."

Changing the subject abruptly, the President asked, "How much do you know about Hinode Worldwide?"

"We know it's Japan's largest industrial combination and that it does a lot of business here and around the world." Syman let Dexter explain preferring to listen and think. "And that several of its subsidiaries are somehow tied up in this mess with the Islamic Brotherhood. In fact, that's how we located the bomb. We went to their office in New York hoping to learn more about their involvement."

The President smiled knowingly and said, "I wondered how it was that you two found the bomb. My sources tell me the office was closed at the time."

Syman and Dexter sat poker faced and said nothing.

The President returned to his original topic. "Hinode is the creation of a man named Kioro Itara, a survivor of the bombing of Nagasaki and a rabid ultra-nationalist. The bomb killed his family and left him crippled. Understandably, he hates the United States."

"But, he doesn't hate the U. S. enough not to do business here," said Dexter, cynically.

"Setting that nuclear bomb off in New York would have been a type of justice for him," observed Syman.

"Itara is apparently a completely ruthless pragmatist judging from what our intelligence people have told me, but no one has seen him for several years and there are rumors he's dead, so we aren't sure if he's the one behind all this."

Hoping the man would get to the point, Syman asked again, "Why are you telling us all this and what can we do to help?"

"Since the discovery of the plague vaccine, a crash project has been underway to replicate the vaccine. As you can well imagine, the scope of the project is staggering. Nevertheless, the United States is doing everything possible to manufacture the millions, in fact ultimately billions of doses of vaccine needed around the world to stop the spread of the disease. Fortunately, I've been told the replication occurs exponentially, but since we've just started the process, we only have the first few hundred thousand doses. As precious as the vaccine is, we're going to send fifty-thousand doses to the Japanese to vaccinate their government people and to seed their vaccine replication effort. As our strongest ally in East Asia their help will be vitally important in overcoming the disease and maintaining stability in that area of the world.

As we speak, the vaccine is being prepared for shipment aboard the space shuttle Endeavor. It will be ready to go at 12 noon from Cape Kennedy. I want you two to accompany the vaccine to Japan."

Dexter and Syman sat and pondered the President's request in surprised silence.

It was Dexter who spoke first, "Why do you want us to go with the vaccine?"

"First, you are two of the handful of people who know all the facts and I want you to explain the situation in detail to the Japanese. We want their full cooperation in stopping the plague and if possible, we want to find the people who are responsible.

Second, and perhaps more importantly, you are both resourceful men of proven ability. Mankind is facing its gravest threat in history and I need good men, intelligent men, with what shall I say? Let's call it flexibility, working with the Japanese. With their enormous industrial and technological capacity, to say nothing of their healthy population, they can be a tremendous help. And the fact is," said the President, sounding a little disheartened, "with the problems we're having with the accelerating spread of the disease here at home, the United States needs all the help it can get if we're going to beat this thing."

"Is the situation really that bad, Mr. President?" Syman asked, gravely.

"Yes, it's that bad, Mr. Pons. Our best estimate is that seventy million Americans have already contracted this goddamn disease! And if it's allowed to run its course untreated, those folks will all be dead in six weeks and the rest of us will have also been infected by then. We know for sure that no one survives this disease without being vaccinated and knowing this, our most optimistic estimate is that everyone not vaccinated, and that's most of mankind, not just the people here in our country, will be dead within 90 days.

Dexter and Syman again sat in silence trying to comprehend this horrific revelation.

Finally, Dexter asked, "Why use the space shuttle? It's a pretty risky way to ship it. Why not fly it to Japan in a regular jet?"

"The reason we're using the space shuttle is time, Mr. Gordon, pure and simple. It's the fastest method available with the necessary cargo capacity. The vaccine will arrive at Kansai International airport in Osaka, where their national microbiology laboratory is located, in just over fifty minutes. The fastest alternative transportation would take a minimum of ten hours and in the fight we're facing, ten hours is an eternity in which millions of lives, possibly including the Emperor's, will be lost. Because of the exponential growth in the disease's spread, time is our most precious commodity right now."

"Won't you have to get a shuttle ready? I thought it took days to get it ready to fly?" Dexter said, wondering at the details.

"Normally, that would be true, but the Shuttle was scheduled to launch today to resupply the International Space Station.

Instead, NASA has been working all night removing the original mission's cargo and loading it with containers of vaccine."

"Taking advantage of the shuttle's speed is a good idea," said Syman.

"We're trying to do absolutely everything possible we can think of to stop the plague. Now that you know how bad things really are, the question remains, will you gentlemen accept the assignment and join us in the effort?"

"Well, Mr. President, I can't speak for Mr. Gordon, but as for myself, I can do no less at a time like this. I'll do whatever I can to help."

"I'm in," said Dexter, a moment later. He looked at his watch, which said 8:48. "It's almost 9 o'clock. If we're being launched from Cape Kennedy, we better get going. We don't have much of that time you were talking about to fly down there if we're going to be aboard for a 12 o'clock lift off."

"Splendid!" said the President. "That being the case, I'll call my physician in here to give you both a shot of the plague vaccine."

Dexter and Syman looked at each other in surprise. Then understanding came to them.

"Quid pro quo, Mr. President? If we work to save the country, then we get to live?" Syman asked, cynically.

"Yes, Mr. Pons. I'm afraid it's down to that. Right now, the vaccine is the most precious substance on Earth. It's our only chance to beat the plague."

Syman frowned and said, "Mr. President, if the situation is really that bad, then I have a favor to ask."

"What is it?"

"I would like you to vaccinate Mr. Gordon's sister, Karrie."

"Only government workers and emergency personnel are slated to receive the first vaccinations, Mr. Pons."

"Sir, if Mr. Gordon and I really have done the nation and the world the service you say we have, then I should think it's small payment to ask in return."

The President thought this over for a moment.

"Put that way, Mr. Pons, I guess I can see my way to authorize that."

"Thank you, Mr. President."

43

The vibrations and the increase in G-force were brutal as the Shuttle went from zero to seventeen-thousand-six-hundred miles per hour in the astonishingly short time of only six minutes. Neither Syman nor Dexter were prepared for the experience and the generic spacesuits (spacesuits were no longer custom made for each person) were a poor and uncomfortable fit indeed. Still, despite the punishing ride to the edges of outerspace Dexter's indomitable sense of humor surfaced when he ask, "Captain, what do you do if you need to use the john during this part of the ride?"

Captain George Winter, pilot in command of the Shuttle Endeavor revealed his own sense of humor when he retorted, "Weep, Mr. Gordon."

All four passengers laughed at that, although Captain Winter's co-pilot, Commander Sarah Jean Leninski wondered to herself what the people on the ground were thinking of their off color remarks. Fortunately, on this trip their voice traffic wasn't being rebroadcast. Still, any ham radio operator with a little skill and a large antenna could listen to their communications with the ground and there were usually several doing just that during any launch.

As abruptly as it started the boost ended and the instant silence was deafening. Ears ringing, joints aching, heart pumping madly, the sudden weightlessness caused a subtle queasiness. For Captain Winter and Commander Leninski the unusual combination of sensations was not new. Both were veteran Shuttle jockeys, but for Syman and Dexter the first few minutes of their trip were nothing you could call pleasant.

"I don't feel so good," said Dexter to no one in particular.

"Are you going to get sick, Mr. Gordon?" asked Leninski.

"I don't think so," said Dexter.

"If you can hang on for a few minutes it will pass. It's caused by the disorientation of your inner ear. It's kind of like car sickness."

"I'll be all right," Dexter replied, not at all sure it was true.

"I can help you take your helmet off if you think you're going to throw up, but this hop is going to be so short the op-order specifies that we, 'keep them on unless there's a compelling reason to remove them'," said Leninski quoting the regs verbatim.

"I'll be okay in a few minutes," Dexter said, desperately hoping it was the truth.

"How are you doing, Mr. Pons?" Leninski asked, brightly.

"I'm doing fine, thank you," Syman replied, smiling in her direction, though he could only see the back of her helmet. His queasiness had disappeared in moments.

"The view is spectacular!" Syman said, as he watched the Earth roll fully into view above their heads. He was truly awe struck by the beauty of the sight. "Now I think I understand why you people love it up here so much, despite all the inconveniences."

"You never get tired of the view, that's for sure," said Captain Winter as he finished his post launch systems check. "We seem to be in good shape, folks. I guess all we have to do now is sit back and enjoy the ride for half an hour. Then we'll start the reentry procedures."

Everyone hung loosely in their seat harnesses watching the earth out the windows. Everyone except Dexter, who kept his eyes closed as diminishing waves of nausea came and went over the next several minutes. As his stomach settled, he took a chance and opened one eye to look at the transcendent view outside. When the nausea didn't increase he opened both eyes. The queasiness continued to abate and after a few minutes he actually began enjoying himself.

The experience of traveling through space, watching the Earth pass below was so novel, even to the pilots, that no one broke the silence. The mood was akin to the atmosphere in a great cathedral, overawing and humbling, inspiring and uplifting at the same time.

Suddenly, Winter and Leninski began to writhe in their seats.

"I can't breath! Oh, god! Oh, god!" Leninski shouted over the com-link.

Winter was grabbing frantically at his helmet's lockring, violently trying to unfasten it. "Can't breath! Help us!"

It took Dexter and Syman a moment to realize the Shuttle pilots were in trouble. Fumbling with their gloved hands, Dexter and Syman wasted seconds trying to unbuckle themselves from their seat harnesses to help the wildly thrashing astronauts. Floating free for the first time in the completely foreign environment of weightlessness made movement difficult and slow. Their air hoses, which tethered them to the bulkhead next to their seats, were only just long enough to allow them to reach Winter and Leninski, impeding them even further.

"Can't breath!" Winter yelled in a strangled voice one last time as his movements slowed and then stopped. Leninski too had stopped struggling.

Dexter and Syman could hear their gasping as they struggled to breath. When Syman reached Winter he immediately began trying to undo the helmet's locking ring. Never easy to open under the best conditions, the gloves he was wearing foiled Syman's every attempt to slide the lockring mechanism.

In desperation, Syman removed the glove from his right hand, but that operation too took precious seconds to accomplish. Finally, after a few moments of concerted bare-handed effort, he was able to depress the latches on the helmet's lockring and turn it, releasing the helmet from the suit.

Dexter was having an equally difficult time with his still gloved hands, but as soon as Syman had removed Winter's helmet, he performed the same operation on Leninski.

"Goddamn spacesuits!" said Dexter, as Leninski's helmet floated free from her head.

There was soot around both pilot's nostrils and they were unconscious or dead, flaccid and unresponsive, with eyes closed and mouths hanging open slightly.

There was a Babel of voices in their ears from Houston that Syman and Dexter had ignored while trying to help Winter and Leninski. Now that the pilots were free, Dexter turned his attention to a distracting light on the control panel blinking in unison with an annoying buzzer. Dexter leaned close and read 'Fire Alert'.

"Sy, this thing is a fire alarm!"

Syman leaned over to take a close look as well and their helmets whacked together.

"Wooo!" said a startled Dexter.

"We've got some problems here, Houston," Syman said in a calm level voice, finally addressing the frantic people on the ground.

"Roger that, Endeavor. Who am I speaking to?" Syman heard in reply.

"This is Syman Pons."

"Where is Captain Winter?" There was alarm in the controller's voice.

"Captain Winter is unconscious and so is Commander Leninski."

"Come again!" said a disbelieving voice.

"Both pilots have been rendered unconscious by some kind of fumes or gas that got into their spacesuits. They have soot around their nostrils and there's a fire warning alarm," said Syman, trying not to sound exasperated with the ground controller.

"Roger that, Mr. Pons. Standby."

There was complete silence on the communications channel now.

"This is Marvin Jenks, Capcom. You've got a fire in the primary air recirculation loop. Winter and Leninski are probably suffering from carbon monoxide poisoning. You and Mr. Gordon are getting your air from the secondary system. Are you okay?"

"We're both fine," said Syman.

"Good. Okay, we need you to go to the lower equipment bay to the locker next to the ladder. It has a blue circle with a red cross in it. That's where the emergency medical supplies are kept. There are small oxygen tanks with face masks. Get two of them and strap them on Winter and Leninski as quickly as possible."

"Roger that," said Syman.

"Undo the air hose from my suit, Sy and I'll get them. You handle the fire."

Syman turned Dexter upside down as he tried to twist the air hose from Dexter's suit. Dexter grabbed the back of Winter's seat and Syman braced against Leninski's and in a moment the hose was detached. Dexter shot away toward the middeck hatch and disappeared down the opening bouncing off the padded cowling enclosing the edge of the deck.

Syman asked Jenks, "Capcom! What about that fire? What can I do about it?"

"This is Sam Leonard, Ecom, Mr. Pons. The fan motor of the primary air scrubber has an electrical short circuit. Look on Leninski's panel for a switch that says primair, that's p-r-i-m-a-i-r."

Syman did as he was instructed and finding it asked," Okay, I've found it. Now what?"

"Turn it to the off position."

Syman flicked the switch.

"Now, remove the air hoses for each of the pilots from the upper socket on the bulkhead and plug them into the lower ones. Those are the ports for the secondary loop, the one you and Mr. Gordon are using."

Syman again followed the instructions and after a minute was done. Dexter came back into the flight deck area and proceeded to strap the masked tanks over the faces of the unconscious pilots.

"They don't look too good, Sy."

"Telemetry shows the fire has gone out," said Ecom Leonard.

Are you getting any smoke in the cabin?"

"Smoke was coming out of Winter and Leninski's suits when I removed their helmets," said Syman, but it's beginning to dissipate, now that I've hooked them to the secondary air system."

"Sounds good. The sensors say the fire's out, but keep an eye on it."

"Roger, that."

"Has either of the pilots regained consciousness?"

"No," said Syman.

"We have another problem." It was the Capcom speaking. "You're supposed to initiate the landing procedure in twelve minutes, but with both pilots unable to fly, we'll have to go round and bring you home to the Cape or to California, where we can land the shuttle by remote control."

Syman and Dexter were silent for a moment and then Syman asked, "Houston, how difficult is this thing to fly and land?"

"Compared to what, Mr. Pons," asked the Capcom.

"Ah, say compared to a bomber."

There was momentary silence from the ground.

"What do you have in mind? Are you thinking you and Mr. Gordon might try to land it?"

"Yes, that's exactly what I have in mind."

"It's difficult, particularly the first time around, Mr. Pons. And it will be dark, just after 3AM in Osaka."

"Well, I'm a retired Air Force pilot, a lieutenant colonel, with a couple of thousand hours flight time in fighters and about a thousand hours in transport and bomber aircraft. Mr. Gordon is flight certified in all of the jet aircraft our company TMI uses for our express product delivery services."

"You're pilots?"

"Yes. And I've done my share of night landings."

"Well, that puts a whole new light on our situation. We just thought you two were a couple of helpless minor politicians."

Dexter and Syman could hear the undisguised amazement in the Capcom's voice.

"Dex, let's get Captain Winter and Commander Leninski into our seats and strap them in."

Dexter began undoing the restraints holding Leninski in the copilot's seat. Syman did the same to Winter.

"Have you ever flown a 747 Colonel Pons?" asked the Capcom.

"No. But I did a few hours in B-52's before I was assigned to fighters."

"Did you do any landings?"

"I did half a dozen in the co-pilot's seat. But I only had the controls for two of the landings."

"Well, we can't exactly call that extensive flight training for flying a shuttle, but it's a lot better than nothing," said the Capcom. "You've got nine minutes to get Winters and Leninski strapped in and I have to get the okay from the flight coordinator. If it's a go, do you think you can be ready on time?"

"We'll be ready," said Syman.

"The flight surgeon says to leave them on pure O-2 until the last possible moment. Then you'll have to put their helmets back on for the descent."

"Roger, that," Syman replied.

"You settle yourself, Sy, and get familiar with the steering wheel and the brakes on this boat and I'll get them suited up when the time is right."

Syman floated over to the pilot's chair and proceeded to buckle himself in.

"Lately, we've gotten ourselves into some of the damnedest pickles," said Dexter.

Syman made no reply. He was busy studying the controls and familiarizing himself with them.

"Houston. Is there anything the co-pilot has to do during the landing or is it all up to the pilot?" Syman asked.

"The only responsibility the co-pilot has is to extend the landing gear and deploy the braking chute. Both controls are between your seats, where you could reach them if need be, but, we'd like Mr. Gordon to handle those two chores. You'll have plenty to keep your mind on just then."

"Roger that, Houston. Incidentally, Mr. Gordon is a retired Navy Commander, SEALs, and we have both been recently reinstated for the duration of the crisis, so for the record this is strictly a military operation."

"Roger that, Endeavor. It sounds like the Shuttle is in good hands. We've got a go on your landing in Osaka, Colonel Pons. If you still want to try it, we're going to have Colonel Charles Gould help talk you down. He's one of our best shuttle pilots."

"Let's do it, Gentleman, I'm getting hungry and a little sushi about now would be just right. You better button them up, Dex," said Syman, in command and sounding like the confident pilot he was.

"Reentry procedure commences in three minutes," said Colonel Gould, as he began guiding Syman through the re-entry procedure.

Dexter double-checked Captain Winter's and Commander Leninski's air hose connections to the secondary air system. He removed the O-2 masks and stowed them in a locker in the bulkhead nearby. Then, he put their helmets back on their suits. The astronauts had not stirred a muscle and Dexter wasn't sure if they'd make it. Though not a particularly religious man, he nevertheless said a quick silent prayer for them before turning away and taking his own position in the empty co-pilot's seat.

Dexter listened without interrupting as Colonel Gould gave Syman a busman's lesson in flying one of the most difficult aircraft in the world.

"Some of the pilots liken it to flying a brick with wings, Colonel Pons. You don't have any power. All you've got is mass with a hell of a lot of inertia, which you can trade for lift as you loose speed," said Gould.

"Just like any good glider," Syman said, wryly.

"Yeah, kind of like that," said Colonel Gould, laughing and then he said," Okay, here we go, Colonel. You have to pitch Endeavor. Twitch the reaction control jets control lever forward, once. Then, watch the pitch indicator on your vid screen. When you're approaching zero degrees on your horizon, twitch the lever in the opposite direction to bring your pitch to a stop."

Syman followed the instructions exactly and performed the maneuver perfectly. Watching their own displays on the ground, the controllers were impressed.

"I think you might be a natural, Colonel," said Gould.

"Let's wait on the critique until I've got this thing on the ground," said Syman, just a touch superstitious.

"Now that the tail is facing forward, we're going to fire the main engine for seventy-two seconds. The reduction in speed will drop you out of orbit. Then you have to turn the shuttle back around immediately before you encounter the uppermost bits of the atmosphere."

"You're coming up on main engine burn in 39 seconds," Colonel Gould informed them as they waited for the main engine to fire. "The computers will control the burn, but if they fail, then you'll have to push the large green fire button under the clear plastic guard directly in front of you on the control panel. The red button below it is the engine cut off. Pull the guard now. I'll tell you if you need to use either."

"Roger, Houston," said Syman.

"And remember, after the burn, you have to turn the shuttle around so it's facing forward again, belly down and you need to initiate that maneuver as soon as the re-entry burn is finished."

"I understand," said Syman, calmly.

They waited tensely in silence.

"Main engine burn in five seconds, three, two, one, ignition," said an earth bound tech half the world away.

Dexter and Syman felt the weight of their bodies again as the powerful rocket motor worked to slow their velocity. After a short time, its job accomplished, the engine fell silent and they were once more weightless.

"You have to turn the shuttle around, Colonel Pons, so it's facing forward," said Gould.

"Roger, that," said Syman as he began the delicate rotation.

"This time, when you're done, you want to have an 11 degree up angle on the shuttle relative to your horizon so the ablative tiles and the nose cone take the brunt of the reentry heating. This is a critical value Colonel Pons. You have to keep it close to that angle as you drop into the lower atmosphere."

"Understood," said Syman, concentrating hard on the artificial horizon indicator as he quickly twitched the reaction control jet joy stick back twice and then forward three times to accomplish the maneuver. The digital counter settled on nine degrees. Syman ever so gently twitched the control forward and then back after a moment. The counter settled on eleven degrees.

"You're four by four on the reentry angle", said Gould. "On the upper right of the vidscreen you'll see a switch that says 'reentry angle lock.' flip it down."

Syman found the switch and toggled it down.

"Roger on the angle lock switch, Colonel Gould."

"You have to monitor the reentry angle as you descend. The computers will keep you in trim, but you shouldn't trust them completely during the descent. The heat and vibration of reentry make it more likely something might go wrong and it's not a good time for a computer to malfunction if you know what I mean."

"Roger that. I'll keep my eye on the angle," replied Syman.

"You'll begin reentry in about 30 seconds," said Gould. "While you're going through the upper atmosphere the ionization from the hot gases generated by your re-entry will make communications impossible."

"We're familiar with that," said Syman,

"When we reestablish communications, in about twelve minutes, I'll tell you how you handle the flight controls. Once you're in the lower atmosphere the computer can help you fly the shuttle down most of the way. You're par...to input inform...need...telem...ing up..."

The shuttle was being buffeted as it slammed through high ranging wisps of the Earth's atmosphere at Mach 17. Syman and Dexter could see fiery blasts of sparks fly up and over the forward facing windows in front of them. The buffeting quickly became more constant and the stream of sparks more intense. A white-orange glow hazed around the lower edges of the shuttle's nose and belly and was frighteningly visible through the glass.

"You think we could stop at a convenience store for a six pack of cold beer?" said Dexter. "It looks like it's going to get a little warm in here."

"No problem, Pardner," said Syman with a short laugh.

Amazingly, although it was six thousand degree Fahrenheit, hot enough to melt virtually any metal in seconds, less than three feet away on the other side of the bulkhead, the carbon nose cone and the aerogel silicon tiles did an excellent job of protecting the shuttle from the fierce heat and the cooling system kept the shuttle's interior at an exact sixty-eight degrees.

As the shuttle entered the atmosphere, an inertial tug of 3 G's from atmospheric braking took hold of the shuttle and its occupants.

Dexter turned awkwardly from side to side to inspect the still unconscious pilots. Though not as violent as the fierce shaking they'd experienced on the ride up, the vibrations were none the less considerable. He watched the unconscious astronauts shake like ragdolls, as their helmets lolled back and forth and their limp arms banged against the armrests of their chairs.

"Winter and Leninski are getting a hell of a bruising back there, Sy."

"Nothing we can do about that," said Syman. "I just hope we get them on the ground quickly enough to save their lives."

During the next twelve minutes, Syman and Dexter traveled two-thousand miles west toward Japan and dropped four-hundred-thousand feet vertically, slowing from 15,600 miles per hour to 2,500 miles per hour. At sixty-thousand feet altitude the radio came back to life.

"Endeavor, this is Houston. Your telemetry is back on line. Do you copy?"

"Roger, Houston," said Syman. "We copy."

"What's your condition, Endeavor?"

"We're in good condition, Houston, but you need to have medical personnel on the ground in Osaka for Winter and Leninski."

"Roger that, Endeavor."

"Colonel Pons. It's time for your next lesson in flying a brick," said Colonel Gould.

"I'm ready," said Syman, with grim determination.

While Gould instructed Syman, Dexter unstrapped himself and began shedding parts of his now unnecessary spacesuit. Free from helmet and gloves, he unbuckled himself from his seat and clambered back to the unconscious shuttle pilots. He removed their helmets and put the O2-tanked face masks back on them in an effort to get as much oxygen into their blood as possible. He was pleased to see that despite their recent battering, they both were breathing evenly on their own and neither showed any signs of distress. It was as if they were asleep, slumped forward, held in place by their seat harnesses with their masked heads hanging above their chests and their arms hanging limply at their sides. Dexter cinched the belts tight to hold them in place during the landing. With nothing else to do, he returned to his seat.

Syman was listening intently to instructions from Colonel Gould, trying to absorb months of sophisticated training experience from a few minutes of verbal explanations. He was sweating and the strain showed on his face. There was only one chance to get it right.

"How is she responding to the controls, Colonel Pons?" Gould asked.

"It feels kind of mushy."

"That's normal. You've got an enormous amount of weight and no power, so you have to anticipate everything in advance."

"We're traveling at Mach .95. When do I begin the pull up to slow us down?"

"Eight miles out from touchdown you'll pick up your glide path. You follow the radio beam down, just like any other aircraft. You'll be moving fast for a landing and you'll be coming in at a very steep angle to maintain your lift. Eight miles before you reach the landing threshold you pull the nose up to bleed off the unnecessary speed. I'll give you a heads up when it's time."

"I understand," said Syman.

"Commander Gordon," said Gould, suddenly.

"I'm here," said Dexter.

"When I tell you, I want you to deploy the landing gear. It's the lever on the lower console between you and Colonel Pons. It has a red and black handle. Do you see it?"

"Affirmative, Colonel Gould. I see it."

"Just push it down, when I tell you."

"Colonel Pons, we're coming up on the speed bleed. Pull the nose up to twenty-eight degrees and hold it there until you're going 240 knots. If you see you're dropping below the glide slope, reduce flaperons and level out to gain speed. When you're back on the glide slope, continue to seesaw the shuttle down until you're going 225 knots."

"Understood," said Pons.

Sweat was beading on Syman's brow and Dexter watched his friend intently. He alternated his glance between Syman and the view out the window as the myriad lights of Japan spread out on the horizon. After flying over the length of southern Honshu, they finally came upon Kansai International Airport looking like a brightly lit aircraft carrier sitting out in Osaka Bay.

To create Kansai Airport, engineers had piled millions of cubic yards of fill inside a huge retaining wall to create the world's first ocean airport. A modern wonder of the world, the long, narrow, manmade island looked minuscule and impossibly small for landing the shuttle.

"Colonel Gould?" Dexter said. "How long is the runway we're going to use?"

"11,700 feet, Commander Gordon," replied Gould.

"Is that going to be long enough?"

"It should be just long enough if you brake hard," said Gould. "First, we want you to deploy the braking chutes, Commander."

"Roger that," said Dexter.

"On the control panel just above the landing gear lever, you'll find the switch to deploy them."

Dexter looked closely at the control panel and found the switch labeled, 'Deploy Parachute.'

"I see it, Colonel. How soon after touch down should I deploy?"

"The moment you're rear wheels are on the ground, Commander," Gould replied. "You'll be moving very fast and the runway is just the minimum needed, so you don't want to wait even a second more than necessary."

"Right," said Dexter, seeing only too clearly that they might not have enough distance to stop before running off the end of the airport's artificial island and into the waters of Osaka Bay.

"What's the recommended runway length for the shuttle?" Dexter asked, putting Gould on the spot.

There was a pregnant pause before Gould replied, "14,000 feet, Commander."

Dexter and Syman looked at each other for a moment without saying anything. The math was basic. The truth was stark. They were almost half a mile short of runway for a normal landing.

"Well, Pardner," said Syman sardonically, "we'll just have to look at the next few minutes as a growth experience."

"Ah, huh," said Dexter, sounding skeptical.

Syman continued seesawing the shuttle down to slow it for landing. He could see on his flight data display that he was right on the glide path.

"Lower the landing gear at the one mile mark, Commander," said Gould.

"Roger that," said Dexter, pushing the control down a few seconds later. There was an electric whine as the hydraulics lowered and locked the wheels with a 'thunk'.

Their speed was a little high, but their approach was other wise perfect. Syman pulled the shuttle's nose up and leveled it out one last time just before clearing the runway threshold. The speed indicator showed 232 knots as the rear wheels of the heavy space plane settled onto the runway.

Dexter instantly popped the chute and waited tensely for the nose wheel to drop to the runway as they rolled toward the far end of the landing strip.

As soon as Syman felt the nose wheel rumble on the pavement, he stepped into the brake peddles with both feet. It took only moments to see they were traveling too fast. Adding his weight to the brake peddles, Dexter glanced at the speed indicator. It read 190 knots. Syman and he watched it count down with agonizing slowness. With only a thousand feet to go, they were still going fifty knots and they could see the shuttle was going to overshoot the runway and end up in the Bay.

"I hope you're wearing your water wings, Pardner, 'cause we're going for a swim," said Syman, resigned to their fate.

"The hell we are!" shot back Dexter. "What we need is a higher friction coefficient!" As he said this, he reached down between their seats and grabbed the landing gear control, giving it a violent upward yank. The landing gear immediately folded under the fifty ton, two-billion dollar shuttle craft as it gracelessly dropped to its belly amidst screeches of angry metal and a shower of sparks and flaking aerogel tiles.

Syman and Dexter were thrown violently forward against the restraining straps of their seats as the shuttle ground to a halt only fifty feet from the dark waters of the Bay.

Seeing the water so close, Dexter took a deep breath and then let it out slowly. He turned to look at Syman.

Looking back at him, Syman said, "This is probably not my best landing."

"Works for me," Dexter retorted

44

I am Akinori Yumi, Forth Assistant to Minister of State Ikeda," said the slight Japanese man to Dexter and Syman. He bowed and continued, "the Minister would be here to greet you himself, but he is overcome with the sickness."

"We've brought you vaccine for the plague, Mr. Yumi. It's in the cargo bay of the Shuttle," said Syman pointing to the belly-flopped Shuttle lying on the runway. "I'm Syman Pons and this is Dexter Gordon."

"I am at your service, Gentlemen," said Minister's Assistant Yumi.

"Our pilots need medical help immediately. We had a fire in the air filtration system, and smoke got into their spacesuits."

As they spoke Winter and Leninski were being loaded into a Medivac helicopter.

"I have been informed that they will be at the hospital in ten minutes. We will do everything possible for them."

"Good!" said Syman.

"You speak excellent English," said Dexter.

"I received my degree in economics from Harvard. I lived in your country for five years."

Syman said, "Mr. Yumi, we need to change out of these suits and then perhaps you can arrange for us to brief your officials on what we know about the plague."

Yumi turned and spoke loudly in Japanese to the driver of his car standing thirty feet away. The driver scurried over carrying two green coveralls. Handing a coverall to each man, the driver relieved Dexter and Syman of their two small suitcases carrying them to a Learjet that had also pulled up next to the Shuttle.

"Please follow me, gentlemen," said Yumi as he crossed the pavement to the jet. "You can change out of your suits and put on the coveralls while we're on the way to Tokyo."

Still encumbered by the bulky spacesuits, Syman and Dexter awkwardly followed Yumi into the aircraft.

When they were seated, Minister's Assistant Yumi continued, "First, we'll fly to Tokyo. There, we will take you to a hotel where you can refresh yourselves. If you like the accommodations, you will be welcomed to stay there as guests of Japan as long as you are in our country."

"Why not take us to the United States embassy?" Dexter asked.

"Normally we would do just that, Mr. Gordon, but many of the embassy staff have the sickness."

Dexter retorted angrily, "This thing is really getting out of hand!"

Assistant Yumi looked at his watch. "It is now Three AM. I have scheduled a meeting with some of our government officials, including people from the Ministry of Justice for eight o'clock this morning. We were informed by your embassy, that you would tell us what you know about Hinode's involvement."

"Hinode is the source of the plague," said Dexter.

"We suspect Kioro Itara is trying to overthrow Japan's legitimate government," said Syman.

Looking shocked, Yumi said, "Kioro Itara is one of our most important business leaders. These are very serious allegations."

"You don't know the half of it," replied Dexter, the bitterness apparent in his voice.

As the Lear rose into the night, Syman's and Dexter's last sight of the Shuttle was of people unloading the boxes of vaccine from the cargo bay.

Following their gazes and perceiving their concern, Assistant Yumi said loudly over the roar of the engine, "The vaccine will be administered immediately, starting with the Emperor."

Dexter and Syman both nodded.

Sitting next to Dexter in the back of the Toyota, Syman watched the busy streets of Tokyo go by. He glanced at his watch. It said 11:20. Though weary, he was none the less looking forward to confronting the man who was the cause of so much misery and death.

At their meeting that morning with Japan's officials, it had been decided to arrest Kioro Itara that afternoon. Because of the seriousness of the charge, a writ would be served requiring him to appear immediately before a magistrate for questioning. He would be taken into custody then and there.

As representatives of the United States, Dexter and Syman would be allowed to observe the writ being served, but that was all. Apprehending and questioning Kioro Itara were Japan's responsibility.

The car came to an abrupt stop in front of an enormous skyscraper. Assistant Yumi opened the front passenger side door and got out. He turned around and stuck his head back inside. "This is Hinode's headquarters building, gentlemen.

Syman and Dexter exited the car.

293

"I must remind you, you are here to observe only. If you interfere we might be forced to release Kioro Itara. As one of the richest and most powerful men in Japan, it will be difficult enough to hold him for questioning for more than a very short time."

"We understand, Mr. Yumi," said Syman.

"Very well. Come!"

Syman, Dexter, and Minister's Assistant Yumi were joined by six others. Yumi's counterpart from the Ministry of Justice, also a Forth Minister's Assistant, had brought two of his subordinates, both lawyers. And because the charge was treason, two heavily armed, uniformed men from Japan's Defense Force and the Tokyo Chief of Police also accompanied the group to deal with any troublesome Hinode security people.

"This is the Justice Minister's Forth Assistant Karuda," said Yumi, introducing the man to Syman and Dexter.

The man stood to attention momentarily and bowed slightly from the waist. Syman and Dexter nodded their responses, unable to respond in Japanese.

Yumi turned away from Syman and Dexter when Assistant Karuda spoke to him waving the folded writ and gesticulating toward the headquarters building. After a few terse words in Japanese, Karuda led the way into Hinode.

Inside the building, Assistant Karuda walked directly to the security guard sitting at a kiosk in the center of the lobby. He told the guard they wanted to see Kioro Itara immediately. The guard picked up the telephone and spoke to someone for several moments. Then the guard told Karuda that Kioro Itara was unavailable and that they would have to make an appointment and come back then. There were sharp words from Assistant Karuda and the guard again picked up the phone. He talked with someone and then listened before hanging up a second time. The guard told the Justice Minister's Assistant that someone would be meeting them in a few minutes. Without hesitation, Karuda turned to the Defense Force personnel and told them to remove the guard from his seat. Leveling their guns at the surprised guard, the soldiers quickly hustled the guard away from the kiosk standing him against the nearest wall. Then Karuda picked up the phone and dialed a number from a list on the guard's desk. He spoke harshly into the phone several times, raising his voice and threatening the person on the other end of the line.

Minister Yumi turned to Syman and Dexter explaining, "Assistant Karuda just told the company official on the other end of the line that he will bring a thousand troops into the building and close it down within the hour if the official does not take us to see Kioro Itara immediately."

Dexter and Syman both nodded their understanding.

Karuda turned and again said something in Japanese to Yumi, but it was obvious that he intended everyone to hear it.

Yumi explained to the Americans, "Assistant Karuda said an official will be here directly to take us to Kioro Itara."

With raised eyebrows Dexter looked at Syman and said, "Well, that was easy."

Syman said, "We'll see."

Despite the threats, two minutes passed as they waited impatiently for the Hinode official to arrive. He spoke to both Assistants and then led the way to an elevator.

At six feet four, Syman was a giant among midgets, the next tallest men being Dexter at five feet eleven inches and the beefy five foot nine Defense Force sergeant, the larger of the two, who had rousted the lobby security guard. Both Minster's Assistants were diminutive, neither much over five feet in height.

From his position in the back corner of the elevator, Syman watched the Hinode official carefully. When everyone was aboard, the official pushed the button for the thirty-first floor.

Seeing from the buttons on the control panel that they were in an eighty floor building, Syman wondered why Kioro Itara would have his office forty-nine floors from the top.

When the elevator arrived at the thirty-first floor, the Hinode official lead them to another elevator door directly across the hall from the one they'd just exited. When they were all aboard the second elevator, the Hinode official inserted and turned a key in a lock on the control panel before pushing an unmarked button directly below it.

To everyone's surprise the elevator began to descend rapidly. Karuda instantly barked at the Hinode official with alarm in his voice. The official spoke to him quietly. Karuda nodded and seemed to relax a little. Yumi translated for Syman and Dexter, "We are being taken to Kioro Itara. He is not in the building. Rather, he is located four-hundred feet underground."

Dexter and Syman exchanged silent looks, both simultaneously wondering if it was smart to just descend into their adversary's lair without informing someone of their location.

Dexter spoke up, "Mr. Yumi, shouldn't we tell someone where we're going before we disappear underground."

Yumi nodded and then spoke to the Hinode official. The elevator stopped its descent abruptly. Yumi removed his cell phone from his jacket and placed a call. Speaking rapidly in Japanese, he explained their situation in a few moments. As he put the telephone back in his jacket, he instructed the Hinode official to proceed and the elevator began its descent once again.

Half a minute later the elevator came to a halt and the door rolled back revealing a hallway of white ceramic tile.

Reminiscent of the ultra-clean rooms at TMI where electronic components were manufactured and assembled, Dexter leaned close to Syman and said,

"Looks a little like building five."

"Wish we were there instead of here," Syman replied.

The Hinode official glanced at them both and then led the way out of the elevator to the left. They walked a dozen yards before coming to a large heavy door, which the official opened with a concerted yank. On the other side, a women and a man dressed in white uniforms were sitting behind a raised counter.

Seeing a large group of strange men file into the room, they were on their feet in a moment. The man raised his voice in loud protest attempting to take command of the situation and halt the group's progress. The Hinode official waved his hand and spoke loudly in return. The man and woman recognized him and their demeanor changed instantly. The official spoke to them for a moment and the man behind the counter shook his head up and down speaking emphatically to the company official as he pointed down the hall to their right. Then the company official spoke to Yumi and Karuda for a moment before turning and leading the way.

Syman sniffed the air as they walked along. It smelled of antiseptic and alcohol and other vaguely medicinal but unidentifiable scents. Everything about this underground bunker made Syman uneasy. After walking fifty feet, they turned left through another heavy door before coming to a halt in a large dimly lit room.

There before them on a hospital bed lay the emaciated body of an old man. Even in the dim light they could clearly see a dozen wires, tubes and hoses were attached to the patient and a ventilator taped to his neck wheezed air into the old body every few seconds. Each arm had needled tubes supplying various fluids. A catheter with pale yellow urine snaked from the diaper covering the old man's groin. A colostomy tube, also coming from under the diaper ran to a plastic bag full of brown excrement clipped to the side of the bed.

After a moment, the Hinode official turned his head slightly to indicate the human wreck in the bed and said in Japanese, "Gentlemen, here is Kioro Itara."

As understanding came upon them, the Minister's Assistants, the lawyers, the guards and Syman and Dexter all stood there speechless as they took in the sight of the pathetic old cripple laying motionless on the bed.

Syman recovered from his surprise a little faster than the others and he immediately began carefully inspecting the scene before him. He realized that this man who had tried to destroy their world had been an immobile, bed ridden hospitalized recluse for a very long time. Except through the virtual reality visor hanging on a hook at the head of the bed, it was obvious that Kioro Itara had had no connection with the outside world in the recent past.

"This is why no one has seen him for so long," Syman said to Dexter.

The old person in the bed looked deformed. The arms and legs were curled in odd ways. The fingers of both hands were clinched and contorted as if Itara were suffering from advanced multiple sclerosis. Laying on his back, his legs were splayed, but with knees bent and the feet extended straight. Itara's body looked as if all his muscles were tensing at the same time locking him in this strange position.

During the entire half minute of silent inspection, not a muscle moved except the eyes, clear and sharp, ferret like in the wrinkled old face. The expression of the eyes was complex and as Syman watched, he saw the succession of surprise, fear, contempt, and anger. Finally, one more unmistakable expression settled in the old man's eyes, that of unconcealed hate.

Perceiving the meaning of Kioro Itara's look, Dexter was unable to bear the old man's venom in silence. Knowing that Hinode's founder spoke fluent English, Dexter walked right up to the bed and leaned over him. With a derisive snort, he said, "So, you're Kioro Itara, the man who would destroy the world, killing billions of innocent people. Well, it's not going to happen and soon you're going to die and go straight to hell, you evil old bastard."

Clearly understanding what had just been said to him, but having never been spoken to in such a disrespectful manner, Kioro Itara was overcome with rage. Unable to move anything other than his head, he did the only thing he could. He spit at Dexter. Stymied by the ventilator in his scrawny neck, it was a pathetic effort and the thin saliva lifted only a few inches before falling back to land all over his own face.

Pleased to see his words had hit the mark, Dexter said with a sneer, "Kioro Itara, you're so vile and disgusting, there are no words to describe you. And in case you don't get it, you lose!" With that, Dexter turned and left the room.

A moment later Syman turned to face the others and said, "We'll call you later, Mr. Yumi. Good by, Gentlemen."

When they reached the elevator, Syman pushed the button on the wall. The doors slid open and they got in the elevator and pushed the button with the up arrow on it. When the doors opened again, they found themselves back on the thirty-first floor. They crossed the hall and took one of the building's normal elevators to the ground floor.

Leaving the Hinode building, they took a taxi back to the hotel.

Finding Kioro Itara and looking him square in the eye was enough for Syman and Dexter. There was nothing else they could do and it was obvious that he wasn't going to flee justice in a mad dash to some other country. Given the sorry shape he was in, he'd be lucky to survive another day.

Back in their hotel room, Syman sat down at the dining table in their suite with a fresh cup of coffee.

"When you told him he'd lost, it reminded me that although we've got him, his lethal little bug is still rampaging around the globe killing people."

"Yeah, my words rang in my ears when I told him that. We won't have really beaten Itara until there's enough vaccine for everybody and it's obvious it's going to take a long time to accomplish that. Maybe half the people on earth will be dead by then."

The grim realization hung in the air between them as they considered it in silence.

After a moment, Syman said, "I've been thinking about that, since we talked to the Japanese this morning and I think I know a way to provide all the vaccine needed quickly."

"If you can do that you'll be the next most popular man in history after Jesus Christ."

"What's needed," said Syman, ignoring Dexter's comment, "is a huge reservoir of antibodies to the disease, enough to manufacture six billion injections of vaccine."

"The President already covered that. It's going to take some real serious time to replicate that amount of antibodies."

"Yes, it would take some serious time, unless that part of the process has already been accomplished."

"You've lost me, Sy"

"Have you thought about the fact that only the government people here in Japan have gotten the plague?"

"Yeah. Itara must have infected them, somehow."

Syman continued, "I'm not sure, but I think that we're missing a more important fact by defining the situation that way, Dex."

"What have we missed?" Dexter asked,

"That somehow, Kioro Itara has already inoculated most of the people in Japan with some of that vaccine we brought back to the United States."

Dexter's brows knit as he considered the implications.

"Well, it is surprising that more people in Japan aren't sick, but there's no way they could have made the hundred-twenty-five million doses needed to vaccinate all the Japanese in that little lab in Libya."

"And they didn't need to. I think Libya was just the containment lab where they developed that nasty little bug. If it had gotten loose and killed everybody in Nalut, who would have known or cared?"

"Yeah?" said Dexter, still trying to get his mind around all the implications of what Syman was saying.

"They probably didn't bring it here to Japan, where they could easily manufacture the vaccine in bulk, until they were sure they could handle it safely."

"Then you're thinking maybe the vaccine is already here in Japan somewhere and we just need to find it?"

"No, Dex, not the vaccine, but rather the antibodies."

"I'm not following you, Sy."

"Kioro Itara somehow inoculated most of the Japanese, so the antibodies needed to inoculate the rest of the people on earth already exist in the blood of the people of Japan. All that is needed is to collect a pint or so from each of the healthy hundred million odd Japanese and you'll have all the antibodies needed to create six billion shots of vaccine."

"Bingo!" said Dexter, with real enthusiasm. "I think you just found the solution to our problem."

The Emperor lay propped up on large, brightly colored, beautifully embroidered pillows. The camera closed in on his face. His skin was pale and his lower lip trembled slightly. Clearly he was very ill.

Dexter and Syman were sitting in the parlor of their hotel suite watching the Japanese-English news channel to hear the Emperor's address to Japan.

As he began to speak, English sub-titles appeared at the bottom of the screen, providing a nearly instantaneous translation.

"My people, it has come to my attention that the epidemic sweeping round the Earth was initiated by one of our own countrymen, Kioro Itara, founder and head of Hinode Worldwide, Japan's largest company."

The Emperor cleared his throat, coughing slightly. In a moment, he was overwhelmed with a wracking fit of coughing. As his chest heaved to draw and expel air, his face reddened and his eyes teared. Attendants appeared and blocked the camera momentarily as they passed in front of it to aid him. He waved them away, shaking his head side to side, indicating that he was all right. Still, it was a minute before he was able to compose himself enough to continue.

"As you may know, most of the elected members in the Japanese Government and I, myself have been infected with this deadly disease. As you also probably know, all other citizens of Japan are free of this disease. This is not a coincidence. Rather, it was intended by Kioro Itara and was accomplished during the nationwide influenza vaccination program sponsored as a public service by Hinode last fall. We now know Hinode's seemingly noble effort was no service to the public. As you will recall, Japan was being swept with a dangerous flu and thousands of people were dying though out Japan. At that time, the pharmaceutical branch of Hinode took it upon itself to inoculate every Japanese against that dreadful disease. Unknown to us all, Hinode had biologically engineer that particular flu strain and released it to create the perfect opportunity to also secretly inoculate the Japanese people against Kioro Itara's terrifyingly lethal biological weapon.

From the beginning, it has been Kioro Itara's intention to manipulate

Japan's people, dispose of Japan's legitimate government and place himself at the head as supreme shogun of all Japan.

In accomplishing these evil things, it was also his intention to exterminate all the other peoples of Earth, committing the most monstrous crime of all.

In attempting to reach his evil goals, Kioro Itara has brought a shame, almost too great to bear, upon us all.

At the moment, most of Japan's citizens are disease free, while the rest of mankind is slowly dying. This is a situation that we can and must remedy. It is within our power to right this terrible wrong and return honor to our people by helping save our brothers and sisters around the world.

Now, I come to the point of my message to you. In a most literal sense, you carry within you the means to stop this tragedy. Within your blood you carry antibodies to Kioro Itara's biological weapon. These antibodies can be used as the basis for a vaccine to protect and cure other unvaccinated people.

As your Emperor, it is my wish that every healthy Japanese citizen go to one of the special blood collection centers being set up around our country and give a small quantity of blood. From your blood the billions of doses of vaccine needed to save the rest of the world can be manufactured in the shortest possible time. As your Emperor, it is my desire that we do all that we can..."

45

Royce slid the map across the table to Dexter and Syman. They turned it around and began studying it intently.

"You could have seen this when you got back from Japan eight weeks ago, if I hadn't caught that goddamn plague. I was really sick. I was throwing up blood at one point. Then I got better, for a while..."

"We're sorry to hear you were so sick, Royce," said Syman sincerely. "And since we got back from Japan we've been overwhelmed by the plague, too, so, we wouldn't have had time to look at this until now, anyway."

"Yeah, half of our employees were sick," said Dexter. "So, it's been kind of hectic."

"Were you guys sick?"

"No. Neither of us has been sick."

"I'm lucky the government came up with a vaccine for it, when they did," Royce said, continuing, "or I'd be dead right now. The strangest thing happened. I was just getting sick again with the second stage of the disease, when the medical center called me and said to come in for a shot. I asked how they'd gotten my name and they said they'd gotten a call from the Surgeon General's office in Washington, D.C. and been told to make sure I got a vaccination. I still don't know how that came about, but I'm sure glad I got the shot when I did. A week later would have been too late. Fortunately, instead of dying, I spent the next three weeks in the hospital recovering."

"We're really sorry to hear you were so sick, Royce," Dexter said, again, meaning every word. "It sounds like it was a real bitch!"

"That doesn't even begin to describe it," said Royce. "I don't remember ever being so ill. I've caught some pretty god-awful stuff during field work around the world, but the plague is in a class by itself."

Syman said, "Well, thank God for the vaccine." He glanced at Dexter for a moment and then turned back to Royce.

"Thank God is right. Neither of you got sick?" Royce asked again.

"Nope," said Dexter.

"Must be the luck of the draw," Royce concluded. "Looking on the bright side, when I wasn't real sick, I was able to spend the time studying the translation of plate. I've plowed through a lot of it, and what it says is amazing."

After a moment, a distant look came over him. "Let's see. What was I going to tell you first? There's so much." He scratched his scalp as he said this.

"You said you'd discovered their rationale for choosing the sites they did for the shelters," Syman reminded him gently as he pointed at the map.

"Oh, that's right," said Royce, turning his attention to the map. "As you can see, there are twenty-five shelters on the Earth, spread unevenly around the globe. Three were apparently destroyed or maybe I should say flooded after the comet's impact. One of these was the one you were in and one is in the Philippines.

The plate says the sea level rose about twenty-five years after the comet hit and they were forced to abandon them."

"That explains why we never found the generators and other equipment needed to power the one at Ilhas Desertas," said Dexter. "The equipment's under water, just like we thought. Syman and I wondered if the Island could have subsided into the ocean, but you say sea level was lower half a million years ago, when they built the place."

"Yes, and the sea level rose and submerged Ilhas Desertas and the shelter in the Philippines."

"You said there are three shelters that were flooded?" Syman asked.

"The third one is a special case. It's located near the island of Menorca, in the Baleric Islands, but there were no islands there when that shelter was built. Actually, it was located on what scientists had thought was once a fertile plain, the hypothetical Baleric plateau. I now know for a fact that here was indeed a Plateau and that it sank after the comet strike, almost doubling the size of the western Mediterranean Sea. Scientists studying the Med have been wondering about the area for years. Core drillings containing pollen spores and other microscopic clues, strongly indicated that the Plateau was once high and dry, but the area is too deep to have ever been above the surface, even during the lowest sea levels. But, now we know what happened there. When the comet struck, the Plateau subsided under the sea."

"Sounds like you've found Atlantis," said Dexter.

"Actually, Dex, from what I've read so far from the history on the plate, Ilhas Desertas and the area of the Madeira Islands where you guys were, probably is what remains of Atlantis, but I'm getting ahead of myself."

"Oh, come on, Royce. You can't be serious. Atlantis?" said Dexter. "Atlantis is a myth, pure and simple."

"Well, Dex, if what I've learned about this ancient civilization is substantially correct, then we're going to discover that a lot of modern man's myths are really the faint recollections of our very distant ancestors preserved

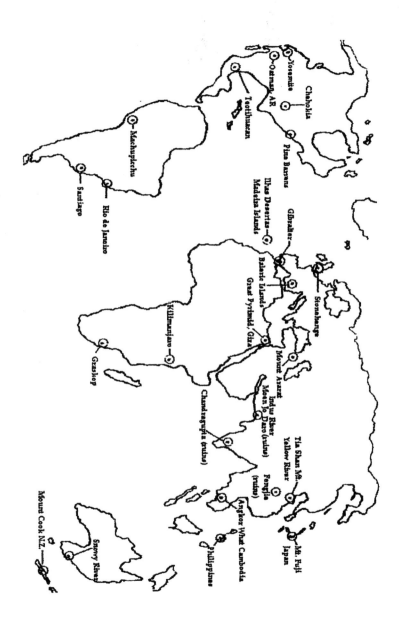

in oral tradition. From what I've read so far, I can already see the basis for many of mankind's myths and ancient legends in the history of these ancient people."

"That we've discovered Atlantis is kind of hard to believe, Royce. Got any other examples?"

"Well, yes, the Old Testament refers to the Nephilim being on Earth before the Flood, Genesis, chapter 6, verse 4, where it says: "The sons of God, went to the daughters of men and had children with them." It also says, "They were the heroes of old, men of renown." And while we're on the subject of the Flood, Noah's Ark comes to mind. You'll note there's a shelter under Mount Ararat in Turkey," said Royce. "And a shelter's purpose was to protect humans and animals from catastrophe."

"Yeah," said Dexter. "That is a funny coincidence."

"If you're having a hard time believing they might be the basis for some of our myths, you're really going to have a hard time with the rest of what the plate says about them."

Dexter replied somewhat defensively, "Oh, really, why is that?"

"Because, in addition to the shelters I've shown on the map, the plate also says there were shelters on the Moon and Mars and a repository of some kind at the South Pole."

"Wait a minute," said Dexter, obviously surprised. "You're saying they had people living on the Moon and Mars, when the comet struck?"

Syman said nothing, only smiling slightly as he listened to his two friends discuss these incredible things. After the past few weeks, he was ready to believe just about anything was possible.

"Well, apparently the moon base, I guess you'd call it that, was actually closed down and its personnel were sent on to the base on Mars, where it was believed they would have a better chance of survival. The plate says that at that point the moon base was also turned into some kind repository. They left some equipment and supplies to help the Mars colonist on their return to the Earth after the strike. The Mars-Moon-South Pole scenario was supposed to be humanity's lifeboat, its absolute last chance in case the Earth was completely devastated by the catastrophe. The plate says that it never got that bad. Still the ancients had done everything they could to prepare, not knowing ahead of time how bad the strike would be.

The repository at the South Pole was intended to further aid those returning from Mars and it was put there because it was the only place they were certain would not be badly damaged by the comet. The South pole repository contained food, seeds, raw materials, equipment, vehicles and everything else that would have helped them reestablish life on the planet, including a library containing all their accumulated knowledge and histories.

"Well," said Dexter. "Whatever they did, I am, therefore it worked."

Royce shook his head from side to side and said, "Sy, how do you get any work done with this child around?"

They all laughed and Dexter said, "Your time is coming, Royce."

Royce retorted, "Un hun," and continued, "The plate also says the people on Mars never returned to Earth and the people who survived the strike lost contact with them after a few years. The fate of the colony was never determined, because with only something like one hundred thousand people still alive on the Earth, there were no longer any resources available to go to Mars to investigate."

"I wonder if anything is left of their settlement on Mars?" said Dexter.

"That's one of the things I've been wondering myself," said Royce.

As he mulled over everything Royce was telling them, Syman scanned the map again. Several manmade sites were named as sites for shelters. He pondered the coincidence and then asked, "What's the rationale for the shelter locations on the Earth you were going to tell us about, Royce?"

Royce turned his attention to an old battered leather briefcase sitting on the table next to him. After rummaging in it for a moment, he handed them each a paper and said, "Look at these groupings I've made for the different locations. You'll see a heading at the top of each of the lists. The first one says 'Remarkable Natural Formations.' In that list," said Royce, reading from his own copy, "is half dome at Yosemite, the rock at Rio de Janeiro, the rock at Gibraltar, Mount Kilimanjaro, Mount Ararat, Mount Fuji, in Japan, and Mount Cook, in New Zealand. Each of these mountains is spectacular by any human standards. A shelter, what the plate's authors call a dandelion, likening their shelter system to the puffball of the flower, was built deep under each of these natural wonders.

Their intention was that each spectacular Formation would act as a magnet to people in the future, repeatedly drawing them back to the vicinity and the shelter under it. It was thought that this would help each group maintain their memory of mankind's past and encourage each group to use the rich information mankind held prior to the comet. But in every case, people eventually forgot about the shelters and their significance. We know from our own history that they all forgot about the priceless knowledge from before, as well. So, instead of memories and knowledge about mankind from before the strike, all that came down to us over the ages were vague superstitions or myths about a few events and places, like the Flood and Mount Ararat."

"Or maybe Atlantis?" said Dexter, still slightly incredulous at the thought.

"Yes, exactly," said Royce." Everything we know about Atlantis came from one source, Plato. His information came from an Egyptian priest, who said Atlantis was destroyed by an earthquake and then sank under the sea nine thousand years before their time.

If Ilhas Desertas is the remains of Atlantis and the source of the myth, then the priest had his timing wrong, but the core of the story was accurate. The builders of the shelters could fly and they seemed to have mastered the basics of nuclear physics, just like we have. To later ill educated generations, the pre-comet level of technical sophistication would have seemed like magic.

Unfortunately, in every case, once the memory of a shelter was lost, it was lost for good and Ilhas Desertas was no exception.

Still, it's likely some of the more spectacular characteristics of the ancient civilization were reported verbally to the succeeding generations, like the ability to fly and having control of the power of the sun. But, with the loss of general education came the loss of understanding.

As the refugees from Ilhas Desertas spread out across Africa and Europe, they would have shared their stories and oral traditions about the old days of their people's greatness. Perhaps what came down to Plato was the last vestige of that old, old confused story about a nearly forgotten but real people and place. The descendants of the people from the other shelters around the world would have run into each other eventually and they would have had their own half forgotten stories turned myth to share about their ancestors.

Ironically, another group of people, the Egyptians, who had forgotten about their own shelter deep under the great pyramid of Giza preserved the oral tradition of the Atlantians, who were probably the shelter group from Ilhas Desertas."

"Maybe the Egyptians are the remnants of the people from Ilhas Desertas," suggested Dexter.

"The shelter under the pyramid mitigates the likelihood of that being true."

"How do you know there is a shelter under the pyramid?" Dexter asked.

"The map inscribed on the plate gives latitude and longitude coordinates in their base five numbers. Starting with the Ilhas Desertas shelter, I converted the coordinates for all the shelters to our method of hours, minutes and seconds. This produced very accurate positions for all the other shelters.

We're lucky you guys knew where the plate came from. If I hadn't had an exact starting point, it would have been impossible to locate the others. We never could have established a correct frame of reference."

"You seem pretty certain about these locations, Royce," said Syman.

"Oh, I am now. At first I was skeptical, of course. The coordinates given were so exact that it quickly became apparent that many of the shelters were located under well known natural and man made wonders, but that was just too damn pat. Especially the manmade monuments. I didn't believe it could be possible that well known manmade monuments could be related to a civilization from half million years in the past, or that the monuments would have lasted so long. But, after thinking about it for a while, I realized that it would have been people's superstitious beliefs that caused them to build up and maintain those very sites for all that time. Having forgotten the true significance of a site, knowing only that it was somehow very important, people probably imbued the site of a forgotten shelter with something akin to sacredness. In several instances, even that was eventually forgotten with the passing of time.

Anyway, wanting some firsthand proof concerning the purported locations on the plate, I decided to do a little field work to prove or disprove the coordinates legitimacy. Last week, I took a geological survey crew to the New Jersey Pine barrens area, to the shelter coordinates nearest to us and did a seismic survey. At the coordinates we found what for the pine barrens was an unusually large hill. I had to spend a little of your money to get the land owner to allow us to do the survey, but since money talks loudly and since the land wasn't being used for anything, he decided to let us do the work.

On the first day, we found indications of a very large cavity two-hundred-forty feet below the surface. Since then, we've drilled down into the cavity and lowered a camera and lights into it. From what we can see, it looks remarkably like the chamber, you described to me, on Ilhas Desertas. I can show you the video if you're interested?"

"Later," said Syman. "We saw enough of the shelter on Ilhas Desertas to last a lifetime and we want to hear about some of the other things you've learned first."

"When it's opened up," said Dexter, "I'd like to take a good look at it and see what a complete shelter looks like."

"One interesting conclusion I've come to is that each shelter, with its limited number of genes to pass on, would have probably reinforced the racial characteristics of each group of people. It would explain why we have so many distinctly different racial types around the world, today."

Syman changed the subject, "You said, they built some type of repository at the South Pole. Was the South Pole frozen when they built it?"

"Yes, it was. And the plate says, aside from the safety issue, they built it there to take advantage of the natural tendency of cold to preserve things. They seemed to have always taken the long view when it came to preserving their history."

"Do you think the repository is still intact?" Syman asked.

"The Plate says what it contained was never needed and indicates that it was probably never disturbed."

"Wow! What an opportunity for an archaeologist. Of course you haven't considered taking a crack at the South Pole repository or anything like that, right Royce?" said Dexter teasing his friend.

"Like hell, I haven't! I've barely thought about anything else since I read about it. But, first I have to put the screws to a couple of tight-wad entrepreneurs I know, to squeeze a little cash out of them to pay for the expedition." Royce said this straight faced, giving back as good as he'd gotten.

They all laughed. Then Dexter said, "Speaking of preservation, Syman and I discovered something so incredible that you'll have a hard time believing it."

"Somehow, I doubt that, if the two of you were involved," said Royce, getting in one more good dig.

"You're going to show him the metal fragments, Dex?" Syman asked.

Dexter nodded and continued, ignoring Royce's comment, "We brought these back with us from Ilhas Desertas." He handed the two fragments to Royce, who took them and examined them. "They're made from stainless steel, a very special stainless steel that's twice as strong as the best stainless known up till now. This stainless is nearly indestructible, which isn't the case with normal run-of-the-mill stainless, which rusts, ironically, when there is a low level of oxygen. This stainless as you can see from the samples in your hand, never rusts and only corrodes after thousands of years and then only slightly."

"That's earth-shattering, Dex," said Royce, still kidding him. Then he said, more seriously, "Now that I think about it, I guess it is rather significant."

"Yes, those characteristics are revolutionary, but there's one more amazing thing about those two rather dull pieces of metal. They contain 8% platinum and 11% palladium, in addition to the normal iron, nickel, and chrome. Since everything in the shelter we saw, the piping, ductwork, doors, structural reinforcement, and anything else made from metal is made from it, Syman and I figured there's probably 150 to 200 tons of platinum and palladium in all that metal work. It's worth about two and a half billion dollars. Now that you've told us that there are twenty-five shelters, that means there's probably about sixty billion dollars in precious metals. It also means, we've just discovered the largest buried treasure in history."

"Not bad for a days work," said Syman, with just the hint of a smile on his face.

"Why am I not surprised," said Royce. Then after a moment's reflection, he asked, "What do you think our next move should be?"

Dexter answered first, "I'd kind of like to see that shelter you found in the Pine Barrens of New Jersey, Royce. How about you?"

"I really want to get down to the South Pole and open up that repository I just told you about. Syman, what do you think?"

"Well, I think we should go pick up Karrie, then fly out to the Plum Club on Long Island where we can all have drinks and a nice dinner."